CIRCA

Adam Greenfield

Circa by Adam Greenfield

ISBN: 978-1-938349-90-4

eISBN: 978-1-938349-91-1

Cover artwork by Abby Weintraub

Layout and book design by Mark Givens

First Pelekinesis Printing 2018

For information:

Pelekinesis, 112 Harvard Ave #65, Claremont, CA 91711 USA

Library of Congress Cataloging-in-Publication Data

Names: Greenfield, Adam, 1973- author.
Title: Circa / by Adam Greenfield.
Description: Claremont, CA : Pelekinesis, [2018]
Identifiers: LCCN 2018027102 (print) | LCCN 2018028432 (ebook) | ISBN 9781938349911 (ePub) | ISBN 9781938349904 (pbk)
Subjects: | GSAFD: Humorous fiction.
Classification: LCC PS3607.R45367 (ebook) | LCC PS3607.R45367 C57 2018 (print) | DDC 813/.6--dc23
LC record available at https://lccn.loc.gov/2018027102

www.pelekinesis.com

Circa

by

Adam Greenfield

For David

who is on every single page

Contents

Chapter 1

THE CUBICLE WAS small, barely the width of a refrigerator, but at least it provided the minimum amount of privacy he needed to make his phone calls about the dead. Well, not the dead exactly, but the nearly dead. Famous people who had lived long enough, who they expected to die at any moment, who would kick the can if they had any decency or respect for the grim science of journalism.

Henry took a deep breath and lifted the receiver. It was the worst part of the job, hands down. Worse than the isolation. Worse than being sandwiched in between Alberto in Classifieds, a gross fatso who breathed sweat and who plodded back and forth to the vending machine to buy moist ham and cheese sandwiches that he clutched like trophies as they slid out of the swinging door.

On the other side was Truman, who worked in Adult Personals. Truman thought of himself as a matchmaker between the broken and the desperate and relished his position and the power he felt he wielded in forging deranged love connections. His voice was slippery, and he spoke quickly. It was almost too much for Henry at times. He had put in many requests for transfer, but no other departments would have him. He was seen as a bad luck charm, sort of a manically depressed version of the Oracle of Delphi. He brought the thought of death with him everywhere, after all, but only because that was his job.

Now, as he was about to make his call, he heard Truman's voice pour over the divider.

"Uh-huh. Tall. Yeah, of course girls like that. It's better than the opposite. It's better than being short. Fuck, man. Let me tell you something: no one trusts a short person. It's like they didn't try hard enough in the womb. Short people were lazy zygotes. It's a fact." There was a silence as he listened. "No no no. Girls don't care about what you're interested in. They don't care that you're up on current events or politically active. In this day and age it's all about the little things. It's the idiosyncrasies that sell the man. Look, we're white Americans...you're white, right? I mean, I've never met a black person named Jeff. Listen, Jeff, we're white. We're privileged, and we've had too much of a good thing for far too long. I don't know about you, but I can get as indignant over my Wi-Fi going on the fritz as I can about what's going on in Darfur. Know what I mean? That's not necessarily a bad thing, Jeff. You just don't want to lead with that. You just don't want to advertise that you've had it too good for too long. It's like you're rubbing their face in it. It's like you're rubbing their face in the white man's messy shit that you've left behind."

He stopped long enough to hock an enormous loogie into a cup on his desk.

"No, that was me. Listen, all I'm saying is, go with what makes you you. Whatever that is, that's what the chicks are gonna respond to. Whether you gave up lube for Lent when you were sixteen and have never gone back to it as a matter of religious conviction, or you bring a bottle of Wild Turkey into the shower with you in the morning, that's what you should go with. That's your lead, my friend."

Truman stood up and poked his head over the cubicle as the

man talked. He pointed to the phone and smiled, mouthing the words, *This guy's nuts.*

"Yeah. I think 'dry jerker seeks unemployed co-dependent' is a total winner. You got it, buddy. Enjoy all that pussy you're about to be knee deep in. Okay. Later."

He put the phone down and walked around to Henry's desk.

"I'm a machine. You know that? I'm a fucking machine." Truman's pot-belly jiggled in the ever so slight, come hither kind of way it had of contracting and contrasting. "You wanna get some lunch today, or what?"

Henry put the phone down and rubbed his face.

"Truman, I'm trying to make a call. Can you give me a minute, please?"

"Sorry, grim reaper, I don't want to stop the perpetual motion machine that is your genius." He wiped his sweaty hands on his T-shirt. "Alberto, lunch? Or wait…let me guess: you're having a ham and cheese orgy with the girls down in ad sales."

Alberto stood up and draped his pale arms over Henry's cubicle wall.

"Ha ha, very funny, pervert. I'll walk out with you, though, I don't want to be here when Henry does his thing." He turned to Henry. "It's unnerving hearing you talk about people like they're dead when they're still alive."

"I know. I know. You hate hearing me interview people. I get it. I just want to be clear, though, that neither of you are exactly charming neighbors, either."

Truman jerked back in false offense. "What do you mean? I hope you're not saying anything about my work in bringing together the less fortunates of the world."

"Is that what you call it?" Henry asked.

"Yeah, that's what I call it. I'm a merchant of love. I'm

cupid with a bazooka. You...you're something different. Don't compare what I do with what you do."

Alberto chimed in. "He's right, Henry. He's sick, but what you do *is* sick. There's an important distinction there. Somewhere. I feel like I'm splitting hairs."

Before he had a chance to retort, Truman slapped Henry on the shoulder and started heading for the elevator.

"Let's do this, Alberto. Let Woodward & Bernstein & Kevorkian do his thing."

Alberto grumbled after him, a tumbleweed with cholesterol problems.

"Try to be done by the time we get back, okay? Thanks, Henry."

Henry sighed. They were right. His job was grim, but it wasn't the worst thing in the world. He'd once seen a documentary on the Discovery Channel about the worst jobs in the world. In it they'd profiled a man in the Philippines whose job it was to dig up the remains of corpses whose families could no longer afford to pay rent on their burial plots. That was worse.

Still, it had its utility. Like any morbid occupation, it was a function of expediency and efficiency. Clear the space for the falling tree. Break a few eggs to make the great human omelet. In truth, he tried not to think too much about it. As Truman was fond of saying, avoidance was the great indulgence of the twenty-first century.

He picked up the phone and dialed the number for the Gorbachev Foundation in San Francisco.

"Hello, this is Cheryl. Thank you for calling the Gorbachev Foundation."

"Ahem...," he cleared his throat to waste time. He always tried to get a mental picture of them before he started in with it. This girl's voice was small but Henry didn't picture her as a diminutive person. Small, but viable, like light from a hallway slicing into a dark room through the crack under the door. Her voice reminded him of light.

"Ahem, hi. Sorry to bother you. My name is Henry Colmes. I'm a reporter with the *Los Angeles Daily Ledger*. I was wondering if I could ask you a few questions for a story I'm doing on Mikhail Gorbachev."

"Um…" her young voice lingered leaving vapor trails of innocence. "I'm not usually the one who talks to the press. Maybe I should…"

"No, no. That's okay. I'm not really a reporter. I'm more of a researcher, and, uh," he paused, savoring the seconds before he dropped the bomb, "I'm working on writing Gorbachev's obituary."

The girl was silent for a moment and then he heard her breath work back up to a steady rate.

"I don't understand," she choked on the words. "I can't believe it…"

He pictured her there, alone in the front office of a grungy non-profit in San Francisco. Prefabricated pieces of wood scabbed and peeling off the walls. Carpeting, the original shade of which no crime lab in the civilized world could uncover. Sourcing DNA was nothing. This carpet held the secret of life. A proclamation from the president of the City Council hanging crookedly over the Xerox machine, the wide-striped calligraphy decreeing it to be Gorbachev Foundation Day in the city. Hear ye. Hear ye. Everyone got a day. Live long enough and you got a street. Live too long and they can't wait for you to die. It's not the evil that you fought against that the people feared, stupid. It was waiting too long for the other shoe to drop. That's what set certain men apart; an absence of anxiety, the sniper's touch.

So, the guy ended the Cold War? Big deal. Who the fuck really cared?

He pictured Cheryl in worn-down jeans, hearts and phone numbers scribbled on top of the kneecaps, a jacket the color of the weather in Portland, shoes made for men who worked with their hands. He imagined light hair, trust-fund blonde, the color of never having to worry about being disappointed by heartbreak. She was probably just out of college, an Ivy Leaguer, no doubt. All of these well-known non-profits had them. They were way stations for the privileged, a time and a place to refer to later in life at the Fourth of July party at your place in the Hamptons.

He took a sip of water and smiled. He would give it one more second before he broke the news that Gorbachev wasn't dead. That he was only collecting bits of research for the obituary that the newspaper would have at the ready when the great man died. When all the great men died. He would tell her that they've written the death of all the greats, that her memories of standing next to the man at a gala dinner were already more than that. That they were already bits of nostalgia that would be winnowed down and presented as pulp. As good as fiction. The best years of your life.

"No, no," he rushed in to save her. "He's not dead or anything. This is standard operating procedure. I'm sorry. Did I upset you?"

"Standard...operating...procedure?" she repeated lithely.

"Yeah, there's someone like me at all the big newspapers. Someone who collects information about famous people, getting biographies together that will one day be used as the basis for their... uh... obituaries. One day. But not now." He rushed the last part, hoping to make up for what he'd just done.

"Oh," she said, hesitatingly, "I see." Pause. "That's a strange job."

"I know. I know. I get that all the time."

His computer went into sleep mode as a lonely deserted beach appeared on the screen. There was a blanket and an umbrella stuck into the sand. Perfectly blue water glittered in the distance. Ironic that Microsoft's version of paradise had no computers in it.

"Well, what do you want to know?"

He stayed on the phone with her for about an hour, asking basic biographical questions, important milestones in the man's life, the history of his non-profit work. She gushed on and on, her reticence succumbing to hero worship, a backhanded compliment of her own choice of vocation. Still, he owed it to her. Owed her the chance to self-aggrandize after the cruel trick he played. It was easier to be patient with people if you felt like you owed them something.

The call finished, and he shook his computer's mouse and the machine buzzed back into being. He began to type up his notes about Gorbachev, methodically and carefully he began to script a narrative, imagining a time in the future when he, and all the great men, would be dead.

*　　*　　*

Five o'clock happened, as it always did, with an anti-climactic click of the clock. No horns, no angels, no forty-seven virgins waiting to punch the clock for you, to part the traffic in two and collapse it on top of your enemies once you were safely through.

Henry, Alberto, and Truman walked around the corner from their building to a bar where they often waited out the traffic. Just a beer or two until things died down out there, a little something to wet the whistle while staving off the trauma of commuting.

They sat at a grimy table and ordered their usuals: beers, chips, French fries. When their order was ready, Ray the bartender called out, "Henry." He got up to get the food. He hated hearing his name called out and regretted ever having used his real name from day one. Henry. Two syllables that didn't go together. It was not a young person's name, even when he was small. Or at least younger than the thirty-seven he was now. *Hennnnnn-ryyyyyyyyy.* There were too many syllables in there somehow, too much flat action. Not the name you'd want hollered out at a bar. It was, however, a name to be screeched from another room, an ailment, a one-word diagnosis. Henry. The only pillow talk it conjured was a death bed's coarse whisper, the last requests of an earnest acquaintance. The bottom line was, he didn't feel like he deserved the name. He didn't quite live up to its dreadful expectations. He was not an unattractive man, and certainly not overweight like his compatriots. He still had most of his hair but opted to keep it short and parted like a schoolboy. Brown eyes sat frozen for most of the day behind a pair of black-rimmed glasses. He dressed plainly, opting usually for a pair of cords or khakis, and a button-down shirt that he invariably struggled to keep tucked in for most of the day. He didn't think he was bad looking, nor did he think he was particularly terrific looking either. He just was. His only really remarkable trait was what a girlfriend had once called his "New York face." He suffered from year-round allergies and was always either wiggling his nose or blinking his eyes against the dryness and itchiness of living in a place where plants not only lived year round but thrived as well. She had said that his constant twitching had reminded her of time-lapse photography of New York where all the cars stop and go in broken little lines, where clouds poured over Central Park and unspooled in rapid succession. He loved the observation and once when they were out they saw an old man, an apparent stroke victim, being pushed in a wheelchair, a blanket up to his neck. The man's face hung languidly, and Henry had leaned into her and whispered, "That's a country home face." He had meant it as a joke, of course, the opposite of his bustling metropolis of a kisser. She didn't take it that way. "That's sick, Henry." She called him cruel and they broke up two weeks later and he felt like the comment was merely an excuse to end things.

He came back to the table with the drinks and they said cheers absentmindedly, the way a Midwestern family might say grace before a meal.

Truman licked his upper lip clean of froth and looked at Henry.

"So," he began, like a gravedigger shoveling out the first scoop of dirt from a plot, "who'd you kill today?"

Henry smiled as his nose twitched, "Gorbachev."

"Very nice. Big fish. You're really getting around the globe these days. Knocking 'em dead from sea to shining sea."

Henry took a sip of his beer and smiled. He liked it when Truman got silly with it, not huffy and strange like before when he wasn't sure whether his friend was being serious or not. Gullibility had always been one of Henry's fatal flaws. It was cute when you were a kid, all wide-eyed and questions, but when you got older, it could easily be the gateway drug to paralyzing anxiety.

"Did you do that thing again where you make them believe the person is dead first?"

"Uh-huh," Henry nodded.

"Why do you do that? You know what you're doing, right?

You know what that does to people."

"Is that a question or a statement?" Henry wondered honestly.

"Break it up, you two," Alberto piped up as he worked french fry after french fry into his busy mouth. The greasy detritus of one or two popped out, and it reminded Henry of those pictures of the helicopters taking off from the top of the U.S. Embassy as Saigon was falling, people scrambling to hang on to the bottom of them, some falling back helplessly to the roof. As if reading his mind, Truman pointed at Alberto.

"Watching you eat makes you kind of want to cheer for some of the food to get away."

"Fuck off," Alberto said, undeterred. "You're an idiot."

"You know, I used to think you might have a tapeworm and that that explained your appetite," Truman pondered aloud, "but now I think I know what it is. You *are* a tapeworm. You're a Mexican tapeworm and no one is safe from you. You even scare the worms that are in the tequila. Those worms hate you."

Alberto stopped eating and stared at Truman.

"You can leave if you don't like it."

"No, I can't. The gravitational pull is too much. We're getting sucked in!" Truman began flailing his arms and legs as he pretended to be getting pulled into the solar system of Alberto's digestive tract. "Aaahhhh!"

Ray, a grizzled old stump of a man that may have once been an oak, looked over and whistled through the gap in his front teeth.

"You two, cut it out. I don't want to have to tell you again. This is a bar, not a fuck shed!"

Truman giggled hysterically.

"Fuck shed! He said fuck shed. I love that! Ray, do you mind if I use that for a bumper sticker? 'This is a bar not a fuck shed.' Or, how about 'This is a manger, not a fuck shed?'"

"I don't give a shit what you do, fruity. Just don't get it caught in your pants when you're shoving it up your ass."

Ray was right. It was a bar, but barely. Cache, located just around the corner from the newspaper, in the heart of Downtown L.A., may have once been a hopping place, but somehow, as restaurants and bars developed schtick and asserted niches to stay competitive, it remained the same. Desultory sports paraphernalia from the late 1980s adorned the walls, as drooping and sad as the old drunks who hid in the corners of the bar like roaches afraid of the light. Smoke moved from all corners, conjured from the tips of the patrons' desperate cigarettes, and drifted lazily to the ceiling all at once like a flock of birds deciding in a split second to head for better weather. Their colleagues at the paper, the "real journalists," would never be caught dead in a place like this; a place that still allowed smoking. Despite its convenience, the others would rather go to their sports, vodka, or martini bars, not one whose niche might have been best advertised as entropy. Henry thought of a slogan, *Come on in and taste the entropy!* It had its appeal, and God knows it would have its audience.

As the night wore on, they continued to drink steadily, sip by sip obliterating the fantasy that they had just stopped in for a nip while they were waiting out the traffic.

Henry admired the resilience with which Truman and Alberto continued to argue. They were two parts of a perpetual motion machine that ran on antagonism. Alberto was talking about his novel in progress, the story of a transient whose Christ complex mystifies the middle-class neighborhood in whose garbage cans he resides, and whose residents inevitably take him in and look to him as a guru.

Truman had begun a novel, too, out of spite, and was arguing for the commercial viability of his concept about a mentally handicapped man who is elected President of the United States.

"Don't take this the wrong way, buddy, but your shit is derivative. *Down and Out in Beverly Hills. Being There.* Sorry, I know the creative process can be a real mindfuck sometimes."

Alberto sputtered, "But your idea is ridiculous. Who would ever in a million years believe that a slightly retarded guy could ever be elected President. It's absurd. Besides," he went on, motioning to a wall he mistook for a waitress to get him another drink, "you're just writing a novel because I am. You're writing angry. You're doomed to fail."

Truman shook his head.

"I feel sad for you. I really do. You're my muse. I wish you could see it that way. You're my big, fat, artery-hardened muse."

He grabbed Alberto in a friendly headlock. Henry watched them and suddenly felt a pang of jealousy. He had no one with whom he could butt heads. No one to tickle his toes while he lay in the coma of everyday life. Once upon a time he did. Once upon a time he had his sister, Grace. He had his friend, Cal. But they were both gone now. Gone, gone, gone. Gone as though they were never here. No, that's not right. That wasn't entirely right.

Just then, Ray called out his two AM benediction, "Last call!" and the few drunks left in the bar, the true believers, groaned a hallelujah chorus of disappointment. It was unanimous. There was no place like home.

Henry pushed himself back from the table and struggled to tuck his shirttails into his pants.

"I'm leaving," he announced with a slur, anointing the air around him with the stench of cheap beer and fried food.

"Of course you are," Truman said as he belched, "it's last call. We're all leaving. You're not so special."

Henry, drunk and magnanimous, wagged his index finger at his two friends.

"You two should be glad you have one another. That's all I want to say. It's good to have someone you can fight with all the time. It's the best reason there is to live."

Truman unhinged his lower jaw and swallowed his last whiskey sour in a dramatic, primordial gulp.

"After a thing like that I feel like it's the end of the world, not just another Monday night."

"Make the most with what you got," Henry slurred back, tired and toxic. "If it's Armageddon you want, don't let anyone stand in your way."

He made a quick salute and turned on his heels. Drunk, he stumbled onto the street, and even though he knew every light in the world was blazing back at him, not one single drop of luminescence reached his eyes.

*   *   *

It's no wonder that he dreamt of war. It had been his secret fantasy since youth, since his time with Cal, and at times when he'd had enough to drink, like tonight for example, he'd been known to drape a skinny arm around the shoulder of a bored cop and whisper a sad confession.

"Don't you ever feel like you've been cheated by not getting to go to war? I mean, Officer...uh, Kozlowski, is it? What good are we if we don't ever get to live up to the memories we think we're owed, let alone what we think the future may or may not have in store for us?"

The cop yawned as he pulled out his nightstick. Henry got wise and disentangled himself from the business of law enforcement.

"Sorry, Officer," he stammered around a tongue puffed up by alcohol. "I thought you were someone else. I'm profoundly color blind."

As he walked back to his car, he kept his eyes tilted upward because he swore there was a sound that skyscrapers made as they flexed their weight into the air, a certain creaking and groaning that clung to oxygen and cleaved the atmosphere as if it had no more substance than a warm pad of butter. In the car he sighed, reminded himself that birthrights were like voices and not everybody had one, took a swig from the flask he stashed in the glove box for special occasions, and listened to the swaying buildings tell him about life at the top.

The car started with a sputtering roar as he powered it into gear. He made a beeline for Hollywood where he took a right up Laurel Canyon and turned on to Mulholland to where the mountains strained to touch the sky like wannabes behind the velvet ropes of some new industry club. Looking at the city from on high, he could see that electricity was at its core as the alternating currents pulsed with incessant regularity. The moon rested above his left shoulder in its quarter state, gleaming like a silver-plated dagger. It was suddenly not out of the range of possibilities for him to end it all right here, to rev the engine, let go of the brake, and pop the clutch, sending the whole kit and caboodle over the cliff and out into the sky. The fall would kill him for sure, and if he was lucky he might even get a nice fireball at the end and take out half the canyon with him.

A brand-new, metallic blue BMW 7-series came to a rest in the spot next to his. He looked over and saw a pretty young girl and her boyfriend start to go at it like diseased Huns, executing with great exuberance the corporal equivalent of a home invasion on one another. The guy's beefy, leather-clad leg was slung over his date's waist, their arms scratched and pulled at body parts that seem to be regenerating from everywhere and nowhere at once, a schizophrenic lizard biting off his own tail every six seconds just to spite itself. Lovemaking in the mercenary position.

Henry's radio was tuned to NPR. It was the tail end of one of those human-interest stories they were always running about quirky people and their subterranean interests, as if liberal slices of life were somehow rich and meaningful enough that one could extrapolate from them a broader perspective of the world and somehow be convinced that it didn't count as cultural imperialism. It was a story about a woman who, as a missionary in Africa in the 1980s, brought over crates of old pop-psychology and self-help books to teach the locals how to speak and read English. "Now," she explained, self-satisfied, "there are whole villages of Hutus in Rwanda and Bushmen from the Kalahari who understand that men are from Mars and that I'm okay if you're okay, and isn't it wonderful," she gushed from her home in suburban Detroit, "that the truths we hold so dear have proven in the long run to be so universal."

What a disaster, was all Henry could think as he imagined some native villager getting his head bashed in by a rival tribesman after using Napoleon Hill's advice about influencing people to finalize a goat trade. What a mess we're in without context, he told himself, switching off the radio and vowing to the gods above that public radio was nothing more than a twelve-step program for the self-obsessed and the next time he thought about making a pledge he'd take a good long look in the mirror and think about the future of indigenous life in Africa.

When he looked over at the BMW again, the couple were staring back at him. Pointing and laughing, the pretty girl rolled down her window and said something he couldn't hear but already knew was going to piss him off but good.

He rolled down his window and got defensive.

"Whaddya want?" He yelled at them in a voice that sounded like the desert.

The girl snickered.

"Jesus. Welcome home, Marine," she said around a mouth full of braces. "All I said was that I hoped you were enjoying the show." They laughed and the man slapped his leather thigh in appreciation.

Henry scowled and gunned the motor a few times to test his nerve. *How'd you like a little unhinged guy begets supernova to spice up your night*, he muttered to no one in particular. *How'd that be for a show, huh? A little fire in the canyon to end your night, leather man and brace face?* He stopped, realizing that he was starting to sound like a comic book super villain.

He spat but missed the window. A brownish, yellow hunk of mucus ran down the inside of his car. So many things had ruined his life, but they were all thoughts, the memories of people and places, things that happened that were monuments to no one but him, that stood for nothing but to the importance he gave them in the soft hours of the night. So many things had ruined his life, but war, and the dream of war, in other words, the gorgeous conflict of others, had defined him now and forever as nothing better than a spectator. He could write the obituaries of a million people, he could cover the earth with spilled ink, fresh as blood, but what would his own say?

Chapter 2

HENRY, AGED THIRTEEN, had given up trying to get his mother to play the new U2 tape on the car's tape deck. He sat back, huffed, and stared out the window. The Southern California sun poured onto his right leg and the right side of his face, tingling the skin like the bristles of a broom.

"Why do I have to play your music on the stereo?" she asked him. "You have your Walkman. Put it on there. I don't have to listen to it, too."

She scowled slightly as she said it, her eyes drawn to little slits behind oversized, white Emmanuelle Khanh sunglasses.

"I don't know," he shrugged. "You might like it."

"No, sweetie," she said, a little more sweetly now, "but thank you. It's nice that you're always thinking of other people."

They were on their way home from the library where Henry hung out after school every day, whiling away his time until dinner by reading reference books and watching a bunch of younger kids play Dungeons & Dragons in one of the utility rooms. Ideally, it was the perfect opportunity for him to be getting his homework done, which was the point of him going there, especially since he had no afterschool activities to speak of: no sports, no drama club, no friends, no nothing. His favorite book was a collection of Nostradamus' predictions and he leafed through it often, focusing especially on the modern predictions, and tried to imagine what Nostradamus would say if he were alive today, in the 1980s, about his future forecasts. Would he see Pac-Man as the harbinger of Armageddon? Darth Vader as the black threat rising in the east, a threat to all mankind? Or would it be the opposite? Would he come and see that his predictions weren't about geo-political events and the fates of nations, but about video games and movies and become disappointed and feel irrelevant? If there was one thing that held true from century to century, it's that there was nothing worse than a morose soothsayer.

There were scribblings in the margins, another thing about the book that he loved, places where kooks had made notes about the predictions, like they were marking up a college textbook getting ready for finals. He imagined these men— because surely no women would ever get caught up in such foolishness, they were far too serious of creatures for that— crouched in dark apartments that reeked of sodium-heavy foods, sharpened pencils at the ready, trying to make sense of their lives by deciphering these prophecies and the relevance of them to their day-to-day existence. It was funny how much stock people put into nonsense, like how his mother insisted on reading Henry and Grace their horoscope every morning before school, dispensing the newspaper's vague allusions as a substitute for motherly advice, which had to be, quite frankly, much more specific and couldn't be relied upon as regularly as the good graces of the cosmos, which had never ceased, by their mere position in the night sky, prognosticating with tenderness since the beginning of time.

The other book that Henry spent an inordinate amount of his time with were the big picture books about the machinery of war, especially the *Jane's* books; massive hardbound picture books with direct but extravagant titles like *Jane's Infantry Weapons, Jane's Guns Recognition Guide,* and *Jane's Urban Transport Systems,* the names of which, like so much technical writing, intimated a kind of pornography by the very nature of their specificity. Originally, it was the size of the books that had caught his eye. As he walked amongst the coldness of the library stacks, letting his fingers trace a line across the bumpy spines of row after row of books, he imagined the library to be not a building crammed full of lifeless words, but a sleeping dragon, these thick tomes its skeletal structure, the ribs and backbone of the recumbent creature. His fingers eventually hit upon the *Jane's* books, which were larger than the rest and therefore protruded further into the aisle. He took one down and was immediately struck not by the immaculate photos of the guns on the cover, but by the name. *Jane's.* He couldn't conceive why a girl would be involved with a book like this, a book that photographed and explained every bit of minutiae of the tools of war, from a weapon's velocity to a diagram of its component parts, all photographed in such excruciating detail you could almost see the oil dripping off the moving parts, the smell of powder as its ordnance was discharged. Later, he read that the book was produced not by a woman named Jane, but by a company that had been founded by a man named John Jane in the early 1900s. Before he realized that, though, he would try to imagine what sort of woman this Jane must be, and as he constructed her in his mind— her love of weapons, her fit military physique, a sick, raunchy sense of humor—he developed a sort of a crush that eventually blossomed into full-on love. Although just an archetype, the book gave her life; the images of the machine guns, tanks, and fighter jets gave her an attitude. It was enough at that age to build a woman up like that, to picture her within the narrow framework of one's own world, because love was only a fantasy then, the materialization of every good thing in the world happening all at one time. Love was overload and wish fulfillment. Love was darkness and the complicity of hands and lips, of swaying and devotion. Love was Jane.

His mother steered the station wagon onto their street, a typically suburban cul-de-sac replete with kids playing all manner of outside games, of houses whose floor plans were all thought up by the same unimaginative domestic engineer, of well-manicured front yards that told you nothing about the inside of the house. Devoid of personality, the only thing the little suburb had that spoke of its tenacity was its color palette. The reds and blues of the birds of paradise that were found in most of the gardens almost bled life, the color so alive it seemed to run down the flowers fresh from the bucket of a careless painter. The flecks of granite and stone in the sidewalk glinted startlingly bright, catching the sun at every angle, reflecting light back in a dizzying kaleidoscope of motion that verged on musical. Even the sun itself was brighter there, more yellow, more intent to succeed here somehow than in other parts of the world. These were colors so rich, so sincere, that in his mind they couldn't occur anywhere else in the world; they were manufactured hues designed not to emulate nature but to somehow surpass it. His mother's car, for example, an ugly, brown, hulking station wagon that wheezed like an injured circus animal when it was forced to stand idle, was more than just brown. Grace called it "baby shit brown," and she was right. It was a brown car like none other. Uglier than any other.

As she came around the corner, piloting the car with an attitude that was somewhere far left of cavalier, she noticed the kids on the street playing their different games.

"Oh, look," she said, trying to make it sound nonchalant as she narrowly missed kids' skateboards, basketballs, and even the kids themselves, "Some of your friends are still out playing. You can play with them for a little while if you want. Before dinner. There's time."

Henry watched with morbid fascination as his mother nearly missed a little girl pushing her dolls in a red wagon, the closeness of the car causing the hem of the girl's dress to puff up, a near vehicular manslaughter version of Marilyn Monroe's up-skirt flirtatiousness.

He didn't answer her. He knew that she was trying to get him to go outside, to play with other kids. But she also knew that that wasn't what he did. She understood that he had very little interest in playing outside, that he wasn't good at sports, that these kids, even though he had lived in close suburban proximity to them almost his entire life, didn't know him just as he didn't know them. Sure, he knew their names. He saw some of them at school and in town when he went to buy packs of *Return of the Jedi* trading cards, but he hadn't been to any of their houses since he was a small kid when everyone played with everyone else, because it wasn't clear yet who fit in and who didn't.

Something landed in the road in front of them and his mother hit it without noticing as she kept on driving. Henry knew she hadn't meant to do it, because if she had she would have shown some sign of recognition, a look in the rearview mirror or the release of a little "Oh my." Besides, she was quick to acknowledge the negative, celebrate it even, which was why when her vivid hypochondria was in bloom, a fireworks display of concern, he knew that everything was all right. He turned around in his seat and saw a dead bird lying in the road behind them.

After she parked, he got out of the car and walked over to where the bird lay dead in the street, its body whole but bleeding, one wing spread out to its full length as if it were attempting to crawl across the road. *Why did the pigeon crawl across the road?* he thought to himself and smiled. It wasn't that he thought the dead bird was funny, but he had to admit to himself that it certainly did die in a very dramatic pose, victorious even, the way a soldier might want to be seen hoisting the American flag above his head as an enemy's bullet sunk into him.

A few of the younger kids walked over to where Henry was standing. A girl with a Strawberry Shortcake T-shirt looked at the bird, looked and him, and then pulled on her friend's arm.

"Come on," she said, coaxingly, the maternal instinct flourishing naturally, "your mommy says you're not allowed to be in the street."

The two little girls walked to the sidewalk and sat on the curb all the while keeping their eyes on the corpse as if they were waiting for it to do something. They were still too young to understand that this was it, that there'd be no flying away, no sad, lonesome sound, no nothing. Then, without any prompting, they began to pick up little stones and bits of gravel that were around their feet and throw them, sometimes accurately, but mostly missing wildly, at the dead animal as if they were willing it away, casting out evil spirits the way it may have been done thousands of years ago in more superstitious times.

More kids began to walk over to see what was happening, and before too long, word went out that it was Henry's car that had killed the bird. Henry had killed it. Other kids joined in the rock throwing until one boy, the oldest of the lot, maybe twelve, threw one of the rocks at Henry. Henry knew who the boy was from seeing him around and he had always looked innocent enough, as towheads so often do, but once he started throwing rocks, he suddenly looked evil and malicious. He thought that all kids looked like that: either angels or devils. Or, they were angels until they became devils. Long story short, he told himself, you should never trust a towhead.

He shielded himself from the projectile, and as soon as the first one bounced away, more started to come his way. Soon, all the children were using Henry as their target, pelting him all over, stinging his legs and uncovered arms. He crossed his arms over his face and lifted a knee to cover his balls. He remained folded like a piece of origami while they used his body for target practice, never once feeling like he had the right to call out or run away, that he had this coming for what his mother had done to the poor bird.

Out of nowhere a deafening cry of "Stop!" echoed around the street and he looked up to see his sister Grace, two years his senior, standing on their front lawn, her arms crossed sternly in front of her. The kids obeyed instantly, as if the word had broken a spell, an irresistible trance that was the quiet consent of violence. She stood staring at them all for a moment, her brown eyes sizzling with anger, her jaw clenched and set like a trap, her pale skinny arms armor over her chest.

"What is going on?" she demanded of them.

When no one spoke, she walked over to Henry and asked him again what had happened.

He shrugged. "Mom hit a bird with her car. I think they're mad at me."

She put her hands on him, checked his arms and face for scratches and welts, and when she was satisfied that he looked relatively unharmed she turned and stormed back into the house. No one moved while she was inside, and in a few moments she was back with a shoebox in her hand. She walked straight to the bird carcass and, with her bare hands, grabbed the thing by the tip of its wing and put it in the shoebox, sliding the lid quickly over the top. She began to walk down the street with Henry at her side, and without a word the other kids followed along, slowly, keeping their distance and with an uncharacteristic silence that children typically had to be coerced into keeping. Even the towhead got off his bike, a thing none of them had ever seen before; that his legs worked as instruments of walking was a marvel to them all.

The procession moved as a group, and the sound of ceramic roller skate wheels clack-clacking against the sidewalk marked their time, a patient grammar they wordlessly agreed to obey as they marched in solemn unison. The most amazing part of it to Henry, the thing he marveled at, was his sister's ability to impose her will on them all, to shame them into behaving and being orderly, himself included. He was suddenly ashamed at himself for having just stood there while they threw rocks at him and could sense that her disappointment extended to him as well.

She led them to the vacant lot at the end of the cul-de-sac, a place they called Rosie's Field for the neighborhood Irish Setter that used it as its primary bathroom. She knelt and dug a shallow hole in the ground and gently placed the box inside. After covering it with dirt she stood, clasped her hands in front of her, and turned finally to look at them.

"Do any of you have anything to say?"

The children looked at one another. They knew that even though she was talking about the bird, about gracing its life with a few simple thoughts, what she was really suggesting was that they take a moment to be ashamed of themselves, that they look upon the dead as just that, the dead, and not as a reason to attack and blame one another for their anger.

She sighed. "Fine. I'll do it." She cleared her throat and

unfolded her arms. "Dear god," she said, her voice high and strong, "we're sorry that this bird died on our street. Please don't let it make you think less of any of us. Birds don't die here all the time, and our mother," at this she looked at Henry and smiled, "she's not always the best at paying attention. Amen."

The kids murmured an assenting "Amen" and stood there until she shooed them away. "Go on, everyone. Get out of here. Nothing else happens. That's it."

Bikes were remounted and roller skates resumed their wobbly trajectories and the field was once again the domain of the neighborhood dogs who would no doubt find the bird's body not too far into the future and that would officially be it. The dogs would have the last say.

Henry and Grace strolled back to the house together, and she let the silence sink in before she asked him, "Why did you let them do that to you? Why didn't you say anything or do anything back? What's wrong with you, Henry?"

It was the inevitable question of a protector, the rhetorical mantra that compelled people like Grace to perpetually worry about people like Henry. He wished he had an answer for her, wished he didn't have to be such a fuck-up, wished she didn't have to ask the questions that he knew he'd never be able to get to the bottom of, even for his own sake. But there wasn't anything to say, which was one of the convenient facts of family, that communication was crucial but ultimately not a requirement. She would always be there for him, his older sister by two years, but besides their being siblings, he couldn't quite figure out why this was. She was infinitely more attractive than he was with her perfect bone structure and skin that was the right shade of pale, and her popularity in school was unparalleled. She got good grades and would certainly get into whatever college she wanted to go to. He secretly wished that it would not be too far away because the thought of living in their house without her made him truly sad.

Once he came close to understanding her love for him. It was the first time his parents fought so badly that his dad punched the wall, denting it with his fist. The china cabinet rattled, and his mom had smiled and said, "Too bad you're so earnest about things no one cares about, Phil. I hope that hurt." His dad had scowled, and Henry remembered being impressed that his mom knew so well how to push his dad's buttons. They were never as intelligent to him as when they fought with one another. That's when all the strategy came into play, mind games, crystal-clear recall of events that seemed, at the time they occurred, to be completely insignificant.

When their dad had punched the wall, Grace had taken Henry by the wrist and led him up the pull-down ladder above the hallway into the little attic where all the artifacts of their attempts at emulating a "normal" family life were stored away for future unearthing: tennis rackets (they were going to play doubles!), tents, and enough board games to choke a horse. He laughed when he imagined the kind of museum they could build with all of the refuse that was the good intentions of families. It would definitely be one of those things you could see from space with the naked eye.

They sat in the attic and talked about nothing, just bullshitting, and when he made a joke about feeling like Anne Frank trapped up in the attic, she laughed and hugged him.

"That's why I love you, Henry. That's why we've always got to stick together. No matter what."

"Okay," he said, quietly, not sure exactly what she meant, but sensing that she loved him deeply.

"You know what else?" she went on, supremely confident in her analysis of things. "This is not how parents should treat their kids. We shouldn't be the ones that have to go and hide. They're the ones that should get a room or whatever..." She started to cry, and it absolutely froze him. He had no clue what to do. She was the one who always looked after him, who comforted him, who told him everything was going to be okay. He stared at the walls, where brand-new fishing poles were lined up, part of the architecture of the house now, at cobwebs that captured the infinitesimal light that leaked into this space and glistened as invisible air trembled its ribs. There were so many things he should have done, things he felt like saying and doing, but couldn't summon up the courage somehow, of worrying that it might come off as somehow inauthentic. That would be the worst sin. If she thought he loved her any less than he actually did. It was better not to say anything. So he didn't.

*   *   *

Everyone wanted to be loved more than they deserved. It was a chronic condition that started in childhood—no, was encouraged in childhood—and continued unchecked throughout life. There was no cure, Henry was sure, because he had heard in school from a teacher who was having them read *Lord of the Flies* that unconditional love didn't exist. It was a figment of your imagination, of your childhood, the teacher said, and the sooner you learned that the better.

Grace was right when she had cried in the attic about their parents, that it was the parents' responsibility to console and protect them and not the other way around. But reality didn't work like that and so Henry tried with all his might to meet his father on the old man's terms—baseball cards, football, and poker—all subjects about which he cared not a thing, but developed an impressive store of knowledge about nevertheless, which would one day serve to shock the hell out of people in bars and in staff meetings.

His father, Phil, was a punching bag of a man; not exactly fat, but there was somehow too much of him somewhere, like his very mass was on the verge of bursting out of its seams. All of his allegiances were sworn to his high school years in the late 1950s when he was, to his own recollection, a star athlete and an unparalleled ladies man, a true Renaissance supernova. True happiness came for him in the telling and retelling of stories about track records being shattered, last-second touchdown runs, and beer busts and girls and cars that could outrun anything (but old age). Henry did his best to keep up with the lore. He remembered the names and the dates, scores and speeds. They became a part of his own childhood, pieces of his own memory, a hallucination they could cherish together.

It was a Saturday morning, and he lay in bed listening to his parents arguing with one another. They were yelling about him.

"Take him with you, Phil. It'll be good for you two to go out and do something together."

"He doesn't want to come," his dad replied like it was a fact of nature. "He doesn't like baseball cards. He comes to these things and he just sort of wanders around all airy-fairy like."

They were talking about baseball cards, the thing that his father held in higher esteem than anything else. Particularly when it came to the 1952 Topps complete set. It was his father's pride and joy. Almost every card was in gem mint condition, sealed in plastic sleeves and stored in notebooks at the back of the closet. 1952 wasn't the most famous year in baseball. In fact, it wasn't even the year that Mantle and Mays were rookies. That was 1951. But something about '52 made it the most sought after, the most prized. All the great ones were in it. Yogi Berra, Roy Campanella, Mantle, Mays, Pee Wee Reese. Shit. You name the guy and if he was worth talking about, hell, even thinking about, then he played in 1952. And even though most of the cards in his dad's set were gem mint, there were a few of the higher numbers (there were over 700 cards in the set that year) that were not quite there. For some reason the higher numbers always seemed to have a slight gum stain shading the back, or a nick in the corner from when some kid in the fifties was stacking his cards up to flip against a friend and accidentally laid the pile down too hard. Who knew? All Henry knew was that he would go downstairs to the kitchen sometimes to get a glass of water before bed and his father would be sitting at the kitchen table, taking out each card and looking it over with a jeweler's loupe in his eye, breathing slightly where there was a gum stain and trying to scratch off the discoloration with a wet Q-tip. He'd hear Henry and look up at him, disappointed almost, Henry sometimes thought, that it wasn't Mickey Mantle or Willie Mays coming down the stairs with some of the high number common cards for him in mint condition. He would see Henry and smile, slightly ashamed, the way Henry was ashamed when his father once opened his door without knocking and found him lip-synching and playing air guitar to Van Halen's "Panama" in front of the mirror.

It was said that the human body was made of something like 92 percent water. If that was the case, then for his dad the other 8 percent was the '52 set. He wondered what could have been so great about 1952 that made his father obsess about this particular year. Because it had to be about that. It couldn't be this particular group of players or that the design of the borders and backs were so innovative. His father would have been ten in '52, which was before high school, so all those glory days were still ahead of him waiting to be collected. He imagined his father at ten, with a crew cut and outfielder's glove, shagging balls in the front yard with his older brother. The two of them would run to Wrigley Field every day in the summer, gloves in hand, getting baseballs signed by all the players, the sun and humidity unimaginable burdens, but in the happiness of the times, they were hardly noticed. When Henry would complain about the heat in the summer and ask his dad if he could turn on the air conditioner, his dad would tell him that they never had air conditioners back when he was a kid and they did just fine. He didn't see how it was possible that people could exist in those kinds of conditions, but as he got a little older, he realized that when you were as happy as his father must have been during that summer, you didn't worry about things like air conditioners and pocket change for the movies. All you worried about was waking up and being the happiest person on earth.

It was all a bit much to try and relate to.

"Just take him with you," his mother said in that way of hers that meant the discussion was done, that to continue arguing would flip a switch in her that would make her go from impatient to angry.

"Fine," his dad mumbled.

"And please watch him around those friends of yours. They're so repulsive."

Henry giggled. He and Grace laughed at their mother's choice of adjectives, which were always slightly off, usually leaning toward the excessive side of whatever point she was trying to make, and they would sometimes call her Senorita Mommy when she did it as an inside joke, as if her verbiage had earned her the suspicion of not really being from this country.

The baseball card conventions were always in a plain-looking ballroom at some local chain hotel, the kind of places where businessmen stayed on overnight trips and it took two calls to the front desk minimum to get a clean towel. The ballroom was always a dingy place with low, claustrophobic ceilings and large picture windows that inevitably gave you a view of the parking lot or a nearby Applebee's. The ballroom contained row after row of six foot tables, cheaply skirted, banners hung over the edges declaring from what state the dealer had schlepped his wares. Pennsylvania. Illinois. Florida. It was amazing to Henry how far they came for these conventions and the camaraderie of their shared obscure interests. He could almost imagine a convoy of these people, getting bigger as it went, heading out west like stagecoaches of old. A trail of tears marked out by stale pieces of rectangular bubble gum and fast food wrappers.

They made a beeline straight for the table of Burl Armstrong, a dealer from Iowa who was one of his father's best friends. Burl specialized in the "good stuff," as his father called it, not all this new shit that wasn't worth a damn. Burl was sitting with a few other collectors and dealers, all people his father knew, and as they saw Henry and his dad approach they began to shout, "It's 1952! Hey, '52!"

His father was all smiles as he shook hands all around, asking about everyone's business, everyone's collections. A couple of the men said "hello" to Henry but for the most part he was ignored and stood there watching his father and marveling at how easily he could become relaxed and happy when he had the inclination.

"How's the stuff here, Burl?" his father asked the broad man.

"So-so. There's a few things here you might like. Jason Baker from Dallas is here, and he's got a few high numbers you should take a look at. Stu Fleishman from Denver. Ira Dillard from Minneapolis. Otherwise," he took a break to pop the last bite of a hot dog into his mouth, "it's a bunch of shit. Not many serious collectors here."

His father nodded and looked at Henry.

"So, you wanna look around? Meet me back here in two hours?"

Before Henry could assent, his father handed him a $20 bill.

"Here," he said, "in case you want to buy anything and get something to eat."

Henry nodded, familiar with the routine.

As he walked away, he looked back and saw his father in a huddle with the men, each of whom, like his dad, had a jeweler's loupe growing out of his eye. They were all so alike these guys, these "serious collectors." They were all around his dad's age, and a lot of them were lawyers like his father. He wondered if each of them had a special year that they focused on, a year they tried to fix up into perfect condition, seal into plastic, and leave in the back of a closet for their sons as hermetically sealed heirlooms. It was awfully presumptuous, he thought, to assume that what your kid was going to want of you once you were gone were memories of his happiest days—of days in which your kid didn't even exist.

Henry wandered the aisles looking at the cards, noticing the big men who hunkered down everywhere in front of glass displays full of memorabilia. They were men who were big in the way the *Enola Gay* or the *Queen Mary* were big; bombastic and unrealistic. These men would never fly. They would never float. This hovering would be it.

He stopped in front of a display case that featured old war memorabilia. Medals, snapshots, and trading cards with pictures of planes on them floated on a sheet of black velvet backing. A man in his forties, gray flecks sprinkled in his bushy moustache and at his temples, making his head look like a pastry, watched Henry studying the display.

"Hey kid," he said, his voice sanded down by years of yelling and cigarette smoke, "you like this stuff?"

Henry looked up and studied the man, suspicious of someone who would bring something non-sports related into this place.

"Is all this stuff for sale?"

The man smiled. "Some of it. Some of it's just for show. You like this stuff, kid? You into war?"

Henry shrugged his shoulders, suddenly bashful and ashamed to admit that he did indeed like "this stuff."

The guy stood up and took his hands out of the pockets of his old Army issue green jacket.

"This one here," he said pointing at one of the medals, "I got for being a superior marksman. See the little bullseye?" Henry nodded, entranced. "This one over here's for bravery. And this one…"

"Is the Purple Heart." Henry interrupted. "Sorry."

"That's okay," the man said. "I'm glad you know what it is."

"Were you in Vietnam?" Henry asked him, getting a little more comfortable, bolstered in his confidence by knowing what the Purple Heart was.

The guy nodded.

"And you got hurt?"

He nodded again.

"What…" Henry paused not knowing quite how to finish the question.

"What was it like?" the man finished the question for him. "Is that what you want to know?"

Henry nodded, embarrassed again.

The guy laughed and thought about it for a minute.

"That's a hard one..." he paused. "What's your name?"

"Henry."

"Nice to meet you, Henry." He stuck out his hand to shake. "I'm Bill."

Henry shook his hand and was surprised by how hard his skin felt, tough and stretched, so unlike his father's or any other hand he had ever touched. "Nice to meet you, too," Henry replied.

"So, getting back to your question. Fuck, dude. I don't know. What's anything like that you want to forget but at the same time remember every little bit of?" He stopped, lit a cigarette, and blew the first drag up to the ceiling, watching the smoke drift away. If there was an answer to be divined in the white puff of smoke, Henry couldn't see it.

"Let me try to put this in a way that might make sense to you. You know when you're at school and everyone's kind of picking on you—your teachers, friends, whoever—and you feel like the whole world is just kind of coming down around you? What do you want to do at times like that?"

Henry knew exactly what he meant. He thought of his parents fighting and his dad's indifference toward him, of school and how little he wanted to be there every day. It occurred to him then, perhaps not for the first time, how often life was about not wanting to be doing what it was you were supposed to be doing.

"When I feel like that I just...I just want to go away to where no one knows my name. I want to go to a place where I can start again. Start over."

Bill puffed on his cigarette again and pulled an imaginary piece of tobacco off his tongue.

"That's awfully deep for a…how old are you?"

"Twelve."

"Let me ask you this: do you think you'd actually be any different if you could start over again? Do you think you could change and be the person you wanted to be just like that? If you could start over why not just start over right now? You don't have to go anywhere to do that."

Henry shrugged as the man looked at him with kind eyes.

"It'd be easier that way, though."

"But then you wouldn't really be yourself, would you? You want to be yourself, don't you, Henry? What's so wrong with Henry?"

Henry shrugged again. He felt like an idiot, but he wasn't sure what he was supposed to say to that. He had the inclination to get his dad and bring him over so he could hear this conversation, since there was no way he'd be able to remember it all later. But who was he kidding? Even if he could remember every word, he'd never bring it up with his father.

"Okay, so in your words, because I think you understand already," Bill went on, not noticing Henry blush with pride for the compliment, "it felt just like you described. It felt like all that stuff happened to another person. Or, if not another person, at least in another life. I wish I could put my finger on it, but that wasn't me," he shook his head from side to side and Henry could sense that Bill was disappointed in himself that he couldn't give a better explanation. "That guy in Vietnam was someone else. Truly. And this me," he stuck the cigarette between his lips as he moved his finger around his general area, "this me is the me, in the words of the great philosopher, Henry the Prepubescent," and here he winked, "that's in the new place where nobody knows my name. This is not the real me. Okay? The real me is back there, stuck in a place where everyone knows my name, and where everyone knows the real me. On one hand I want to get back there, like, to put my hands on myself, and really make sure that I was real. But on the other I don't. On the other hand I couldn't be happier that that guy is someone else now."

Henry looked at him, confused, and Bill, sympathetic but not able to make it any easier imitated the kid and gave an earnest shrug of the shoulders.

"Look, Henry, I don't kno,w what to tell you. A guy beats off, he hits the hay…that's everyday life. It's all violent and violence. That's who we are. People never really get over anything. Not really. Maybe that's the way to think about it. Maybe this is all a war and our only job is to get ourselves to the next part. To the next life. Whatever you want to call it. Maybe that's how you should think about it. Does that make any more sense?"

Henry smiled and nodded out of politeness, even though he barely could process what had just been explained to him.

"But look," Bill said, clapping his hands together, "I don't want to bum you out. You wanted to know what was for sale, right? Okay, here's what I've got." He took out a pack of trading cards that showed profiles of different fighter jets from down through the ages. "Take this. Forget this baseball shit, right?"

Henry smiled. "Right."

He took the pack of cards and gave Bill a dollar. They said goodbye to one another, and Henry walked away wishing that he could somehow keep talking to the man, hang out with him and get to know more about what the war had been like and how he got his medals.

Back at Burl's table he found his father who was sitting there showing some cards to the other three or four men gathered around. His father looked up and nodded at him.

"Hey, kid. How'd you do?"

"Good."

"Did you get anything?"

He took the pack of fighter plane cards out of his pocket and showed them to his dad: the MiG, the F-16, Mustangs and Messerschmitts.

"What is all that crap?" one of the men asked.

His father shook his head.

"I don't know. Room full of baseball cards and the kid finds the one thing that has nothing to do with anything else." He looked at Henry. "Always with this war shit. I don't get it."

Henry put the cards down, but before he could answer, he felt a large, hairy arm snake around the front of his neck and get him in a tight chokehold. He immediately sagged and began pulling at whoever was behind him. He heard Burl laugh, the hairs of his arm tickling Henry's face. "First rule of war, kid. Don't ever turn your back to a room. See what can happen."

The men all laughed as Burl held him there, helpless, and he looked at his dad expecting for him to call an end to the fun, but like the other men, he laughed along at the joke, whether that be the joke of this large expressway of a man holding a twelve-year-old boy by his neck or just the joke that was his son.

The ride home was silent, and when they pulled into the driveway Henry opened the door and tore into the house and straight into his room, slamming the door behind him. His heart raced as he looked for something to break. Something to scream at. Someone to punch. He remembered the cards in his pocket. He took them out and began to tear them up, one at a time, scattering their remains around the room. He gritted his teeth as he tried to shred more than a few at a time, but he wasn't strong enough and the cards only bent.

He was huffing and puffing when he heard a knock at his door. Grace peeked her head inside.

"What happened? Are you okay?"

"I don't care anymore," he said, hyperventilating. "I don't care about anyone anymore."

"Okay, calm down," she took his arm and sat him down on his bed. "Do you want to tell me what happened?"

He shook his head. "No. I just don't want to go to these things with Dad anymore. I don't care about his shit." His voice came out in gulps as he tried not to cry.

She hugged him and patted his back. She looked around the room at all of the posters of guns and tanks and planes that adorned his walls and thought that it must be hard for a boy to be nothing like his dad.

"You don't have to," she cooed to him. "You don't have to ever again."

Chapter 3

THE NEWSROOM LIVED up in every way to his expectations of what working for a newspaper should feel like. An omnipresent tapping of keyboards and human static leaked over everything like slow hurricane damage, and the low mantra of over-eager fluorescent lights peeled away the truth like a reporter with his pad. A stale coffee smell lacquered the walls; it was decrepit to just the right degree, ancient and squeaky the way an antique car was, perfectly living up to the expectations of the bright young people who worked there. Calculated decay, was how Henry thought of it, and he bought into it just like the rest of them, bought into the idea of themselves that made self-confidence seem like more of a vice than an asset.

Henry wasn't sure why he was asked to attend this, his first staff meeting, but instead of excitement his nerves took over and he panicked inwardly as he tried to formulate an explanation. Was he to be publicly humiliated and then fired in front of his co-workers? Called out for some error, some small factual mistake in his research that had reverberated throughout the system, leading to the erosion of the newspaper's credibility and ultimate demise, like a Rube Goldberg machine that could be traced directly back to him, back to something stupid he had unknowingly done. Maybe his being asked to be there had been a mistake, the email invite in his inbox nothing but a bureaucratic oversight, the kind of benign but malicious mistake that led public libraries to send out overdue book notices decades after the fact.

The small talk was loud and vigorous around the table as they waited for the editor, Ken Fowler, to show up, competitive chit-chat, more a general fear of dead air than the need to contribute anything of real substance. When Ken finally showed up and took a seat, Henry was near to having a nervous breakdown. He stared at his hands, which were trembling uncontrollably in his lap, and as much as he willed them to stop, they wouldn't obey, so he shoved them roughly under his butt hoping no one would notice the guy in the corner who looked like he was getting ready for a late-morning prostate exam.

The meeting began, and one by one they went around the table talking about their current assignments, sometimes asking for suggestions from their peers and Ken, sometimes visibly bristling when opinions were offered unsolicited. They were a competitive bunch, it was clear, and he wondered just how much resentment they'd have for a newcomer to their precious coven.

Ken pointed at the guy sitting next to Henry, a young hotshot reporter named Jeff Schofield, the current star of the newsroom who had received a Pulitzer nomination the year before for a piece he had written on transgender police officers. Jeff was dressed as always in a tie and an argyle sweater, beanpole skinny. Truman called him the Scottish tie rack.

"How's the three-parter on black tar heroin coming, Jeff?" Ken asked, looking at some rough drafts he held in his hand.

Jeff leaned back and cleared his throat.

"Good. I'm hoping to finish it by Wednesday and start working on the piece about steroids in the Olympics by end of week."

"Good job. I'm anxious to read it. I guess sources means a whole different thing when you're talking about heroin, huh?"

A courtesy laugh went around the table like a wave at a football game.

"Okay," Ken went on, "I believe that takes us to Mr. Colmes." He cocked his hand like a gun and fired a finger at Henry. "Mr. Colmes, what slice of bad luck are you currently concocting?"

Henry's mouth went dry as he answered. "I...uh...I've been working on Gorbachev the last few days. Interviewing some people and...uh...doing a write-up. Basically..." he felt himself floundering, "basically, that's it."

Out of the corner of his eye he could see Jeff snicker, and he felt indignation rise in him like a fast-moving sickness. Since when did black tar heroin become more important than the guy who ended the fucking Cold War, he thought to himself. But it wasn't about that. As much as he wanted to be one of these hot-shots, one of these kids who'd gotten their master's at Northwestern or Columbia, he wasn't. He had graduated from high school, barely, but college wasn't in the cards. The urge to write was always there and when a friend had told him about the job, he had quickly put together a portfolio of short stories and essays he had written for himself over the years, and that seemed to impress Ken enough to give him a job. He suddenly resented being at the table with these people he so clearly didn't belong with. If it was humiliation Ken was after, he had accomplished it.

"That's it?" Ken asked.

"Uh," he racked his brain, trying to think of anything he could add that wouldn't make him sound like a complete idiot, but couldn't come up with a thing, "yeah, that's it."

"Okay," Ken said. "If that's it, then that's it. I guess we need more for you to do around here. Do you do windows?"

More laughter as Henry's ears grew so hot with shame, they felt like they would melt off his head. "I'm kidding, Henry. Don't look so serious," he said as he fixed his eyes at the next person down. "Next victim, I mean, person." Another laugh from the group. They were drowning in fucking laughter.

*   *   *

Henry stood up as the meeting adjourned and absent-mindedly pushed his shirttails into his pants. Pushing his shirt down had become more a nervous habit as much as a point of grooming, and he saw Jeff smile again as he did it. A cold shiver of anger crept over him, the haunting of an adolescent impulse, as he glared at Jeff, who was already on to his next assignment—making a clumsy pass at Ken's assistant, Jocelyn Davidson, who was, without a doubt, the most beautiful woman on their floor, if not at the entire newspaper. She was graceful and gorgeous, painfully so, expensive furniture with legs. One felt lonely just for wanting her. He felt the anger ebb away as he watched them talk, wishing he had the guts to make small talk like that, to just walk up to a girl and start talking about a bunch of bullshit. Some people called it an art, talking to women, and if this was art, this laughing too hard and taking any opportunity to touch her shoulder, if this was art, then he was seriously painting with a broken brush.

"Hey, Henry," Ken Fowler called from the door of his office, "Can you come in here for a minute?"

Henry stared as Ken disappeared back inside his office and slowly started to collect his things. He brushed by Jeff and Jocelyn on his way out of the conference room and heard Jeff joke to her as he passed, "They must have gotten a call from the Pulitzer Committee." She tittered in complicity, proving that, when you got down to it, scorn was most effective when it was a conspiracy.

Once in his office Ken pointed at a chair. "Sit down."

Henry sat and looked around the room as Ken finished typing an email. Framed articles, yellowing under glass, were hung on the walls along with pictures of Ken with his family: a trip to Epcot Center, making fudge, someone's graduation. It was strange to think that this is where all that history, personal and otherwise, finally culminated; hanging on the walls of a shabby office, going unnoticed except at the most awkward of moments, when nervous eyes had nowhere to go except for the walls, bookshelves, anywhere but straight ahead.

There were a lot of reasons why Ken might call him into his office for a private conversation, almost none of them good. He knew there were cutbacks at some of the sections and he knew that as far as extraneous went he was the cat's meow. He had also, not too long ago, masturbated in the men's bathroom after a 15-minute fantasy blackout wherein he imagined pummeling Jocelyn from behind while she was laid out over a stack of bundled newspapers, the *PennySaver* clinging to her small sweaty breasts like some bargain basement S&M get-up. There was no way they could have known that, though, unless there were cameras in the bathroom, which didn't seem likely.

Ken sent his email and pushed himself away from his desk. The swivel chair conveyed his bulky form so that he was facing Henry.

"Boy. Mondays, huh? I mean, when is this day going to finally go fuck itself? Am I right?"

Henry nodded and tried to force a smile to his dry lips. He couldn't get the image of himself masturbating in the bathroom stall out of his mind and was beginning to feel sick. He wondered what the worst they could do to you for getting caught beating off at work. A firing seemed like the least of it. He'd probably have to register with the authorities every time he moved or tried to buy tickets to a PG movie. Or worse, they'd write a huge scarlet 'M' on his record so that when the next job called to check his references Ken would be obliged to say, "Henry? Great worker. Terrible masturbator."

"What I wanted to talk to you about is this…" Henry tried to keep his eyes on Ken's mouth to keep them from wandering back to the wall where the pictures hung in solidarity with an irreconcilable past. That felt like a little too much to ask for given the circumstances. Better to brace yourself for the worst and hope for something slightly better than ritual disembowelment, or for them to hand you a pink slip that had the words 'aggressive heterosexuality' written as the cause for termination.

"You've been here for a while, and I know you didn't take this job to be a researcher for the rest of your life. You're a good writer," he lifted a folder from his desk and took out Henry's old writing samples. "I was just going back and reading some of the stuff you submitted when you first came here. I wanted to give you a writing job then, but there wasn't anything at the time." He put the papers back in the folder concluding the visual aid portion of this nerve-wracking conversation. "So, what I want to offer you is this: a chance to write a large obit retrospective piece that, when it runs, will probably start you on the front page—below the fold, of course. Are you interested?"

He was so amazed for a second at what he had just been told that all he could do was stare blankly at Ken.

"I'm not sure how to take your reaction," Ken said.

"Yeah, yeah," Henry said quickly, trying to regain his composure, "I'd love it." He tried to restrain his enthusiasm, knowing it was the surest way to make someone regret having done something nice for you. Too much emoting made most people nervous.

"Okay, well you don't even know who it is yet. Do you want me to tell you?"

"Uh-huh," Henry nodded and spoke at the same time like he was his own ventriloquist's dummy.

"Do you remember the Reverend Doug Potter?"

Henry blinked. It had to be a rhetorical question. Everyone alive over the age of thirty knew who Potter was. Younger than thirty, and you just thought you knew who he was from the creepy T-shirts and posters kids had of him on their dorm walls like they might of Charles Manson or John Wayne Gacy in his clown get-up, believing somehow that reverence of these terrible men was the most effective kind of youthful rebellion. After all, the bogeyman wasn't real, was he?

"Sure. I remember him. I actually thought he was already dead."

"No, not yet. Unfortunately."

Potter was, depending on your political affiliation and age, any one of the following: Satan, a Soviet, AIDS, thermonuclear war, or if you were doing a lot of cocaine, all of the above. He was anything and everything in the ephemera that couldn't be touched, every childhood fear wrapped into one tight innocent-looking package. And to make matters worse for Henry, Potter and his "children" had lived in California, not too far from the Nevada border, which was, to Henry's young mind, not too far from LA, which meant of course he was probably just down the street. Maybe even in the next house.

Henry could remember images of Potter on TV and in magazines, always in his gentleman farmer's getup: overalls, a corncob pipe, straw hat, a smile that could be measured in acreage, a most charming piece of arable land. And beneath the smile a chipped tooth suggesting he was not above getting his hands dirty and not so vain that he didn't realize a little thing like a chipped tooth wasn't so much a blemish as it was character building.

The Reverend Doug Potter was also the leader of an infamous California cult called the Children of Light. It seemed innocent when they first came on the scene. The reverend espoused a new kind of philosophy that was rooted in a reverence for nature, an agrarian point of view that saw the world as god's farm, and his followers the flowers and crops, the beautiful sustenance, spiritual and physical, that would nourish the world as it went through its inevitable trials and tribulations.

Potter had started his movement in the sixties, born from the egalitarian spirit of the times, and at first it was seen as just another vehicle on the frenetic highway of spiritual enlightenment that had so thoroughly infused society at the time. The Children of Light lasted, though, where others failed because of Potter's willingness to change with the times, to keep his movement and his people as relevant as possible no matter the political or societal realities of the day. When the hippie-dippy energy that had fueled so much of the flower power movement ran low, Potter had adeptly repositioned the Children of Light as a kind of self-help implement, a place where recovering hippies could nurse their bruised egos while the sixties became the seventies, and even after that, when the iceberg that was the seventies slowly melted, feeding into the great big ocean that became the eighties. In the early seventies a COL follower had died and left a huge piece of desert land to Potter that was just on the California side of the California-Nevada border. Potter and his followers quickly built a makeshift town there and almost a hundred people picked up and moved overnight to the place, which was quickly dubbed Pottersville. Starting in the late seventies, Potter began running spiritual retreats for wayward searchers, a generous description given that most of the men and women who showed up at the compound's gates were people at the end of their mortal ropes, human coffee grounds who had come out of the other side of a decade of bingeing on cocaine and so much casual sex their self-esteem resembled an inner-city trauma center. Seedlings, Potter generously called them, looking for a plot of land. Many of these refugees never returned to their mediocre lives, deciding instead to stay in the scorching hot non-judgmental paradise they had either heard about in AA coffee klatches or read about in the backs of free city newspapers, next to the ads for massage parlors, escort services, and people needed for medical experiments. In short, Pottersville grew.

In the early eighties, Potter again reconceived the group, infusing it this time with political overtones, knowing it would need to be attractive to young people once again if it was to survive. For the first time COL members were noticed at anti-nuclear and anti-death penalty protests standing along-side real social justice advocates who were there for political, environmental, and religious reasons, honorable convictions that had to be respected if not accepted. There was footage of Martin Sheen and Jane Fonda standing with Potter at the gates of the San Onofre Nuclear Generating Station, each of them holding a large sign demanding an ambiguous version of "justice." They passed a small bullhorn back and forth as they each took a turn leading the crowd of several thousand outraged people in angry chants, primal scream therapy for those who had engaged in nothing but self-indulgence since the late sixties. Fonda and a small entourage had even visited Pottersville once but left before Potter could sit down with her for some one-on-one "cultivation," a term the COL used to describe someone's first introduction to the group. She had described the vibe to the media later as "spooky."

The group's upward trajectory stalled out permanently though in 1984, a year Henry remembered perfectly well, even though he was only eleven at the time, because of the Summer Olympics being in town. The traffic was a thing of nightmares that summer, the heat particularly searing, but those weren't the things an eleven-year-old boy remembered. An eleven-year-old remembered the freshly painted murals along the freeway depicting happy people of all races and nationalities coming together in a show of unity next to the choking stench of the 101 and 405 freeways. He remembered the omnipresent Olympic rings, which had quickly been co-opted as a ubiquitous marketing tool for every kind of business and product in town, from the bagel shop with its obvious carbohydrate tribute to the dry cleaners and their five linked wire hangers in the window. He could recall with crystal clear clarity the nightly news countdown that would begin its broadcast by cutting live to the torch's exact location, celebrities of the day like Mr. T, O.J. Simpson, and Michael Jackson taking their turns with it for a few photo opportunistic steps as it drew closer and closer. A few kids at school got to carry the torch, and when Henry asked his father if he could have a turn his dad told him that those kids' fathers had paid $500 and it would be a cold day in hell when he would spend that kind of money for his son to have his picture taken with a glorified flashlight.

His family gathered around the TV to watch the opening ceremonies, and despite how blasé he tried to seem about it, Henry could tell his father was impressed by the whole thing. He watched from the corner of his eye as his father's lips moved along with the National Anthem. His father pointed out Carl Lewis as he walked the track of the Coliseum during the Parade of Athletes, telling them to pay attention to that one, that he was going to blow them all away. They had just bought their first microwave and the rich smell of buttery popcorn reached them from the kitchen. "Oh my gosh, that smells so good," his mother whined with happiness as she got up to fetch their first irradiated snack. "It smells just like a movie theater in here." When the broadcast ended, his father was the first to get up. He hitched up his jeans and gathered the empty popcorn bowls to take back into the kitchen. "It's not going to be the same without the Soviets," he declared as he left the room. "It's not the same thing," he said, leaving them with that one last bitter admonition, a warning that they might think it was great what they were watching, what they believed in, but that it didn't really count. Not in the long run and not compared to the past.

The only piece of news that could penetrate the nightly broadcast of the Games was when the scandal broke at Pottersville on the fifth day of the Olympics. They were watching women's gymnastics when the local NBC affiliate went live to the desert with breaking news as police surrounded the gates of the compound, guns drawn everywhere, police car lights rotating weakly in the desert sun, all pointed at the gate. It was like watching an old Western, Henry remembered thinking at the time, the kind of standoff that could only end in a river of blood because resolution in such a desolate locale equaled bloodshed. Afterwards, there would no doubt be buzzards that would descend and strut around like they owned the place, not to mention a mangy dog that would only lift its head to bark at ghosts. After the first hour or so when it appeared that nothing exciting was imminent, NBC had resumed its broadcast of the Games. Henry's dad began compulsively flipping the channels between the Olympics and the standoff, which other networks were covering live, consumed with the fear of missing something dramatic, be it a gold medal or a gunfight.

"Stop it, Phil," Henry's mother finally erupted, "you're making me nauseous. Pick one and leave it."

His father fired a stern look at her that was more hurt than anger and then disappeared into the kitchen in a huff. He was such a child. Henry looked over at Grace, who grinned widely at him and he smiled back and it almost became laughter, which, he knew would turn into uncontrollable laughter, and if his father came back and saw that, he was unsure what might happen, so he put his fingers up to his mouth and started chomping on his nails, unwilling to run the risk of unleashing some sort of middle-aged temper tantrum.

They heard a loud noise and in a minute Henry's father was back carrying the small black and white set they watched sometimes when they ate their dinner, reruns of *Three's Company* and *Alice*, cheap morality plays that did more than an adequate job as a surrogate for real life conversation. He stacked the small TV on top of the larger color one, plugged it in, and turned on the standoff. "Voila," he announced. "Best of both worlds." He turned the volume all the way down on the set with the Olympics and sat back down in his plump reclining chair, a self-satisfied look plastered across his face as though he had just cured cancer.

"Unbelievable," his mother responded, crossing her arms and leaning back. "You're something else."

Grace caught Henry's eye again, smiled, and mouthed the word "crazy." Henry nodded and smiled back.

They sat in silence and watched as nothing continued to happen, and nothingness was indeed what it was, the continuous and active articulation of anticipation. Someone, his sister maybe, went into the kitchen and soon there was the now familiar sound of the microwave grinding to life and then the smell of popcorn that quickly brought him back to a couple of days before when they had all been sitting like this to watch the opening ceremonies: same seats, same expectant posture, same movie theater smell marinating their expectations. Henry looked from his father's face to his mother's and then to his sister, waiting for someone to say something poignant or reassuring about what they were seeing unfold, maybe tell him it was going to be okay, maybe explain how this enthusiasm was different than the excitement they had felt for Carl Lewis just a few days before. But no one said a word, and Henry, left to his own devices, came to the conclusion that perhaps this was life at its best, going from one spectacle to the next, leaving no room to breathe or to think. Downtime was to be feared worse than anything that might be lurking behind Pottersville's dusty gates. All that was missing was the music.

They learned, from a reporter's somber voice coming from the tinny speakers of the smaller TV, that the police had been called because of allegations of sexual abuse brought by a girl who had lived in the compound with her parents and recently escaped. The girl, whose name was later revealed to be Flora, went to her uncle and aunt's house and regaled them with horrific tales of abuse, of children being shared among the senior members in the compound, ruthless corporal punishment doled out for the slightest of infractions of what sounded to be an indecipherable set of rules that seemed to change all the time, almost made up on the fly, the girl suggested. Flora talked about being singled out as a "Special Seed" at an early age, one of a group of about a dozen girls who'd had bestowed upon them new names by Potter himself, the names of flowers, and were destined for something better. What "something better" meant was unclear, but Flora didn't wait around to find out. She knew it was close because two days before she decided to leave, the twelve Special Seeds were given matching white dresses, a flowing light thing, she told her aunt and uncle, that made her feel like something bad was going to happen to her and the others, because dresses that pretty meant you were going somewhere special and having lived in Pottersville for the better part of her life, she knew firsthand that there was no place special to go in the dusty compound. That "special place," she knew, was a place in Potter's mind, a mind she had grown to fear the older she got, the more her thoughts became her own and her future became more ominous than glowing. Her mother and father treated her with extra care in those last few days, doting on her, petting her, reminding her to think wonderful thoughts. They were proud of her, she had recalled, of that she had no doubt, expectant and hopeful, and their expectations were the final nail in the coffin, because like the dress that hung on the back of the cheap plywood door of their cabin, they were expectations she knew she could never dream of fulfilling, not because she wasn't an able and smart girl, but because Potter often asked them to be things and think of things that were out of their control. There was such a thing, she had said to the authorities, as the wrong kind of hope.

A year or so later, after the standoff was over (eighteen hours in total. "Almost as long as the fucking opening ceremonies," his dad had joked to no one in particular) and three of Potter's men were shot dead by the police and Potter himself had been sentenced to fourteen years in jail on weapons charges, Flora, whose real name it turned out was Claudia, appeared on *20/20* with Barbara Walters. Henry and his family, like every household in America, tuned in to watch Claudia, who was now seventeen, tell her story to Barbara, the camera pulling back to show her nervously clawing apart a Kleenex in her lap, dissecting it almost down to its molecular level, patiently and detachedly explaining the nuances of her situation, her fear a sketch of fear, her relief at being free just the idea of relief. There was something not right about her, America thought, something *off*.

"Such a phony," Grace snorted when the camera switched to show Barbara's face, all pinched up with worry and concern, patiently waiting for Claudia to finish her thought before firing another leading question she hoped would take them into the land of gory details, the only real estate really worth investing in.

"Shh," her mother warned her, never taking her eyes from the set.

"Which one?" Henry asked her. "The girl or Ba-ba Wa-wa?"

Grace thought about it for a moment and then said, "Both."

"I told you both to be quiet," their mother turned to face them. "I'm interested in this. If you're not, then you can leave the room."

"Sorry," Henry mumbled, unused to seeing his mother get so upset. That was airspace usually reserved for his father.

Grace, though, was unfazed. She snorted derisively and walked upstairs to her room, slamming the door behind her for good measure.

The interview went on, and with about ten minutes to go before the show would end and *Webster* and *Mr. Belvedere* would return them all to their regularly scheduled lives, Barbara took a photo from a folder on her lap and held it up to Claudia.

"Do you know what this is?" Barbara asked her before the camera shifted around to show the image to the audience.

"No," Claudia answered, but her face, which in an instant had become a pale smudge of tremulous features, said otherwise.

"Are you sure?" Barbara went on. She was a dog with a bone, and it was only then, as Claudia's posture collapsed like a deck of cards and her hands stopped tearing the Kleenex because suddenly she was no longer nervous, she was something else, or rather *somewhere* else, that Barbara let the camera show the picture, which, she explained as she let the audience drink it in, showed a windowless room with concrete walls, completely undecorated save for twelve nooses that hung from the ceiling in two perfectly even rows of six, each with a simple footstool beneath it.

"Are you sure you've never seen this room before, Claudia?" Barbara asked again as the girl continued to stare at the photo. The camera lingered on Claudia's face, waiting for some kind of reaction that would satisfy the weight of the implication, but the ten quiet, static seconds that followed, which to Henry and the rest of the country felt like an eternity, yielded nothing illuminating and maybe, Henry thought, as he reflected in Ken's office, that's what made it seem so terrifying at the time, that there was nothing else to say, that the picture said it all.

"Maybe you shouldn't be watching this," Henry's mom said, turning first to him and then to his father. "Maybe Henry shouldn't be watching this."

But his dad said nothing because like everyone else watching the interview he couldn't tear his eyes from the screen.

Later that night, Henry had a dream he remembered vividly when he woke the next morning about Claudia in her long white dress, an apparition floating breezily across the endless desert at dusk. He watched her from a distance and the closer she got to him the more excited he remembered feeling. Excited to meet her, to touch her hand, to ask her how she moved so effortlessly. But when she was finally near enough to him that he could touch her, the white of her dress had faded and he saw that she wasn't a girl at all, but a thorny sagebrush bouncing its way across the landscape, a product of the wind that pushed it. And when he woke up, hot tears were streaming down his face, and even odder than that, an overwhelming sense of loss that it was his fault somehow that he would never have the chance to meet her.

*   *   *

Back in Ken's office, Henry remembered the dream all too vividly and the sadness he had felt at the time suddenly revisited him and then just as quickly was gone again.

"What's wrong with him?" Henry asked.

"Not sure exactly. We've heard cancer and we've also heard AIDS. The Children of Light are so damn secretive, it's hard to know anything for sure. It's a good story, though. People are still interested in him. People love cults, or anything else that has the potential to fuck them up and spit them out, for that matter. I think it's a big story for California. When he dies, I mean."

"I think so, too."

"So," Ken said, exhaling the word more than saying it, "do you think you can get me 10,000 words in two weeks?"

Henry finally let himself smile. "Definitely."

"I realize that you're probably thinking that this is your big break," Ken said, "and you're right. You're going to do a good job, Henry. Not because of the pressure, but because you're up to the challenge."

"Thanks," Henry replied. The flattery had caught him off-guard. It'd been a long time since he got a pat on the head for anything.

"All right then," Ken said, standing up to shake his hand, "get out of here. You've got ink to spill, kid."

Ken patted him on the back and opened the door. As he walked out, Ken said, "God. I wish I could get away with dressing like you at work."

It struck Henry as a completely passive-aggressive thing to say, but he immediately and almost unconsciously began to push down the edges of his shirt into his pants. Ken saw him doing it and smirked, enough of a look to make Henry feel the bitter humiliation of being caught wanting a thing too much.

*   *   *

Later that night he sat at the Golden Hue with Alberto, slowly sipping something red, not his customary poison, but more attractive for sure, celebratory as far as these things went. Truman had yet to show up and Henry felt a tension in Alberto, a closed-upness that didn't exist when Truman was around. Alberto pushed a bottle of Bud around, moving it like a hockey puck across the wet table, hiccupping terribly from some indigestible meal no doubt.

Henry glanced around the bar, bored, and noticed how old the place felt, how resistant to change it was. Some people might call that quality quaint, but quaintness to Henry didn't necessarily describe benign indifference. Things that wanted to change did. Those that didn't, didn't. Both acts were conscious. In light of what had happened to him earlier, this chance at something more at the paper, he suddenly started to feel a little depressed, ashamed at himself for not wanting more earlier, ascribing to the panorama of self-doubt that had been his preference all along.

"So," Henry looked at Alberto, plunging into the shark-plagued waters of small talk, "how's the novel coming?"

"Oh, I bailed on that," Alberto said matter-of-factly, waving his hand around like he was swatting flies. "It wasn't going anywhere. Besides, I'm doing this new thing with Truman. You should ask him about it."

Henry smiled at the notion of there only being time in Alberto's life for one non-work-related activity at a time. It was probably how he had let himself get so disgustingly heavy, this prioritization method of his.

"Are you saying Truman talked you out of it."

He thought he was being funny, but Alberto stopped moving his beer and glared at Henry over the top of his tortoise-shell glasses. He quickly lobbed a peanut in between his lips that were turned down at the corners.

"You've got to be kidding me," Alberto said sternly.

Henry waited for more, but that was it. That was all the retort he was apparently entitled to. He broke the awkward silence by standing up and heading to the bathroom in the back of the bar. He passed through a dimly lit hall that was scratched up with sex-starved graffiti, the hieroglyphics of want. He pushed the door open and ran head on into a woman he knew coming out of the women's room. Her name was Kelly, a regular at the Golden Hue, and once long ago in a drunken restlessness Henry had taken her home to his little apartment in Koreatown. She had a certain charm that was undeniable, a siren on a bar stool, the kind of woman who was clearly "older" but her exact age would forever be a mystery. The only way she'd ever give it up would be involuntarily, by cutting her in half and counting the rings of sadness inside.

Henry smiled at her, and she glanced at him quickly, drew air in through her teeth as if about to speak and then, deciding not to, smiled back and pushed through into the bar.

He wondered what had happened to earn him such a strange response. He checked his breath by blowing against his palm, smoothed down his hair, tucked in his shirt. The good news of earlier today was being eroded by the second, but he decided not to let it get him down. Life was, after all, a sea only insofar as you could never see the other side. Moments weren't buoys. People weren't life jackets. That was why Alberto had become angry when he had made the comment about Truman, Kelly brushing him off, Ken Fowler insulting him: who wanted to show anyone that they needed someone?

He got back to the table and as soon as he had put his hand up for another drink, the door flew open and Truman blew in like a Santa Ana wind. When he was close enough to hear, Alberto feigned looking at his watch and said, "Oh. Is it rape o'clock already?"

Truman laughed and slapped his friend on the back. "Is that new? I love it. It's going to be the title of my autobiography. Rape O'Clock, the Truman Porter Story. I'll dedicate it to you guys. To my good friends, Ready, Willing, and Unable. Wait, that's three people. Alberto, you'll have to be two of the three. Can you handle that? Do you want to be ready and willing? Or unable?"

Alberto shook his head and whinnied a laugh through his nose. To the naked eye, their give-and-take bordered on the romantic.

Henry stuck his hand up again. "The usual," he hollered, in what he hoped sounded like an authoritative want.

The bartender scoffed. "You've got to be kidding me," he yelled back, refusing to acknowledge Henry's dedication to alcohol from over the years.

What did it take exactly, Henry wondered, to be recognized as a reprobate? There were no easy cliques to get into anymore, the world was becoming too self-conscious for anyone's own good.

"How about a vodka grapefruit," Henry called back.

"You call that a regular?" The bartender yelled back. "Regular douche, maybe."

He led a chorus of laughter at Henry's expense, humiliation tacked on to the end of a brilliant bar tab, but Henry decided to shake it off, that the good news he had run into in Ken Fowler's office would lift him up and over happy hour and beyond.

Truman noticed the confidence and, as he ate a handful of stale peanuts, said, "You look particularly chipper. What's your problem?"

Henry told them both about his conversation with Ken Fowler and about his assignment. When he was done he pulled the straw from his drink and took a long sip.

"Congratulations," Alberto said, raising his drink in salute.

"Yeah," Truman added, sipping his own boozy concoction. "Congratulations. I've gotta say, though, I'm kind of surprised. I never mistook you for someone with ambition."

"Thanks," Henry said, trying to decide if he should attempt to muster up a semblance of indignation. "You're the third person today who's kind of made me feel like shit about myself."

Truman looked surprise. "Only the third?"

Truman did have a point. Ambition had never been Henry's strong suit, and he probably shouldn't have been surprised that his co-workers had picked up on that over the years. It wasn't exactly something he expressed aloud, this lack of ambition. It was more a kinetic thing, inert but not forgotten, the simmering possibilities of what might not be. Entropy was exhausting.

But when Henry thought about it, he could almost imagine himself succeeding at this assignment, being promoted to features, and then maybe news stories. One day, perhaps he would be elevated to war correspondent, caught in some foreign land with pen and pad, inhaling the fumes of conflict; jet exhaust and scorched desert, the sizzling oil and dung smell of a foreign marketplace. And he would be in the middle of it, looking around, uncovering the truth, calling out the names of planes and the size of artillery exploding in the distance, giddy as a bird watcher in an aviary.

Alberto laughed and raised his glass again, "Congratulations."

"What was that for?" Henry asked him.

"Probably nothing. Reflex."

Truman went on.

"I just meant ambition is a slippery slope, Henry. Typically it's a slide and you can see it coming for a while. I haven't seen it coming from you, is all. I never even knew you had the desire to be a writer, to do anything but what you were doing. Can you blame me? Do you think I'm wrong?"

He had to admit to himself that Truman was not wrong. Ambition had never exactly been one of his strong suits, neither imagined nor vocalized, and it wasn't that he didn't have any, it was just that it wasn't fully realized. He normally didn't let himself go down the road of thinking good things about himself and what might be. It was a gambler's logic, to think of the worst possible outcome to protect yourself so that when failure eventually came it could never match up to the projected catastrophe. But also it was superstition. Pure and simple. Making an offering of hope, the sacrifice of optimism, giving these things up to assuage the gods in exchange for the promise of mediocrity and the great honor of just getting by. He didn't fool himself that his panoramic doubt wasn't a silent prayer in some ways, playing dumb blonde to the universe's sugar daddy, but then again, opportunity like what had happened today didn't exactly come along all that often. Up until this afternoon the dream of war was the only one he had, a firm belief in things bigger than himself, cosmic events that lured all people in with its promise of camaraderie and never dying alone. That was important. The possibility of war loomed here, too, though. One day he might find himself a great war journalist, pen pressed to pad, scavenging for life in the flat-bottomed boat ride of combat. There was some sort of relaxation in chaos, a certain unburdening of examination that was appealing. It was enough just to live. That was an appealing notion, too.

"Just because I never said it doesn't mean it's not true."

Truman slapped his head. "Oh, I get it. You're pleading simplicity, is that it? You're saying you didn't want to complicate the public perception of you?"

"I didn't say that. All I meant was that I didn't want to complicate things at work by being too much of a complainer."

Truman clenched his jaw. "Okay, let me get this straight." He picked up his beer and, like a boa devouring its prey, seemed to unhinge his lower jaw as he drank the whole thing in one constant, horrendous swallow. "You're saying that you were just lying back, waiting for Ken to notice you, not wanting to cause any trouble in the meantime, because you didn't want to make life hard for yourself?" He wiped his mouth with the sleeve of his shirt. "Let me tell you something, my friend, there is nothing hard about life. The problem these days is that everything it too easy."

Henry winced. It was almost unbearable when Truman got into a groove like this, all preachy and philosophical, bending logic to fit his triumphantly unbendable universal truths. Truman lived by his own maxims, a liturgy of shady assertions that guided his everyday life and made him utterly unaccountable to anyone else's opinions or beliefs. Also, these "truths" were so convoluted and complex that to try and follow them, even for the sake of avoiding future sermons on one's own idiocy, was almost impossible.

"Look at you with your *dijonnaise*," Truman scolded Henry as he took a bite of his club sandwich. "Was the stress of mustard and mayo too much for you?"

Henry rolled his eyes as he chewed.

"Don't roll your eyes at me, you lazy scornful fuck. I'm serious here. Look at Alberto, for example." Truman turned so that he was facing his friend. "How many times have I told you that it's never okay to wear denim above the waist? Yet, you persist. Don't you? Don't you?" Truman shook his head as he waved a finger at Alberto. His universe was realized. The Big Bang Theory cum fashion faux pas.

Alberto giggled as he sipped his drink through a stirring straw. It was a funny sight watching a voluminously fat man sucking a gin and tonic through a tiny straw. It reminded Henry of all the slow mechanics of nature, the eons it took for wind and sand to erode mountains in the desert. And he was about to get mad, then, to tell Alberto to say something back, to hit Truman, sit on him, push the boundaries of their friendship through assault, when it struck him that Alberto was entertained by these rants. This was symbiosis, plain and simple. The world could not exist without this horrid type of give and take.

A crude silence descended.

At another table three guys in their mid-twenties sat hunched over beers in serious discussion. Henry listened in on their conversation, which was an argument about a porn password the three of them shared but could not use simultaneously. They were coordinating a masturbation rotation.

"You always blame me," one of them said in soft defense, tightening his grasp on a trendily low-rent beer. "How can you be so sure it's me and not Stan?"

"Because," another spat back, "the search history was all zaftig chicks. You're the only one that beats off to fat women."

Truman, who had been listening in as well, shook his head in mock disgust.

"That's what the recession has done to us. Scrambling over jerk-off time." He lit a cigarette and then quickly put it out; his smoking habit was kept alive by this deft act of quick rebellion. "It doesn't matter. The sad thing is in another age those three would be plotting a revolution."

Henry looked around at the bar and admitted to himself that it didn't exactly seem like the type of place that might inspire the birth of any great social movements or earth-shattering intellectual treatises anytime soon.

Old calendars and pictures of women with tits larger than African children adorned the walls. Outside was the continuous busy chatter of Orthodox Jews who seemed to do nothing but walk to and fro all day long in their Pippi Longstocking tights. And at eleven, the church next door opened its doors, spilling out that night's AA meeting attendees. It was then that the bar's customers would get together by the front door, sipping their drinks with luxurious diligence, lording their bad habits over the recently recovered. It was evil, but communal, and that made if feel like it was okay.

The bar's ambience was that it had no ambience. It was a black hole of possibilities.

Henry stretched out his arms and let out a ragged yawn.

"You've got too many rules, and I've gotta say, your intellectual jailbait is starting to make me crazy."

"Rules?" Truman was incredulous. Alberto sat quietly, smug, blowing bubbles into his forlorn cocktail. "How dare you!" Truman went on. "These aren't rules. These aren't just suggestions and rants. What I've done here is transcended. I've become the zeitgeist. Listen, I don't like to boast, but I think what we're seeing here, and what Alberto and I wanted to share with you tonight, is the start of something bigger. A complete revolution of thought and critical analysis."

"What are you talking about?"

"I'm talking about the next phase of being. I'm talking about what comes after postmodernism. I'm talking about total deconstruction here. Post-postmodernism. A double-negative. Reversing gravity."

Truman was high on his own grandiosity, and although slightly annoyed, Henry's buzz had given him the patience and openness to at least appreciate this performance on an artistic level.

"Post-postmodern?"

"He's not bullshitting you, Henry," Alberto spoke softly, a sharp contrast to Truman's bomb door of a mouth. "This is a really good idea he came up with. And it's not only going to make us a lot of money, but it's going to change a lot of things, too."

They looked around and saw that Truman was walking over to the table where the three conspiratorial masturbators sat plotting their soon-to-be well-scheduled ejaculations. He leaned over them spreading his hands out on their table to support himself, and they looked up almost simultaneously, alarm coming over their faces.

"Remember this, men: the pursuit of happiness IS the

fucking rat race."

*　　*　　*

Henry sat in the backseat of Truman's little Honda. Alberto was in the passenger seat fiddling with the radio dial.

"What are you doing? Stop that." Truman spat at him.

"I'm looking for the Allman Brothers. Try and tell me the Allman Brothers aren't on right now. I can't believe that."

Truman nodded a benign assent. He was not one to rein in dogma.

The car swerved slightly as they drove drunk from downtown into some part of LA that Henry couldn't immediately identify. It was one of those parts of town that had no name: not West Hollywood, that tricked out municipal closet, nor Hollywood proper with its drug addicts sunning themselves in the heat of their own hype. No, this was just LA. Plain LA. Urban pre-come. Potent, but not the least bit threatening. Just there getting your underwear wet for no good reason. It was neglected, this no-named part of town, but not blighted. That would give it too much character. It was transitory, half-assed, full to bursting with bus stops and no-named shops: *panaderías* and medical marijuana dispensaries. The tax base was a crying fucking shame.

Truman parked the car and walked to one of the condo buildings that lined a residential street. They took the elevator up to the third floor to a hallway lined with doors to different units. Truman stopped in front of number seventeen, stuck the key in the lock, and turned to face Henry.

"We want to show you something and then ask you a question. Are you ready?"

Henry was drunk and feeling light. He was ready for anything. He was going to be a war reporter, after all. He might as well start the battle at home.

"If it's a dead hooker, then I can already tell you the answer is New Jersey."

Truman laughed. "Wow. You really are happy. All nubile and showing your teeth. Careful, Henry, that's how fetishes are born."

Truman pushed the door open to an empty apartment, and together, he and Alberto unveiled their grand scheme. Their plan was simple: priced out of home ownership in Los Angeles, Alberto and Truman had rented apartments adjacent to one another. They let no one know that they were friends and were both planning on moving in over the next couple of weeks. As time wore on, they would begin to publically not get along, and the basis of their disagreements would all be centered around the fact that Alberto was Hispanic and Truman was white. They would keep up the racial turmoil, increasing it ever so slightly as time wore on until they had established that there was a clear and undeniable racial problem in their building and hopefully, if the plan worked, in their immediate neighborhood. The neighborhood's resulting bad reputation would drive down property value to the point where Alberto and Truman could scoop up the places at a steal and, after mending fences, sell at an enormous profit.

"The opposite of gentrification. We're going to facilitate decay for the betterment of others," Truman said.

"What others?" Henry asked incredulously.

Truman pointed at Alberto as Alberto pointed back at Truman.

"You guys are insane. This is really," Henry searched for the word to express his disbelief, "wrong."

"Wrong?" Alberto snapped back. "What's wrong is that we haven't done this until now. This is the thing that we deserve.

It's about time that me and Truman were rewarded for our interracial friendship. It's not every day you see a Latino and a Gringo get along so well. Society owes us something for that, doesn't it?"

"Gringo," Truman nodded. "I like that. Let's make sure we use it in one of the opening salvos. It'll be a great precursor to me lighting a piñata on fire on your doorstep."

Alberto nodded his head. "The escalation needs to be gradual. You're absolutely right."

"You guys are nuts. I mean, this is seriously deranged. Someone's going to get hurt." Henry was trying to assimilate all of this information.

"Post-postmodernism, dude. Welcome to the real world," Truman said matter-of-factly. "If you can't beat 'em, give 'em what they want. Besides," he went on, "crazy ideas are completely overrated in my opinion. Surviving a lifetime of overrated experiences is what makes us American in the first place. I'm a fucking patriot."

The idea, as shocking as it first was to Henry, seemed to make more and more sense as Truman and Alberto confidently defended it. Perhaps they were right, perhaps this was the way to get ahead. Maybe their version of what war meant to Henry was right here, doing this crazy scheme together, faking out everyone else with their apocalyptic inside joke. And besides, as Henry had begun to understand only recently, their friendship was based on need more than anything else, a dismal condition that depended on their mutual abhorrence of one another's success above all other things. One could not fail without the other. Their friendship was a life raft made for three with two people occupying it pushing out other potential survivors.

"Okay. Fine," Henry didn't want to argue with them. It was

exhausting. He was feeling fried and he wanted to go home. "What was it you wanted to ask me?"

"We just wanted to know what you thought," Alberto said, "but I guess we know now." He thought for a moment and then went on. "Do you know what friendship is, Henry? I'm talking about real friendship?"

Henry just wanted to go home. He could feel his heart pounding in his chest, every inch of skin his sore spot, his blood like a voice, reminding him about things he didn't want to think about. He didn't feel anything like malice toward Truman and Alberto. He was just tired and didn't want to have to think anymore about why nothing was easy, why nothing could be straightforward. Any way you sliced it, there were meanings and motives inside everything. Nuance was the nucleus of all action and if war for Henry was the orientation point for life, then who was he to judge a little social upheaval for the sake of profit. After all, it felt American enough.

Truman stepped up and slapped an arm over Alberto's shoulder as Alberto replied, "I'll tell you what it is." Henry braced himself for the onslaught. "It's having a person you can go to when you've done something terrible. Something really terrible."

Truman nodded and then interrupted.

"Like fucking an animal terrible," he said gravely.

*   *   *

The next morning Henry woke up early to a surprisingly bad hangover. His mouth was parched and he was sweating uncontrollably, soaking through two shirts merely trying to pour a glass of orange juice. After struggling for fifteen minutes with the coffee maker, he bit the bullet and called in sick. He was worried about being perceived by Ken as shirking after his new assignment, but his editor seemed to care less.

"Yeah. Fine. Whatever. Get better. See you tomorrow." The best kind of absolution came in fragmented sentences.

He was going to say that he would work from home once he felt a bit better, but Ken didn't give him a chance, hanging up the phone as if it was an involuntary reflex.

With an entire day of headaches and an overactive gag reflex looming before him, he dug around the fridge for the hair of the dog, thinking that he if he could just get past the first sip, a little vodka and grapefruit might just settle him down, give him context. There was no vodka, but he had the juice, and when he took a sip it tasted all clotty in his mouth and he spit it out violently into the sink where he stood for a few minutes, his head hung down, his body heaving, out of breath for no good reason but the effort it took to hold down throw-up.

He walked outside and gulped down a few mouthfuls of LA's early morning air. It was winter, which meant the smog felt festive, a bit tighter across the chest the way a comfy sweater might keep someone warm in the snow. Drops of dew had colonized lawns all over the neighborhood and one or two trees dimmed their greenery, subscribing to the idea of seasonal change if only in the abstract. On mornings like this his car would be crypt cold. His joints felt stiff and he longed for coffee. It was a sham, though, this mockery of the seasons, because day and night were the only two seasons in Los Angeles and it was all anyone should need to mark the passage of time. He turned slowly to walk back inside. His joints creaked as they let off the pressure of living. Today, he would be a shill for lethargy.

He wandered around his apartment for a few minutes, touching objects as if he were in a museum; the otherworldliness of his throbbing head gave him a wonderful sense of third-personness. He fantasized about thirty days in rehab, thirty days of self-indulgence, catharsis, the permission to act like a self-centered animal and blame it all on the process. He imagined going to Shakey's one day with Truman and Alberto for the buffet and seeing his intervention on their welcome sign out front, along with the birthday parties and *quinceañeras* they also hosted. It was mornings like this, disassociated slices of life, that made teenage girls want to cut themselves.

He decided to clean his house and put on a mix of old hardcore music to get him inspired. He had a mix for everything: music to listen to from the other room while he was shitting, music to jerk off to, music for drinking. It was the benefit of living in the digital age, that there was this ease to perfecting any moment with the billions of little flourishes and touches right at one's fingertips. The catch was, though, that there was a built-in expectation that went along with the promise of perfection, so nothing was really organic anymore, nothing could just happen. Also, it was just plain fucked-up to realize that the music that fueled his teen angst was now the soundtrack to his domestic compulsion.

He gave up on the cleaning and after a two-hour nap he felt near enough himself to get up and do a little work on the computer. He shook the mouse, waking his old PC from its electronic slumber, and was confronted immediately by a picture of his sister, Grace, that was the wallpaper on his desktop. Grace in happier times. It sounded like an era when he thought of it like that, an epoch, a layer of the great fossil record like the dinosaurs or the Nazis.

He started to surf the web about the Children of Light and found article after article about the group, mostly dealing with Potter's arrest and his calm demeanor on the steps of the State courthouse. Potter had declared war with a smile that day, issued a fatwa as he forgave, threatened with open arms. There were testimonials from former members of the group, couples who had been broken apart by Potter's schemes insisting that he be allowed to have sex with their wives as a show of fealty, not to him, but to the cause. Never to him. His appetite for sex, which seemed to range from prostitutes to, by many accounts, underage boys and girls, was just one symptom of his lust, a lust which spilled over to material possessions like cars, houses, and extravagant jewelry. It was said that at one time, before the raid in '84, that the group (meaning Potter) was worth more than $20 million. And it was obvious to Henry, as he sat there nursing a hangover reading all of this, that this was a person truly worthy of hate. That if even one-tenth of all the stuff that was written about him was true, he would still deserve to be drawn and quartered at the very least. His ire grew as the day went on, as the fuzziness in his mouth started to deteriorate, as he absent-mindedly ate a peanut butter and jelly sandwich while he read, not even conscious of having made the sandwich in the first place.

Henry didn't have a nemesis, but he now knew that this man could be one. Even if you threw out all of the horrible shit Potter had been accused of doing over the course of his life, which, as a journalist he knew was neither here nor there, because once they were out as public accusations they were as good as true. Even if he didn't count that stuff, the really reprehensible part, the part that tore at Henry more than any other, was Potter's dishonesty toward the people who had put so much of their faith in him. It was that deception, that knowing betrayal, that rankled him more than anything. It was hard to be a follower all your life. There were certain expectations of the leader. Passive people aren't always satisfied with passive lives. Actually, they're usually dissatisfied with them, only they're too lazy to do anything about it.

He started to feel a real anger build up inside of him. The clock on the wall told him that he'd been at the desk for almost 8 hours without consciously taking a break.

He dragged himself into the shower and roughly rinsed himself off. He scribbled in a hurried "I ♥ U" into the steam of the shower as it painted the glass door like he always did. It was an offering, a daily ritual that somehow grounded him. It was the little things that made him think of Grace, little bread crumbs he left behind for himself to come across later when he least expected them. Some people's tendency might be to try and forget after losing someone—losing someone like *that*—but, Henry yearned to be reminded, and more than that, startled by it as often as possible.

And, though he didn't have a nemesis in his life, he could see how useful it could be. Having an enemy, a mortal foe, gave one a certain necessary weight. Ballast. He had people in his life that he loved to varying degrees: from Grace, who was near the top, down to his parents who he felt a responsibility to care about more than actual love. So many shades of indifference. What he didn't have was a polar opposite. What he didn't have was someone he needed as his life mission to ruin. He could see that in Potter. He could see himself hating the man for any number of the horrendous atrocities he'd committed during his life as a supposed humanitarian. The only problem was his objectivity as a journalist. He couldn't go into his first real journalistic assignment with such a tremendous prejudice. That would be counterintuitive. No, it would have to be someone else. There was a reason to live out there somewhere.

Chapter 4

I **T ONLY TOOK** until the first day of his sophomore year of high school for him to realize just how monumentally anonymous these years of his life were going to be. There were times during his freshman year that Henry felt more invisible than others, like when he was at his locker putting some books away and some older boys had run into him as they were horsing around in the hall, unintentionally knocking him into the wall of metal lockers and causing him to chip a tooth. They got up, still laughing and pushing one another, completely oblivious to the crumpled heap of a freshman bleeding and groaning beneath them.

He had a big mess of hair, a Jew-fro he had heard it called, which sat atop his tall gangly frame like a crow's nest looming large over the deck of a skinny ship. His features were ordinary—brown eyes, brown hair, and dark eyebrows—and they would only give someone pause if they stopped to look at him. His wardrobe was bland, inconspicuous, something from the Witness Relocation winter collection: jeans, flannel shirts, black Converse High Tops. His only requirement was that nothing should have labels or be attention-grabbing, because as discombobulating as being anonymous was, it was worse to be noticed for the wrong reasons—like trying to be fashionable or fit in.

The first thing he noticed, walking through the rusting

gates of Burlington High School on the first day of tenth grade, was the flag whipping around at half mast. He racked his brain trying to think who had recently died. He hadn't heard about any of the ex-presidents, astronauts or Bob Hope kicking the bucket. He took the brown paper bag lunch his mother made for him out of his backpack and began to dig into an anemic-looking turkey sandwich. If he ate the whole thing now, he thought, he would have to get creative at lunch. Was it so hard for his mom to understand that he was growing like crazy and could eat his weight in carbs every six hours given the opportunity. Maybe he could beg off Grace, who, now that she was dating, seemed to have an increasingly diminished interest in food.

As more kids started to arrive, they began to jostle one another for information about who had died and when word started to leak around that it was someone from their school, he became interested again and walked near a group of students standing near the cafeteria chatting about it.

"His name was Tyler something. I think he was in special-ed classes," said a tall skinny blonde girl named Stacy who he recognized as a friend of his sister's. She saw Henry watching them and looked away, not wanting to admit with a nod of recognition that she knew who he was from being a regular visitor to their house since the time she was eight.

He moved away quickly, though, because he already knew exactly who she was talking about. Tyler Martin was his age and they had shared many classes together both in middle school and last year as freshmen. He wasn't in special-ed, though. He had MS and used one of those old polio crutches that had a cuff that wrapped around the arm. Henry used to feel bad watching him as he struggled around campus; the school was set at the top of a canyon that gave the campus a gradual slope upwards so that if you had a class at the bottom of campus and had to go immediately to the top for your next period, chances were that even unencumbered by neurological deficiencies you would be huffing and puffing to avoid being tardy. That's not to mention the school's close proximity to the beach, which was barely a mile drive down the canyon. Surfing and volleyball were worshipful activities, as was evidenced by the perfect tans and bodies of many of his classmates who spent their mornings before school surfing the break that was a short bicycle ride from campus. It was ideal, if that was what you were into, beset on one side by lush green mountains and the ocean on the other, the sea air pollinating already rabid hormones and inflated senses of self-worth. The fact that these people would assume that Tyler was somehow mentally deficient because he walked around on crutches made perfect sense.

He didn't know Tyler well and wasn't quite sure what to do with the information that Tyler had passed away. Henry wondered if Tyler knew from the time he was a kid that he didn't have a long life ahead of him, if it had been part of the "birds and bees" conversation his parents had with him early on, something they casually slipped in between foreplay and unwanted pregnancies. Whatever the case was, Henry knew that Tyler had a good sense of humor because he'd seen him once hit the back of his mother's station wagon with his crutch as she came to pick him up after school and crumple to the ground pretending she'd just hit him. His mother jammed the car into park and came running around the side, already in tears, already hyperventilating, and when she knelt down to put her hands on his leg and on his back, he popped up and broke into riotous laughter, the kind of pure laughter than can only come at someone else's expense. Tyler's mother slapped him on the arm, and Henry could catch snippets of her screaming and then little by little relenting and finally smiling, the joke settling in like a well-administered anesthetic.

The next day in their TV Production class, where they sat next to each other by default, because the rest of the kids, who were mostly black and Hispanic, had hijacked the room's TV and watched the movie *House Party* over and over until Henry knew every line by heart, Henry had leaned over to Tyler and nervously told him that he had seen the joke he played on his mother. Tyler was clearly surprised by this overture at conversation. It was the first time Henry had ever spoken to him.

"The funny thing about that," Tyler said, eagerly taking up the invitation to a conversation after getting over the initial shock of someone speaking to him, "is I've done that to her before. A few times. It's weird how she always falls for it." They both laughed at the gullibility of mothers.

It was already close to the end of the semester and they spent that last week in class talking to one another quite a bit. They found out that they were both hugely into *Star Wars* as well as the short-lived sitcom *Sledgehammer,* a show about a reckless, trigger-happy cop whose inclination was to rely on his .44 to solve any and all of his crime fighting problems. The bumper sticker on the back of his car read *A Mind Is a Terrible Thing to Waste Someone With.* For the rest of that week, before school let out for the summer break, they had spent the entire hour of TV Production class talking about music, games, and TV shows. They had a lot in common, and during that summer break before sophomore year, Henry thought about calling Tyler many times. They could have gone to the movies, to the game store to check out the newest D&D module, or they could have just hung out. He never did call, though, for one reason or the other, and spent most of the summer in the library instead, whiling away the hours of the day scouring the stacks for new books on the guns of the Viet Cong or the kinds of artillery that was used during the Battle of Gettysburg. It wasn't that he wasn't lonely at all, or that he didn't want to do something other than take the same seven-block walk every afternoon, past packs of kids hanging out at the Mobil station, copping cigarettes and making plans for the rest of the summer, surfing trips to Mexico and Grateful Dead concerts in Oakland, their heads pressed close together in tight catacombs of lovely whispers, teenage conspiracies hatching left, right, and center.

He was lonely for all that, and when he thought of calling Tyler, of actually picking up the phone and asking the kid to hang out, he just couldn't do it, couldn't admit out loud that he needed anyone else. That was what he was thinking about when he looked up and saw Grace crossing the main quad toward him. Like the rest of the student body, she bore all the markings of a summer spent at the beach. He could tell that she was worried about him, as usual. She walked up to him and her friends casually peeled back, not interested in the family dynamics that compelled Grace to openly address her strange sibling in front of the rest of the school.

"That kid who died. Did you know him?"

Henry bit his lower lip, suddenly feeling the urge to cry, and nodded his head. It wasn't clear to him whether or not it was because the reality of Tyler's death was finally hitting him or because he felt as though his sister was expecting it. She hugged him tightly and stepped back, giving him a moment to speak if he wanted it. He looked over her shoulder and saw her friends watching him. Stacy, who he had overheard just a little while before cranking up the gossip mill, watched them closely, twirling her hair around her finger absentmindedly. He couldn't tell if her stare was one of close scrutiny, trying to pick up strands of information, or simply a dullness that could not be repressed.

"I'm sorry," she said. She shielded her eyes and looked up as a dull grey cloud floated across an otherwise flawless blue sky like a cataract of bad weather.

Watching Stacy stirred something up in him, something angry, and he lashed out at Grace.

"Why did you think I knew him? Because he was on crutches? Is that the only friend you think I could get?"

She backed away and sighed.

"That's not what I meant and you know it, Henry."

Behind her Stacy was getting impatient.

"Come on, Grace. We're gonna be late for first period."

"One minute." She sounded aggravated. "Or you can just go by yourself."

That made Henry smile. He loved that she didn't need someone to cling on to all the time. Almost everyone their age seemed to travel in packs and it made him proud to see that she was above that, that she had her own mind.

All around them kids were moving toward their first classes, breaking off bits of cookies and doughnuts to pop into their mouths, washing the whole thing down with a Coke, a sugar high built to last the span of civilization, but would really only get them through the next hour or two of their day until they could sneak away for a cigarette in the parking lot or a bong load in someone's garage. Teenage consciousness was built on these short intervals of stimulation, and caffeine was their generation's great social movement.

Grace took his hand and squeezed it.

"Are you going to be okay?"

She was genuinely worried about him and he had no choice but to murmur a soft yes. He'd do anything to make her not worry.

As Grace and Stacy made off for their first class of the year a boy came up and grabbed Grace around the waist. She gave off a shrill, surprised scream and then laughed and threw her arms around his neck. Henry wasn't sure who he was and not just because he looked like all of the other skin cancer petri dishes around him. He knew most of her friends, or at least could recognize them by sight, but this was someone new. And given the degree of their familiarity, he guessed that this was probably the boyfriend she'd spent so much time with this summer.

It shook him a little to think that Grace might have a boyfriend, but it also made sense. She was one of the most popular people in school, something you'd never know by looking at her if you went off what movies and TV shows said about the upper crust of teen society. There was no popular kids area of the quad or the cafeteria where that group hung out to plot the subjugation of the weak, to work out a rotary schedule for bullying, or to plan exclusive parties that the lesser folks only caught wind of but were never privileged enough to attend. Jocks didn't wear their letterman jackets and hunt down nerds in the hallways, devouring their prey with the ease of a grizzly standing along the banks of a river of spawning salmon and simply dipping its paw in the water to pull out morsel after succulent morsel. Nothing about high school conformed to any of these classist archetypes. TV had let him down. The movies had let him down. His identity was built on a foundation of these stereotypes, none of which were proving true. It was a defeating feeling for him to not be able to hate who he thought he should hate. The enemy was invisible, like the Viet Cong had been, hiding and stealthy, but there. Definitely there.

The boy's hands dropped off her waist and he took up one of her hands in his. She turned to look back at Henry, but he averted his eyes, pretending to focus instead on a banner that someone had hung on a building welcoming them back to school. He didn't want to embarrass her by watching. Here they were, getting older, doing the things that people were supposed to do as they grew up and the only feeling he could muster was disdain that they were changing in such predictable ways. No, not disdain exactly. More like embarrassment. That's what growing up was, he thought to himself, an embarrassment. An embarrassment because there was no new way to do it.

So this was puberty. A battle royale of feelings where resentment came out on top, smashing sympathy over the head with a folding chair, kicking pity in the nuts when the ref wasn't looking. His first class of the day was biology. He would have to run this theory by the teacher, this notion that the structure of his DNA wasn't a double helix but a steel cage. Peach fuzz was beginning to grow in on his upper lip, and heimagined it sprouting like a Hitler moustache, his Adam's apple dropping from the bomb bay doors of the *Enola Gay*. Like the vet at the baseball card convention had told him not that long ago, he had a lifetime of hitting the hay and beating his meat ahead of him, war was everything, war was never having to say you're sorry.

On his way to class he passed by the room where he and Tyler had taken TV Production together. The door was a faded pinkish color, taken straight from the Glidden incarceration palate: institutional hues that subdued while simultaneously drove you slowly insane. He remembered seeing Tyler pop up behind his mother's car and thought how great it would be if he did that now, just popped up in the middle of the quad during lunch break, smiling, middle fingers ablaze, happy as shit that the joke had worked again. That kind of joke would always work. It would never get old.

That first day went by in a blur, and as a ghost, Henry drifted in and out of lives, haunting the hallways with as little presence as he could muster. He wasn't just a fly on the wall—he was the ghost of the fly on the wall. And as such, he noticed everything that went on. He saw the ragged-looking teachers in their polyester pants, their faces bloated from spending the summer at the bottom of a bottle of Captain Morgan. He heard the swagger in the locker room, mushroom clouds of guy talk, seniors prodding one another about conquests to come.

That night at dinner his father and mother got into a huge argument over whether or not soup was an acceptable entrée. Henry and Grace ate their dinner quietly, their heads bent low over their bowls like British orphans, not wanting to get involved in a fight that clearly had other, stranger, meanings.

After dinner they retreated into Henry's room together and closed the door, barely able to contain their laughter.

"God, he's a weird guy, isn't he?" Grace said, wiping her eyes that were wet from laughter.

"You don't know the half of it. Try being his son. At least he ignores you. I get all of the unfulfilled expectations dumped on me. He probably doesn't even know you're dating."

"How do you know I'm dating someone?"

"Because, genius," he said, tossing a Nerf ball up in the air and catching it, "I saw some guy put his arm around you at school today. How slick do you think you are? Is he nice?"

"He is. I like him a lot. More than I thought I would when we first got together."

"What do you mean?"

"I've known him a long time and always thought he was

cute. I knew he was into me, and since this is senior year and I've never really had a proper boyfriend before I thought that would be enough. But now that I've gotten to know him better..." the sentence trailed off as she snatched the Nerf from his hands. "He really likes me, Henry. I didn't think it was important for me to be liked like that by a boy, but it is." She took a deep breath and pitched the ball into his lap. "And you'd like him, too. He's smart and funny. And he's really into books and music."

"I'd like him because he's into books?"

"Don't be an asshole. That's just part of it. I want you guys to like each other. It's important to me."

Henry tried to ignore the part of him that all of a sudden felt wobbly and empty, the part that felt deserted and blindsided. He wished he had the ability to feel happy for someone else the way he could sympathize with other people, but maybe that came later in life and with the practice of disappointment. "What's his name?" he asked trying to sound interested and not like the self-centered asshole every molecule of his body was telling him to be.

"Peter. Peter Gossett."

"Do Mom and Dad know?"

"Mom does, but Dad," she shook her head and grimaced, "I'm not sure how he'd take it. He doesn't really do that well with reality, does he? He probably thinks I have all my baby teeth and am still really into Barbie."

"I dare you to go downstairs and ask him where babies come from."

She giggled hysterically. "No way. He can't be that clueless, can he?"

"Wanna bet?"

From outside a man's voice broke the nighttime suburban sound barrier. Granted it was a low threshold, it still made Henry jump a little when the word "trust" careened into the room like a stray bullet. And just as painfully, and as if natural selection wasn't bad enough, a woman's voice ricocheted back, and all Henry could make out of her response was the word "comeuppance" and that was just the counterbalance he needed to make it all seem okay in the way that nothing felt superfluous.

She bit her lower lip. "Okay. How much?"

"If I win, you have to tell me something about Stacy that would really embarrass her if she knew I knew."

Her eyes closed as she thought. After a few seconds she said, "Okay. I know what I can tell you. That's fine. What do I get if I win?"

He looked around his room and pointed at a stack of Rush cassettes.

"If you win you can take my stack of Rush albums for a month."

She clapped her hands together excitedly. "That's a bet. There's no way you're going to win this, Henry. No way."

"You're so wrong. You don't know him like I do. You're totally screwed."

When she went downstairs he lay back in his bed, laced his fingers behind his head, and felt the happy indigestion of giggles percolate deep within him. He looked down at the end of the bed and noticed for the first time that his feet were hanging over the edge. It had happened at some point without him even realizing it, and as the giggles finally overflowed out of him, he couldn't help but wonder what else had changed that he hadn't noticed.

In a few moments his door exploded open and she ran to his bed, her face bright red. He realized she was on the verge of hyperventilating with laughter.

"What happened?" he asked, desperate to be let in on the joke. "What did he say?"

She took a few deep breaths and tried to fan herself with her hand. She was laughing so hard that sweat was starting to sprout on her upper lip and forehead.

"He was working on the couch and the TV was on. I asked him if he could tell me how babies were made and he muted the game and tore a fresh piece of paper off his legal pad. Then…" A fresh set of laughter overtook her again, "…then he started drawing the female reproductive system, only," and she turned her head sideways as if she was trying to recreate the sketch in her mind, dislodge it from a crooked corner of her brain. "It was all fucked up. He had the urethra running almost horizontally away from the vagina and there were eggs just floating around everywhere and this teardrop looking thing that I guess were supposed to be sperm. It looked a little like one of those Rorschach patterns."

"What did you see when you looked at it?" Henry was laughing now, too.

"I don't know. The death of my childhood?"

They busted up into a fit of laughter the likes of which only occurred between family members who implicitly knew the shared absurdity of heredity, the irreconcilability of roots.

"Is that when you left?" he asked her.

"No. I left when he started drawing happy faces on the sperm. I thought I was going to lose it. Really lose it. Like, never come back lose it." She flopped back on his bed and used her finger to wipe away the tears streaming down her face.

He watched her happily, so at ease to have a true ally, and it occurred to him, that he would always remember her like this, in this moment; Grace in happier times, an era, like the Victorian age or the Industrial Revolution.

"Why were you so sure he would fall for that? Is it that he doesn't know how old we are or that he just doesn't care?"

"No, it's not that," he said trying to make sense of it in his own head. "It's that it's not relevant to him."

"That's sad," she said, trying to regain her composure. "Doesn't that make you sad?"

He thought about it.

"It used to, but I've grown to accept it. I'm fucking enlightened. Also, it might be different for me since I'm the boy."

"How so?" She looked at him in a way that made him feel like the older sibling.

"Remember that time we drove to Vegas over Christmas break?"

"Yeah."

"We were going through the desert and there was this big building off in the distance, just a speck off the freeway. I remember watching it, kind of thinking about what it might be, and I looked up and saw Dad staring at me in the rearview mirror. He saw what I was looking at, and I guess this was his way of trying to relate, and he said 'That's where they've got Evel Knievel locked up. You like him, right? I think he hit a guy with a baseball bat.'"

Grace started to laugh again. "It's not funny," Henry went on, barely suppressing a smile himself, remembering all the cactus sticking up, the desert's middle fingers raised to the sky, the truest hostile climate. "I mean, who tells an eight-year-old shit like that? I loved Evel Knievel. After that, though, every time I thought about him I didn't think of motorcycles and the Grand Canyon—I thought of a guy in an American flag jumpsuit bashing in someone's head with a Louisville Slugger."

He sprung up, exhilarated by the rush of catharsis, and grabbed a wiffle ball bat that was stashed in a corner of his room. He brought it back and struck the edge of his bed with it as hard as he could, the plastic bat whistling through the air as he brought it down, connecting with his bedspread with a barely satisfying thud. THUD "Thanks, Dad." THUD "The end of childhood." THUD "Look at me, I'm finally playing sports. Aren't you happy, Dad?"

Out of breath, he dropped the bat and fell onto the bed next to Grace. A car pulled into the cul-de-sac behind their house, and they watched as its headlights slowly rode the slipstream of darkness across the ceiling and down his bedroom wall.

"So," he turned his head toward her once the lights disappeared, "what's the big secret you're going to tell me?"

She walked across the room and sat down on his desk chair.

"Okay," she said, "you cannot tell anyone what I'm about to tell you. Understand?"

He nodded. "Okay."

"No, Henry. Seriously." She was as earnest as a teenage girl could be.

"Fine," he told her, exaggerating his exasperation. "It's not like I've got anyone to tell it to, anyway. My only friend died, remember?"

"Okay," she finally conceded. "Stacy...Stacy cuts herself."

"What? On purpose?"

"Yes on purpose. Jesus, Henry. Don't you know that's something chicks sometimes do in high school when they're really depressed?"

The thought made him nauseous.

"No. I mean…how the hell am I supposed to know that?" He was slightly incredulous, but also shocked to a degree, shocked that there were people who did this, people that he knew, and that he didn't know it was happening. An image of Stacy getting ready for school flashed in front of him: Stacy picking out jeans, brushing her teeth, packing a lunch, and… oops, can't leave without a little slice of thigh.

"It makes her feel better. I mean, who knows why people do the things they do? There's no reason why what feels good to someone might be completely incomprehensible to someone else. Right?"

"I guess." He looked at her with concern. "You never do that, do you?"

She laughed and walked over to him. "No," she said, stroking his hair, "don't worry about me. I had a hard enough time with dissecting the frog in Mr. Howard's class last year, let alone getting a knife near me like that."

They caught the tendrils of sound from the TV, a crowd cheering something glorious and fleeting.

"I can't believe you still have that skateboard," she said, pointing to a corner of his room to an old Sims deck painted with the Union Jack. "Remember when Dad bought that for you?"

"Remember? Are you kidding me? How could I ever forget? It was all I wanted for Christmas and he made me promise him right there in the store, in front of all those skater guys, that I would use it no matter what. He made me promise like a thousand times, telling me over and over that it was a hundred bucks, and those guys were all laughing, wagging their fingers at me behind his back."

From the moment he got it home, strapped on the pads, and tried to ride it down the sidewalk, he knew that he would never use the skateboard for more than a couple of hours, and that the holiday present he had sworn to use, was actually a life sentence, a burden to carry with him until the day he died. It wouldn't take an archeologist one day to find the artifacts of disappointment around the house; the skateboards and baseball gloves, all the things he'd tried and abandoned in the name of his father, left to rot in the shadowy corners of his room.

"When he finally bought it for me, I felt like it was the holy fucking Ark. Something too precious to actually use."

"I have an amazing idea," she said leaping up from the bed. "Let's take it outside and break it."

"What? No..." But before he could stop her, she was already at the door with the board in her hand, racing down the stairs, her footsteps making a hollow galloping sound down their home's bones.

He ran after her, but she was already outside by the time he heard his father bellow, "What are you two doing? Cut it out!"

She turned around in the middle of the street, out of breath from running, and thrust the skateboard at him.

"Break it, Henry. Come on."

He stopped and put his hands up, backed up slowly, not wanting to touch the thing, afraid of it as though it might rear up and strike like a poisonous snake.

"Break it," she said again. A streetlight painted a jagged shadow across her face. "Break the motherfucker!"

Her enthusiasm for malice tickled him pink. He had never really seen her like this, all vengeful and angry, and as he wiped his sweaty palms on his jeans, thinking about what this meant, she seemed to read his mind and said, "Don't think about it. Just do it."

She egged him on, a muse with a mean streak. He turned to leave, to end this game, when she blurted out, "Don't go. Stacy gave John Lutz a blowjob in the backseat of her father's BMW and he came all over the seat. She couldn't get the stain out and had to tell her dad it was ice cream." She watched him for a reaction, and seeing none, went on. "Matt Sharpe was molested by his scoutmaster on a camping trip in Joshua Tree. Valerie Cannetti let Doug Gilbert finger her during Algebra II so he would write her English final. I could go on." She slapped a hand over her mouth and widened her eyes and he could tell that she was genuinely surprised by what she'd just done. "Sorry," she said, moving her hand away slowly, "I just want you to trust me."

"I do trust you, Grace. It's just…"

"If you trust me, then break it. Break it and I'll tell you every secret I know."

And then she was off again, her voice an old stock ticker, the stories falling in great loops of tape around their feet. Sitting still, smiling, nodding, he let her feel what she needed to feel: unburdened for a while. The more she went on, though, the worse he began to feel. Knowing one or two things about people at school was great, something to snicker at and make you feel superior, but knowing everyone's dirt, that everyone was a wreck, made him feel insecure and sad, like there would be no one to turn to for help in case the shit ever hit the fan. She was ratting out their generation and the only way to make her stop was for him to jump up and land right in the middle of the board, which he did, splitting the thing into two even pieces with a resounding and deeply satisfying CRACK. The sound echoed, the secrets stopped, and he was grateful.

Smiling, she hugged him, and then stooped to pick up the two halves of the board. She threw them in the dumpster behind a neighbor's house as they walked back home. Together, under the moonlight, nothing but silence and the scent of night-blooming jasmine, they were unending penitents at the church of family.

*   *   *

The afternoon sun exploded off a row of lockers and for a good long moment he was completely blinded.

It was a strange day, the air was thick and still. Earthquake weather, his mother had declared that morning, packing him an extra granola bar and a Band-Aid, fortification to see him through whatever apocalyptic times lay ahead.

Speaking of the apocalypse, he loved walking around school during class when the campus was quiet and sullen, abandoned looking, like a military outpost that had long since been overrun and plundered. Rusted metal and peeling paint proved that neglect could look like some of Mother Nature's best work.

A girl walked by, her shy hands clutching a hall pass, her footsteps echoing against the cold concrete. Other than that, the only sound was the swish of her skirt, an erotic call and response, the sound you would hear if you put your ear against a seashell going through puberty. He dreamt about moments like this, rather than of specific girls, moments that were absolute islands of distance where everything was perfect inside his own head, never mind what was actually out there. Never mind that the school sat in the most pristine of settings; between the mountains and the sea, going more fallow by the day. Paint peeled off benches and tables, revealing ugly sores of rust underneath. Graffiti adorned almost every surface that could be reached by human hand (and then some), ubiquitously decorating the walls and doors of class-rooms the way lace hemmed the edges of everything during the Victorian age. The only bit of color that hadn't yet faded was the bright red aluminum fruit born of the soda machine. It was no wonder junk food was so popular with kids their age. Other than soda cans, the only real color was perched at the top of the mountains or out on the horizon at the sea, both just out of reach, driving home the unrelenting dogma that the grass was always greener.

"You might not want to stare at her ass like that," a voice behind him said. "She was carrying a copy of *Atlas Shrugged*. Her ass is a capitalist pig. She might come back and charge you for the leer."

He turned around, startled. Speaking to him was Cal Demott, a kid from his history class he knew by name only.

"That was awesome, by the way, that you got Mr. Johnson to kick you out like that. How do you know all that stuff?"

Henry stuffed his hands in his pockets. He had been asked to leave his honors history class after the teacher had mistak-enly identified the World War One battle where tanks had first been introduced into modern warfare as the Battle of the Bulge. Henry, who rarely spoke up, corrected him, telling Mr. Johnson that it had been the Battle of the Somme, not the Battle of the Bulge. The thing had escalated as the teacher became more and more angry at Henry's matter-of-factness about his opposition. Finally, the teacher, who after five minutes of one-sided arguing, yelled at Henry to get out. He hadn't specified where Henry should go, though, so he chose to wander around the school until the bell sent him to lunch.

"I wasn't checking out her ass. I was just..." he thought about saying he was thinking about the sound her skirt made as she walked, but the shame of lust made him waffle. That and his skills as a bow-legged conversationalist. "Forget it."

"I don't care. One way or the other, it doesn't matter to me. And I don't mean that in an apathetic way. I'm just indifferent. And they're not the same, by the way. Apathy and indifference. Apathy is more, like, not even bothering to take the time to care about a thing. See, I thought about it, and I just don't care. That's a whole process, an intellectual process, I bet you never even thought about."

Cal spoke fast and decisively, not leaving Henry any time to dwell on his shame.

"An ass is an ass," he went on, "I just think there are better, less Fascist asses you could be focusing your attention on."

"Fine."

"Henry," Cal touched his shoulder, "I know your name's Henry, by the way, from roll call—a total, fucking, bullshit invasion of privacy, by the way. How the fuck did you know that shit back there in class?"

It was hard for Henry to keep up with everything that was being sad to him, all of Cal's epiphanies and revelations that came to him in no logical sequence or order, like sucker punches in a street fight.

"Just reading," Henry shrugged, wishing there was some great mystery to it other than his having spent untold hours with his nose pressed into history books, the world's worst moments at his fingertips. "I like war." As soon as he said it he realized how stupid it sounded and wished he could take it back.

"That's fucking awesome," Cal's enthusiasm was as big as he was, steak dinner big, and his voice boomed through the empty hallways. "That's the greatest fucking thing I've ever heard. 'I like war'. Now that's a real fucking extracurricular activity. Fuck marching band and varsity soccer. War. Yeah, war."

"Is that why you left class?" Henry looked behind him to see if there were any teachers on their way to send them to the vice principal's office. "To ask me a bunch of bullshit?"

"Bullshit?" Cal feigned surprise. "It's not bullshit. We've got what…three classes together this semester? I haven't seen you talk to one person in all that time. I bet they tell you the same shit that they tell me, that you've got a lot of potential and that you're on the sensitive side. Am I right? You know what that means, don't you? It means they're disappointed in you. They're disappointed in guys like you and me, because we don't talk a lot and we don't like the things everyone likes, but all of the idiots who go around reading half-assed philosophy books and Holden Caulfield, they wind up doing okay. How's that fair? How's it okay to be so dumb and predictable that you actually feel like it's a badge of honor? I bet you don't have a cum-soaked copy of *Catcher in the Rye* lying next to your bed. I bet not one of them likes war. I bet not one of them can correct a teacher and not back fucking down because he knows he's right."

"Who's the 'they' you're talking about? Are you talking about teachers or…"

Cal interrupted. "You're missing the point. The point is… the point is fuck *Atlas Shrugged* ass and fuck hall passes and fuck them all," he bit his lip and Henry realized he was trying to get himself to calm down. After pausing a second, Cal laughed and said, "Besides, I heard that chick talking in my English class about Sylvia Plath and ovens and asked her friend if *The Bell Jar* is a cookbook."

Henry allowed a smile to creep over his face, and Cal took it as an opening, a crack in the armor. He slapped Henry's stomach.

"Come on, that's funny, right? You know that's funny..."
And before he knew it, Henry was laughing, and not just chuckling, but seriously laughing his fucking ass off.

"I hope someone stopped her before she tried to make any of those recipes," Henry said through breathless gasps.

"Fuck that," Cal laughed back, "I hope she bumped her head trying to light the pilot."

Cal began to walk down the hall and Henry hustled to catch him. The clock showed them that the bell for lunch would ring in about five minutes.

"What's for lunch?"

"Huh?"

"What are we doing for lunch?" Cal rephrased the question.

"I don't know. I don't have anything." He thought about the emergency supplies in his backpack. "Wait, I have this." He took out the granola bar and, openly defying his own survival, handed it to Cal.

Cal shoved the entire thing into his mouth and had it wolfed down in three seconds. "That isn't going to cut it."

Henry thought for a moment.

"We can go beg my sister for food. She's always got something."

Cal stopped and looked at him sideways.

"You have a sister that goes here?"

"Yeah," Henry said, racking his brain for where else they might find sustenance.

"What grade is she in?"

"She's a senior. Grace."

"Huh?"

"Grace. That's her name. Grace Colmes."

"Yeah, I figured that was her name," Cal said as he continued walking, this time toward the main quad. "I didn't think it was a descriptor considering the quality of the bitches around here."

Henry exploded, "Don't say shit like that," and then in a softer voice, "My sister's not a bitch." He hated to show his vulnerabilities like that and could almost imagine Cal settling into his sensitivity about his sister, easing into it like a comfy chair.

"Okay, okay," Cal held his hand up. "I'm sorry. I don't have any siblings so all I know is what I see on TV. You know, how the older sister always tortures her younger brother, tells on him, shit like that. I'm a product of my generation."

"Yeah, well shit isn't always the way it is on TV."

Cal smiled and patted Henry on the back. "You're telling me," causing them both to laugh yet again.

The lunch bell rang, and kids began to stream out of their classrooms, their voices already a thickly stirred concoction of white noise. Henry led them through the restless bodies toward the table near the cafeteria where his sister always sat and ate lunch with her friends.

"The heart of darkness," Cal mumbled to him as Grace noticed Henry and gave a little wave.

"Hi, Henry." She looked at Cal.

"Hey," he waved back. "This is my friend, Cal."

"Hi, Cal."

Cal pushed up on his heels and raised his eyebrows, but didn't say anything.

"Hey, Grace. Do you have any food? I forgot to pack a lunch today and I'm really hungry."

"Didn't you get Mom's earthquake snacks?"

"Ate it already."

"Do you have any money?"

"Nope."

He looked away, embarrassed that in a sense he was lying to her, since he wasn't really that hungry.

She shrugged and handed him a sandwich neatly wrapped in a Zip-Loc bag.

"Here. But you should try to get up a little earlier and pack something for yourself. It's not like those extra ten minutes in the morning do anything for you."

Cal laughed a little too hard and both Henry and Grace stared at him.

"It wasn't that funny," Grace said.

"I thought it was," Cal replied, his smile looking wholly out of place, like it had tricked its way onto his face.

They said goodbye and walked away from the table, wandering around the quad, neither one of them too keen on committing to such a public location for lunch.

"You know what I just noticed?" Cal asked him, not waiting for an answer. "We're both wearing army jackets and black Chucks. That's kind of funny, right?"

Henry looked down at himself and saw that Cal was right. Except where his jacket was adorned with the insignia of the 3rd Battalion, 4th Regiment, the "Thundering Third" as they were known, whose L Company was the last to leave Vietnam, Cal's was decorated with the patches of punk bands: Germs, Circle Jerks, Minor Threat, Dead Kennedys, and more.

"What kind of music do you listen to?" Cal asked him.

"I don't really listen to that much music, to be honest." He pointed at the patches on Cal's jacket. "Do you listen to all these bands?"

Cal nodded. "I'm going to make you a mixtape. A lot of the bands I listen to are from around here. Bad Religion, TSOL, the Adolescents. All punk rock. We should go see a show sometime. A lot of pushing and shoving. Ever been in a mosh pit before?"

"No."

"It's intense, but it's a really good feeling. You're going to love it."

They continued to walk around the quad and Henry noticed a few people starting to look at them. Before today, he would never have been given a second glance, but now that he and Cal were walking with their army jackets and matching black shoes, he felt like all eyes were on them, a jarring change from the anonymity he was used to.

"Let's go eat behind the E Building," he said to Cal, suddenly feeling very uncomfortable.

Cal looked around and saw that they were being watched. "Fine," he laughed, unwrapping the sandwich, "but fuck these assholes. You shouldn't care what people say behind your back."

"Behind my back?"

Cal winked at him. "Don't worry. I've got your back now." He handed Henry a piece of his sister's sandwich; chicken salad.

As they headed off toward one of the far ends of campus, Henry stopped and turned to Cal. "The weirdest thing happened to me right here, one time. I was walking across the quad, going to catch the bus after school, and…"

Cal stopped him. "Wait," he said, putting out his hand. "Let me guess. You were walking across the quad, minding your own business, and out of nowhere a black kid came up to you and hit you in the face. Am I right?"

Henry was shocked. It was exactly what he was going to say, except that he had never told anyone about it. It had been such a strange thing, so jarring and out of nowhere, like a dream, that he wasn't even sure sometimes if it had ever actually happened. The punch hadn't been hard enough to knock him down, and when it was over, and the kid had quickly walked away, he looked around to confirm that it had happened, but no one had stopped or even looked over at him. It was the most surreal thing that had ever happened to him.

"How did you know?"

"Because," Cal said, "it happened to me, too. I found out later that it's a gang initiation thing. These black kids have to walk up to the biggest white guy they can find and punch him in the face."

The warning bell rang throughout the school, warning them that they had ten more minutes to finish their lunch.

"That's amazing that you knew that's what I was going to say."

"Well, you're tall. I'm tall. We're in the middle of the quad and I didn't think you were going to tell me that this is where a cheerleader asked if she could give you a handjob." Cal burped and shifted his backpack to his other shoulder. "Besides, they wouldn't do that now, would they? Not when there's two of us."

Chapter 5

TRUMAN LIFTED THE pair of headphones off Henry's head and placed them on his own. His face took on a look of studious concentration as he crossed his arms and tapped his foot lightly, and not at all in time, against the floor. After a minute he handed the headphones back.

"I don't get it. That music helps you work?" Truman's upper lip and blue Izod shirt sported matching mustard stains.

"Yeah." Henry took the earphones back and covertly wiped the little ear buds on his pant leg, not wanting to consider the varieties of auditory infections Truman exposed himself to over the course of a day of conversations with the kind of people who placed personal ads in the paper. "It's what I used to listen to when I was a kid," he explained, thinking back to his indoctrination into the world of punk rock by Cal, the thousands of times he had heard these songs, manifestos to a teen, nostalgic wallpaper now as an adult. "It makes me sentimental."

Truman shook his head. "For what? Incest?"

"Very funny."

Truman bent over to look at the pictures of cult leaders Henry had hung on the walls of his cubicle. "Inspiration?" he asked, scribbling a Hitler mustache onto a photo of a beaming Rev. Moon that was right next to the picture of Grace. Victim and violator. He liked the symmetry.

"Something like that." He knocked the pen out of Truman's hand. "Hey, stop it. I don't come over to your cubicle and…"

"Let me guess," Truman interrupted him. "Knock the dicks out of my mouth? Is that what you were going to say? Peasant." And then without missing a beat. "Can you imagine listening to anything these panty sniffers had to say? What kind of bullshit has to be going on in your life that you'd think one of these assholes has all the answers?"

"That's what I'm trying to figure out," Henry said, staring now at the wall of photos as well. "I have a feeling, though, that the answer is going to be disappointing. I don't think it's going to be as simple as that."

"Who's that?" Truman asked, stabbing a finger at the picture of Grace. "Some sort of cult babe pin cushion?"

"That's my sister," Henry said. "Was my sister," he added, correcting himself.

"Oh," Truman replied, sheathing his digit, "Don't I feel silly?" And then, because shame was for suckers. "How'd she die?"

Henry felt himself tense up at the question. He didn't often talk about Grace, and when he did he found himself sometimes making up stories about her death so he wouldn't have to go into it all. It was a long story, exhausting in a way nothing else in his life was. He decided to give the short answer.

"She was murdered. Shot, actually. She was shot."

"Jesus, Henry. That's…I don't know what to say. Gnarly?"

Henry leaned back in his chair, folding his hands on his stomach. He took a deep breath.

"You can say 'gnarly'. Gnarly works."

Truman walked over to the elevator. "How's this for a segue? Wanna get some lunch?"

"Yeah, I could do that," Henry said, breaking the picture's trance. "Where's Alberto?"

"I don't know," Truman pushed the down button at the elevator, "we don't talk anymore." He looked around the room to see if anyone was listening. "Just get in the elevator."

On their way down, the elevator's old winch turning crankily, Truman told him that he and Alberto were no longer talking in public as part of the plan to make their real estate scheme seem as real as possible.

They left the building and headed south, down streets that white flight hadn't just made irrelevant, but had somehow made feel as though they'd never existed in the first place; weeds and trees, nature's wild mercenaries, ran roughshod over anything that dared stand still for long enough. Henry saw a red Ford Fiesta, long since abandoned, sprouting lush green foliage from within its hood where its engine block had once been. A grey cat arched its back and rubbed its face against the car's tire, ample proof that even Mother Nature knew to buy American. Urban sprawl was turning back on itself, inverting; entropy was the new back to nature. A new-looking banner, festooned with colorful, bubbly writing, was strung above Broadway announcing tryouts for a new season of Little League. It was almost a joke, the civic fathers' way of paying child support.

"Where are you taking me?" Henry asked, not terribly interested in the answer.

"We're meeting Alberto."

They ran a gauntlet of homeless men, expressionless husks with infinite stares. Henry wasn't sure where they could be going. It seemed impossible that there could be anything for them to see or do in this part of the city with its forlorn massage parlors and restaurants promising authentic home cooking from countries that didn't even exist anymore. But then they turned a corner and he saw where they had been headed. It was an enormous new grocery store, a *supermercado*, a towering and broad structure that took up almost the entire block. In its shadow these decrepit old stores seemed quaint, a throwback to a time and a place when public safety didn't matter as much as a good meal or the privileges of nepotism.

"How could I not know this thing was here?" Henry asked no one in particular.

Truman hitched up his pants. "I know. It's amazing. It's like finding a lost city or a ship full of sunken treasure."

"I don't know about that," Henry squinted up at the giant edifice.

"You're looking at it the wrong way," Truman said as he led them across the Saharan parking lot. "This place has it all. It's the conveniarchy. We need things like this in our life. We need not to be so fragile. If this store was a boyfriend you would ask it, 'Why are you hitting me?' And you know what it would say?"

"No, I have no idea," Henry replied, still taken aback by the sheer volume of his discovery.

"It would say, 'I'm hitting you, baby, because I don't like the way you make me feel.' That's what it would say."

"Interesting analogy. So you're saying shopping here is like getting beaten by your boyfriend?"

"All I'm saying is if you want to be a real man, if you want to join something worth fighting for, then come with me." He clapped a hand on Henry's shoulder. "Come shopping with me."

They met Alberto at the entrance and exchanged a quick hello. Inside, the grocery store was a Tower of Babel, which, instead of multiple languages, perpetrated a cacophony of odors and sights that had no business existing together in the same enclosed space. It was a marketplace of groping senses, the smell of chemical cleaners competing for space with the rustic sadness of freshly baked bread, multi-colored labels basking under fluorescent lighting that registered in the optic nerve as something halfway between the physical manifestation of second sight and ether. There was a forlorn Starbucks next to the pharmacy, which sat adjacent to a florist's outpost. This wasn't convenience, it was an all-out assault on the senses, and Henry, who did his shopping at a local convenience store, felt immediately overwhelmed by it all.

"Is this what grocery stores are like now? I feel like I'm in an interrogation room and I'm about to confess to something that I'll regret later." Henry tugged gently at the collar of his shirt.

Alberto nodded, but Truman had already taken a place in line for coffee, smiling delightedly at Henry's discomfort.

"It's just a market, Henry. Relax. This is how the other half lives." He craned his neck around to see what was taking so long at the register. "Come on," he hollered at the lady at the front of the line. "Hurry up, I'm dying for coffee here." He smiled at Alberto and Henry. "You can be as alarmist as you want at these places, and no one takes it for impatience. It's erotic almost, when you think about it. Did you hear what she was ordering? It's hard to tell if that's coffee or sorcery."

"He loves being overwhelmed," Alberto confided in Henry. "It's when he does his best work."

The woman took her coffee and walked by Truman, giving him a worried stare.

"Are you going to drink that thing or fuck it?" he asked her as she scurried past.

He turned again toward Henry and Alberto and shrugged his shoulders. "What? How can anyone expect personal accountability when there's this much stimulation to contend with?"

They strolled the aisles as Truman licked playfully at his whipped cream-topped coffee.

"What are we doing here?" Henry asked glancing at his watch.

"We're getting supplies for the condo," Alberto answered, checking his shopping list and dumping some S.O.S pads into his cart. Truman tossed in a plunger and an extension cord on top it.

"Okay," Henry joked, "You want to be ready for when the shit goes down, huh? Get it. Plunger? Shit goes down?"

Truman stopped and turned to him, wiping the rest of the whipped cream off his lip with his sleeve.

"You can make jokes all you want, Henry, but we gave you the chance to be part of this thing and you turned us down. Don't fuck with what you can't comprehend!" and with that Truman stormed off ahead of them down the aisle.

"What's wrong with him?" Henry asked, genuinely confused.

Alberto shrugged his buttery shoulders. "He's bummed out that you didn't want to do his thing with him. He's a big baby; you know that. He considers you a good friend."

"He has a funny way of showing it."

"You know how men are," Alberto responded, blithely.

Henry looked at him strangely. "That's a weird thing to say."

Alberto shrugged again. It was becoming his signature move. "Post-postmodernism. It's a freer world, dude."

Henry checked his watch again and thought about getting back to the office. He had made a few calls that morning, one to a cult survivor's group and another to Reverend Potter's old attorney. His writing so far had been confined to getting the facts down, a very pro forma timeline of Potter's life. What he was still missing was some personal insight, stories, experiences that might frame Potter's actions, give his deeds some kind of explanation or justification.

He joined Truman who was standing in front of the greeting cards, flipping idly through them, seemingly looking for something in particular.

"Where's the card that says I'd rather you not have a birthday at all than for me to have missed it?" Truman asked him sincerely. "Where's the truth?"

A sudden rush of affection coursed through Henry, affection for Truman's honesty and for his eagerness, for his undiminished optimism and faith in the American dream.

"Come on," Henry said, "Let's find the dairy section. I want to show you something."

He led them through a maze of aisles to the back of the market to where the dairy cases were lined up breathing swirling sprays of mist into the aisle. Henry looked up and down the aisle, and seeing no one, grabbed an armful of whipped cream cans and beckoned for Truman and Alberto to follow him. They turned down the ethnic foods aisle, with its matzah and udon noodles, all but abandoned in the name of decency and globalization. Popping the top off one of the cans, he looked his friends in the eye, smiled, and pushed the button, sucking in a gigantic hit of nitrous oxide. In an instant his sinuses were full of liquid steel, and he felt a black hole open up in his forehead, emitting a lightning bolt made of pure neon. He sat down and sighed out the gas, his fingers and toes buzzing like lightning bugs.

"Aaahhh...my fingers and toes are electricity. It's like they're throwing a party, celebrating the destruction of my brain cells."

Truman smiled widely and looked at Alberto. They each took a can and inhaled a mouthful of laughing gas. Truman gripped his knees, mumbling to himself, his eyes swooning in his head, words of exultation stacked up high behind trembling lips, waiting to spill out and declare fealty to Lord Nitrous of Oxide. Alberto was losing a similar battle against his nerve endings. He leaned his back against a wall and slid slowly down to his ass. "I feel like a pie," he said as he went down, his hand bobbing up slightly and then crashing down to the floor next to him.

"What was that?" Truman asked, "That thing with your hand?"

"I was trying to make air quotes," Alberto giggled, "but I don't have the upper body strength."

Truman was already working on his next can. "Your girth is preventing you from being literal. Obesity has condemned you to a lifetime of irony."

"Life," Alberto seemed to be thinking about it, toying with the word as though it was a concept not yet put into practice, "is a broken time machine."

A hot young Asian woman came around the corner, her index finger extended as she read over the labels of the thirty types of fish sauce she had to choose from. She stopped when she looked down the aisle and saw them, Truman with his head bent over a can of Reddi-Whip, Henry laughing at his own teeth, and Alberto laying on the floor, trying to push an imaginary 'Rewind' button. They heard her and looked up, frozen as if they had come across a deer in the forest, not wanting to scare her off. Her eyes widened as she tried to make sense of what she was seeing. But before she could turn and run, or scream, or give up on the cuisine of her homeland, Alberto grabbed his crotch like he had just pulled the pin on a grenade, and pantomimed lobbing it over at her as she hurried away.

"That's incredible," Henry said, as if he was hearing his own voice from far away.

"Thanks," Alberto said, reaching for someone's hand to help hoist him up. "It's how I deal with the notion of unattainable women. If my cock can't have them, then no one will."

"And your dick blowing up?"

Alberto shrugged. "Collateral damage."

Henry felt good, alive, as he laughed his way in and out of numbness, and he knew that this little idea of his had been a good one when Truman, smoothing down his thinning black hair, a perfect part that guarded over the two very separate parts of his brain, snapped at Alberto, "We don't have time for this, people. Alberto, if you want to spend the rest of your life playing Fight Club with your cock, that's your business. But I'm here to get the things we're going to need to ride out the storm, man. I'm trying to prepare us…"

"Preach on, preacher man," Alberto said, throwing a box of macaroons into their shopping cart.

Before he could respond, Henry snatched the grocery list out of Truman's hand.

"Let's see here," Henry tried to focus his still dilated pupils on the words. "What exactly is on a shopping list for when you're getting ready for the apocalypse."

"Don't be dramatic," Truman said, snatching back the piece of paper. "It's just a race war. It's hardly the end of the world." Truman smiled and slung an arm around Henry's shoulder. "Thanks, buddy," he whispered, "this was a lot of fun."

"My pleasure."

"Don't forget about us, okay? Come and visit once in a while."

"I will," Henry said, satisfied that he had done the right thing for his friend.

*   *   *

Back at his desk the cold frost of a hangover began to take the shape of a headache that forced him to close his eyes, put his head on his desk, and begin to massage his temples lightly, in little circles. From over the partition of his cubicle, he heard Truman rumble to his feet and hang his own wretched noggin over the wall.

"It looks like you're rubbing a clit. Two clits. You must be a god in bed." Truman drew in a sharp breath. "Is my head supposed to hurt this much? Am I ever going to feel my lips again?" He asked the questions with perfect innocence, like a kindergartener wondering why the sky was blue.

"Yes and no," Henry replied, wading through a pool of his own pain. "Any question you ask me for the rest of the day is going to have the same answer; yes and no."

Truman thought for a moment and then sat back down. "I can live with that."

Henry went back to massaging his head and when the phone rang he snatched at it, angrily, holding the receiver tight like it was the head of a rattlesnake.

"Hello, this is Henry." The words slid wretchedly from the back of his throat like a muddy landslide.

"My name is Daisy," a slight voice said, "I'm returning your call."

"Huh?" Henry rubbed his head and a dusting of dandruff fell on his desk. He stared down at the flakes as if he was reading tea leaves for the answer to who this Daisy might be.

"I'm calling from CHoSEN. The Children of Light Survivors Network. You left us a message." Her voice was flat. Atonal. "You're a reporter?"

It finally clicked. This was the ex-cultist place he had left a message at earlier in the day.

"Yeah," he searched his desk frantically for something to write on. "I'm doing a story...well, actually, I'm doing some research on Reverend Potter for a piece I'm writing on him and I'd love to get some input from a former..." He didn't know what to call them. Were they members? Victims? Morons, as Truman might suggest.

"Member? Yeah, ok." She paused as if she was checking on something. "I could meet you in about an hour. Do you know the restaurant Drama on Vermont?"

"Uh-huh."

His face was tingling in a not too pleasant way, like someone was trying to vacuum his face from his head.

"Okay, I'll see you in an hour then. By the way, don't bring any cameras or voice recorders. If you do, I'm out of there."

The line went dead as she hung up the phone.

He knew the restaurant, or at least had known it at one time, when it was a fifties-themed diner called The Gravelly Bottom. Now, in its present incarnation as Drama, it had been transformed with very little effort into a faux French bistro type of place. Gone were the fifties-style pennants and old yearbook photos only to be replaced with black-and-whites of romantic intellectual types, smoldering within the elegant suits that European men throughout the ages seemed to always wear no matter their socio-economic status or the occasion, as if there was a dress code to merely exist on the continent. He chose a booth under a picture of Sartre sitting at an outdoor café in Paris, spectacles framing his compassionless eyes, a cigarette burning eternally in one hand. Henry picked up a menu and flipped it open. At first glance it seemed not to have changed at all, but upon closer inspection he noticed that what he had first thought were the doodles of an unwatched kid were actually accents written in at random over the diner fare. Hamburgers were now hambùrgers. Home fries were home friés. Cultural imperialism had run amuck and was delicious.

He laid out the tools of his trade on the table: a pad of paper, a finely sharpened number two pencil, a business card. It was hardly intimidating, but it was all he had and he hoped they would be enough to give him the upper hand. Judging from her voice on the phone, a desperate sort of nonchalance, along with the opportunity he was giving her to air the truth, he guessed that he would have it. He wondered how he would know her when she came in and cursed himself silently for not asking her for a description. In his head, and from her voice, he pictured someone stringy and bland, a tall ugly woman with a complexion the color of spoilt milk. He pictured a victim, sadness incarnate, someone who might have listed psoriasis as an interest in her online dating profile. He imagined the human equivalent of a loose thread hanging from a sweater just waiting to be pulled. Maybe that's all Potter had to do to get her. Just pull that thread.

He felt a tap on his shoulder just as his nose began to twitch. He wiped it with his sleeve as he turned around to see a beautiful blonde woman.

"Hi," she said. "You've gotta be Henry, right?"

"Yeah. Hi." He struggled to get his twitching nose under control. "You're Daisy?"

She looked at him as if waiting for him to say something like, 'Yeah, duh. Of course you are,' but before he could get the words out she had already nodded and sat down at the table.

She was tall and athletic, lean, and wore not an ounce of make-up, more beautiful because of it rather than in spite of it. Her looks and dress suggested an earthiness that was vibrant and lush, not the ditziness he usually associated with the word. She had long blonde hair that swept down past her shoulders and deeply red lips, the very color of life.

She looked up at the wall and pointed to a picture of Hegel.

"Do you think they know that he's not French?"

Henry looked and shrugged. "It doesn't matter. It's black and white. That seems to be enough for them. Did you notice the umlauts over the grilled cheese? The whole thing's a mess. Old Europe."

"So," she said, picking up the menu, glancing at it casually, "what is it we're doing here? You said something about writing an article about Reverend Potter?"

"Yeah," he said, suddenly sitting up a little straighter. "I write for the *Los Angeles Daily Ledger*." He handed her his business card. "I'm writing up the obituary of Reverend Potter, it's something all the big papers do for older notable figures, and I wanted to talk to you about your experiences with him. About your time in the..." he struggled with how to put it, not wanting to offend, "...group."

"Group," she snorted as she put down her menu. "You mean cult? It's okay, you can say it. It doesn't offend me."

"Okay," he grabbed his pad and made a note. He was nervous, shaken by her appearance and by her assertiveness. He had so wanted to be the one in control of this interview, but he could already feel it slipping away from him.

"Cult." He mouthed the word as he wrote it.

She summoned the waitress over and ordered a veggie burger. Henry ordered the same with absolutely no intention of eating.

"Well, why did you get into it then, if you knew it was a cult?"

"Wait," she said, holding up a hand to stop him. "Quick question before we start."

"Okay," he replied, putting the pencil down.

"Are you a huffer?"

"What?"

"I just mean, well, your lips are all blue. I knew some guys in college that used to huff shoe polish and they always had blue lips like that. So I was just wondering..."

"No," he exclaimed, putting a hand to his numb kisser. "I get cold really easily. I have a thing with my extremities."

"Okay," she smiled. "Just wanted to know what I was dealing with."

"How did you know I was me, by the way? We never talked about how we'd recognize one another on the phone."

She shrugged. "You just kind of looked the way I imagined a journalist would look. Kind of scruffy. Kind of unkempt. But intelligent looking."

"Oh." He didn't know quite how to take it and without even realizing he was doing it, began pushing his hair over to the side. An uncomfortable silence passed in which Edith Piaf's rough voice scratched its way out of an unseen stereo like fingers clawing at the inside of a sealed coffin.

"Edith Piaf's always sounded to me like someone with a gun to their head being forced to sing love songs. Still," she went on, fiddling with a straw, "a love song's a love song."

Clearing his throat, he tried to take control of the meeting.

"So, back to my question if you don't mind."

"I don't mind," she said, matter-of-factly.

"If you knew it was a cult, and I guess we can assume the word *cult* has a negative connotation to it, why did you join in the first place?"

"Well, like with any big decision in life, you can say I fucked my way into it."

He tried not to look too surprised by her answer.

"What do you mean by that?"

"I've always been kind of a joiner. I was involved with every group in college you can get into and then I met a guy who was one of the Children and that was that. Good sex is incredibly persuasive. At least at the beginning."

"What do you mean you were a joiner?"

"Just that," she said. "I was always into things. Cheerleading in high school. College Democrats. Then I did the Free Palestine thing. I was always on to the next thing. I'm cause-oriented."

"So it escalated like that?"

"What do you mean?" she asked.

"It's just the trajectory you're charting here kind of goes from the frivolous to the political to the very political. You never noticed a pattern there?"

"Frivolous? What do you know about Ohio cheerleading?"

He laughed.

"I'm serious," she said, drumming her fingers on the edge of the table. "It's all in how you look at it."

"One chick's cult is another chick's cheerleading squad," he tried to joke, but she didn't crack a smile.

"Is this going to be one of those interviews," she asked seriously, "where you tell me what you think you know about how things are, or are you going to actually listen to what

I have to say? I'm risking an awful lot by being here. You don't understand how serious these people are about former members talking to the media." She sighed deeply. "You know what they call people who leave the Children?"

"What?" he asked, pen poised, trying to regain any respect she may have had for him.

"The Dead."

For the first time he noticed a light freckling of sweat dotting her forehead and her upper lip, just the slightest suggestion of discomfort, and he realized that her posturing wasn't just about being assertive, but that she was genuinely nervous about being seen with him.

"What about you? At least I was doing things, experiencing life. Your whole profession is about observing. Sitting back while the world goes by."

He picked up his glass and tasted the Arnold Palmer he didn't remember ordering. It was cold, but utterly tasteless. He wondered, not terribly worriedly, if inhaling the nitrous oxide had somehow destroyed his sense of taste.

"I don't just sit back. That's not what being a journalist is. I record."

"You endure by not doing," she shot back.

"Are you saying I can't have a full life because I'm a journalist?"

"Animals endure. Man overcomes."

"I'm up and coming," he said meekly and then coughed. He tried to summon up some sense of determination and indignation but found only a chest full of phlegm.

Daisy sat back and ran a hand through her hair, causing a few strands to avalanche down her forehead and across her face like the opening of a fault line across the earth.

Their food came in greasy heaps and she immediately and

ferociously set to unleashing a hailstorm of pepper across her plate, truly a seasoning of Biblical proportions. They ate in silence, Henry picking at his fries, waiting for an opening to resume the conversation, Daisy devouring her meal in quick and hungry bites, stopping only to wipe her mouth when ketchup spurted from the burger leaking down her chin.

When she was done, she began speaking again as if the interruption in the interview had been something they had agreed upon ahead of time.

"My life was pretty ordinary, I think."

"That's pretty subjective, don't you think? It's not really an answer."

She grinned as she stole a french fry from his plate.

"Put it this way, we always had dinner together and we'd go around the table and ask one another how our days had gone and everyone always had the same answer. Fine. Great. And they were. It wasn't a lie. We weren't trying to throw one another off the scent of anything serious. There was just literally nothing to say."

She went on for another half an hour about her life; her upbringing in the Midwest, the picture perfectness of her family. She seemed to have been born into complacency, a happy contentedness, so maybe it wasn't that hard to make the leap from that kind of happy upbringing to where she wound up; nervous and argumentative, looking over her shoulder every time the front door clicked open. Maybe this was the comeuppance of complacency.

"So, tell me about the Children of Light. You say you joined," he wanted to put it delicately, "because of a guy. What was it like? How soon after that did you realize that you belonged there, not just because of who you were dating at the time?"

She chuckled. "Dating. That's funny."

"Why's that funny?"

"Because," she explained, "you don't really date once you're there. There's no such thing as boyfriend and girlfriend or even husband and wife. You're part of the group once you're there. You're living each day as if it was new, as if every time you woke up you were waking up to a brand-new world, the earth reborn. Relationships tend to take on different dimensions when that's your mindset."

Mindset. He felt bad for her, having to try to boil down something that had been such an integral part of her life for so long into condensed ideas.

"So, if you guys weren't together like that, why didn't you leave at that point? If you joined for a guy, why didn't you take off once you two weren't together anymore?"

"Because," she looked at him as if he should already understand, "by that time I was one of Potter's children. I was a child of light and he was the shaper, helping us renew the universe every day, showing us how to experience all of life in every second. In every breath. The days could be so wonderful there," she went on, dreaming with her eyes open. "Mornings in the garden. Walks through the woods. Sex in the afternoon. What's not to love about being totally free?" And then focusing on him, she asked, "I mean, doesn't that sound perfect to you?"

He thought of his own dreams then, nightmares he conflated with memories. "I think it sounds nice."

"Nice, huh? That's it? Just nice?"

"It sounds like one version of perfect. Put it that way."

"Okay," she smiled and then looked around quickly, scrutinizing the room again. "One version of perfect. That's a nice way to put it. One thing, though, I want you to know before I have to leave." *Leave? He didn't want her to leave.* "Don't think of all the people there as victims. That's important. Most of them chose to be there. It wasn't like a last resort. People may have had a lot of different reasons for being there, but that's like anything else. That's like therapy." She smiled at him. "Ever been in therapy?"

"Sure," he laughed. "Why not?"

"I bet you were one of those guys who used to think about killing himself all the time before you saw a shrink. And then once you started talking about your feelings and your mommy and daddy, then you realized you didn't want to kill yourself, but that you wanted to kill everyone else. Am I right? Isn't that how therapy goes?"

A stack of plates smashed to the floor somewhere back in the kitchen and an exclamation of curses ignited the air in what sounded like a dozen different languages. It was less jarring than her question but gave him a chance to think of a snappy reply.

"No, actually. We never talked about my homicidal tendencies. She was more interested in whether or not I was a chronic masturbator."

Daisy laughed, relaxing back into her seat.

"Chronic masturbator? Has she ever met a man before?" They both laughed.

"Okay then," he probed carefully, "if it was so great, why'd you leave? What happened?"

He thought it was an innocent enough question, especially given how comfortable they seemed to be getting with one another, but her face went ashen and she looked away.

"I don't want to talk about that. I don't mean to be secretive or anything, but I just don't want to talk…"

He waved his hands. "No, no. That's okay. That's okay. I

shouldn't have asked. This is supposed to be about Potter anyway," he said, looking down at his notes where all that was written was the word 'cults.' He circled it for lack of anything better to do with his hands.

She stood up and dug her hand in her pocket for her money. The check hadn't yet come, but she was finished. She wanted to leave. He stood up and shook his head.

"I'll get this." He pried loose a couple of threadbare five-dollar bills from his wallet. "Can I call you again? I mean..." she smiled and he got flustered, "...to talk about this stuff. I feel like we've barely scratched the surface."

"You don't know the half of it," she said a bit hopelessly, as if to start from the beginning might take more time than either of them had. Her posture was perfect, he noticed, like a ballerina in repose, and he self-consciously forced himself to stand up straight, forcing evolution on himself so as to at least appear that he was from the same species. "It's my hope, more than anything else, that the truth comes out about this group and this man. You're in a very powerful position, Henry. But I know you know that.

"I want to speak again. In fact, it's important that we do, but," and here she leaned in close, her voice a tingly thing in his ear, loose wires, that feeling of good drugs kicking in. From out of nowhere he imagined what sweet talk would feel like coming from those lips, ruby red, a color that can only be dug from the earth. It would be feverish dedications and lip-locked scriptures, desperation incarnate, the best kind of love, "I think we're being watched," and without another word she left.

He sat back down, and waiting for his change, replayed in his mind where it had all gone wrong. He had come to find out about Potter, to gain some insight into the man whose obituary was due on his editor's desk in less than ten days, and had in the course of an afternoon, learned absolutely nothing. No, that wasn't quite true. What he had learned was how easy it was to offend people. He hadn't meant to say anything that would hurt her feelings. All he wanted was some version of the truth. It didn't seem like too much to ask for. He hadn't even thought for a second that she might have her own story to tell, a story that wasn't about what life was like living in a cultist commune in the Mojave Desert, but rather a story that somehow defended her intelligence despite having made what any outsider would think of as a terrible mistake.

Back in the kitchen he could hear the unmistakable resonance of mariachi music coming in over the radio. The stations that played this kind of old-style Mexican music had the best reception by far in Los Angeles. He had several punched in as presets in his car just for the clarity of the reception.

Walking back to his office he had the vague sensation that he was being watched. He shoved his hands in his pockets and locked his neck in place, careful not to let his head turn for fear that someone would sense that he was watching the watchers. The art of acting inconspicuous was suddenly paralyzing despite a lifetime of relative anonymity. The more he thought of acting naturally, of walking down the street like any other guy, the harder it became to do. He felt his knees start to lock up making it difficult to walk. His shoulder tensed, his biceps flexed. He was turning into a piece of rebar and before he simply turned to stone, he ducked off the main street into an alley, and let himself catch a breath, realizing now that he had barely taken a single breath since he left the restaurant a block or so ago. Remembering that he had been running from something, he quickly looked up and saw a homeless guy staring at him from atop a pile of crushed cardboard boxes. The man wore a thick wool winter coat, crusted over with a deep strata of stains and other bad choices, and a dirty hat with ear flaps, winter gear he had the foresight to hang on to despite its now being the middle of summer. His face was deeply tan, peeling in places from too much time in the sun.

"I was going to ask you for a dollar, but…" the man looked warily at Henry.

Henry glanced around frantically, and then slowly let himself calm down, sure now that he wasn't going to be found.

"They're after me," Henry said by way of explanation.

"I know the feeling," the homeless guy replied, shaking a cigarette in Henry's direction. Normally not a smoker, Henry took it and let the man light it from a disposable red Bic. "Who is it?" the man asked him, sincerely. "Who's after you? The government? Black ops? Aliens?"

Nothing in his voice made Henry feel as though he were patronized. In fact, if anything, the man's sincerity made him feel calm and relaxed. He leaned back against a filthy brick wall and pulled his knees up to his body, hugging them tightly to his chest.

"Cultists," he answered. "I think there's some cultists after me."

The homeless man nodded knowingly as he sucked on his cigarette watching Henry through narrow eyes.

"Which cult?"

"Children of Light."

He nodded again. "Reverend Potter. He's got a dangerous organization. Secret police force. Deep intelligence-gathering apparatus. It's not his style to come right after people, though. I don't think you have to worry about taking one right between the eyes," he jammed his index finger at the spot between his eyes, mimicking the impact of a well-placed gunshot. "Potter's a lot more subtle than that. He'll fuck you up. It'll just take longer and be more painful in the end."

"Are they after you, too?" Henry asked him.

"No." The man waved his hand away, chasing wisps of smoke and a Biblical body odor in Henry's direction. "They may have been. In the seventies. I'm not sure. Now, I've lost track of who's after me. That's what happens when you get old. You start to forget who wants you dead."

Henry was about to ask something else, something about Potter, when the door that the man was sitting in front of suddenly opened, flinging him off his perch and toppling his tall stack of cardboard real estate. A Chinese cook in an apron and cook's hat came out holding two bags of garbage, and when he saw the homeless guy trying to pick himself off the ground, began to swear at him in Chinese, gesturing wildly to a sign above the door that was also in Chinese. Henry looked up at the sign and guessed that it probably said 'exit' or 'do not block' or something of that nature. The script was so ornate and extravagant, though, it hardly seemed possible that that's all it could mean. If that's all it meant, then it hardly seemed worth it.

The homeless guy picked up his stuff and the two of them walked together down the alley, a flood of angry Chinese people at their backs, heading deeper into Downtown. They walked past Grand Central Market, Angel's Flight and MOCA, up to the twisted heap of metal that was Disney Hall, which, the first time Henry saw it, made him wonder if he hadn't stumbled upon a plane crash. They strolled through China-town, Henry trailing slightly behind Lou, which Henry had found out was the homeless man's name, carrying some of his belongings for him like a porter at the airport. Past China-town they came to a part of the city outside of the scope of the urban renewal that the Downtown area was supposedly undergoing. Here, in the outskirts, they passed vacant buildings sunning themselves into decomposition, brick becoming sand again, the birthright of property superseded by the self-satisfaction of indifference. Abandoned shopping carts rusted on sidewalks and in the middle of the street like a deactivated, junkie, robot army. And everywhere, weeds and ivy, wild plants that intruded into everything like misfits running rampant in the bad part of town. Henry and Lou stopped under a freeway overpass where a latticework of vegetation grew up the walls and across the underside of the highway. This was the architecture of neglect, nature filling in where man had gotten lazy and left off. Strange flowers bloomed from the cracks in the concrete. Tall plants nestled into the shady corners, nursing at the fetid and smoke-filled air. Lou talked non-stop about his persecution at the hands of the Chinese, his latest tormentors. They walked around and over other homeless men and women, people in the midst of conversation, eating, drinking, sorting endlessly through their belongings as if the very act of moving things from one pile to another and back again would somehow make them more useful, more meaningful. It was the momentum of ritual, the very fabric of life.

Lou found an unoccupied patch of sidewalk and dropped his stuff summarily to the ground. It was less dramatic than the explorers planting the flags of their colonial sponsors into fresh new soil, but the idea was the same.

"The thing about the Chinese," he went on, unfurling his sleeping bag on the sidewalk, "is…" But before he could finish the thought, one of his new neighbors, a grizzled looking piece of flesh in a Dodgers hat piped up.

"Oh yeah, the Chinese. Fucking Chinese…"

"See," Lou said to Henry, shaking his head, "that's the problem with these homeless fucks. Incestuous amplification. That's a military term. One asshole says something, and because of the chain of command, because one guy's on top of another, that thing, whether it's right or wrong, gets repeated over and over. Incestuous amplification." He said the phrase again after he had explained it like it was a word in a spelling bee.

Henry played with the words inside his head. He liked the way they felt.

"That's good," he said, "mind if I use that in something I'm writing?"

"Writing?" Lou became a little more lucid. "What was it you said you did for a living?"

"I'm a journalist," Henry told him, looking around for a bottle of Purell, trying to manifest one out of thin air. He wondered if it would be a faux pas to ask Lou if he had one. "I write for the *Los Angeles Daily Ledger*."

Without a word, Lou grabbed the bags Henry had been carrying from him out of his hands and waved him away. "I don't talk to reporters."

"Wha—" but he was cut off.

"I don't talk to reporters. Ever. End of story."

He took his things and stormed off waving a 'no comment' hand behind him as he went. Henry looked around embarrassed at having been abandoned now for the second time that day. The incestuous amplifier, who to this point, had been railing on about the Chinese, suddenly stopped and glared at Henry. Picking up the last thread of conversation he curled his upper lip and spat at the ground by Henry's feet. "We don't never talk to reporters. Never."

The next day at his desk Henry sat in front of a blank computer screen, pure white, the color he had come to associate with being completely unproductive. He hadn't heard from Daisy since the restaurant despite having left her several messages. The CHoSEN offices seemed to be permanently closed. Perhaps they had gone on some sort of office retreat together, he thought, but the idea of a bunch of ex-cultists going off together for intensive discussion seemed about as logical as an Alcoholics Anonymous field trip to a brewery. He thought of her incessantly, not just needing to speak to her so that he could get the rest of the information he needed for his story, but also to know that she was okay, to know whether or not he had been right to worry about being followed himself. He thought of her alone somewhere, trapped in a damp and soundproofed room, bruises welling up on her face, her teeth working frantically to gnaw through the straps at her wrists. Shaking his head, he told himself not to give in to the tendency to create worst-case scenarios, however safe that felt, that conjuring up the most dire of situations was probably a huge part of his problem in feeling that so few moments of his life felt real to him anymore. Besides, she had so easily taken over the conversation at the restaurant despite his intimidating armament of sharpened graphite and two-color business cards, he figured it wouldn't be the easiest thing in the world to wrestle her into the trunk of a car. Google brought up nothing on her, not even a high school photo, nothing about high school honor roles or college demonstrations, the typical innocuous flora of digital finger-printing. That shouldn't have surprised him, though, because the way she had described herself there was very little that was typical about her, very little that suggested she'd have a Facebook account or have published her top-ten summer reads list on Amazon.

His fingers went to the keyboard again and wilted, not knowing how to start the story of Potter's life and death. Fingers back to the keyboard again and he typed a sentence he heard Alberto say during their nitrous binge the day before: *Life is a broken time machine*. At the time, he remembered feeling that those words would be the perfect lead sentence for Potter's obituary, but now, instead of inspiring the rest of it, or at least a little more, the words just sat there floating uselessly against a sea of white empty space. It could hardly be said to be writer's block, though—for that you needed to have started something and been caught in the process, not knowing what to do next. This was something more chronic, a fundamental lack of momentum, physics defeated by gloominess and anxiety. He sighed and leaned back in his chair, feeling stuck and tired, the way the needle at the end of a record slides along and then bobs sadly in that space in the middle, crackling for help, for a nudge back to usefulness.

Alberto's head sprouted up over the cubicle wall. He leaned over and rested his chin on his folded arms.

"What's wrong?" he asked Henry, who was rapidly rubbing his face with his hands, "Writer's block?"

"Ha," Henry laughed. "That would mean I'd actually have to have started writing something, which," he gestured to his computer monitor, "as you can see, is not exactly the case."

From the other side of him, Truman's voice suddenly appeared.

"Can the two of you take the small talk somewhere else? Some of us are trying to get some work done over here."

Henry peeked his head around the corner to find Truman scrutinizing a picture of a naked Asian girl spread eagle on a bed, a Hello Kitty ball gag jammed in her mouth.

"This is work?" Henry asked.

Truman shrugged, never taking his eyes off the screen. "It's call 'Guess Her Muff'. They show you a picture of a girl completely clothed and then you have to guess what state of repair her muff is in. I'm twenty for twenty so far. This could be my super power."

"Super power?"

"Yeah," he looked up at Henry. "I'm like a snatch savant. That's gotta be good for something in today's day and age, right?"

Henry thought about it. "Probably," he answered without too much irony.

"Snack," Alberto asked him, ignoring the twat talk.

"Is that a question?" Henry asked him.

Before he could answer, though, Truman again butted in.

"With him it might be a threat. Watch yourself."

Henry grabbed his wallet and walked to the elevator. Around them, deep in fluorescent trances, reporters, editors, and designers walked with purpose, their heads bent low to read whatever urgent missive or draft they held in their hands. It was a strange posture, but, thinking about it, Henry thought that perhaps it was more evolved than he gave it credit for; with their heads down they were maximizing their time so they could read while in transit. Maybe it was the most bent people who were the most enlightened, necks curled like commas, their elliptical forms welcoming subtext and innuendo into the warmth of their open parentheses.

Alberto called over to him from the other side of the room, "Let's take the stairs," he said, patting his stomach. "But just on the way down."

The sound of their steps dented the silence of the stair-well. Henry followed Alberto, surprised by the larger man's agility and quickness. He wasn't sure if that said good things about Alberto or terrible things about himself. The stairwell was an airless no-man's land of shallow light and extravagant graffiti, all of it text-based and lengthy. The theme of these manifestos either centered on how fucked the corporation was that owned the newspaper, sex with co-workers, or the wish to kill co-workers. Often times the three themes could be found in one piece of writing, such as a large paragraph on the third floor landing that Henry couldn't tear himself away from that dealt with the violent dog fucking and then murder by paper shredder of an editorial assistant he remembered from a few years back.

"I should really take the stairs more often," Henry said, his face bent close to the wall, following the angry narrative like an archeologist reading a mummy's curse in a newly unearthed pyramid. "This stuff is intense. Also, I think this might be Ken's writing. In fact I'm sure of it. And look," he said, pointing out one part of it for Alberto to look at, "someone took the time to copy edit this." Whoever had written it had crossed out the phrase 'pelvic annihilation' and written in 'hate fuck' instead, but the editor had written the word 'stet' over the original, an editing comment meaning to leave in what was originally written.

Alberto shook his head. "The stairwell is a really fucked-up place," he said matter-of-factly, as though he had thought about the subject before, maybe even rated the most fucked-up places in the world in his spare time and kept the list in his wallet, waiting for a conversation starter like this for years.

They kept on toward the lobby, past more angry literature written mostly on the wall where the paint had peeled away in huge irregular shapes, the original calming sky-blue color giving way to the direness of concrete, a hue that was an incitement to violence if ever there was one. The concrete-colored shapes on the wall looked a bit like countries to him, nations on a new atlas, a new world order created by the arrogance of time and the unintended consequences of benign neglect. Against that map, his voluminous black shirt floating along, puffed out like a sail full of wind, Alberto was a ship exploring the promise of new land.

"Sorry about your writer's block," he called back to Henry, sincere as ever. "I'm sure that must be difficult."

"It's not really writer's block," Henry answered, and after weighing whether or not to tell him about his lunch with Daisy, went ahead and told him the whole story of how she had instantly taken over the interview and put him on the defensive and how she had put it into his head that they were being surveilled by the Children of Light goon squad. Alberto didn't have much of a response, even when Henry told him about being chased by invisible cultist secret police.

"That's exciting," he said, opening the door to the lobby and ducking into the snack shop. He grabbed a lemon Hostess pie, the kind that has an expiration date that says 'End Times,' and a Diet Coke. "I knew you'd find your own war. That's what I told Truman. I said to him, 'Don't worry about Henry. He's gonna find his own war. You'll see.'"

"That's awful sweet," Henry said eyeing a package of Pepto-Bismol tablets on the shelf that he considered buying for the indigestion he was getting by looking at Alberto's purchase, "but I'm not really looking for a big thing to get involved in. I need to find this chick because I need to finish my story. Without her I don't have the ex-member's perspective. I don't want any cultists after me. I don't need that in my life."

Alberto interrupted. "We never need cultists after us. Sometimes..." he shrugged his shoulders and laughed.

Henry shook his head.

"What I need is to finish this story, do a good job, and move on. Move up. I don't need a war."

Getting off the elevator on the sixth floor, he noticed the conference room beginning to fill up and suddenly remembered the weekly editorial meeting. He would be expected to bring a draft of his story on Potter and discuss his progress with the staff. It was the first time he'd ever actually had a story to talk about at one of these meetings and with dread he knew he was sunk.

Back at his computer, and with mounting anxiety, he looked frantically around his desk and grabbed the first few sheets of printed paper he could find.

"Shit, shit, shit." He chanted the words like a true zealot, the holiest prayer of the church of the most terminally fucked.

Truman stuck his head over the partition. The grin on his face was toothy and genuinely evil, sparkling like change falling out a child's pocket on a sunny day.

"I can name that tune in six notes," he said.

"Not now," Henry said, barely interrupting the flow of his chant. "Shit, shit, shit…"

"Is it 'the Gregorian Monks Go to a Donkey Show?' Concept album, right?"

From within the glass wall of the conference room Henry could see Ken motioning at his watch to Henry that it was time for the meeting to start.

Henry quickly ducked his head down and went on to a new desperate refrain.

"No no no…"

"Is this one of those cries for help?" Truman taunted him.

"I'm supposed to be presenting what I've done on the Potter obituary and I've got nothing," he hissed, bringing his face right up next to Truman's. "I'm totally fucked."

At that moment he heard Ken's voice call his name from across the room.

"Let's go, Henry. We're all waiting on you. And bring what you have on Potter."

That was it. The lethal injection. The tension in his shoulders and jaw released and his whole body went limp and numb as if every muscle had been simultaneously washed away in a great flood of chemicals that was the opposite of adrenaline. He half walked, half floated to the room where his colleagues, fresh-faced and eager all, were seated around the large, glass, rectangular table. There was something about glass and newspaper offices. Maybe it was the symbolism of transparency, he thought, as he laid down the stack of papers (which, now that he looked at them, realized were MapQuest directions he had printed out to a pot dispensary) he was hoping would get him through the next sixty or so minutes. All faces turned to look at him as he slunk into his seat, a single drop of sweat trickling sickeningly down his spine that made him feel like he was a Ziploc baggie being opened. A blast of cold from the overactive air conditioner hit his back, cauterizing the spot, sending a chill up the length of his body. He shivered profoundly and let out an audible exhale of air, attracting the attention of the entire table.

"Jesus, Henry," Jeff smiled, "did you just have a stroke?"

As soon as he said it, he looked immediately at Jocelyn, Ken's assistant, to see if the joke had made her laugh. When he saw that it had, he twirled his pen around excitedly in his hand.

"Are you okay, Henry?" Ken asked him sincerely.

"Yeah," he answered, shakily pouring a glass of water for himself from a glass pitcher that was also sweating crystalline lines of illuminated perspiration.

"Okay," Ken said, taking one last look at Henry before launching into the meeting. "What've we got? Jeff, do you want to start? How's the heroin piece coming?"

Without hesitation, Jeff launched into an update on his story about heroin. He described the dealers and the addicts he had met with, the time he had spent on Skid Row getting to know the "life," as he obnoxiously called it. In the middle of relaying one anecdote where he had been suddenly surrounded by gang members, some of whom had flashed their guns at him, Henry forced his mind to wander to keep from getting angry and snapped to a little while later, just in time for his turn to give his update. He sat up and shuffled the papers around in front of him, pretending to study them for a little last-minute preparation. The old-style clock on the wall ticked loudly, a heartbeat. If he were back in high school, it might save him by ringing, deliver him a reprieve out of nowhere with ground zero subtlety. But this wasn't school and there was no bell.

"Okay," Ken began, "last but not least, Mr. Colmes." He looked down the long table at Henry. "What have you got for us, Henry?"

"Well," Henry started, looking around at the faces of his colleagues, some of whom looked tired, some bored, some just wanting to get the fuck back to what it was they were doing before the meeting started. He noticed, not surprising, that Jeff was smiling at him in an expectant kind of way, like in the old comedy movies when the banana peel had been dropped and the guy carrying the ladder just came on screen. "Potter is an interesting fellow."

"We know," Ken said. "That's why we're writing his obituary in advance. Come on, Henry," it was the end of the meeting and he was clearly getting impatient. He extended his arm across the table, his hand out, "What have you got so far?

Let's see what you've written."

Time slowed down to a sickeningly slow crawl as he stretched his arm out to hand the MapQuest directions down to Ken. He felt himself grow light-headed and queasy as the edges of his vision blurred becoming inky swirls of gray smoke. He was going to pass out. Shit himself. Something was going to happen. Every one of his nerves was screaming its safe word when he heard Ken suddenly shout, "Holy shit, what the fuck is going on?"

Everyone's heads turned to look out at the main room where a wash of black smoke was rising from the far wall.

"Is your desk on fire, Henry?"

Ken and Henry rushed out of the room with the rest of the writers close on their heels. At the other side of the room it was apparent that the fire was indeed coming from Henry's desk, or rather his garbage can, in withering waves of black heat. Truman stood next to the fire with his arms crossed, his bottom lip between his teeth.

"What the fuck happened?" Ken asked.

"The trash can caught fire," Truman responded.

"Did you do this?"

"Yeah," he said sheepishly and not without a hint of pride, "but I never meant for it to get this big."

The reporters stood around transfixed, as though they were all new to being part of something dramatic instead of just observing, like they were just born and their reaction reflexes hadn't fully kicked in yet. To be fair, though, it was mesmerizing: black plumes of smoke billowed upwards in mushroom like waves hitting the ceiling and then disseminating in great black storms, scattering like frightened apparitions.

Carl, the office security guard, rushed by with a fire extinguisher. "Dumb motherfucker," he muttered as he walked by Henry so only he could hear it.

Rather than try to defend himself, Henry looked at Truman and was about to choke out an explanation when Jeff let out a laugh. The crowd assembled, and by extension, the room, turned and looked at him as he stared at Henry's computer monitor.

"Life is a broken time machine," he read off the screen. He laughed again. "Is this what you've got so far, Henry? Is this the story? Or wait, maybe it's a suicide note. If it was a suicide note you should have brought it into the meeting. We might have been able to help you wordsmith it a little."

Truman let out a sudden and loud laugh. He was the only one.

About half an hour later, Truman and Henry had left Ken's office; Henry had been officially reprimanded for the lack of progress in his work and Truman fired for his arson. More than being horrified by what Truman had done, Ken was frankly more surprised that Truman still had a job with the paper.

"I thought I fired you six months ago," Ken had said to him during the meeting.

"You may have," Truman responded, neither upset nor worried.

It was dark by the time they left. Henry helped Truman carry out his personal belongings in a couple of battered old cardboard boxes. Large halogen lights illuminated the evening in a foggy brightness and above them dark clouds of insects congregated at the altar of its luminescence feeding off the blurry light.

"I suppose, in a weird way, I should thank you," Henry said to Truman, staring at the bugs, amazed that he and Truman weren't being bitten to death, that the nourishment of light took precedence over the lure of their blood. "I know you were just trying to cover for me."

"No problem," Truman shrugged. "I don't have a single regret." He shoved a cardboard box full of his workplace things into the back of his cheap car. "Well, I do have one regret."

"What?" Henry asked.

"That I didn't cheat on every girlfriend I ever had. I mean, because in the long run, we wound up breaking up anyway."

Henry smiled at him. Any trace of anger at having been outed to Ken was gone.

"Oh," Truman said in mock surprise, "you thought I might have a regret about that." He pointed at the building. "Fuck no. I'd light a desk on fire for you anytime, buddy," he patted Henry on the shoulder in false modesty, like a fireman who had just saved a family of immigrants from a three-alarm fire and was pretending like it was all in a day's work. "Any time." He started to get into his car and then turned back to Henry. "You know what's funny?"

"What?" Henry asked.

"I used to have all these fantasies about what I'd do when I was leaving a job. How I would tell the boss to fuck off, take a shit on his desk, email a picture of me jizzing in his coffee cup. In the grand scheme of things, lighting your desk on fire was pretty mild, don't you think?"

Henry nodded. "Wish fulfillment. You did yourself proud. It was the definition of win-win."

"Oh, by the way," Truman said, struggling to pull something from his back pocket. "I grabbed that picture of your sister for you. I figured you'd want that."

"Thanks," Henry said, feeling oddly touched for an arson victim.

Truman smiled and rolled up his window, giving Henry a thumbs-up as he did his best to peel out of the parking lot. Henry watched him go and then turned to go back to the building. He saw that the cloud of bugs had thickened considerably and that now the building looked like it was being consumed by the creatures, dissolving within the steady thrum of their unquenchable appetite.

The night shift was coming on: editors and writers who stayed through the evening to make sure the paper was ready to go to the presses, that there were no final edits or corrections that needed to be made. Henry had never seen them before, usually leaving well before the time that their thankless shift began. They were the monsters in the night. The elves that fixed the shoes for the kind cobbler.

Upstairs he cleaned away the ash from his cubicle, wiping away piles of soot and dust that had only recently been his papers, a few pictures, a clipped-out newspaper article about the Clash coming to town from the early eighties. The night shift shot him graveyard looks as they came in, already bleary-eyed, permanently exhausted, unshaven and unkempt. Enthusiasm among this bunch was an outlawed deity. A couple of them lit up cigarettes as they took their seats, and he could imagine the justice of a workplace beer at this hour. Other than a few stares, though, no one acknowledged either him or the fact that there had clearly been a fire in the room.

Christ, his head was suddenly clear. The anxiety of the past few days had quietly melted away; there was no worry about finishing his article, or finding Daisy, or the cultists that might or might not be after him. Now, there was only this room, these piles of ash, these blank non-judgmental stares. He felt strong and clear-headed, like all of the tiny problems that had been plaguing him had all been expunged by the fire, and if not entirely incinerated, then illuminated, picked apart, and considered one by one as manageable parts instead of an inseparable and unmanageable whole. He wished there was someone to tell, but his co-workers didn't look like the type to be impressed by catharsis. If only moments could be muses. If only words could speak themselves true. That's what he'd say, if he thought anyone would listen. Really listen.

Ken had already gone home, so Henry left as well, resolving to get a good night's sleep and start fresh in the morning, proceed with or without Daisy, ignore the paranoid shadows that would otherwise keep him from finishing his assignment.

He got in his car and drove home, the night sky a blue tarp stained with the light of a full moon left out to dry on an unusually clear night. He parked his car behind his apartment complex and got out, inhaling deeply the smell of jasmine that made his neighborhood smell like a candy store on these warm summer nights. On his way around the side of the building he plucked a kumquat off the neighbor's tree, popping the small round fruit into his mouth, savoring the sting of flavor as it flooded his mouth with saliva and sent a shiver up his spine. For once, none of these nuances were lost on him. It was as if all of his nerves were exposed and taking the night's temperature.

In the very next moment two sounds occurred to him at the exact same time: first, there was the unmistakable sound of car tires peeling out on pavement, a terrible noise, like a mad scientist had gotten hold of a scream, took its pieces apart, and reassembled it into a Frankenstein monster sound, truly horrifying not for what it was, but for what it would result in, the inevitable collision, the horrifying assessment of the damage done. Instinctively, Henry got up and began running to the back door, aware that something terrible was about to happen, but unsure of exactly what it was. As his hand touched the doorknob, he felt the second noise, which was a blast of heat at his back, as the force of a homemade bomb of some sort crashed through his front window, detonating, and then unceremoniously igniting the front room of his house. His hand fell limply from the doorknob as the force of the explosion pushed him forward, headfirst, into the door. The last thing he remembered thinking before blacking out was that he was finally under attack.

Chapter 6

THERE TURNED OUT to be a lot more to being friends with Cal than Henry had first expected, the least of which was his laborious and time-consuming indoctrination into the world of punk rock. More than punk rock, though, it was the entire process of befriending Cal that was time intensive and utterly immersive, like a new recruit getting used to the hardships of basic training. But instead of just a crash course in a new culture, something to just tide someone over during a brief period of adjustment, his transition into this new way of being was utterly overwhelming and durable, with pieces of his own self chipping off as he made his fat way through the narrow doorway into Cal's world. Although, when he thought about it, there really hadn't been that much he was so passionate about that it was hard to say goodbye to as Cal plied him with mixtapes, magazines, and patches bearing the names of bands that he sewed onto his military coat, new epaulettes and awards of distinction that bore a close resemblance to the military insignia he collected over the years. What else did he have really but his war stuff, and that seemed to fit right in with the rest of it.

The music came at him in waves, a new batch of records and mixtapes handed off on almost a daily basis during third-period history. The Ramones, the Clash, and the Sex Pistols to start. The building blocks of punk, Cal called them, feeding them to Henry as if he were the newbie's musical nutritionist, breaking down his old diet of new wave garbage and Top 40 crap as if they were poison that went in through the ears. It was a little hard to relate to, this British stuff. Not the music, that part was great. "Fuck this and fuck that" could cut across almost any cultural barrier, and for a teenager, it was instant gratification at its most primal. The thing that was hard to relate to were the icons themselves, Johnny Rotten and Sid Vicious, cartoon characters: Rotten in his bright-red bondage pants and spiky orange hair and Vicious with his black leather jacket holding his bass that hung as low as his lip curled up. They weren't scary, these guys, they were ridiculous. Henry remembered seeing KISS on the Jerry Lewis telethon when he was a little kid and being completely afraid of them, running out of the room until Grace could reassure him that they were done and he could safely watch some kid with MD get lowered into a swimming pool filled with Jell-O, which had been the boy's greatest dream. It seemed like a great dream to Henry as well, and that very well may have been his height of envy, watching a little kid with no muscle tone float around in a sea of green eternity.

The Clash's political realism was a little better (less of the rage for rage's sake) and he found himself drawing their red star logo all over his notebook and book covers, the writing of it a hypnotic exercise, almost a tic after a time, as desks and chairs in his classrooms broke out in the angry red mark. Still, the Clash were all about history lessons and human rights, stuff that was interesting but not immediately relatable. It wasn't until his introduction to the more local stuff, hardcore bands from Southern California, that he really latched on and understood the power of this music. The Circle Jerks, Social Distortion, Adolescents, Descendents…the list went on. There seemed to be no shortage of angst from his quarter of the world, but it was anger that he could at least relate to. Feelings of alienation from family and peers, frustration at not being able to get your hands on a six-pack; these bands made all of that seem important and even though it wasn't as important as human rights in Central America or the US's secret wars, it was still legitimate, if not completely justified. It was the anger of boredom and frustration, the boredom of want and of believing that life, right now, didn't count, that it was a warm up for the real thing, which came later. It was easy to understand that anger, hating your parents and not being able to get laid. It was small-time in the grand scheme of things, a bystander's frustration, but it was all they had and it was all theirs.

Henry now went everywhere with a Walkman when he wasn't hanging out with Cal, and it gave him a whole new perspective on school. He strode quickly down a long hall, the Misfits blaring in his ears: "I ain't no goddamned son of a bitch...You better listen to me baby." It put a spring in his step and the vector of his personality wasn't quite so wide now. Instead of dodging everyone that was coming toward him in the opposite direction, he let his shoulder bump against theirs, pushing them both off to the side a little bit. Even though he didn't exactly feel like one of these people, his classmates, running along, slapping one another on the shoulder, laughing uproariously like the secret of life was their inside joke, he had a sense of what they might be feeling. Lightness. Contentedness. The music, instead of adding to the chaos, making it seem impenetrable, actually seemed to make some sense of it, orchestrate it in a way, so that what he saw and what he heard flowed together.

One day after school in late fall Henry and Cal walked to Henry's house to hang out. It was the first time Cal would be coming to Henry's, and it felt to Henry like a big step in their friendship. Being friends with someone at school was easy, kind of a convenience, but taking that next step to hang out after school, and especially to show someone where you lived, that was stepping it up to the next level. It meant that the friendship was more than just a friendship by default, that it was something intentional and genuine, and it made Henry feel good to know that Cal not only would come over and spend his time with Henry outside of the confines of periods one through six, but that Cal himself had suggested it.

The walk home took them through a series of placid streets where tired homes watched them from the ends of vibrant lawns that had been given an almost neon green finish by the almost constant use of sprinklers in the neighborhood. This was an old neighborhood that was slowly becoming infiltrated by more and more affluent families who were looking and willing to pay for the privilege of living in a quaint suburb, the closest a high-functioning human could get to existing in a state of suspended animation and still be said to be alive. There was a sense that this charming decrepitude was only temporary, precarious, and that sooner rather than later, things would change. Wrecking crews. Fleets of Mercedes. A bumper crop of McMansions sprouting from the ground. The houses had a helpless look, a someone's grandma being left at an old-age home look, an aura of hopelessness and a full realization of their eminent and certain replicability. It was a sad last moment of consciousness, Henry thought, knowing that as soon as you're gone another, better one can so easily take your place, commiserating for a second with the houses, thinking of the small children of new families that were already starting to populate his street, the better models of a tired brand. His father complained about it every time a house in the neighborhood went up for sale, telling them almost threateningly that he didn't know how much longer they could afford to stay in their own house. It wasn't a case of their mortgage or their property taxes being unaffordable, it was the sheer value of their home, what he thought he could get for it if he put it up on the market. The calculations made him batshit crazy. Whenever she heard him talking like this, Henry's mom would roll her eyes, and catching her, his dad would say, "You think I'm not serious? You don't think I'd do it, do you?" It never went much further than this, but it left Henry wondering what it was his dad wanted that he didn't already have.

Cal picked a wet leaf off a parked car and flung it at Henry.

"Used tampon!" he yelled as it hit Henry square in the face.

"Ew!" Henry screamed, a little more like a girl than he intended. "That's fucking disgusting." He gave Cal a playful shove as he fell away laughing.

"Dude," Cal said, twirling the end of his backpack's loose strap in his fingers, "do you know that chick, Allison Martell?"

Of course he knew her. Every boy in class knew her, knew every shapely second of her, from her blond hair that hung in a springy ponytail you wanted to tie around your neck like a noose you loved her so much, to her perfect chest that had appeared overnight as full-fledged breasts without ever having gone through the pitiful excuse of puberty and, down past that, all the way down to the tips of her ruby-red painted toenails that would give any sane man an instant and lifelong foot fetish.

Henry scrunched up his face and pretended to think about it for a second. "Oh yeah. I think I know who that is."

"'Oh yeah. I think I know who that is.'," Cal mocked. "You know exactly who the fuck that is. Everyone knows."

"Fine," Henry shrugged, embarrassed. "What about her?"

"Wait a minute," Cal stopped walking and held out a hand in front of Henry to stop him as well. "Do you think she's hot?"

He didn't want to say it, afraid of somehow disappointing his sister by acting like a "typical male," a phrase she liked to throw around when describing the boys at school.

Cal raised his eyebrows as if to say "well." He wasn't going to drop the thing about Allison Martell.

"Sure, she's hot," Henry finally admitted, just wanting the interrogation to stop. He resumed walking.

"Jesus, Henry. Don't get so mad about it. Do you like her, or something?"

He turned around quickly and got in Cal's face.

"No, I don't like her. I just don't want to talk about it." He paused and hooked his thumbs under the straps of his backpack. "You don't know what's it like having a sister…" He regretted having said it and cut himself off. He didn't want it to come off like he blamed Grace for not wanting to talk about girls, or admit to Cal, or anyone else for that matter, that he thought about them in a sexual way, but it was hard, because he felt that he owed her so much and the least he could do was somehow proselytize civility.

"Bullshit," Cal said. "That's the stupidest thing I ever heard in my life. You're just a pussy."

Henry shook his head. "I hate that word."

"What word? Pussy?"

"Uh-huh."

"Why do you hate the word pussy so much?"

"I know what you're doing," Henry said, trying to show Cal that he was ignoring him.

"What am I doing?"

"You're saying that word over and over because now you know I don't like it. But you're saying it in an innocent way so that it'll seem like you're not really saying it."

"That's not true," Cal said, barely able to conceal his grin. "I won't say pussy if you really don't like the word pussy. I just want to be clear about it."

"Cal…"

"Is it because of your sister's pussy?"

Henry turned around quickly and put his nose against Cal's.

"Don't talk about my sister that way," he clenched his fists, felt his nails digging into the flesh of his palms.

"Then don't use her as a fucking excuse for something. If you don't like me or anyone else using that word around you, just tell them to fuck off. Don't pretend like you're doing it for your sister, though."

It wasn't clear to him why Cal felt the need to do this kind of prodding, why it felt like everyone in the world had a lesson to teach him.

"Just say what you mean," Cal said, picking up his backpack and walking ahead. "That's all I'm saying."

It wasn't that easy, saying what he meant. To him, hormones were just conversations he wished he could have, glad-handing with a closed fist, a gentle shove until the body broke. If he could say what he meant, he would. He just wasn't sure what that was.

Kids on dented and scratched bikes rode by them in a ragged line, a zig-zagging pecking order. Just by looking at them Henry could see why the kids at the front would be the most popular, pushing the pedals with ease, standing as they rode, impervious to road hazards or the proximity of their friends. The ones at the back rode hard to keep up. In a few years, the free-for-all that was after-school play would end. Those at the back wouldn't be invited to hang out with the ones at the front. Henry hoped they enjoyed it now, these kids at the back, because in not too much time, this laissez-faire egalitarianism would pass, and they would not only not be included, but forgotten about entirely.

They turned a corner and Henry pointed to the end of the street. "That's my house." He felt a bit like an explorer coming upon the end of the continent.

"Which one?" Cal asked, squinting.

"The one at the end of the cul-de-sac."

"You say that like you're proud. Cul-de-sac is just the white man's way of saying dead end."

"Aren't we white?" Henry asked, as curious as he was sick of the dogma.

"Not that kind of white."

At the front door, Henry looked over his shoulder as he stooped to fetch the hidden key. Cal laughed.

"Let me guess. Is it in the planter?"

Henry laughed, too. Maybe it was better not to have secrets, he thought, because there was nothing new anyway.

He opened the door and walked into the front hallway. The house was quiet and dark. No one had remembered to open the curtains that morning. Flecks of dust swam in the narrow wedges of sharp sunlight that slashed their way through tiny gaps in the curtains. Both boys fell silent as they laid down their backpacks.

"Take your shoes off," Henry said to Cal, kicking off his own without first untying the laces. He walked over to the curtains, and grabbing high on the cord, jerked down hard, causing the curtains to open with a wild flourish as sunlight poured in over them like water from a hose. Cal jumped a little, startled, and Henry smiled to himself.

Henry hit the "play" button on the answering machine as Cal walked past him into the kitchen, taking the liberty to open the fridge and peer inside. Reaching in he pulled out a beer, and without asking, pulled the tab on one of Henry's dad's cans of Coors. Cal took a long sip and then used the back of his hand to wipe away foam from his lips.

"Help yourself," Henry said, slightly annoyed. He wondered if his dad counted the cans and would notice that one was missing.

"Want one?" Cal offered a can to him with all the magnanimity of the wholly dispossessed. Henry shook his head. Cal shrugged and put it back in the fridge. He took another sip from his can and examined the label as he swallowed.

"What's a banquet beer?" he asked with sage-like sincerity. The tone of his voice was one of genuine curiosity.

Henry ignored him and shut the door of the fridge. He wasn't sure which his father would be madder about, Cal taking his beer or leaving the refrigerator door open. Cal examined the door once it had shut. It was covered from top to bottom with photos, calendars, old artwork, and cut-out comics that proffered maxims of the most simplistic kind. They were hung there without irony. Irony had no place on the family fridge. Henry stood behind Cal as he noiselessly looked at everything; a picture of Grace on an eighth-grade ski trip sticking her tongue out at the camera from beneath a fuzzy woolen cap, Grace's last report card that was all A's except for one B+ in AP Calculus, a self-portrait Grace had drawn of herself in art class. Henry braced himself for a sarcastic comment, but Cal said nothing, only sipped his beer, scrutinizing it all with the sullenness of a professional critic.

The thing he had been most afraid of Cal pointing out was that everything on the fridge was about Grace. There may have been a picture or two of Henry thrown in, family photos, pictures of him and Grace together, but nothing on his own. Cal didn't need to say it. They both knew that it was what the other one was thinking about, that the fridge didn't lie.

Henry led him upstairs to his room. The stairs shook under their heavy footsteps, and Cal noticing it, stomped harder, causing the light over the staircase to sway, deep thuds echoing from the house's hollow bones. This place, his home, suddenly felt small to Henry, too shallow, unreal like a doll's house, like it could be packed up and moved at a moment's notice. These thuds proved it, their tall and still growing bodies proved it, heads barely missing hitting the top of the doorframe as they walked in his room. It had never seemed that way before, but now he felt crowded in it. There was something about having Cal around that made him feel uncomfortable in his own skin, skin he never even knew he wore before Cal made it seem obsolete.

He hadn't thought to be ashamed of his room until he led the way in for Cal. The things that made him happy as a kid all seemed like rubbish now. Star Wars toys, posters of the rock group Rush, a few stuffed animals collecting dust in the corner, remnants from outings that had subconscious sentimental meanings that prevented him from throwing them away.

"Wow," Cal said, walking around the room, picking things up, aiming a toy blaster at him and pulling the trigger. "This is…"

"I know," Henry said, facing away from Cal. He did know. From the second he walked in the room he knew.

"Can I ask you a question?"

"What?" Henry shot back, suspiciously.

"Were you planning on going through puberty sometime this decade, or are you saving it for a rainy day or something?"

"Shut up. I've had this stuff in here for a long time." He was making an excuse and corrected himself. "Oh, is that what puberty is? When I figure out how stupid I used to be? When I get to be as smart as you?"

"It's more realizing it than figuring it out," Cal responded. "I know they're just toys, Henry, but come on. We're sixteen years old. What's wrong with you? Is it just that you don't care?"

Henry sat on his bed and stared out the window into the backyard.

"It's not that important to me. I guess I don't have as much of an idea about who I am as most people. Maybe that's what it is."

Cal put down the toy gun and walked over to the bookshelf. The shelf was lined with various books about weaponry and military history and in front of the books was a display of models Henry had painstakingly put together over the years; tanks, planes, and a few boats.

"These are cool," Cal said, picking up a model of a P-41 Mustang.

Henry grabbed the model out of Cal's hands before he could do anything to it. "Not the war stuff," he told him, breathing rapidly. "Don't touch the war stuff."

Cal shrugged. "You are the way you are because of the people around you, Henry. It's not your fault that you're one way or the other. Parents, the kids at school, shit you read and the..." here he grabbed an edge of the Star Wars poster and ripped it off the wall in one gigantic tear, "...stupid movies you watch. I bet your parents are like mine. Not that bad and not that good." His voice was taking on a certain preacher's urgency and Henry turned his head, ashamed of watching him, as he heard his breath grow thin and stretched, his face flushed. "But let me tell you something, the only thing that makes them decent people are their anxieties. Think about it. If they weren't sick with worry all the time about money, and how you and your sister are doing in school, and whether or not you guys are on drugs, if they didn't have all that to freak out about, not to mention a million other things that they never let on to you about, do you think they'd still be decent to you? Do you think they'd even pretend to care? And they're feeding all of that into you, same as the kids at school, same as the teachers, same as every damn fucking person. They all seem decent and like they're trying to do the right thing, but they're not. They're using you because you're a nice person and you don't argue with them. You never say no. You never say fuck you."

There was a silence as Cal seethed. Some of what he said made sense to Henry, the stuff about his parents being overwrought with neurosis could be true. He hadn't ever thought of them like that before, going around and acting the way they did like it was knocking on wood, like the family dynamic was nothing but an overwrought OCD ritual. The kids at school he wasn't so sure about. Or about the teachers. It was too easy to just get by and not be noticed day after day and year after year. And definitely not when it came to Grace. She might be kind of melancholy these days, but he knew that it had nothing to do with him. In the long run, he would always be able to count on her.

"I'm not that nice," he replied, somewhat meekly. "My dad always says that I'm too sensitive. That's not the same as nice. It's something else."

Cal sat down at Henry's desk and began dreamily chomping

on his fingernails as his eyes dissolved into a paradise of concentration. He was there, but not there, his mind busy evolving some sort of strategy, processing, assessing, the devil and his details.

"That's a terrible thing to say to someone," he said lightly, the words tiptoeing out of his mouth as if afraid to wake up a sleeping giant. His eyes were still somewhere far away, and Henry thought that perhaps he had misjudged him, that it wasn't a plan that Cal was formulating, but rather reconciling a fantasy about sympathy and empathy, a misery of collusion and desperation. Henry wanted to ask him what he was really thinking, what had just happened to him, but he thought better of it. Instead, he walked to his closet, and reaching up high to the top shelf, past Clue and Monopoly, past a baseball glove and a Tupperware bowl filled with change that marked a brief foray into numismatics (a hobby, even in his greatest periods of boredom, he could not comprehend), he grabbed a cardboard banker's box and carried it over to the bed. Inside the box were dozens of plastic bags, each bulging with a squadron of toy soldiers, separated by period of history. One by one, Henry ripped apart the bags and began to dump the soldiers into a giant pile in the center of his bed, the squadrons becoming an army, a jumbled pile of mismatched warfare. Finally, Cal came to and turned his attention to the bed.

"What are you doing?" he asked.

"Putting this stuff back up," Henry replied, not pausing in his task. "I love this stuff, and I don't know why I don't have it up on my shelves. I don't care about this other crap. I used to think that the war stuff freaked my family out, but now I don't care."

Cal sprang out of the chair and began rummaging around through the pile of mixtapes he had made for Henry in the past few months. He found one and put it on the tape player. The first jangly chords of the Adolescents' "I Hate Children" grew in the air and they both began jumping around within the confines of its perfect time, and whether or not the music gave them a reason to be angry or was accompaniment to a catharsis, it was an energy Henry had never felt before, a happiness he couldn't name. Cal jumped up on Henry's bed and after a few riffs of air guitar, grabbed one of the edges of the Rush poster and tore it down. He went to the next one and ripped that down, too, while Henry pushed onto the floor all of the action figures, the cheap plastic trophies he got as a kid for playing youth basketball, Boy Scout patches, and everything else that was taking up space in his room because he didn't have anything legitimate to be proud of.

Soon, his walls were bare. Cal was breathing heavily, still stomping the floor to death in time to the ear-splitting music, as if suburbia were a bug he could smash. Henry started to put the toy soldiers up on his shelves, singing along, surprising himself by knowing more of the words than he thought he did. When "Land of Competition" by Bad Religion came on he shouted to Cal to turn it up. Cal didn't answer, though, and the volume didn't change, so when he turned around to see what Cal was doing he was slightly surprised to find that he was no longer in the room. He turned down the music and called out. "Cal!" No answer. His face flushed with anxiety as he took off down the hall toward his sister's room, a bad feeling rising steadily in him.

He ducked his head into his sister's room. Not there, thank god. He walked further down the hall to his parents' room and stepped inside. Cal wasn't in there, either. But just as he was about to leave, he noticed a light coming from his parents' closet. He walked silently over as if he would scare off the light by startling it, and poked his head inside. Cal was there, in the dimly lit and narrow space, sitting on the floor, touching his father's baseball cards. The 1952's to be exact. Panic leapt out of Henry.

"Don't do that!" He ran toward Cal, who was on the verge of taking one of the cards out of its plastic holders, and snatched it from his hands. "You can't be in here, you fucking idiot. You can't touch this stuff. If my dad finds out about this he'd fucking kill me."

"Okay, okay," Cal held his hands up. "Relax. I was just looking at them. I'm not a fucking idiot."

Henry looked at the cards at the top of the stack to make sure none were missing or damaged, and when he was satisfied, he put everything back into the large box where his dad kept them as neatly as he imagined they were stacked when Cal found them, and slid it back into its place at the back of the closet.

"All right, I'm sorry," he said to Cal. "I didn't mean to call you that. It just freaked me out. My dad loves those things more than life itself."

"Come on, Henry," Cal said with a smile, "stop being so sensitive."

Henry allowed himself a smile, begrudgingly, like an alcoholic giving in and allowing himself one small glass of wine at a party. "Fuck off, dick. What are you doing in here, anyway?"

He hadn't been in his father's closet for a very long time. It had always been a door in the house to avoid, both because of the baseball cards he knew his dad kept in there, as well as the pure ambience of the place: narrow, dark, and musty smelling. No natural light. No ventilation. It was a tomb. A dusty gross cavern. It didn't need a maid, it needed a spelunker.

All around them was the fossil record of his father's life, the most recent and relevant shirts, ties, and shoes stationed at the front by the door where you first walked in, going on back through the past. He let his fingers touch the shirts and coats as he walked the length of the space, traversing different eras, butterfly collars when the dinosaurs died and more recently French cuffs and the dawn of man. Many of the shirts sparked nebulous memories, vague sensations like the kind psychics get when they touch the belongings of the dead. About halfway back on the floor was an enormous jar of pennies filled to the top with good luck. He wondered when his father had stopped picking them up, when he had decided, consciously or not, that he didn't need the cosmic leg up anymore. A few years back he had seen the movie *Altered States* on the Z Channel and had been fascinated with the isolation tanks William Hurt's character had spent time devolving in, or whatever the fuck that was that turned him into a raving monkey man. The closet reminded him of one of those isolation tanks, and he could almost imagine his father coming in here and lying down in the dimness, staring up at the cottage cheese ceiling that had the hallucinogenic properties of ten hits of acid, losing himself entirely in this space that had the ideal acoustics for a nervous breakdown.

"Why did you come in here, anyway?" Henry asked Cal again.

Cal stood up and started to leaf through his father's old sports coats.

"I thought we could find something cool for you to wear," Cal said as he continued to examine the clothes, "something like this."

He pulled out an old white sports coat of his father's from somewhere in the middle of the closet.

"Do you think your dad would miss this?"

Hal looked at the spot Cal had plucked the coat from and judged it to be roughly a 1978 vintage, which had been a very good year for bowling leagues, menthols, and white evening wear. He shook his head.

"No. I don't think he's worn that since the last time he brought cocaine to take to a party at John Travolta's house." The jacket was terrifically ugly. "What are you going to do with it?"

Cal took the jacket into Henry's room and laid it out flat on the floor. Without any hesitation, he grabbed a pair of scissors and cut the sleeves off the hideous thing. He took a black Sharpie and started to scribble all over the lapels and collar and then flipped it over and drew the anarchy symbol so that it covered the entire back.

The whole operation took less than two minutes, but when Cal stood up to admire his work, he was as proud as if he had created an entire spring collection for the young and dispossessed.

"That's awesome," he whispered. And then turning to Henry. "Try it on."

"Me?"

"Yeah," Cal said, picking the jacket off the floor. "This is for you."

Henry let Cal help him into the jacket and then stood back to look at himself in the mirror. "It's cool. Thanks, dude." Even though the jacket was his father's and not really Cal's to give away, it was one of the nicest presents he'd ever received.

"Looks good on you, man. Slowly but surely, we're getting you there. Slowly but surely."

They walked back to Henry's room where the floor was covered with the sloughed-off snakeskin of his youth.

"Help me throw this shit away," Henry said, kneeling down as he began to gather the bits of ripped-up poster and Boy

Scout commendations in his arms.

"No, wait," Cal put his hand on Henry's shoulder. "I have a better idea."

"What?"

"We should burn it," he jumped up, energized by his new idea. "No, we have to burn it! There's gotta be a ceremony."

"A ceremony?" Henry studied the refuse, trying to figure out what Cal was seeing that he wasn't. "Why?"

"Because," Cal said, crystal-eyed, "if you don't have a ceremony then it's not important. And this," he pointed at the floor, "this is important."

Henry had an inkling of what Cal was talking about, but he didn't ask for any further explanation. He understood what it was to be indiscriminately passionate, to have Shari'ah-like sincerity about something that barely mattered to anyone else.

They gathered up the detritus, two heaping armfuls of good intentions.

"Where should we burn this?" Cal asked, the eager pyromaniac. "The backyard?"

"No. I've got a better idea. There's a dried-up reservoir up the street a little bit. Let's do it there."

Cal nodded and the two of them left the house and walked to the end of the street, which dead-ended at a trailhead. Henry went first, and Cal followed as they walked along a dusty path a few hundred yards into the Santa Monica Mountains. It was a cloudless day, blue overflowed from the sky, spilling the late fall heat onto the top of their heads and down their backs. The almost-full moon was visible in the perfect daylight, a pale specter in lurking repose. Birds sang, celebrating the stillness, and the boys walked silently out of a subconscious respect for it. The reservoir appeared after a few minutes, a huge concrete bowl carved into the hill making the mountain seem as though it had a bald spot. As long as Henry could remember these hills had always been dry except after the heaviest of rains when the side of the hills would run sloppy with mud, too much water to be of any use to anyone or anything. And for good measure a huge brush fire tore through the scrub every fifteen years or so, flooding the sky with choking smoke, blacking out the sun like a plague of locusts, raining ash on cars and houses, the tops of their heads as they all evacuated to the high school gym. These fires and mudslides were the Southern California equivalent of a snow day, all thanks to the mountains, which, when they weren't the centerpiece in a play about the end of the world, were in a perpetual coma of potential catastrophe. The brush around them was dry and spiky and Henry cut his leg on a branch as they climbed down the gradual slope to the bottom of the reservoir.

"Shit!" he yelled, his voice echoing outwards in all directions like radiation. A panicked knot of birds flew up into the air, as much outraged as frightened by the sudden intrusion.

"Cool," Cal said, throwing his armful of posters and sci-fi paraphernalia onto the concrete ground. "Fuck!" he screamed, and the word bounced across the reservoir and up into the hills.

Henry laughed as he threw his load of things on top of what Cal had brought.

"I always thought it was the hills have eyes," Henry said, touching the fresh cut on his ankle, tracing the faint line of blood. "Not, the hills have a potty mouth."

Cal laughed and then in a loud voice sang out once more, "The hills are alive with the sound of SHIT and FUCK!" He held his arms straight out and twirled around just like Julie Andrews in the movie.

Henry hadn't been to the reservoir in a long time, not since he was a kid, when he and his sister would bring their bikes back here, wheeling them along the trail, careful not to pop the tires. They would ride around and around at the top part of the bowl, pretending to be racing in a velodrome or caught up in a swirling black hole. Now, garbage and graffiti covered the ground, all paraphernalia of youthful experimentation. The place had somewhere along the line become the Bell Labs of depravity. Ground zero for the invention of sin. Henry saw a couple of used condoms rotting in a dead pile of leaves. Countless numbers of crumpled cigarette packs were strewn around, Marlboro Reds and Winston's mostly, brands he knew the kids at school smoked. A fetid looking mattress lay ominously near the stuff they had just piled up. Metal springs broke through everywhere, signaling that it probably hadn't been used in some time, and that if it had, someone around here was inordinately kinky. Henry tried to fathom the degree of determination someone must have had to drag that down the path from the trailhead. Molotov hormones. It would have been no small feat. The girl must have been a knockout. A smashed bong lay in pieces nearby, shattering the myth of potheads as peaceful couch potatoes.

"Do you have a lighter?" Henry asked Cal, patting his pockets in vain. It was a stupid question. Kids like Cal always had lighters.

Cal pulled a cheap plastic Bic from his pants pocket and handed it over to Henry. "Do you want to do this?"

Henry grabbed it and knelt next to the pile and poked at it with a stick, trying to find the best spot to touch with the flame.

"Anywhere," Cal said, getting impatient. "Light it anywhere."

Tentatively, Henry lit the corner of the Rush poster and

jumped back quickly, worried that irrationally the thing might all of a sudden go up in a great big fireball. The poster caught fire easily and the flame spread eagerly over and through the rest of the stuff, proving that it was meant to be, that there was a reason behind the enthusiastic immolation. Black smoke, the stench of burning plastic, a heat that was artificial and fulfilling. They were both mesmerized by the spectacle of it, by the smoke signals pumping their youthful confessions into the sky, and they forced their eyes to stay open so they wouldn't miss a minute. Even as the smoke stung them, drew out their tears as though it were a divining rod. Even then they watched, helpless not to. Overcome by an absence of feeling, Henry searched himself for sentimentality, for regret, but found nothing, nothing but the perfect sense of location, of knowing one thing and knowing it well. Neither of them smiled, too lost in contemplation, too overcome with the knowledge that the quest for immortality was a cheerless endeavor. Henry sought to break the silence, to peer through the crackling of the flames. He wanted desperately to know if Cal felt the same as he did, that this was a beginning of sorts, an orientation by which to plot future movement. He was about to say something to that effect, to try and give it some words, but Cal spoke first and spoke suddenly.

"Do you ever think about killing yourself?" Cal looked straight ahead as though he were addressing the fire, the quickly growing pile of black ash.

"What?" Henry laughed. "No." He hesitated reciprocating, but given the lack of anything else to say, he asked, "Do you?"

A moment passed, a moment in which he saw Cal struggling to answer, as though the fire were holding him back, restraining him from telling the truth. "Yeah," Cal said lightly. "I do. All the time."

Henry swallowed. His Adam's apple suddenly too big for

his throat.

"Really? Are you being serious?" If this were a joke, he would be pissed. He was feeling too good to be taken out of the moment for a bunch of bullshit.

Cal's face didn't change expression. "Yeah. I'm being serious."

"Why?" Henry asked.

"I don't know. I just think about it. I think about not being around anymore. I think about how I'd like to do it. I like the idea of knowing where I'm going to die. I like imagining the place."

Henry's teeth began to chatter, and he folded his arms against his chest. He didn't want Cal to see that he was frightened. But Cal was not looking at him. He was still talking to the fire.

"What place?"

Cal bit his lower lip. It looked like he was fighting something or someone that he couldn't control, someone forcing the very living truth out of him.

"The staircase in my house. You haven't been there, but there's a staircase that leads right up to my room. I think about hanging myself in the stairwell in the middle of the night, and I think about my parents waking up for work and finding me. I think about the way my body would be swaying just a little bit, since I'd have been dead for hours. I think about the black and blue marks around my neck."

Henry thought about it, too. The gentle creaking of the rope straining under its heavy load. Cal's parents going from surprise, to thinking it must be a practical joke, and then rapidly to terror as they realized it wasn't some sort of Halloween decoration, but that it was actually their son hanging there, dead by his own hand. He could barely control the chattering of his own teeth now. His lower jaw wobbled like a rubber band. Turning from Cal, he looked up at the sky where the smoke was thickening, staining the blue sky like an overturned inkwell. From where he stood, it looked like the entire sky was being overrun by the spillage, and that it would only be a matter of time before the palette was ruined. It was remarkable how the smallest of actions could have the largest of consequences, but of course that was a matter of perspective, of how far away you were from the thing that was happening. He tried to think of something to say, but words failed him, failed him like they never had before. Saying "no" or "don't do it" seemed worse than nothing and trying to understand felt patronizing and pithy. He stayed silent, the best solution of all, rehearsing in his mind ten thousand conversations that he would never have.

"We should put this out," Henry said, walking to the trail to pick up a couple of handfuls of sand. Cal followed suit and soon they had thrown enough dust on the pyre to see it go out, to see the last wisps of smoke overcome, carried away by a slight breeze that was always lurking in these hills. Later, as Cal was getting ready to leave, Henry put a hand on his shoulder and, overcome with sincerity, said, "Be careful, okay? Don't do anything stupid."

Cal stopped, looked at him puzzled, and then laughed. "Jesus. Don't be an idiot, Henry."

A few nights later, after dinner, he took out the garbage, which was really his only household chore, and barely a chore at that since his family seemed to generate very little waste. He had always thought it was a bit forced to call it a chore, barely qualifying as onerous, but never challenged the terminology, figuring that it was his parents way to rationalize the ten dollars a week allowance they still gave him. On his way in through the garage, he slammed the back door without realizing that his mother had been standing on the other side watering her plants. Her fingers were hooked in the door frame and when Henry shut it, the door closed on them, eliciting a huge howl from his mom who then crumpled to the floor with her fingers in her mouth, sobbing as blood trickled out over her lips and down her chin. Henry knelt down quickly and tried to pull his mother's fingers from her mouth, but she wouldn't let him care for her. She was beyond his consolation. Grace and his father were soon by his mom's side and she finally allowed Grace to take her hand from between her lips. The tips of her middle and second finger had both been caught and were already flushing a deep black blue color, the bruise darkening as they looked at it, a time lapsed examination of pain.

"Jesus, Henry!" his dad yelled, getting up and running to the kitchen. He brought back a plastic bag filled with ice and when he touched it to his mom's hand she shuddered in pain as though the thing were a live wire. Grace stroked her hair, and when the whimpering stopped, she continued to cry, innocent crying, the kind that can't be helped.

"You've gotta be more careful, Henry," Grace scolded him. "What the hell were you doing?"

Henry stood up and backed away from them, his family, huddled together on the floor, Grace and his father doing double duty, trying to soothe his mom while shooting him reproachful stares and the most menacing of body language.

"I didn't mean it. Shit!"

"Watch your language, Henry," his dad scolded him.

"Fuck all of you!" Henry spat back, full of fire. He didn't wait for a response but turned instead and ran up the stairs and into his room, slamming the door behind him. Without looking he pulled one of Cal's mix tapes from a pile on his desk, put it in the stereo and hit play. It was the Circle Jerks' *Wild in the Streets*. The music was a blast of energy he didn't need, his adrenaline already a lethal dose of rattlesnake venom rushing to his heart. He didn't know what to do with his body, with the anger coiled up inside of him, and without thinking, balled up his fist and hit the wall as hard as he could. Instantly the surge of energy faded as his body's attention rushed to his hand and the pain gathering there, pain like the body giving up, pain in the worst way. He clenched his fist harder and put it to his lips, breathed heavily on it, let it brush against his lips. Gritting his teeth, he looked at his wall. He'd made an impressive dent there, layered inwards, crater-like. The carpet at his feet was dusted with pulverized plaster. He sat down heavily on his bed, waiting for the pain in his hand to stop and wondered idly if he had broken it.

A few minutes later there was a knock at his door. He didn't care who it was. If it was his dad, he wouldn't say anything to him. He would let him yell at him, punish him, whatever he had to do to save face and then Henry would never speak to him again.

"What?" he called.

The door opened slowly, and his mother stuck her head in the gap.

"May I come in?" Her voice was soft, sincere, and he felt himself suddenly on the verge of tears. He nodded and she came in and sat down next to him. Her hand was bandaged, carefully done up in a white dressing. Grace had to have done that. There's no way his father could ever be patient enough to accomplish such a thing.

"I didn't mean to do it," he said, staring straight ahead. "I was going to say that. And tell you that I was sorry. But no one gave me the chance."

"I know, sweetie." She put her arm around his shoulder and hugged him close. He let his head rest on her arm. A few tears loosed themselves from his eyes and splashed against his legs. He didn't try to stop them. "And I know you've had a lot of problems with your father lately, too. I know it's hard for you to remember, Henry, but he was a good father to you guys when you were younger. He would take you out on the weekends to Kiddieland, football games, play catch with you in the yard. I don't expect you to remember, but I do expect you to take my word for it. I don't know what's happened, though…" She paused, giving the mystery its proper room to breathe. "It's you too. I don't want you to take this the wrong way, Henry, you know that I care about you, but you've changed, too. You're not always the sweet boy you used to be. The music you listen to. These clothes you wear. That kid you hang out with. I don't know what it's going to take to get you two back to where you were, but I hope you'll try. I hope you'll both try."

He turned to face her now and saw that her eyes were ringed by heavy dark circles. Crow's feet and wrinkles seemed to have sprung up overnight, the details of her face never so clear to him, her words the sincerest he had ever heard her spoken. Motherly advice, suddenly, wasn't just a diagnosis. He had wondered if his parents had noticed any changes in him, if there actually was anything about him that was different since he started hanging out with Cal, and now here was his answer. He wanted to say something back to her, something as honest as what she'd just told him, and for a moment he considered telling his mom about Cal, about the fact that he thought often about killing himself. In a way it'd be the most real thing he'd said to her in years.

"Wow," she said, looking around. "You really did a number on your room." He wasn't sure if she was talking about the wall or the fact that his shelves and walls were now almost bare.

He decided then that he wouldn't tell her about Cal, that it wasn't his thing to tell. His eyes moistened again as he thought of her fingers, of doing something that made her cry like that, of how he might have been wrong about her for not being a real person for the past decade or so.

"Mom," he said, trying desperately to not sound like a child, "do you still love me?"

"Sweetie," she said, surprised. She lifted her injured hand and looked at it as though it didn't belong to her, as though it was attached to someone or something else. "I'll always love you, Henry. I may not always like you, but I'll always love you."

He tried not to take it personally.

Chapter 7

TWO WEEKS SINCE his house had blown up. Two weeks since he had seen Daisy. A two-week deadline on ten thousand measly words. Two weeks and not a damn thing had happened.

He had done his best to clean his cubicle, to scrub away the fire and brimstone, the benevolent firebombing (as opposed to the other firebombing in his life, which, to his great relief had been deemed a gas leak by the bored fire inspector who had come by a few days later to imperiously walk the rubble), the large swaths of black fire damage that made his work place look like the scene of a ritualistic murder or a porn shoot after party. His tiny walls were still streaked black, their cheap cloth torn and burnt away to form disturbing patterns and images that he'd been obsessing over for the last forty-five minutes while he waited to be called into Ken's office. He rubbed his eyes and forced himself to face straight ahead, at his darkened monitor that reflected his image back to him; tired, nose running, eyes with deep dark circles above and below and sunken way back in his head, the windows to his soul looking like the neighborhood kids threw a baseball through them and then ran away laughing, delighted by the carnage. He had turned in the draft of the Potter obituary to Ken about forty-five minutes earlier, just as the clock struck nine, wanting to seem eager, a go-getter. Ken had grabbed the papers out of his hands without a word, his own eyes two red and puffy ravioli stuffed with disappointment.

"How are you?" Henry had asked, as nonchalantly as he could muster, knowing that the story he was turning in was not going to cut it. Everything depended on getting another crack at talking to Daisy, but he hadn't been able to turn up hide nor hair of her.

"I'm great," Ken deadpanned. "If I was any greater, I'd have to shoot my own face off."

He walked into his office and shut his door, but before Henry could take three steps back to purgatory Ken had opened the door and popped his head out. "Don't go anywhere. I want you to sit at your desk while I read this. When I'm done, I'll call you."

"Okay," Henry said, softly, not wanting to know who else in the room was watching them. The fact that Ken was wearing a Hawaiian shirt only made things worse. Men in Hawaiian shirts were capable of all sorts of evil. Nameless evil. Evil that came quickly so the evil-doer could get back to swimming with dolphins or parasailing or whatever the fuck it was he was relaxing at before he had to make the problem go away.

"Not even coffee, Henry. I'm fucking serious."

"Okay," he said again, continuing the Bataan Death March back to his desk.

He tried to sit still, but it was impossible. Ken hadn't said anything about not getting up to take a leak. He stood and made his way through the maze of cubicles that always made him feel like a poor man's Jack Torrance whenever he had to pee, and as he walked past the desks of his colleagues, he noticed for the first time just how littered they were with sentimental refuse: vacation photos, bumper stickers proclaiming their kids' relative intelligence, homemade pencil holders (as if anyone wrote anymore). These overwrought artifacts only intensified his nervousness. They made him think of peasant offerings, lamb's blood on the door to ward off the angel with the itchy trigger finger. He didn't have anything like that at his desk. Maybe that was his problem. No purple squeezy balls, no giant Staples red panic button, no picture of a kid in an AYSO uniform kneeling majestically on a soccer ball looking like a proud bicycle-kicking castrato. They were hasty totems that seemed put together at the spur of the moment as though HR had handed down an edict that desks had to be filled with crappy off-gassing garbage and, as a result, there'd been a mad rush to the same stores, similar trips planned to Disneyland to crouch and smile in the presence of Mickey. It was sentimentality that felt all wrong. Where did the bad man touch you nostalgia. Old people reminiscing about the good old days of separate water fountains.

Perhaps, though, it had nothing to do with sentimentality or uniformity. Maybe it was just good old-fashioned superstition, tradition that was passed down through the ages until it just became accepted as wisdom. And wisdom? Wisdom then was accepting that tradition as fact, not even bothering to think whether or not it should be done, or why it was done in the first place. True wisdom was when you didn't even question the thing anymore.

His feet felt leaden as he walked over the sad, stained carpet, the original color of which was most certainly at one time an aesthetic preference but had been trod upon in the decades that followed to create an original hue, something a shade or two lighter than entropy on the PMS scale.

His nose twitched with nervousness. The story was shit and he knew it. And to make matters worse, he knew that Ken would know it also. Sweat began to dampen his underarms as he imagined different scenarios of Ken reaming him out. The best of all would be the straight-out screaming followed by a "Sorry I lost my cool for a minute, but I just know there's so much potential in there." That he could deal with. What he couldn't deal with was a quiet "You've really let me down, Henry. I went to bat for you, man." The quieter the discipline, the worse the psychic damage. Throw in a sports analogy and it was Armageddon.

Walking over to the long row of windows that looked down onto the street he tried to open one, but it wouldn't budge. He tried them all, becoming more and more panicked as he went, and it dawned on him, as desperation mounted, that not only did they not open, but, in the two years he had worked there, they had never been opened. Two years of the same stale air, of bad breath, and taco wagon farts, two years of carpet and paint leaching toxic fumes that had long ago been deemed inhumane by international treaties. He noticed scratch marks on the window frame and thought of the poor proofers and classified ad takers before him, men who didn't have internet porn to go home to or the white light of SSRIs at the end of the long tunnel of manic depression and generalized anxiety disorder.

"Doesn't seem fair, does it?" a woman's voice behind him asked, startling him.

"Huh?" he said, turning around. "I mean, what?"

She was a plain-looking woman in her mid-forties dressed in well-fitting jeans and a cheap blouse. He had seen her before but had never spoken to her, just another nameless face haunting the hallways, trying to hang in there until it was time to collect her pension and move to a drier climate, god's ultimate Happy Hour.

"That the windows don't open," she said, standing next to him, looking down at the busy downtown street. "I get why a casino does it, but at least they have the decency to pump in oxygen. I'm not sure what the paper gets out of it."

"Maybe it's a suicide prevention thing," he said, wondering if he was inadvertently showing his cards too soon.

Shrugging, she pulled a rubber band out of her pocket and in one deft move pulled her hair back securing it expertly in a ponytail. Henry had seen girls put their hair up like that a million times—Grace used to wear her hair like that often—but something about the way she did it reminded him of a military action, the precision moves of a soldier restraining and cuffing a terror suspect.

"Suicide hotline's gotta eat, too," she said, winking at him.

With her hair back, her face more exposed, he was no longer so sure about her age. Her skin was very fair and she had quite a few moles on her cheeks and on her neck, which, when contrasted with the translucency of her skin, made them seem much more prominent than they probably would on anyone else.

"Yeah," he said, repeating her joke, "suicide hotline's gotta eat, too."

She laughed and waved away an invisible fly from in front of her face.

"You're the guy with the desk, right?"

"The desk?" His mind was only half in it. The other half was trying to guess what was going through Ken's mind and whether or not he could keep himself from crying after he was fired.

"You know," she said looking at him like he was stupid, "the desk that caught on fire."

A slamming door by the elevators made him turn his head suddenly, but it wasn't Ken.

"Yeah," he said, still staring at Ken's door to make sure it wasn't going to fling open just as he turned his head back to this woman. "That was my desk."

"I didn't think that was right. What they did to you. They should have cleaned that up for you. It's probably giving you cancer sitting there."

He turned his head back and noticed her again as if for the first time.

"I hope not," he said, deciding finally that she was pretty. Pretty in the way being home is beautiful: comfortable, ensconced in eternity. It was the same kind of pretty as summer days that had no end, and parallel lines collapsing into one another, the most desperate kind of embrace.

"I know I don't know you," she began, "but it seems something's bothering you. Are you okay?"

"I'm a little nervous," he said, but then quickly stopped himself. If she was hitting on him, and he couldn't say for certain if she was or she wasn't, then revealing himself to be an anxious wreck might not be the best first move.

"About what?"

"Oh, this and that," he answered as nonchalantly as possible. He wished he had some kind of prop to play with, something to show his supreme confidence, like a Swiss army knife he could whip out and start picking at his nails with. "I'm just waiting for my editor to get back to me with some notes on a story I wrote."

"A story?" She looked confused. "I thought you worked in Classifieds and Marketing."

"Technically speaking," he started, halting as he thought of how to paint himself in the best possible light, "that's true. But I was actually hired by Metro originally to do research.

I only sit in C&M because of logistical issues."

She scrunched up her face.

"You mean, you work for Metro, but they put you in C&M because they didn't have room for you?"

"Uh, technically…" he gave up halfway in. "Yeah," he said. "Pretty much."

"Gotcha," she said and turned back to look at the window some more. "It's weird back here, isn't it? In the cubicle forest?" She lowered her voice down to a whisper and leaned in close to his ear. "The people are fucking strange."

Her soft voice tickled his ear and a shiver ran up his spine giving him goosebumps all up and down his arms. Her breath smelled sweet and delicate and he imagined reaching out and drawing imaginary lines connecting the moles on her face, naming the constellations, a galaxy of love and lust.

"What do you mean?" he asked her, pulling his head away from her mouth, afraid people might be watching.

"They're just weird. All the Disney shit on their desks, the pictures, the stickers of Calvin and Hobbes pissing on things. What's up with that anyway?" She leaned in again to whisper. Clearly she was a fan of confidence. "You know there have to be a lot of weirdos who work here, and the thought of them doing normal things, like going to Disneyland or the Grand Canyon or whatever, is creepier than thinking of them doing creepy things. Does that make sense?"

He nodded. That was it exactly. It was precisely what he had been thinking before but hadn't quite been able to put into words.

"Are you normal?" he asked her, smiling, trying his best to be cute.

"Yeah," she shot back. "Completely. I've been divorced. I've been quirky. I've been realistic about life and it took." She seemed to go away for a minute and then came back. "I once walked the entire length of Bourbon Street in my bare feet. How's that?" she asked triumphantly, as if it was the slam dunk piece of evidence.

"That's pretty good," he said, and then thought about his own life, about Cal and everything that happened when he was younger, the cultists firebombing his house, this assignment that was most surely going to be the end of him.

A pause in the conversation that couldn't quite be characterized as an awkward silence descended, the difference being that neither of them was tense about how the rest of the conversation would go. The underlying sounds of the busy newsroom flowed into the spaces; the constant tapping of word processing and the wordless churning of ten thousand conversations going at once combining to form one pitch perfect voice. Stillness but not quite nothing.

Looking down into the street was like staring into a fire, the sun reflecting off of cars and buildings, the tops of people's heads, burning everything with its brightness. Henry concentrated on what he knew to be a tiny El Salvadoran woman manning a food cart that sold bacon-wrapped hot dogs. They were his secret lunchtime passion, one he indulged only when he was on his own, and he would sleep after lunch on the rare days he bought one or two, putting his head on his desk as the grease and sodium made mincemeat of his productivity.

"Look," she said, pointing downwards, and she might as well have been pointing out a grain of sand at the beach.

"What?" He struggled to locate what it was that caught her attention.

"That woman, over there," she said, pointing more emphatically as if that would help him see more clearly, "in front of that building. She's having headshots taken, I think."

Henry strained to see and finally located the photographer and the woman. A brunette was posing in a series of exaggerated poses as a guy laid down on the sidewalk in front of her, snapping dramatically, clearly encouraging her through his own dramatic behavior.

"Oh yeah," he whispered, as if speaking too loudly would interrupt the photo session six floors below.

"Think she'll make it big?"

"I don't know," Henry answered, transfixed by how small they looked yet how vital what they were doing seemed. "Probably not," he revised his answer.

"Why do you say that?" she asked, turning toward him, putting her hands in the back pocket of her jeans.

He shrugged. "Most people don't get to be what they want." He hadn't thought how negative that sounded until after it had come out and moved quickly to cover his pessimistic tracks. "That being said, she has just as good a shot..."

She interrupted him by drawing in a sharp burst of air and thrust her hands out in front of her as if willing the world to stop in its tracks. Her yelling, "OH NO!!" finished off the pantomime, and Henry instinctively winced and covered his head with his arms as the tinny sound of metal on metal reached their ears from the street below. They both peered down and saw a massive wreck; an old BMW had seemingly run a red light and T-boned a small SUV. Metal was flung everywhere and a river of shattered glass flowed across the street glinting in the sun as if it was water and not glass.

The woman started to run for the elevator and when she realized that Henry was not following her, she turned and yelled to him from across the room.

"Come on!" she said, "let's go."

"I can't," he replied. "I've gotta wait here for Ken." His eyes went to Ken's door, afraid that even the suggestion of him leaving would incur some kind of extra sensory wrath.

"Are you kidding me?" she asked him incredulously.

"No," he shifted nervously, turning back to the window to scan the accident. "He told me to wait."

"Fuck what Ken said. This is…" she searched for the word, "…real life."

Real life. The words hit him in the gut, and he turned without saying a word, and ran past her to the elevator. She got on and they were on their way down, each in their own silence, the sharp corners the mind took on its own. The elevator creaked its way down to the street slowly, rheumatic gears straining to prove their usefulness. Henry jabbed his finger at the first-floor button a few times to do what? Prove a point to their outdated lift?

"That doesn't do anything," she said, staring at the lights above the doors that flashed as they passed each floor.

He said nothing.

When the door opened, they sprinted across the lobby and out the front door. The accident scene was already crowded with onlookers and helpers, a few people kneeling to help the wounded and the rest hoisting camera phones aloft to chronicle the carnage for future dinner parties and social networking, a picture definitely worth a few dozen thumbs-up on Facebook. A collage of blood, metal, and glass covered the street. Henry thought to himself that if he didn't know it was an accident, his first guess would have been that this was a public art display either gone horribly wrong or horribly well, another well-coordinated effort to replicate the zeitgeist rather than take responsibility for it.

The woman, his new friend whose name he didn't even know, caught sight of something across the street and took off like a bolt toward the opposite sidewalk. Henry followed her, sprinting to keep up, and when he caught up with her she was standing a few feet from the model and the photographer they had seen from upstairs just a few minutes before. Now, instead of posing like an orphaned contortionist, the photographer was egging his muse on to lay in the street with the accident in the near background and pretend she was a critically injured accident victim.

"More," he said, the camera bobbing up and down in front of his face. "More victim-y."

The model let her tongue loll slightly out of her mouth, which prompted a happy response from the photographer.

"Yes!" he shouted, ecstatically, "that's it. You've got it, baby. Critical, baby."

"I can't believe this," the woman said, turning to Henry. "Can you fucking fathom what you're seeing?"

Sirens blared at them from all angles as cops and ambulances converged, everywhere people were shouting, and he could swear that from somewhere deep within it all, that he could hear his own name emerge, from the heart of all this, as though he was somehow the source of all this destruction.

"No," he shook his head, he couldn't fathom it, but not for the reasons she couldn't. Where she was repulsed, he was suddenly overwhelmed and anxious as though ten tons of guilt had just collapsed on his head, and when he looked past her at the car wreckage and caught sight of what looked like a head, trapped like a fly in the spiderweb the windshield had become, he went down to one knee and began to dry heave.

"Henry!"

It was his name again, but this time louder, clearer. He

pulled a long string of saliva off his lower lip and flung it to the ground. Looking up, he saw Ken coming toward him, his Potter story clutched tightly in the editor's hand.

"I thought I told you not to fucking go anywhere," Ken said, standing over him, his arms crossed, the look on his face that of a self-satisfied tyrant.

"I didn't," Henry said, rising slowly to his feet. "I mean, I wouldn't have if…" he looked toward his new friend who was engaged in a ferocious yelling match with the photographer, the both of them dogs with their hackles of righteous indignation at full mast.

"If what?" Ken asked him, looking around. "Are you a doctor? You gonna help these people out? Or are you a fucking fireman? Cause you're sure as hell not a writer," he yelled, letting Henry's story fall casually out of his hand and sailed to the ground.

"Leave him alone, Ken." The woman had given up her common-sense jihad and was now standing next to Henry. "Don't be ridiculous," she added for good measure.

"Stay out of this, Bea," Ken turned to her.

Bea. Her name was Bea.

"Don't tell me what to fucking do. You're not my boss anymore."

Ken shook his head and turned his gaze back on Henry.

"Here's the deal, Henry," Ken said, holding up his index finger. "You've got one week to get an interview with Potter and rewrite this piece of shit. One week, otherwise you're out on your ass. I don't care how you do it. I don't care if you have to join the fucking cult and pray to a bust of Howdy Doody for six hours a day. Get the interview. Write the story. Save your job. Otherwise, forget it."

He turned, never once having looked at the accident, and as he walked away, his Hawaiian shirt became an oasis, a place to look forward to in the impossible distance.

*   *   *

Later that afternoon, Henry sat at his desk looking forlornly at his computer monitor. The Google homepage was up and he had no ideas, no place springing to mind that could help him, nothing to punch in. He literally had the world at his fingertips and all he wanted to do was sleep. He could now add his job to the long list of things he had to panic about in his life, which included (in no special order): the homicidal cult that firebombed his apartment in an apparent attempt to murder him, a girl he feared was in mortal danger for talking to him, and his present living arrangement, which was in Truman's spare bedroom in his condo that had begun to resemble an anti-federal government version of Burning Man. On top of it all, the Santa Ana winds had begun to kick up, throwing his nose and eyes into spastic overdrive, giving him the overall appearance of a malfunctioning android.

He was about to get up to get a cup of coffee, hoping the caffeine would somehow change his body chemistry, when Bea wandered over to his desk. She looked at his charred walls and the carpet under his chair that had melted down to the concrete flooring and let out a long whistle.

"This is worse than it looks from across the room." She put her elbow up on the cubicle wall.

"Yeah. You really have to get in close to grasp the full extent of the carnage. The President flew over, but it's not the same as taking a tour of the devastated area."

She laughed.

"Hey, what's wrong with your face?" she pointed at her own

face, moving her finger around to indicate the whole thing.

"Allergies," he replied, hoping it would suffice. He didn't want her asking "allergic to what?" because that would require him to say "pretty much everything outside," and that was no way to begin a friendship. Thankfully, she didn't press him.

"Listen," she started, and he felt an apology coming on, although for the life of him he couldn't figure out what for. He felt he had come off as a spineless turd when he argued with her about rushing down to the scene of the accident because Ken had told him not to move. "I didn't mean to yell at you earlier. I get excited sometimes and I kind of just block out other people. That wasn't right of me. You've got pressures, a job to protect. I shouldn't have…"

He waved her off and stood up.

"No, no, no," he said, putting a hand on her shoulder. "I'm the one who should apologize. You were absolutely in the right. I mean, what am I, fourteen? I mean, if Ken told me to jump off a bridge…"

"Or if Ken told you to sit in a work space that looked like Lucifer's taint, would you do that?" She crossed her arms and smiled, moving back a little to let his hand slide from her shoulder and back to his side.

"Who'd be crazy enough to do that?" he mock laughed. "That'd be stupid."

"Really stupid." She pushed her black-rimmed glasses back up the length of her button nose, just a short distance to her razor sharp blue eyes.

"When did you used to work for Ken?" he asked her. "Were you transferred?"

"Kind of," she said, looking around distractedly as though this was a story she'd told a million times before and wasn't particularly in the mood to tell again. "Ken and I were cub reporters together a long time ago, right after we both got out of journalism school. He stuck with it, rose up through the ranks, and I pooped out on it."

"What do you mean, pooped out?"

"I got sick of it. I was married to a reporter, was working as a reporter, the paper was my life, and I didn't want that. I didn't want the life I had here. So," she reached up and pulled out the hair band that had been holding back her hair, letting it rain down ten shades of gold and blonde across her shoulders, "I divorced my husband, figured out I was a lesbian, and took a job in C&M. Now I have a personal life,and I'm a lot lot happier. And that's it. That's the whole story. Believe it or not."

"Why wouldn't I believe it?" he asked.

"When I tell people they sometimes think there must be something else, some scandal or something. I try to convince them there's not, but people don't want to believe that. Somehow it's easier to believe that I freaked out, ripped off all my clothes, and went running down Figueroa screaming out the Lord's Prayer than what really happened."

"Which was what?" he asked, feeling a pit in his stomach as though her answer might explain a thing or two for him.

"I decided, rationally and calmly, to make a change. It does happen, you know, from time to time. Not every epiphany has to resemble a massive stroke."

He nodded, not really knowing what to say.

"So, what was all that about between you and Ken? He seemed pretty pissed, but then again, he was always in sort of a bad mood. Just one of those people who can't get happy."

He told her what had happened to him with the assignment

thus far, leading up to Ken's ultimatum that Henry somehow pull the interview of the decade out of his ass.

She thought a minute, almost as if weighing whether or not she should make a suggestion and get involved, before saying, "You know who you should talk to? Oscar Booth. He's the last reporter to get an interview with Potter and he works here in this building. He might have an idea or two for you."

The idea of going to see Booth had never crossed his mind. Booth was the paper's most decorated reporter, the recipient of two Pulitzers and a series of on-the-ground stories from Vietnam where he'd been embedded with the Marines that had been compiled into a bestselling memoir later optioned by Tom Hanks. Booth was also known to be excruciatingly temperamental and nasty, a drunk whose better days were definitely behind him, and a relationship with senior management that was less than civil. Henry had heard a story of Booth once getting outrageously drunk at a Christmas party in the building, and after getting into a yelling match with one of the editors over a cut in the budget for international affairs writing, had grabbed the man and tried to force him into a paper shredder dick first.

"I've heard he's a little…" Henry tried to be diplomatic, "… rough around the edges."

She stuffed a hand in the pocket of her faded blue jeans and pulled out a pack of Fruit Stripe gum. "A lot of that stuff is overplayed for effect. All that 'curmudgeon-in-residence' bullshit. Every paper needs to have a living legend." She unwrapped a piece of the gum and folded it into her mouth. She stuck the pack out at Henry.

"No, thanks," he said, waving it off. "Loses its flavor too quickly."

"So?" And when she realized he wasn't going to say anything, added on an imperious, "Men." for good measure.

"If you're talking about the story of the editor and the paper shredder, there was a lot of alcohol involved. Also, he never would have gotten him into that shredder. It was more for effect. Don't worry, you'll be fine. I'll send him an email and tell him that he should be nice to you when you come down."

"How do you know so much about him? Can you personally guarantee the safety of my dick?" Henry asked her.

She laughed. "Your dick is in your own hands," she said, snapping the gum around in her mouth. "You'll be fine, Henry. Besides, he's my ex-husband and he still owes me a lot of back alimony. He has to do what I say."

She tapped one of her ground-down fingernails against her teeth and pointed at one of his cubicle walls.

"Maybe we're thinking about this all wrong," she said, still looking at the charred remains of the fourth estate. "If this place were outside, I could almost see it becoming a monument. Kids might hang around it, smoke, carve their initials, write political graffiti, get engaged, fall apart, fuck, get high. People would leave, like, flowers on secret anniversaries and if you were lucky, you might even get a suicide or two just to really cement the whole sanctification of it. That's how I'm going to look at it for now on," she said, her eyes finally coming back to rest on Henry, her daydream spitting her back out on familiar shores, "like a monument."

He nodded and smiled politely, but what he didn't ask, because he knew she wouldn't have an answer for him, was, a monument to what?

*   *   *

He took the stairs down to the fifth floor where Oscar's office was, and on the way down came across one of the newspaper's senior editors adding to the graffiti on the wall, so deep in thought that he didn't even notice Henry until the two of them were nearly standing next to one another. The editor, his grey hair a sentient being in the dim passage, covered up what he had been writing as he waited for Henry to pass him on the way down to the next floor. Henry worried for a moment that he had seen something he wasn't supposed to, some sort of managerial privilege like how some companies had an executive washroom or use of a company car for executives, and, having pulled back that veil, might be let go or disciplined somehow for having seen too much. All was well, though, because as Henry passed him up, the editor gave a hangnail of a smile and nodded his head toward him conspiratorially, as if they somehow were in league together, in the same splinter cell, because neither one of them was above taking the stairs once in a while. It was a weird club to be part of, Henry thought, as he nodded back confidently, as though this happened to him all the time. As though he was privy and sympathetic to all deviance in the building no matter how big or little.

The fifth floor, when he pushed open the door, looked remarkably like the sixth. He didn't know what he had expected, but somehow a replica of the drab confines of the sixth wasn't the first thing that popped into his head. As he walked the halls looking for Oscar's office, he passed an endless chorus of ringing phones and ticking clocks from dozens of time zones and just the general hurriedness of foreign affairs and then national news. It was what he always imagined a newspaper to be: a giant body with limbs spasming every which way, a schizophrenic collision of voices, a general rush of movement, uncontrollable, like adrenaline hijacking the system and everything moving by sheer biology, free will surpassed and pink-slipped on the way to more streamlined solutions.

He found Oscar's office despite the nameplate on the door being tampered with so that it read "car Boot". The other thing that gave it away was the hand-drawn sign on the door that said "No girls allowed." It occurred to him that there might be a secret knock or arcane password he would need to enter, something so shrouded in mystery it would make the Masons and the Knights Templar seem like a society of quilters.

He brushed off the sneaky feeling that his immortal soul was about to belly up to some kind of other-worldly glory hole and rapped lightly on the door.

"Who is it?" A gruff and muffled voice asked him through the door, a voice that had been marinated in thousands of cigarettes and countless bottles of booze.

"It's Henry Colmes. Bea said that I should come talk to you."

He hoped that she was as good as her word and that a trap door wasn't about to open under his feet, sending him into a meat grinder or a shark tank.

The door opened a tiny bit as Henry saw a tall figure turn away and walk to the back of the office.

"Come in," Booth said.

He pushed the door open slowly, letting it creak open, and walked cautiously into an office that was inordinately dark, almost impossibly dark, ambush dark. He could just vaguely make out Booth sitting on the edge of his desk, smoking a cigarette, blowing smoke to the ceiling where it gathered like fog on a mountaintop. You would need a sherpa to change the light bulb.

"Go ahead and sit down," Booth told him, kicking a chair in Henry's general direction.

He no longer felt like he was in the same building as he had been just seconds ago. The office was a portal to somewhere else, somewhere defined by its faintness and blurriness. Almost every overflowing inch was saturated with memorabilia from a long and storied career. Framed photos on the wall were bleary black-and-white glimpses on the past, rough narratives, grainy shots of Booth standing by an M48 Patton tank in Vietnam, holding an AK-47 in another that looked like Afghanistan, or it could have been Central America—combat had a way of making the terrain of these places all so similar. All in all, it was a decorating style located somewhere between feng shui and the Big Bang.

Booth had been stretched thin by war, literally, it seemed. He was a wisp of a man, taller than he needed to be, almost like he was trying to prove a point tall, and deeply tanned to the point where it could be said his skin was closer in consistency to leather than epidermis. His face was lined with deep creases, and to Henry, studying him for the first time in this dim office, he almost seemed like an origami version of himself. Like this wasn't the real Oscar Booth, but just an arts and crafts version of the real man, popsicle sticks and tissue paper, meant to fool the bosses while the real Oscar clung for dear life to a bar stool somewhere, yelling out complicated and intricate drink orders that sounded like surgical instructions or roadside directions to one of those towns in Wales that had no consonants in it.

Henry took the chair and smiled up at Oscar, who remained still, perched lethargically on the edge of his desk, alternating smoking and then, in violent eruptions, coughing so violently it looked as though he might actually snap his skinny frame in half.

Out of nervousness, and with no other thoughts about how to start a conversation, Henry pointed to the ceiling and said, "A/C just went on. Must be the first day of summer. Happy solstice."

Booth took the cigarette out of his mouth, coughed, and furrowed his brow.

"Huh?" he asked, clearly puzzled.

"It's the first day of summer," Henry repeated, pointing dumbly again at the ceiling. "Summer solstice." He already wished he could start over. He had just been trying to make small talk and now regretted it deeply.

"I know what the solstice is," Booth said calmly. "I've just never had anyone wish me a happy solstice. It's kind of fruity, don't you think?"

"Yeah," he answered, wanting to say the right thing, "it is. I grew up by the beach, though, and it was kind of a holiday for people. I guess it just stuck with me."

"Okay, well, I don't get down with cultural imperialism, and I definitely don't recognize any holiday that's celebrated with a drum circle, but that's not why you're here." Oscar looked at his watch and scratched a patch of stubble on his neck that could have as easily been two hours' worth of growth as two weeks. "Why are you here?"

Henry swallowed and felt his Adam's Apple bob heavily almost choking him.

"Bea asked you if I could come and talk to you. It's for a story I'm writing about Reverend Potter and the Children of Light."

Booth stared at him through the thickening fog of smoke until finally he nodded, and it made Henry think of that old Mousetrap game where every lever and trigger had to go off just right to get the cage to fall on the mouse at the end.

"Right, right," he said as if he knew the answer all along. "How is Bea? I haven't seen her in a couple of years."

"But you work one floor down from her," Henry pointed out haltingly.

"That's true," Booth replied as he turned around to search for something on his desk. "You know how it is, though. Work builds up. Gets hard to leave the office." He turned back around brandishing a coffee mug with the sentence *My heart is into paving but my ass belongs to Jan* inscribed on it. He took a swig of the contents and smacked his lips.

"She's good," Henry said, trying to think of something to say about the woman he had met for the first time earlier that day. "We saw a car accident together."

"You were in a car accident?" Booth asked him, examining the bottom of the mug as if he was trying to find any hidden or wayward drops.

"No, we just saw one. It's actually not that..."

"Interesting?" Booth interrupted. "No, it's not."

Henry was sure he was on the verge of getting thrown out of the office at any moment and didn't know quite how to get to the point.

"Who do you work for?" Booth asked him.

"Ken. I write...well, I usually research the big obituaries, so that they're ready to go when the person dies, but I just got my first assignment. Ken wants me to write one on Potter. That's why Bea..."

Oscar made a face.

"That's really fucked up. You write obituaries about people that aren't even dead yet?"

"Yeah," Henry said, unfolding his hands from his lap. "I know it's kind of weird, but..."

"I didn't say weird," Booth corrected him. "I said fucked up. There's a difference. Weirdness doesn't really imply any kind of karmic ramifications. Fucked up, on the other hand, is a whole lot of trouble in the next life."

Henry sat up straight. He was sick of people telling him that what he did was wrong or strange.

"What's the matter? Don't you believe in karma?"

"I tend not to believe in things that are celebrated with vegan catering." He smiled, hoping the joke would help break the ice. This seemed to be his last shot at writing this story. If Booth told him to fuck off he might as well start researching his own obit and kiss his chances of finding Daisy goodbye.

Booth cracked a smile. "That's funny," he said, using the end of his cigarette to light a fresh one. He let the old one fall to the bottom of the mug where it sizzled for a second and then expired. "So tell me, what is it I can do for you?"

Henry started explaining the circumstances leading up to his need to find Potter but found that he couldn't tell the story without going into the whole thing: Daisy gone missing, the bombing of his apartment, how this assignment was his one and only hope of ever amounting to anything in his life. Fifteen minutes later he leaned back in his chair and slid a hand under his thigh, which had fallen asleep.

"Sounds like you're putting an awful lot on yourself to finish this story. Wouldn't it be easier to walk away from it and try to find work at another paper? You're not exactly next in line for a Pulitzer, and maybe these COL goons would leave you alone if they knew you were off the trail."

In all his obsessing about what to do, Henry had never once thought about ditching the whole thing. There was too much at stake now, too much riding on him finishing.

"I can't," he said, shaking his head. "I've gotta finish it."

"I get it," Booth clapped his hands together and rocked

back a little delightedly, surprising the hell out of Henry, who had it in his head that Booth couldn't actually move, but was merely an animatronic smoking and drinking machine. "It's the girl. You wanna fuck the chick. Buddy, trust me, there's plenty of pussy out there that you don't need to get firebombed to fuck. When I was in Vietnam, I had an amazing girl who shivved me in the arm for my wallet after we'd just fucked. That was almost worth it. Firebombing," he shook his head, thoughtfully, "no fucking way."

Henry was about to object. There was a certain exaggeration of shame for him in being suspected of acting irrational or odd because of women (a trait left over from childhood, no doubt), but stopped himself when he realized that Booth was at least partly right. He wasn't desperate to fuck Daisy (although he wouldn't mind); he was desperate to save her. Something in him was pushing him on to find her and help her, to do for her what he couldn't do for Grace, who, he suddenly found himself thinking about and missing deeply, painfully.

"Well, whatever the case may be," Booth went on, getting up now and walking over to a pile of papers on the side of his desk, "Ken shouldn't have done that to you. That's fucking ridiculous. Especially coming from someone who couldn't write their way out of a fucking paper bag." Booth knelt as he leafed through one yellowing stack of paper after another. "I remember reading some of his college samples when he applied for a job here originally. Terrible. Even after twenty-five years the terribleness of it sticks in my mind. Vietnam, Afghanistan, Nicaragua…all that and I still remember something about an intramural cream the cookie league, or some fucking shit…" He trailed off, and Henry wanted to laugh, but his mind was stuck now, looping over and over on itself, justifying motives and making plans amidst this sudden diaspora of reason.

"Aha!" Booth shouted. He held up an old piece of paper that had some sort of a stain on it that resembled Alfred Hitchcock's profile. "Write this name and number down. Alan Downes. 310-477-9089."

Henry patted himself down for a pen and a scrap of paper but found none. He looked up pathetically at Booth.

"Are you kidding me?" Booth asked him. "You don't carry a pen and pad everywhere with you? That's sacrilegious, buddy." He leaned back over his desk and lobbed a pen and a small scratch pad to Henry. "Consider that a gift."

He read the name and number again as Henry copied it down.

"Who is this?" Henry asked him, worried momentarily that it was someone he was supposed to know.

"Downes is a former COL member. One of the very few who'll actually talk to people about it. He was there for all the good stuff: the raid on the compound, the suicides, Potter being sent off to prison. He runs a support group now that helps ex-cultists get over their shit. Or something like that. He's a good guy. Tell him I sent you and he'll talk to you."

"Thanks," Henry said as he got up to leave, sensing he should seize the opportunity to get out before Booth decided he was the enemy and put him in some sort of primal chokehold.

"Hey," Booth called out just as Henry was about to open the door, "did Bea tell you that I made her gay?"

"Huh? Uh…no," Henry was still lost in thought and could barely keep up with the jai alai-esque trajectory of the conversation.

"Hmm," Oscar said, nodding as he lit yet another cigarette, "I kind of wish she would."

Chapter 8

TRUE TO ITS name, the nuclear family was a messy proposition. There were meltdowns and infections, collateral damage, cover-ups and crises that got so close to being the end that people wouldn't believe it if you told them. But, also true to its name, and at its core, the nuclear family was a perpetual motion machine, powered by fits and bursts of temporary ecstasy, exploding and exploding again.

In the couple of weeks that followed Henry accidentally breaking his mom's finger, a general détente spread over them, a kind of relaxation of tensions that implied everyone was willing to give this family thing another chance or that it was simply too exhausting to go around being an anxious collective wreck all the time. Henry and Grace's mother was going out of her way to be overly maternal, showing up in their rooms or in front of the TV before dinner with peeled carrot sticks sprinkled with a dash of salt, the kind of good-for-you snack she used to bring them when they were little and worried over their health constantly. Her index and middle fingers were still taped together, but no one ever mentioned the accident or that night at all. It wasn't as if it never happened, but it was clear that it was the genesis of this palpable civility, which was enough. Why look a gift horse in the mouth? Especially one that had a history of bucking off riders and then kicking them in the head with its back legs.

For his part, Henry's father invited him down to the couch where he parked himself to watch TV every night to play a game or two of chess. He would hear his father's voice boom up the stairs, "Henry! Chess!" Half question, half command, he would come down to find his father smoking with the chessboard set out in front of him, the pieces already in their beginning positions, his father's work shirt loosened at the collar, toes still in their black dress socks digging into the peach carpet. He had taught Henry chess when he was in the fourth grade and was excited when Henry immediately took to it. Of course, Henry never got as good as his dad, who had played chess for his college club, but it was something they could share, sitting in silence across the board from one another, moving pieces back and forth as they tested the limits of one another's defenses and foresight. Henry had only beat his father once in all the hundreds of games they had played together but losing never bothered him.

His father would sometimes give him hints when he was about to make a bad move. He would clear his throat or ask in a passive voice, "You sure about that?" and Henry would move his piece back quickly before his dad could change his mind, and he'd reset his thoughts, focusing harder on what looked like a good idea at first. Most of the time, though, when he'd make a bad move, his father would counter quickly, snatching up one of Henry's power pieces without a word. It was a strange calculus, trying to figure out when and why his dad would let him off the hook sometimes and show no mercy others, but he didn't dwell on it for long. Most of the time he was happy to just play, to sit there in silence with him, to stare at the board and not one another. Once in a while he would catch his dad looking at him, a small smile sticking up the ends of his lips. Henry had shaved his head the week before and wondered if that was what his dad found amusing, that this was what Henry thought rebelling was, and how sad it was compared to the things he had done to his parents when he was a kid. There was no evidence, of course, that this is what he had been thinking, but sometimes Henry let his mind go there, and when he did, he would look back quickly at the board again and try to channel that paranoid reasoning into his next move.

Grace also seemed to be loosening up. She and Peter had recently gotten back together after a brief breakup, and she was happier than Henry had seen her in a long time. He could hear her talking with her boyfriend on the phone until all hours of the night, usually just a muffled drone of happy chatter that was occasionally punctuated by loud squeals of laughter and insincere admonishments. "Stop it, Peter." If she said it once a night, she said it a million times. It was like their mating call to one another. Henry had never thought of her as particularly girlie, one of those chicks who hung on to her boyfriend's arm and did whatever he wanted to do and laughed at all of his stupid jokes, but here she was, succumbing to the ecstasy of young love, and even though he would sometimes tease her, launching into a loud and erotic round of "Yes, Peter. Whatever you say, Peter" moans from his room when he knew she was on the phone with him, he was not disappointed in her for acting that way. He was happy for her. Happy and also a bit jealous that not only did he not have that kind of love for himself, but that his sister was no longer his and his alone.

When she wasn't on the phone or out with Peter, she would stop by his room to talk and listen to music the way they used to. She was making more of an effort to understand the kind of music he was into, the color storm of flyers for bands she had never heard of decorating his room, his new haircut, his new clothes. They were becoming different people, they both realized, but that didn't mean they had to be different to one another. Also, they would always have their parents in common. Genetics was, after all, the ultimate inside joke. Once, after one of their mom's nightly carrot drop-offs, Grace knocked on Henry's door, and when he opened it, she pushed her cheeks together and spit an enormous mouthful of shredded orange carrot bits all over his face and shirt. She ran away, shrieking, and he chased after her into the bathroom, where he pushed her into the shower with her clothes on and turned on the water, dousing them both in a jumbled, laughing heap on the floor, both of them laughing so hard that when their parents came running in, worried at first that something had happened, and seeing their children tangled together in a wet heap on the floor of the shower, had shaken their heads and started laughing themselves, unsure of what was so funny other than it seemed like, for now anyway, they were all happy.

Maybe it was all the punk rock he was listening to, with its non-stop rhetoric about how fucked up white middle-class families were, a conspiracy theory set to a breakneck rhythm launched by a guy clicking together drumsticks and yelling "One, two, three, four," a reverse countdown to a blast-off that was all screaming the "truth" about dads who didn't give a fuck about anything but sports and bullying their kids and moms who popped pills to cope with reality while lecturing their own kids about the dangers of drug abuse. The suburbs of punk rock were a paranoid and angry place and enemies lurked everywhere, or so the propaganda went. The chances of surviving it were slim, so fuck shit up while you had the chance, because it was the only way anyone would ever know you were ever here.

Maybe it was the music, or maybe it was just his track record of fucking up from time immemorial, but the recent familial peace left Henry feeling a bit wary, that it was all predicated on something very shaky and tenuous, temporary and fragile. He was glad that everyone seemed to be in such a good mood these days, but the mood didn't seem real, and while that would be enough for some people, to enjoy the stability while it lasted, for Henry it was a reason to be even more on guard than usual, to steel himself for the inevitable collapse he was sure must be just around the corner.

The other thing that had left him feeling a bit out of sorts was all of the college applications that had been coming for Grace over the past couple of weeks. Colorful booklets arrived on almost a daily basis now from universities around the country. Grace had great grades and would probably get in to whatever school she wanted to go to. Henry sometimes flipped through the books when no one else was around and imagined himself bundled up with a scarf around his neck, walking over snowy paths, the grey stone buildings of some Ivy League school peppered around a quad with other similarly dressed smart students moving with great purpose and in great camaraderie, reverential of their surroundings but feeling entitled to be there, that they belonged. There was no doubt that come fall Grace would no longer be living in this house. Henry would be beginning his junior year and Grace would be thousands of miles away, finally with other people like her: smart people, concerned people, people who were in almost every way better than the ones they went to school with and even, he thought, her own family. She was getting more and more excited with the arrival of each new application and he knew that she must be biding her time now, counting down the minutes until she could leave them behind to suffer each other's dull and brutal company while she was somewhere far away being exposed to new ideas and great works. The only new ideas he could depend on were the ones being fed to him by Cal, an exhausting stream of paranoia that was as much without end as it was without reason.

One evening after dinner he was in his room doing some homework for a change when he heard his father's voice boom through the house.

"Henry, get down here for a second!"

He dropped his pencil and looked straight ahead wondering what he had done, wondering if the détente was over and the war had recommenced over some negligible violation of an untranslatable treaty. Slowly he got to his feet and ambled downstairs to the kitchen where he heard his family speaking and the TV on. He stopped suddenly when he saw his father, mother and sister seated at the kitchen table laughing and giddy about something he couldn't even begin to guess the origin of.

"Did someone we hate die?" he asked, not knowing what else to say, and the three of them broke into an even louder chorus of laughter, his mother actually pounding her fist on the table she was cracking up so hard. Earlier that day there had been a slight earthquake, just a tremor really, barely enough to be felt, and certainly not bad enough to do any damage. Their mom, though, had gone into a slight panic about it and had been running around since he got home from school trying to put together emergency kits. "We're not ready...we're not ready..." she could be heard muttering as she dashed this way and that, rifling through medicine cabinets and beneath all the sinks in the house. No one was. It was the collective hallucination of living in Southern California that they weren't all living on the precipice of some imminent disaster, a catastrophic daydream in the making. They would all be caught unaware one day, and that was what made it okay, that they would all be screwed together when the big one finally came. It was almost a relief for him to see her in a frenzy, but now here she was again, totally relaxed, like she didn't have a care in the world.

"Sit down," Grace said, pushing out the last chair for him. "We're about to be rich."

"Huh?" he asked, beyond puzzled now. Had they all taken drugs and not told him? Was it family shroom night? He pulled up the collar of his Circle Jerks T-shirt and stuck it in his mouth. "What's going on?"

"Nothing," Grace said, patting the chair. Henry noticed she was wearing a Harvard sweatshirt and he suddenly felt a huge lump in his throat. It was like she was advertising her disdain for them. Why not rent out the blimp and fly it over school with the message FUCK YOU HENRY scrolling across its oblong body? "Dad bought some lottery tickets for the big drawing tonight. $120 million. We were just talking about what we'd do with the money if we won."

"Oh," Henry said, slumping into the chair. A clock on the TV was counting down the minutes until the drawing. Above him a ceiling fan whirred shakily, its chain tapping out a patient grammar as it struck against the light bulb in coincidental time with the countdown on the screen. It made Henry feel tense, like time was edging away toward something inevitable and unkind.

"Dad said he'd build us a huge house like the Winchester Mystery House. Remember that place?"

Henry nodded. They had visited the old house on a family road trip years earlier. The house had been built by the widow of the man who founded the Winchester rifle company, and after he died, she was convinced that the ghosts of all the people who had been killed by her husband's rifles were coming after her. She built a sprawling estate to hide from the evil spirits, instructing carpenters to build hallways, stairways, and doors that often led to nothing, a maze that spiraled out in confusing patterns to throw the ghosts off her trail. The building went on until she died, the house now a tourist attraction not to be missed by anyone who liked to spend their summer vacation visiting a modern marvel of paranoid schizophrenia. Next stop…the Queen Mary.

"Why?" he asked.

"So he can hide from us on Sundays," his mother said, trying to collect herself, "when football is on."

Grace, his mom, and dad broke into another round of laughter. He smiled. He had never seen them act so relaxed together. So happy.

"What about you, Mom?" Henry asked, "What would you do with all that money?"

She fanned herself with a napkin as she stared up at the ceiling, contemplating the question.

"I think I would send myself to one of those spas in the desert for about a year. The kind of place the celebrities are always jetting off to so they could lose weight and rejuvenate themselves, where they cook you fresh food and squeeze fresh juice every morning. That would be nice," she said, perhaps a little wistfully, "to have that feeling like I was starting over."

"You'd trip and fall into a cactus, Joan," his father said, stirring up another round of chuckles.

"Probably," she said, taking his passive cue and dismissing the notion with a roll of the eyes. She took a sip of lemonade from a sweaty glass on the table.

"Grace?" Henry asked, looking at his sister. He held his breath as he waited for her answer, hoping that it would somehow involve him, a plan that would let them stay together, protecting one another from whatever would come their way.

"A trip," Grace said. "I would take Peter on a trip around the world. We would start in South America and work our way west through Southeast Asia, Japan, China, India, the Middle East, Africa and Europe. We would go everywhere and see everything." She said it decisively and quickly. Too quickly. College wouldn't get her far enough away from them. She wanted to leave the country, the continent, go to a place where there were no words for family or brother. He felt a hole open up in his stomach, a strange pit into which he could feel his energy slowly sliding, his last lick of breath contrasting into that sullen space.

"What about you?" Grace kicked his grimy Chuck Taylor with her own. "What would you do with all that money?"

He shrugged. His eyes caught on a bowl of blackening bananas in the center of the table. A couple of tiny flies hovered over the fruit. No one else seemed to notice.

He was about to answer when suddenly his mom perked up. The Big Spin was starting. They turned their heads, transfixed by the little white balls popping around inside a huge tumbler, the cheesy emcee grinning from ear to ear like an elf on dope, telling them the odds of winning, never breaking his smile. Six million to one, he said, and as Henry watched his mother, father, and sister, each secretly cheering for the impossible, for their own individual getaway schemes, he thought that those odds weren't just about winning a hundred million dollars but were the chances they'd ever be this happy again.

He stood up and walked past Tweety, their unoriginally named pet parakeet's cage. It was the only pet they had ever had, and it took a full-scale pity assault to get their parents to cave in and buy it for them. It was never about agreeing. Always a capitulation. The thing must have been ten years old by now. Molted feathers gathered in dusty clumps at the bottom of the cage. Above it hung a little container of yellowing water. Next to it, some birdseed that looked to be covered in bird shit. He decided that he was going to change the paper in the cage, refill the water, get some new food for the bird. He was as much to blame as the rest of them, and suddenly, the thought of this neglected bird made his eyes start to well up with tears. He opened the cage and grabbed the disintegrating newspaper that covered the bottom. The bird watched him from its perch, it's little black eyes unmoving, it's body shaking, steadily. It was the only way he could tell for sure that it was actually alive. He threw the paper away and spilled out the old water in the sink, rubbed the container with a sponge, and then refilled it with fresh water. As he walked back to the cage a sudden and collective groan went up from the table that startled him, making him spill the water on the floor. Their numbers hadn't come up. It looked like they were doomed to be together, after all.

Henry returned to his room and a little later he heard a knock at the front door and then Peter's booming voice. They were all talking together downstairs, laughing, maybe reminiscing about their near flush experience, explaining to Peter that he was this close to kicking back in first class on a trip around the world. There was more laughter—what was so fucking funny? he wondered—and then the sounds of people coming up the stairs and finally Grace's door closing. He put his ear to the wall, but couldn't make out any sounds, incriminating or otherwise, and then another flurry of laughter.

He lay down on his bed and reached underneath it, groping blindly for something. Finally, his fingers felt the cover of the giant old book and he slid it out and dropped it on the bed. It was the old copy of *Jane's Infantry Weapons* that he'd liberated from the library several years before. He felt guilty about stealing the book back then, but when he looked at the front of it and saw that he was the only one who checked it out in the previous ten years or so before that, he rationalized that it would be better off with him, that he would use it more than anyone else. Maybe he was the only one who ever appreciated it. He had planned to steal the rest of them, as well; naval weapons, aircraft, but he had lost his nerve after taking the first one.

He blew a thin membrane of dust off the cover and opened up to a random page and started reading. It was a section on the M16: its development, technical specs, the history of its introduction and adoption by American troops just in time for the Vietnam War. He knew these things by heart. They were his bedtime stories, his fairy tales, and before he knew what hit him, he fell asleep with his head in the book, like a child curled up with his favorite blanket.

*   *   *

Some time later he awoke with a start. Someone had turned off the lights in his room and for a moment he had no idea where he was. His face stung and he rubbed his cheek where he felt an imprint. Then he remembered that he had fallen asleep on the book, in his own bed, in his own house. He had no idea what time it was and swung around to look at the clock by his bedside. It was only a little after ten, which meant that he had been asleep for just over an hour. It felt like much longer. He switched on a light and peeled off his tee shirt, jeans and socks. Standing in front of the mirror he looked at himself and chuckled. He was tall and skinny, the first tufts of chest hair were beginning to sprout in haphazard patches in the center of his chest. A small tuft of hair grew around his belly button, leading down past the elastic band of his pale blue boxers to his dick and balls, where it flourished with even greater carelessness. The whole thing was a mess. Puberty wasn't a change; it was a slow-moving cataclysm.

It was much earlier than his normal bedtime, but he was exhausted. He walked down the hall to the bathroom that he and Grace shared and hurriedly brushed his teeth and washed his face. Their bathroom was right next to the door to their parents' room and as he started to make his way back to his own room he heard his father and mother talking in low voices. He couldn't remember the last time he had seen them together in their room, sitting on the bed, talking without the TV on or without his mother on the phone. Normally his father stayed downstairs on the couch with the TV on a predictable loop of local news and then sports. Upstairs, his mother lay on the bed with a Danielle Steel novel propped open on her lap and the TV tuned to whatever domestic disaster the networks had decided to re-create as a movie of the week. These weren't routines to Henry as much as they were facts of life, and to see them like this, spying on them through the crack in their door, huddled together and touching, laughing and looking at one another while they talked, was blowing his fucking mind.

He was about to turn away and go back to sleep, chalk the whole night up to a strange alignment of the planets, or a slow gas leak that would soon turn them all into homicidal maniacs, when he heard his father say his name.

"Henry, Henry, Henry. I'd say he was gay, but all that gun stuff doesn't seem like something a gay kid would be into."

"He's not gay," his mother said, laughing. And then alarmed sounding, "Is he?"

"I don't know. I've never seen a girl around here and I've never heard him talk about any either. You'd think he would have come to me for advice or something if he was interested, but nothing."

"Oh, Paul," his mother teased. "What a ladies' man."

"I'm serious. Isn't a boy supposed to ask his dad about stuff like that? Isn't that what's fun about a father-son relationship. That's what I always dreamed it would be like."

"Maybe he hasn't gotten to that point yet," his mom ventured. "He's always been shy, Paul. He's just slow to develop."

"All that military stuff wasn't slow to develop. I'm telling you, Joan. When I walked in there to check on him, he was face first in a giant book that had pictures of guns all over it. That's weird," his father turned to face her. "Right? No *Playboy* or *Penthouse* to be seen. Guns."

They laughed together and his mother put her fingers to her lips to hush him, "Shh. We don't want him waking up." She reached up and stroked her fingers through his hair. "Okay, maybe he's a little weird."

"A little?" his dad said, pressing himself up with his arms. He leaned over her and their faces came together.

It was the first time Henry could ever remember his parents kissing one another on the lips.

Blood boiling, he made his way back to his room, careful not to make a sound. He could hear it in his ears, his blood, seething and pulsing, his body wasn't big enough to hold this much anger. He felt the physical heat of too much rage, of narrow options, his vision was a mess of blurry shapes squeezed behind the veins of his eyes. He couldn't calm himself down. As much as he tried, it wouldn't subside. He stalked around his room looking for something to break. Catching sight of himself in front of the mirror again he didn't recognize now what he saw. White dots of saliva flew off his lips as he struggled to control his breath and he imagined himself a lit fuse, burning its way down from the top of his head and out to the ends of his fingers and toes.

Time froze as he looked around for something to destroy. He

was a bomb. A missile. He was an accident gleaned through the shrinking aperture of faith. He closed the big *Jane's* book and without a conscious thought slammed it against his head. The blow staggered him and when he regained his footing he did it again and again. Two, three more times. A thread of blood tickled his nose as it slid down his face and smeared across the front and spine of the book, where the tome's Dewey Decimal number was clinically laminated. In front of the mirror again he saw a gash had opened up on his forehead and both of his eyes were swelling up, well on their way to become full-fledged shiners. It was amazing to see it, because he could barely feel a thing. In fact, if anything, he felt better now than he had a few minutes ago. He was able to breathe now and feel his skin, his senses coming back in overwhelming waves, and he suddenly felt dizzy and exhausted. He went to sit on the edge of the bed but misjudged the distance and fell to the floor with a resounding thud. Laughing, he dragged his fingers through his blood-matted hair and the ridiculous thought occurred to him that if it wasn't before, the book was his now for sure. This was how you claimed ownership.

Sensing someone else was in the room he looked up and saw Grace standing in the door, her mouth agape, eyes staring at him in utter disbelief.

"It's okay," he tried to tell her. "I've never felt better in my life." But he couldn't get the words together and out of his mouth.

She backed away from the door and raised her hands to her forehead and then to her eyes. Tears began to rush down her face, and he realized that she was unconsciously imitating his hands as they traced the geography of his own face, feeling his eyes swelling and his forehead spilling out a steady stream of warm sticky blood. They were playing Simon Says except he hadn't said, "Simon says touch your broken orbital socket.

Simon says wipe the blood away so you can see except it feels kind of good spilling down in a tickling sort of way, like someone running their fingernails lightly over your back." The thought of it made him smile and he was about to ask her if she remembered how, when they were kids, he would give her an Indian burn and she would chase him around the house demanding that he twist it back the other way, that he "put it back," and how weird that was she wanted him to hurt her again, but that now he understood it. Now it made sense. But before he could get the words out, Peter appeared at the door. He was wearing a stupid Quiksilver T-shirt and his shorts were unbuttoned. Who knew what they'd been up to. The thought made Henry queasy, and it gave some shape to his rage, a handhold he sorely needed because he was losing his grip on what he should be feeling.

Henry stood up slowly and before Peter could ask whatever stupid thing he was going to ask Henry launched himself at him, knocking Peter to the ground and falling on top of him in a furious twist of tan flesh and pasty limbs. Somewhere in the distance Grace began to scream, but it didn't stop Henry from digging his fingers into whatever flesh he could find as though he would tumble off the edge of a cliff if he didn't hold on.

In a fight, time slowed down to almost nothing. He knew where he was and he had a sense of what he was doing, the exertion involved, the bells of panic tolling from the next town over, but to him it was, for once, perfect clarity. Some of the things he thought about as he flailed wildly at Peter, as he pushed himself closer and closer against his sister's boyfriend, as though the only way he could win this fight would be to take him over completely, cells conquering cells, the will failing, pouring gas on what has burned so far, included:

Music would be great right now. Music was made for moments

like this. Adolescents. The blue album. That would do the trick. If there was makeout music, didn't it stand to reason that there would be music to punch by? Concept albums by which to divide and conquer?

He continued to flail away even as he felt his father's arms close around him, lifting him off, gritting his teeth next to his ear, whispering to him, "That's enough. That's enough, Henry," like he was trying to break a wild horse. Henry couldn't stop screaming, though, as much as he tried. Even when he tried to answer his father, he couldn't make the words come out right. He was speaking in tongues, he was the Holy Spirit with a haymaker.

"You fucking freak!" Peter screamed as he got to his feet. He took a general inventory of his injuries and realized that most of the blood on him was Henry's. It was on his face, his shirt, dabbed ceremoniously on his face so that it looked like a terrifying rite of passage might have just taken place, something that might propel them into adulthood if it wasn't so tragic, if Henry could stop sobbing long enough to thump his chest.

Peter left soon afterwards. He didn't want anyone to help him clean up, and he pushed Grace's hand away when she tried to dab his face with a washcloth. As he left the house, he was bombarded with apologies from their parents begging him to stay, to forgive Henry, to try and understand that he was going through a hard time. They were all excuses, but they happened to be true.

Later, after Grace disappeared into her room, Henry allowed himself to be led by his mother into the bathroom where the first sting of antiseptic on his forehead made him bawl uncontrollably. She cleaned his injuries without a word and afterwards led him back to his bed where she tucked him in and kissed him on the top of the head like she used to do when he was little, and left without saying a word, turning the light off as she noiselessly slipped out the door. Within seconds, Henry fell into the deep folds of teenage sleep; sleep so deep not even dreams could reach him.

CIRCA

Chapter 9

H E HAD BEEN living with Truman since the night of the assault on his apartment, and in the couple of weeks that had passed since moving in the condo had begun to fill up with a wide assortment of conspiracy freaks, para- noid delusionals, and fringe believers Truman had reached out to in an effort to populate his place with "whites who knew what it took" to get the job done.

"I left it vague on purpose,"Truman told Henry about the ad he put on Craigslist. "It didn't really fit in the roommates or real estate section. It was kind of in that grey area between 'men seeking men' and 'Civil War re-enactors on mescaline.' And then before I knew it, the thing went viral, man. It's a good thing."

Viral was an understatement. The ad had gone for a ride on the underground railroad of freaks and had even wound up as a classified in a small newspaper outside of Montreal, where a rather stringent Québécois separatist name François had seen it and moved south to organize and gain "le perspective."

There were California Separatists, Freegans, a Jew who jumped every time he heard a car horn honk for fear that it was the Rapture. They were scattered throughout the condo, taking up space in the living room, the kitchen…one of the Freegans had even laid down a futon in the bathtub. It was a flophouse for fanatics, but the surprising thing to Henry was how quiet the place was. Those who had comrades tended to stick together in close huddles, whispering to one another in hushed tones about what they already knew, incestuous enclaves of schemers that made codependency seem like a game for infants. Those who didn't have friends tended to keep to themselves.

These folks, the fringe fanatics, untouchables in the caste system of crazies, were so used to being told to "shut up" and "go away" that they tended to keep their ideas to themselves, letting their paranoia grow and eventually manifest in more physical ways. Their eyes spoke of loquacious needs, the white parts yellowing with frustration. There was a lot of hand washing in the condo. Stuttering and body tics were common as well. Henry was sure it wouldn't last, though, the perfect silence, and he dreaded the time when the nuts would all start cycling together, the paranoid hormones becoming perfectly in sync with one another, unleashing a cacophonous tidal wave of OCD that would sink the city, leaving it a submerged legend.

He knocked on Truman's door, and without waiting for an answer, went in. Truman was sitting on the edge of his bed engrossed with his phone and looked up only briefly enough to register that it was Henry coming in and not some sort of survivalist home invasion. He wore his Whole Foods Security T-shirt, which meant that he was either just back from or about to leave for his job standing watch over the bulk food bins in the Brentwood grocery store. Henry took a seat on a folding chair and waited for Truman to greet him.

"That Freegan is going to have to let people bathe in there one of these days. This place is starting to stink to high heaven," Henry said, looking for a way to engage.

"You think?" Truman responded, still hell bent on whatever

it was he was doing.

"When'd you get an iPhone?" Henry asked him. He was a bit suspicious of the combination of craziness and technology. The only thing people like Truman should be early adopters of was experimental medication.

"They gave them to all of the security guards at the store. So we can keep in touch. The problem with this thing, though," he said, finally looking up at Henry, "is that it keeps auto-correcting my spelling. I'm trying to program this thing so it doesn't correct me when I need to tell the other guards that there's some cocksucker…not corksucker…with his hands buried in the ancient grains. That just makes me look stupid."

"You seem stressed," Henry said, leaning back on the plastic chair.

Truman put the phone down. "Of course I'm stressed, dude. I've got a new career to deal with, not to mention some serious mission creep in the condo."

"What do you mean?"

"I didn't want to tell you this," Truman said, looking around, "but I found a jizzed-on copy of *Dianetics* in the bathroom this morning. Near the Freegan's zone. This thing is becoming too many things to too many people. I've gotta get it back on track. There's a real estate assessor coming over in a bit to evaluate the price of this place. I need to focus on that."

"Focus? How?"

"Hello, Henry!" he knocked his fist mockingly against his skull. "What do you think I'm doing here? I gotta get these guys focused on hating the Latinos one floor up. I can't let the assessor see all this Freegan survivalist bullshit. I've looked into this stuff and there's nothing like good old-fashioned race hatred to kill property values in a neighborhood. We need to focus on the fundamentals."

Henry reached back for his drink only to find that he hadn't been drinking. He could have sworn he had been halfway into a shot of Maker's. "Race hatred's a fundamental?"

"Yeah," Truman said, angrily, showing his true Luddite colors. He bent back over his phone for a few seconds and then threw the thing impatiently on the floor. "Fuck! How do I get the emoticon with the ball gag in its mouth? Is that eight-semicolon-hyphen?"

"I don't know," Henry answered, a little bit in awe of Truman's laser-like focus. "I'm not so good with computers and stuff."

"Yeah, yeah," Truman waved a hand at him and then picked up the phone. "By the way, I need to ask you to do me a favor."

"What is it?" Henry said, taking out his laptop. Their apartment didn't have wi-fi and there were no networks around that weren't password protected. He clicked on a random one called PussyPower and tried to guess at a password.

"I need you to go talk to Alberto and tell him about the assessor coming over. Tell him that he needs to be ready for him when he gets here."

"I'm not going up there," Henry said as he punched in the word 'twatstrength.' It didn't work.

"Why not?"

"It's dangerous up there. The last time I was up there, I had the distinct impression that I wasn't wanted."

"I need you to do this, Henry. Please. You're the only white guy left he'll listen to. He's been weird and nasty to me lately. He sent me a prostate-shaped piñata for my birthday last week that was filled with urine. He's taking jabs at my age, and he's trying to infect me with Brown Pride piss. He's out for blood."

"Urine is sterile," Henry said, finally succeeding in logging on using the password 'rawtuna,' more intuition than lucky shot in the dark. "I noticed he was getting to be a little Che-like, too, the last time I went up there. But this is all your fault, remember? Your mess."

"Don't talk to me like I'm the CIA, dude," Truman stood up and walked over to where Henry was sitting and leaned over him. He was clearly approaching panic mode. "Let me ask you something, man. What's your relationship like with your parents?"

Henry flinched. It was the first time anyone had asked him anything about his past in a long time. The question made him sit up, rigid, in his chair.

"It's complicated," he said, suspiciously.

"Oh. Are you one of these people who gets all weird when someone brings up their families?"

"No," Henry said. He could feel his shoulder muscles gathering in rough knots by his neck, tension suddenly torching his mood.

"Besides, isn't 'it's complicated' usually code for, 'we're fucking, but not talking about it?'"

Henry relaxed a little and rubbed his eyes with his hand.

"Right. That's what that means. My relationship with my parents is that we haven't talked in a long time."

"Okay," Truman said, clapping his hands together as if he just proved the existence of god.

"What about you?" Henry asked him, sincerely wanting to know. "Do you talk to your folks?"

"Eh," Truman said, "once in a while. Every month, month and a half or so. I like to call them up after I've seen a really fucked-up movie and recommend it to them. Just to shake them up a little bit. I think they go because they want to show me that they care about my opinion and can be interested in the same things I'm interested in. I suggested *Hostel* a few months ago, and I think it really freaked my mom out. She hasn't really been the same since."

"Where do they live?"

"I grew up in Vegas, but they moved to Salt Lake a couple of years ago. It's like a dry run for retirement," Truman replied. "My dad was a doctor. He practiced there for about thirty-five years."

Henry chuckled. "I didn't know they had doctors in Vegas. I always imagined that when people got sick they just got thrown away."

"Funny. Anyway," Truman went on, "my point is, I have a rule with my parents when it comes to catching up."

"I can't wait to hear this," Henry said.

"I never give them more information about my life than I would to someone I've met two times. I call it the two-time rule. But now," he went on, standing up straight and smoothing down his curly hair, "I'm like the parent. To all these people out here. I convinced them to come out here, and now I've gotta make sure we can stay. They're depending on me."

"You're telling me you're going to let all these nuts stay here after you've bought the place?"

In the other room a smoke alarm began to sound, a steady beeping that was barely urgent.

"Fuck," Truman said. He got on his hands and knees and began to root around under his bed. In a few seconds he stood up holding a golf club. "I thought I'd gotten rid of all those fuckers a while back." He began to leave but stopped in the doorway and turned around. "Please, Henry. Please go talk to Alberto for me. Will you?"

"You didn't answer my question," Henry said, leaning back in the chair again, his feet dangling in front of him. He looked like an ancient way to tell time. "Are you going to let them stay?"

Truman turned around and raised an eyebrow. "Are you fucking serious?" He left the room and in a few second Henry heard the sharp whack of the smoke detector being demolished. It sounded like victory.

*   *   *

It wasn't fear that made him not want to go up to Alberto's floor and talk to him about the real estate appraiser. It was more his instinct to not get more involved in a situation that had very little to do with him in the first place. Instinct told him to be a bystander, a wallflower, but when he finally gave in, as he so often did, it wasn't his instincts failing him, because instincts never truly disappeared. They did, however, digress from time to time, wavering between survival and relenting, one as natural as the other. That's what the last few weeks had been. A digression.

He took the stairs down one floor and in the stairwell saw that someone had spray painted the words BROWN PRIDE in huge letters across the wall.

The door to Alberto's floor opened onto a cluttered hallway that reminded Henry of pictures he had seen of plundered museums in Iraq after the US invasion. Random propaganda supporting everything from the United Farm Workers (¡Uvas No!) to Cheech and Chong concert posters lay strewn around or were haphazardly tacked to the walls, ceiling, and doors of the condos that lined the hall. Someone had begun a Día de los Muertos mural against the far wall and it took him a moment to notice that it was a sketch of Alberto's head on a svelte skeletal body that was the central element of the piece. Given time, they would build the pyramids in here. Who he supposed were the muralists took a break beneath a makeshift canopy made of Guatemalan blankets and as his eyes adjusted to the darkness, he could tell that they were huddled around a small fire. Eventually someone noticed him, and the blanket flap was lifted and a squat, sturdy thirty-something Latino walked the length of the hall to meet him. He wore a pair of beige Dockers that had been raggedly cut off at the knees and what looked like a button-up shirt from the Gap that was half tucked in to his pants, top button undone. A cheap woven leather belt cinched him at the waist. He was mid-management all the way. This was clearly a vacation for him from whatever sad reality couldn't compete with being present for the immaculate conception of a banana republic. For all Henry knew, this guy worked at the ubiquitous tech company one floor up from the newspaper in a cubicle no bigger than his own.

He stared hard at Henry and asked, "¿Qué pasa?"

As he always did in the face of confrontation, Henry automatically averted his eyes as he responded. "Is Alberto here?" The guy's smart phone holster hung empty at his waist. A definite oversight in the authenticity department. Henry thought about pointing it out to him but was a little bit petrified to break the fourth wall.

"¿Cómo te llamas?" he asked. His Spanish accent was thick. Too thick. It had to be a put-on.

"Just tell him it's Henry, and that I come in peace." Henry grinned, trying to make the guy understand that he meant no harm and that he was in on the joke, but a dirty scowl told him that it wasn't appreciated. Henry put his hand to his face and felt the rough whiskers of a beard just coming in. He thought that perhaps he would let it grow out. At this point, what could it hurt?

The guard walked back to the makeshift teepee or whatever it was and lifted back the flap to duck his head inside. In the few seconds that Henry could see inside he thought he saw a gun lying there, a revolver on the floor next to one of the men. This was getting out of hand.

After a minute or two the guard came back, this time holding a large sombrero, the kind of oversized, wide-brimmed hat that Speedy Gonzales used to wear in the old *Looney Toons* cartoons.

He thrust the hat at Henry. "Put this on," he said. Henry took the hat and looked back at the guy, searching for confirmation of his humiliation. "I'm serious, gringo. If you wanna come in here and talk to Alberto, you better put this thing on your fucking cabeza." Now when he spoke Henry noticed a distinctly suburban white-bred drawl, a sharp suburban twang, which did nothing to soften the malice in his voice.

Henry shoved the ridiculous hat on his head and allowed himself to be led down the crowded hallway which was really nothing more than a crooked timeline of their history, a history to which they had no real connection but this ridiculous posturing, this outpouring of overwrought dedication that, if left unchecked, could one day metastasize and become real fanaticism. He understood why they did it, though. Or at least he thought he did. It was the same reason he still kept those old stolen copies of the *Jane's* books under the bathroom sink in his apartment, the dreams of war, memories of lives they wished they had lived. They all sought to be part of something bigger, something that would bring them together with others, bind them in a way that was essential and undeniable. He tried to imagine the lives they had left behind to be part of this ridiculous charade. Stacks of bills and mortgages, all electronically scheduled so that they would never actually have to see the statements and pay the bills. Children lost to the toxic glow of video games screens. Wives who were once as adventurous as they were given over completely to the conveniarchy of online shopping and text message gossip.

The guard slowed his pace, allowing Henry to catch up, and when they were walking side by side he addressed Henry on the sly out of the corner of his mouth in his best water cooler gossip whisper.

"Some of the guys are saying that they have a lot of guns upstairs. That they're really crazy." The guard's sleep-deprived eyes darted around to make sure that no one saw him cavorting with the enemy. "Are they fucking nuts, man? Do they really want to kill us? I have a wife and kid. The kid's at paparazzi camp for the summer and my wife is visiting her folks in Denver. One of my paintball buddies convinced me to take some vacation time and hang out. Get in touch with my roots." He looked around again and then widened his eyes. "Dude, I'm not even from LA. I grew up in Atlanta."

It was then that Henry understood what he had felt all along but could not name; these weren't the bridge and tunnel Cossacks with translucent scores to settle that he had once thought they were. In the brief amount of time he had spent in Alberto's place, there was a clear difference in the character of the recruits he had assembled versus the ones living with Truman. Whereas Truman had succeeded in creating a safety net for those purged during the great natural selection pogroms of the last several millenia, Alberto's co-conspirators were much more well-adjusted, having only taken leave of their senses for a brief Rumspringa of terror, racial warfare, and ethnic rediscovery that they couldn't get in their daily, humdrum existence. These men were weekend warriors, tourists in the land of violence, armed to the teeth with righteous indignation and now chronically in over their heads.

And for a moment Henry allowed himself to feel the dignity of fellowship, imagining he was just like them, succumbing to the slow paralysis of indoctrination, patient zero infected by a new airborne strain of Stockholm Syndrome. He thought of himself as a victim, a weary messenger caught in the middle of a situation he had no stake in and would wind up on the losing side of the conflict, no matter whose side he found himself on in the end.

But this idea of perpetual innocence was short-lived, because even though he might not have a horse in this race, he had put all his money, so to speak, into a race with the Children of Light and Reverend Potter. Time was running out for him, and he imagined Potter in some over-decorated, post-modern bunker somewhere, launching SEAL teams of loyalist psychotics to get Henry while he luxuriated in a hammock made of virgins, plotting his next indignity from a bucket list Hitler would have been proud to call his own.

The guard stopped a few feet short of a door at the end of the hall where another soldier, an obese sack of guts perched on a stool with folded arms, watched them carefully. He leaned into Henry's ear one more time and Henry felt him slip something into pocket as he spoke.

"This note is for my wife. In case I don't make it. It says I love her and the kid. But do me a favor, okay?" Henry nodded. He was willing to agree to almost anything to get through the overwrought moment.

"Tell them I died for something really important, okay? Don't let them know that it was just this."

Henry nodded again as the guard peeled off to walk slowly back to the front lines. He felt something like pity for the man, but not quite. The fat sentry pushed the door to Alberto's room open without a word and nodded to Henry that he should go in.

Instead of the combat bunker he had expected to find, Alberto's condo looked a lot like what he suspected a college freshman's dorm room might look like. Posters of naked and half naked women bent over the hoods of expensive sports cars provided much of the decoration, accented with empty cans of diet soda and pizza boxes strewn around haphazardly as though they were supplies that had washed up on the shore of a deserted island and pillaged by the desperate survivors. A cheap curtain of beads separating the entrance from the living room rustled slightly, touched by an invisible breeze that had followed Henry in. He pushed the beads apart and saw Alberto sitting on the other side of the room in a giant black leather recliner mashing the buttons of a joystick as he played some kind of war video game on a gigantic flat screen TV. He wasn't sure if Alberto had heard him come in or not, but as he got closer, realized that he had on a set of heavy-duty DJ headphones and was muttering gutterally into a small microphone that protruded a few inches in front of his mouth.

"Fuck you! No, fuck you, you little shit. I'm gonna take a shit in my hand and stab your mother with it." There was a pause. "Good. I'm glad she has breast cancer, you fucking cheating fourteen-year-old bastard."

Henry realized that he was talking to someone in the game and tapped him on the shoulder. Alberto snatched the headphones off his head and craned his neck around to see who was behind him.

"Oh. Hey, Henry. I'm playing *Call of Duty* with some little fuck from Texas. Wanna jump in for a round?"

Henry shook his head no.

"Can I talk to you for a second, man?"

"Sure," Alberto answered, as cheerfully as ever.

"Consider yourself lucky, you little piece of shit. My homey's here and I've gotta bolt. You gonna be on later tonight?" There was a pause as Alberto listened to the answer. "Sweet. I'll check you later, dude."

He tossed the controller onto the floor and then used the toe of his shoe to switch off the Xbox. He raised a chubby arm to Henry.

"Help me up, man. My leg's asleep."

Henry grabbed his wrist and pulled as hard as he could.

"Come on, Henry. Harder. You're not gonna break me," Alberto chided him, using his own girth to goad him on. Henry wondered if the monolith on the stool outside the door had heard that and what he might be thinking right now.

When Alberto was finally standing, he waddled into the kitchen, ritualistically rubbing and punching his legs to get the circulation to return. He pulled a red beret down onto his head and checked to see that the buttons on his bilious white shirt were all fastened and that he wasn't obscenely sticking out somewhere. Henry didn't know where he had managed to find a shirt that was actually too big for him, but this one was, giving him the appearance, if you saw him from some ways in the distance, that he might be the tent in some fantastic desert oasis, a mirage from which you could quench your thirst with Diet Mountain Dew and enough pizza to derail a train.

"I need to talk to you. Well," Henry corrected himself, "Truman asked me to come talk to you. It's about the property assessor. He just wants to make sure you're ready."

Alberto nodded and helped himself to a bong on the kitchen counter, sucking down a huge draft of smoke, holding it for a few seconds, and then expelling it with a fit of coughing directly into Henry's face like a steam ship chugging through cold seas.

Henry fanned away the smoke, coughing.

"Sorry," Alberto said. He held the bong out to Henry and asked graciously, "Want a hit?"

"No, thanks," Henry fanned away the smoke. "Did you hear what I said, though, about the assessor? Truman wanted to make sure that you guys were ready."

"Don't we look ready?" Alberto asked, as he rummaged around the counter for something, finally laying his fingers on another enormous nugget of weed, which he crammed into the bowl of the bong. He lit it and once again sucked deeply as the water in the pipe bubbled ominously like the first rumblings of a gigantic tremor that would soon engulf them in a seismic cataclysm, the first chapter in the book of the end of the world.

Henry nodded. His mind was elsewhere, and he wanted to kick himself for getting roped into a situation that really had nothing to do with him in the first place. It shouldn't be this hard to prove neutrality.

"The sweat lodge in the hallway is a great touch. You've really done a bang-up job here."

"Oh, you saw that? Good. I wanted to be sure we were being inclusive of the native people, too, you know, not just Latinos. There's being here first and then there's *being here first*, you know what I mean?"

"Uh-huh," Henry said absentmindedly. His thoughts were on the dead end he had reached in his investigation both of Potter as well as finding Daisy. It was almost impossible to believe that in this day and age where you could track down the first girl who ever gave you the clap in less than five minutes on the internet, that he couldn't find hide nor hair of either of these two people; they had transcended anonymity and deflated the ego of mystique. They were just gone. No more and no less. He walked over to a window that looked out over the street below.

Henry flicked the side of a two-liter Mountain Dew bottle on the window sill, in which a bright red betta fish hung in suspended animation, to see if the thing was alive or dead. It took a couple of taps before the fish suddenly lurched forward and began to swim around again, probably wondering what in the world had roused it from its perfect silence, and after it had circumnavigated its world a couple of times, settled down once again into near perfect stillness, content to have explored what there was left to explore. The perspective made Henry a bit jealous, not just the simplicity of it, but the acceptance of that simplicity. He knew that in his own way he was witnessing something that was not new and impressive, but rather it was the immaculate conception of mediocrity, the realization that the only miracles going forward was that there would be no more miracles.

"What's wrong, man?" Alberto had joined him at the window. He reached his hand toward Henry and Henry flinched back and bumped the Mountain Dew bottle, stopping it from toppling over at just the last second. "Relax," Alberto said, holding his hands out, "I was just going to take that sombrero off your head. Unless, of course, you want to keep it on."

"Oh, thanks." Henry reached up pulled the silly hat off his head and tossed it onto the couch.

They stood silently, side by side, looking out the window as a garbage truck stopped in front of the building and began its loud digestion of the overflowing garbage that spilled out from their dumpsters. The view was a time-lapsed vista of urban blight. The tops of a row of what Henry guessed were once kumquat trees were dusted with a thick layer of dirt, an accumulation of car exhaust and other urban fertilizers that squandered the promise of manifest destiny. A car sat rusting in the shade of the trees, a new Denver boot strapped elegantly to one of its tires looking like the latest in automotive fashion accessories. The view depressed him, and he was beginning to wonder why Alberto and Truman even wanted to live here in the first place. He had wanted to believe it was more than just owning a house for the sake of owning a house, but that would be underestimating Truman's allegiance to his own brand of intellectualism, a school of thought that relied more on knee-jerk emotional reactions than the Socratic method.

"How's it going with the story? Any luck finding Potter?"

"Nope," Henry stared at the trees. Maybe not kumquats. Maybe they were lemon trees.

"How about the girl?"

"No. Not her, either."

"Sorry, man. I know how bad you want this."

He turned and looked at Alberto.

"Thanks. I appreciate that."

"Sure," Alberto said, patting Henry roughly on the shoulder. "Empathy can be a real battery recharger. I know how it is."

Henry nodded. It was nice to know there was someone out there who could at least pretend to know what he was feeling.

"Speaking of empathy," Henry said, as he walked away from the window back toward the kitchen, "I wasn't going to say anything, but I am a little worried about this whole situation."

"In what way?" Alberto asked, following him.

"I'm a little worried that this whole thing has gotten a little carried away."

"Nah," Alberto said, laughing. "That's sweet of you, but it's cool. Me and Truman know what we're doing."

"I don't know, man," Henry looked for a clean glass in the cabinets and finding none grabbed a dirty one and took it to the sink. He turned the tap, but no water came out. He put the glass down and turned around. "Some of those guys Truman's got on his floor are a little wacko. Also, I think I saw a gun on one of your guys in the sweat lodge just now. You just don't want to push people into a desperate situation, is what I'm saying. Getting an apartment at a cheap price is one thing...This, though," he looked around the condo trying to find something he could point to that would be particularly illustrative of his point, but finding nothing close by, picked up the bong, "this is something else."

Alberto smiled. "That's a bong, Henry. It's not a dirty bomb."

"I know," he said, putting the bong back down on the counter. "I just couldn't find anything else to grab."

Alberto opened up a cabinet and pulled out a paper cup from a large cache of paper goods. He filled it with Mountain Dew and handed it to Henry.

"I appreciate your concern. Really, I do. And I know Truman does, too, even though I haven't talked to him in a couple of weeks. But everything here is going to be fine. This is what we want. This was Truman's vision from the beginning. You didn't think it was just about the condo, did you?"

Henry shook his head and took a sip of the Mountain Dew. He knew that this whole scheme wasn't just about finding a cheap place to live. It was more intellectual than that. More philosophical. The warm sugary soda tasted like a school of small fish swimming through his mouth. He grimaced, swallowed, and put the cup down on the kitchen counter.

"Do me favor when you go back down, will you, Henry?"

"What's that?"

"Tell him that you're really worried about me. Tell him I look crazy, like you're really concerned I'm going off the deep end. Maybe throw in a Colonel Kurtz reference or two. He'll love it."

"Are you sure?" Henry asked worriedly. He didn't want to be responsible for making things worse than they already were.

Alberto laughed a deep phlegmy chuckle.

"I'm sure. He might not seem like he's appreciative, but trust me, it'll be the nicest thing you've ever done for the guy."

*   *   *

Before heading off to the ex-cultists support group meeting, he stopped downstairs to tell Truman about his meeting with Alberto. True to his word, he embellished the situation, told Truman that Alberto was beginning to remind him of one of those creepy dictators that have weird child-like compulsions. "It's just a matter of time before he's paying Lionel Richie to come entertain him and the troops, something to make him feel whole again, because 'Hello' was the first song he ever electrocuted someone's nuts to."

Truman nodded knowingly, and then whispered, "Awesome."

He's in perfect awe of himself, Henry though as he scooted away, getting himself ready to track down Alan Downes, the former Children of Light member Oscar told him to go see. The address where the ex-cultists recovery group met led him to a row of churches on a desolate street in Hollywood he had never been on before, hidden back in an industrial corner of town near a cement factory and a handful of warehouses that rented out film equipment. The irony wasn't lost on Henry that this was what had become of an area of churches in Hollywood, that there had been a sort of white flight of morality leaving the holy places to suffer the ignominy of urban blight. Or maybe this was the perfect place for them, dilapidation always being a friend of holy places, giving them street cred, a sense of suffering appreciated and expected by those who pretended to the austerity of moral authority.

But this wasn't the romantic dilapidation usually associated with churches: there were no Gothic accoutrements, spires feeding upwards piercing the chilly air, nor were there the de rigueur windows brocaded with lacy shadows of dusk's perpetual doom-giving pallor. This was authentic dilapidation. The kind repudiated by local politicians in election-year stump speeches to which they swore to return areas like this to their former glory, only to be quickly whisked away by minions to the next stop on the campaign trail, the short-term memory loss of campaign promises just an annoying buzz in the public's collective ear. And as they fanned their ears, they tried to recall just what had been here before it was an empty lot. Was it a shoe store? A check cashing place? Could it be that it had always been vacant? Some sort of natural preserve that had escaped development and had remained a safe place to shoot up, to turn a trick for whatever you've got in your pocket. Some other eyesore, probably. Their eyesore. But whatever it was, it had to have been better than this, right? Wasn't everything once better than it was now? Wasn't that the secret con of speculation? That it was the past that was for sale, real or imagined, and not the future at all. Not the future one little bit.

Several people hung around the front door smoking cigarettes or spitting casually onto the sidewalk. No one spoke. Theoretically, they were all here for the same sort of reason, for the promise of rehabilitation, fresh starts and guilt-free finishes. In the distance the sun was treading water in the west, leaking a migraine orange hue across the sky, soaking the city in earth tones knitted from a sky of smog. Soon it would be night, and these folks would be no more difficult to see then they were now. Less than shadows, they were the malcontents whose wispy energy powered the city, the spare change of humanity.

As he was deciding whether to go in or not, a stubby dude dressed in mechanics overalls and a Nike swoosh baseball hat pitched his cigarette to the ground and stomped it out with a decisive grind of the boot. He made eye contact with Henry and immediately walked over to him.

"Hey man. Got a cigarette?" he asked, pronouncing the 'c' in cigarette through a wind tunnel of a lisp.

"No," Henry said, looking away a moment too late, forgetting that eye contact to those that were even slightly off-kilter was like honey to a bear. "I don't smoke."

"How about gum?" the guy asked, hocking up a lungful of snot and spitting it expertly a few feet away from them on the sidewalk. "You chew gum?"

"Yeah. I chew gum."

"Well," the guy waited, "do you have any?"

Henry shook his head. "Nope."

"Mints?"

"Nope."

"A plug of tobacco?"

"Uh-uh."

"Cup of coffee?"

Just as Henry was about to ask what about him reminded the guy of a vending machine, the guy sneered disgustedly at him, turned away and walked back to the exact spot on the sidewalk where he had been when Henry first showed up.

He fished around in his pockets and pulled out a cigarette, which he lit without once looking back at Henry.

The interaction was just mystifying and aggravating enough to Henry that he pulled the heavy wooden door to the church open and walked inside, resisting the impulse to scream out "Sanctuary!" "From what?" a priest might ask him and that's when Henry would break down. "From the Santa Anas, Father, and from the smog. From texting and traffic and *pico de gallo* and street food. From bumping bass and daylight savings and summer hours and casual Fridays. 'From what?' is not the question," he would be shouting by then, his voice a flock of pigeons rising up from a bustling piazza full of tourists, "The question is 'What's worth saving?'"

But of course there was no priest there to greet him, no emissary from the lord of any kind. There was just a wall of fliers advertising an enormous range of support groups, meet-ups, and singles events. It was the physical personification of Craig's List, this holy place, and as he read about Dungeons and Dragons groups in need of clerics and missed connections at a local marijuana dispensary, it dawned on him that there were no more sacred spaces, because there was no more need for them. Man had reached its full potential as far as self-sufficiency went. God had been downsized, the job of passive observer of the cosmos shipped off to India. Profits had been maximized. The shareholders were finally pleased as punch.

He walked through the church looking for Alan Downes and his group. Each door had a sign taped to the front announcing the meeting that was currently going on inside, but he didn't need to read those, because the doors also had little windows built into them and at the third door along the main hallway he peeked into one of the classrooms and knew at once that this had to be Downes and his coven of glassy-eyed wallflowers.

A stained-glass window spilled its colorful guts across the floor of the room. On a chalkboard at the front of the room he saw evidence of a free association session gone terribly awry. A trail of mismatched words had taken the group from 'Mother' to 'Pediatric Gynecology' and back to 'Mother' again with a violent crossing out of what came next. About a dozen men were seated in a semicircle facing the board, all of them focusing intently on a man he assumed was Downes but also simultaneously twitching, coughing, picking fingernails—a convening of subconscious nervous energy so enormous it would make the Large Hadron Collider blush with envy.

He couldn't hear what was being said, but it was obvious from Downes' posture and his red face that he was in the middle of either an epiphany or a mini-stroke, bringing these natives fire for the first time. Downes, who was otherwise plain-looking, had sandy-brown hair which dropped straight down off his head in a bowl cut and a nose, forehead, and cheeks that looked recently sun-burned, his skin beginning to flake in a way that looked healthy and not overtly transformative.

The semicircle of rapturous, dilapidated faces slouched toward him at an incremental rate; they were planets being drawn into the orbit of something bigger than themselves, some truth that would alter their telemetry, and Henry wondered if this wasn't a common occurrence at these meetings given their shared reason for being here. Because unlike him, who could never give all of himself to anyone or anything, these men had all, at one time or another and with varying degrees of success, given everything of themselves to an idea or a cause Whatever it was, they had once been whole because of it, he realized watching them and their earnest appreciation for whatever version of the truth Downes was spewing whole, in a way that he never was and probably never could be.

Henry cracked the door just a millimeter or so, desperate to hear what was being said. But instead of being allowed to passively observe, the hinge emitted an end of days sounding blast, and all eyes quickly turned to him, their twitching and fumbling coming to an abrupt stop as his presence took them all out of their collective moment.

Downes turned to Henry, waited a moment, allowing the embarrassment of interrupting to fully envelop him, and then asked, "Can we help you with something?" And then, without giving Henry an opportunity to make an excuse for himself, Downes turned back to the group and clapped his bony hands together, "I think that about does it for today. Friends," he intoned earnestly, the oxygen for irony long ago depleted from this barren, caring landscape, "please take a moment to put up the chairs and throw away the trash before we meet for closing words."

As the men got up to do what they had been asked Downes walked slowly over to Henry and extended a hand. "Hello, friend. What can I do to help you today?"

Henry looked at the bony hand, hesitant to touch it, afraid that he might crush it or worse, catch something. He was suddenly overwhelmed by the feeling of being covered in a layer of thick contagious dust, the dust of tombs and stagnation, of forgotten places rediscovered, old diseases let out to fester and flourish once again. Reminding himself that he was here to get information, he pressed his hand against Downes' and shook it, but Downes was loathe to let go, holding on to Henry's palm as he looked deeply into his eyes.

"It's nice to meet you," Henry said, hoping that he had intoned the right spell to be released from the awkward moment.

"Are you Oscar's friend?" Downes asked him, squinting a

little as though trying to make out what was real and what was a mirage. "The reporter?"

"Yeah," Henry said, taking the opportunity to pull his hand away and unsling the brown messenger bag from his shoulder. "My name's Henry Colmes. I write for the *LA Daily Ledger*." He knelt down next to his bag and fished around for his notebook and pen. There wasn't too much in the bag, but he let himself pause there for a moment, pretending he couldn't find it right away, to let himself recover for an extra second or two from the awkward moment. He stood up and flipped open the notebook to a blank page, which meant trying to quickly fan past the doodles that made up the majority of its contents. "I was hoping I could ask you a few questions. If you wouldn't mind."

"Of course not," Downes said, finally breaking his gaze from Henry, "I figured that's what you were here for. Being a reporter."

"Right," Henry replied, glancing down at the empty page, noting that Downes was capable of sarcasm and not just the hollow jolliness of someone who might describe themselves as being 'put on this earth to help others' as he might have guessed at first. "I wanted to ask you a few questions about the Children of Light, and specifically, I wanted to ask you about Reverend Potter. If you still don't mind, of course."

Downes grinned and nodded, "I don't mind at all."

Henry quickly told him about his assignment, the obituary, his need to find Potter. Downes laughed.

"Sorry, friend. I have no idea how to find Reverend Potter. It's been a long time for me—ten years—since I've seen that man. Ten years, fifty churches like this, countless semicircles of men and women in folding chairs. Truth be told," Downes went on, sounding a little more tired now than he had a few seconds ago, "and I probably should have told Oscar this when he asked if you could come by, I haven't had a good answer for anything in many, many years. I appreciate your dilemma, friend, I really do, but I'm sorry, I have no idea where Potter might be now."

"What about these men?" Henry made a motion at the group members who were busying themselves straightening up the room for the next group to come in and make a stab at recovery, forgetting, rationalizing, whatever the case might be. Whatever the solution might call for.

"I don't have answers for these guys," Downes said, shaking his head. "All I can do is offer them advice and tell them my story."

"And then?" Henry asked.

Downes shrugged.

"And then they tell me their stories. They tell their stories to each other. They go home and tell the stories to whatever family and friends they have left. Their stories get perfected in this way, changing incrementally every time, or more than that, sometimes changing massively. Whatever it takes. I'm just here to listen. I'm just here to help them craft their stories."

Henry was disappointed but not surprised. Answers, it seemed, were as elusive as Potter himself, the motives many, and the truth a state of mind. That's what Downes was trying to tell him without getting too metaphysical.

"So what is your story?" Henry asked. He dropped the tip of the pen to his notebook, ready to record whatever clues might be loosened.

"You mean, how did I get involved with the Children of Light? Is that what you mean to ask, friend?"

"Yeah," Henry answered, looking down at the blank page,

embarrassed for the second time in a just a few minutes.

Downes took a moment before beginning. "I was just like you, friend. I was just a normal man. I had a normal life, a girlfriend I was planning on marrying, a job in an office. I had everything I ever wanted. I craved the average life, and I had it. I saw nothing wrong with it. I wanted contentment, so I set my bar to a certain level that some might call low, and I strove to achieve it. And I did. And I was happy."

"And then what?" Henry asked, trying to figure out what was worth writing down. "You woke up one day and realized you needed more?"

Downes laughed.

"That's what everyone thinks. More, more, more. No. That's what was so beautiful about what I had. I wanted no more than that. I was happy. Truly happy, friend," Downes reached up and unbuttoned the collar of his heavy brown flannel shirt. Henry hadn't noticed until then that it had been fastened, hiding Downes' neck away, and when the collar fell open, he saw two long purple scars stitched across the skin, faded like the latitude lines on a child's old globe. If Downes noticed Henry staring, he said nothing about it and went on with his story.

"I did wake up one day, though, as you put it. But not with an unslakable thirst in my mouth, my throat dry for what life had not yet given me. I woke up and wanted to celebrate what I had. Reinforce it somehow if that makes sense. Does it?"

Around them Downes' acolytes were folding up and stacking their chairs in perfect lines. One man pushed a large broom around the floor, conspicuously sweeping every square centimeter. Another man trailed him closely with a dustpan in hand. The two didn't talk. They were singularly focused on their task. Henry wondered if Downes had worked with them to perfect the execution of their chore, if he had gone over it with them again and again until its perfect ordinariness was assured.

Henry waited for Downes to continue, understanding that the question he had asked was a rhetorical one, the way séances are rhetorical exercises.

"So, when I heard about the Children of Light from an old high school friend I ran into, I was intrigued. This was before all of the problems, mind you. This was before everything went bad."

Old high school friend. What a strange expression, Henry thought, as he imagined himself running into Cal now, the two of them having a catch-up conversation that at some point would have to go, "So, what's been happening these last twenty years?" "Well, I joined this cult. Based on what I remember about you from twenty years ago you should totally check it out." "Yeah?" "Totally!" "Okay, I will. By the way, how's your mom?"

"Back then," Downes went on, unemotionally, "and this is what's hard for people to understand, Potter really did believe he was just a gardener. Nothing more and nothing less. He would tell us stories about being in his yard with his mother, kneeling in the rich, musty dirt of Central Illinois, the sun a beating mineral in the sky, transfusing them, the land, those flowers that he almost didn't have the language to describe. That's what he wanted for us. Back then. He said he wanted us to feel what the sun felt like, what the earth smelled and felt like. What it meant to him to be there with his mother, just the two of them, willing life into being with their very contentedness, as if that was the missing ingredient, what thousands of years of horticulturalists and agriculture experts had never discovered."

"Sounds nice," Henry remarked.

Downes, who had been lost for a moment in the revelry of hindsight, suddenly snapped back into focus.

"Nice?" he laughed, and Henry realized his comment had sounded pithy and completely unintelligent. "Yes, friend, it was 'nice' as you say. But it was more than that. For me it was those gardens. Rows and rows of plants, vegetables, flowers, all perfectly spaced out, laid out in something that was more than precision to me. It was the perfection of all the order I had ever wanted, and the difference between the contentment I had and what was still possible to achieve. It showed me that I was miles away from happy. Do you understand?"

Henry nodded that he did.

"So, I left my job, and my girlfriend told me that it was her or the Children. Well, you can imagine how much I appreciated the simplicity of an ultimatum. I lived out there with them right up until the girls died. I didn't know that was going to happen," he turned to look out the window, his voice descending an octave into the musical range of regret.

"You had no idea those girls were going to kill themselves?" Henry asked, taking advantage of Downes' apparent wistfulness.

Downes chuckled. "They didn't kill themselves, friend," his voice was tense, as close to agitated as Henry had heard it so far. "Remember the trial? The conviction? Those girls were murdered. As sure as if Potter had tied twelve nooses and then kicked the chairs away himself. He set the soil in that miserable little room that most of us hadn't even known was there. He tilled it, fed it, mulched it, and when it was ready, when his words had made it the most fertile piece of land on the ranch, he planted a row of flowers, twelve perfect little flowers, that were to be the pride of his garden."

"Twelve?" Henry asked. He pulled out one of the research

notebooks from his bag and scanned his notes. He found the section about the girls and double-checked his notes. "It was ten girls. They pulled ten girls out of that room."

"It was supposed to be twelve. There were twelve nooses, twelve stools. But two of them ran away before…," he lost himself as he searched for the words, "they could be planted."

Henry was confused. "What happened to them? To the ones who didn't end up killing themselves?"

Downes shook his head. "Not killed themselves," he repeated, "were murdered. He murdered those little flower girls just as sure as he kicked them off the stools himself."

"When you say flower girls, do you mean they were literally named for flowers?"

"Uh-huh. It fit them so perfectly, too. Rose and Petunia, cute as buttons those two were, sisters from Sacramento. They did everything together. Wore their hair in pigtails everyday, matching colors. They were Irish Twins, but you could tell they wished they had come out at the same time. That they had been twins. I think that was why they tried to be exactly alike all the time, to somehow revise the accident of their not being identical. All of the girls were like that," he went on. "The only blemish on their innocence was the tattoo they all had. A black circle on the back of their necks. It was supposed to represent the center of a flower, the most important part. He loved little hidden things like that. He thought it was so clever. Like a little boy with a secret."

"Of the two who ran away," Henry asked Downes "was one of the girls named Daisy?"

"No," Downes shook his head. "Iris and Violet. The two who got away. Potter made us dig up all the irises and violets on the ranch. Such a waste of color. We burned them in a pile that same day. All that color and still the smoke was so black."

"What happened to them? What happened to Iris and Violet?"

"Well, they left, friend. The night before the other girls were murdered. They ran away. I heard later that one of them tried to come back, but I'm not sure, I was gone by then."

"Someone told you that?" Henry asked.

"Yes. A friend who left the Children after me."

"Someone in CHoSEN?"

Downes narrowed his eyes. For the first time in the conversation he seemed genuinely mystified by what Henry was asking. "What's that?"

"The Children of Light Survivors Network. I got plugged into them when I started working on this story."

"I've never heard of it," Downes shook his head. "I'd know if there was a group of ex-Children."

"Are you sure?" Henry asked, his mouth going dry as parchment paper.

"Trust me, friend," Downes said, smiling his toothiest grin, the bullshit of it building up and flowing out from his inner being, "it doesn't exist."

Chapter 10

I N THE ABSENCE of any real difference between the seasons (other than the sudden appearance of full winter wetsuits lying to dry in the back seats of the cars in the parking lot where only a week ago there had been the half spring suits), it was left to the individual to tap into his or her own prehistoric instincts to mark the passage of time, to find an inner metronome that could measure the pulse of some greater notion of movement. For Henry it would always be the mustering of landscapers that would remind him of the time of year. It seemed like leaf blowers were in almost constant use around the school between the months of October and February, responsible for the neurotic task of blowing piles of organic debris from place to place, bagging it up, and then returning the next day for more, their machines the whining background music to every facet of childhood between those greyish months. For the rest of his life it would be the sound of landscaping equipment and the smell of freshly cut grass that would clear his mind and leave him thirsty for some new knowledge. White noise would never quite cut it. It needed to have that exhaust smell for his synapses to really kick in.

Henry and Cal were on their hands and knees in the cafeteria, searching through the discarded lunch tickets for one that might be good for the day. The bell that signaled the end of their nutrition period had just rung and their peers had moved along to their third-period classes, knowing that they had seven minutes to get to class before they would be marked tardy. Three tardies and a note went home. Five and it was anybody's guess. Drawn and quartered by the football team. Forced to lick the floor of the boys' locker room clean. The possibilities were endless. School afforded ample solutions to the age-old idle threat of a fate worth than death. There were lots of fates worse than death. All you had to do was look around.

Every day at the end of nutrition there were literally hundreds of lunch tickets left scattered around by kids who were on the free lunch program. But invariably every one of them was dated one day earlier than whatever day it currently was. Henry never did understand where all these tickets came from a day late. Had that many kids really gone without their lunch the previous afternoon? Or, as he sometimes liked to imagine, did the administrators sprinkle these useless little colorful scraps of paper around every night so they could watch idiots like Cal and him crawl around on their hands and knees in the vain hope of finding that golden ticket that would save them a dollar and a half in the cafeteria line that afternoon. Henry raised his head and looked at the administration building hoping to catch the blinds suddenly drop in front of a quickly glimpsed gaggle of laughing faces. But of course there was no one there. No one was watching them. No one really cared.

They each wore a pair of headphones attached to their Walkmans. Henry was listening to Agent Orange, the old South Bay surf punk band. The album was just so-so, but he loved the first song, "Bloodstains," and had been listening to it over and over non-stop for the past few days, rewinding the tape each time he came to the end of the track so he could listen to it again and again—the guitars were gears that ground him up, mulched his bones, his insides, turning his whole self into a vibrating pulp, a ridiculously simple compound that could explode with just the smallest addition of outside influence.

He heard Cal snicker, looked up, and saw him pointing at his sleeve, which he had just let fall into a wayward puddle of hot sauce.

"Fuck," Henry muttered, checking himself from his first reaction, which was to stick the sleeve in his mouth and suck it clean. "Why are you laughing?"

Pulling his earphones off his head, Cal sat up and laughed harder. "Because it's funny."

"No, it's not. What's so funny about it?"

"Not your jacket. You. It's funny how pissed you're getting." Cal put his arms across his stomach as he did his best impression of someone in the throes of hysterics.

"You're such a dick," Henry said, pulling off his jacket and walking over to the drinking fountain to scrub in vain at the toxic stain he knew he'd never be able to wash out. There was a lot of negative things to be said about the quality of public school cafeteria food. It's ability to permanently stain was not one of them. The stuff had staying power. You had to give it that.

As he walked back to collect his backpack he noticed the haphazard ringing of the cord on the flag pole slapping against the metal pole and looked up. The wind was having its way with the flag, balling it up, stretching it out, not really the stars and stripes from down here, but some sort of in-between nation, a country in transition.

Something about it seemed strange, and it took him a moment to realize that it wasn't the spastic acrobatics of it, rather it was that the flag was once again at the top of the pole instead of waving at half-mast as it had been at the beginning of the year after Tyler had died. There had been no announcement from the staff that the time to remember him had passed, no hushed whispers now, no celebrity of association. The time to mourn and remember had passed and the flag had been recalled to its regular place at the top of the pole, and like everyone else he hadn't noticed it happen. Even worse was that he had been friends with Tyler. How long had it been like that for? How come no one had told him? Shouldn't there have been some sort of announcement? Some recognition of the end of the recognition? It didn't seem right to let something that important just slip away, be changed in the middle of the night without telling them. Without reminding them. If that were the case, though, if there was no expiration date for grief, then there would truly be no good way to remember anyone, nor any right way to forget.

Other sounds that were marginalia just a second ago came slamming forcefully to the forefront: the droning whoosh of cars travelling up and down the canyon road that ran next to the school, the dull insectoid clicking of the football team's shoulder pads colliding over and over as they drilled their violence to the approval of periodic shrill whistles and yells of encouragement from the coach. Headache noises. All of it was pure randomness, yet it was consistent. He had to give the world that much. It didn't leave much room for pauses. No jet-black moments of pure stillness. Rare as real obsidian.

"What are you looking at?" Cal asked him, following Henry's gaze to where it landed at the flag. "You getting all patriotic on me? Gonna jerk off to Old Glory?"

Cal began to move his hand up and down in front of his dick, thrusting his hips backwards and forwards as he moaned. "Oh yeah. I love the way you gallantly wave, bitch. Uh-huh. Do you want to see my bombs bursting in air? I bet you do.

Yeah, bitch."

Henry tried not to smile but he couldn't help it. He grabbed his backpack and slung it over his shoulder. "You're fucking sick, dude."

"Wait," Cal moaned, still in the throes of his pelvic Pledge of Allegiance. "Don't screw me up. I'm about to make a mess all over the land of the brave..."

Henry laughed and felt the disappointment about the flag drain away. Those sounds that had been sharp arrows in his temples a moment before were now gone, dulled down to blunt sticks, resting harmlessly in their quiver.

A girl's voice behind him spun him around like a dance partner in a steroid rage. "Jesus, Grace. Is that your brother?"

It was Grace and Stacy and they had walked by right in the middle of Cal's campus sex show.

Cal quickly stopped his act and walked over to stand next to Henry, who wished he would have just stayed where he was. There had been such a pleasant détente at home the last few weeks since the thing with Peter and both he and Grace had done everything they could not to stir the pot with one another. But now he had embarrassed her in front of her friends once again and knew that he had set the needle back. Grace squished her face together and looked at Henry as though he was disintegrating before her very eyes, like she couldn't believe what she was seeing.

"What are you doing, Henry?" she asked.

"What do you mean, what am I doing?" His defense was to act incredulous. "I wasn't doing anything. It was..." He didn't say Cal's name, but he hoped she understood what he was trying to imply.

"Hey, Grace," Cal said nonchalantly, totally oblivious to

how angry she was.

Continuing to look only at Henry, she asked again, "What are you doing?" This time her voice had lost its edge and he could tell she was genuinely trying to understand not just how much like children they were acting, but also the obscenity of it. It was the kind of behavior she despised and had no patience for, this kind of disrespecting of women, and he knew it. There was no answer he could give that would make up for her catching them acting like this, least of all in front of Stacy, and so he ventured none, not sure he could speak anyway.

"Hey, Grace," Cal said again, and Henry wished he would stop, that shamed silence was their best bet, but Cal didn't understand and he went on. "We were just messing around. Henry was staring at the flag and when I saw him…"

She didn't let him finish, though. She swung her head around to stare at him, her eyes deep fissures of hate, and in a voice he had never heard before, something between panic and mob rule, shouted, "Don't you fucking talk to me and I want you to stop hanging out with my brother! Do you fucking understand me, you fucking weirdo psycho? Do you?"

Cal's mouth hung open as he stared back at her.

"I'm not kidding," she said. "Come on, Stacy." And they were off. Just like that.

"Whoa," Cal said after a minute had gone by. "What's up with her? Is she on the rag or something?"

There was no way for him to explain to Cal how angry she had been. How genuine her hate was for him. He saw that now. He still didn't quite understand it, but now at least he got it. She hated Cal and was going to do whatever she could to make her brother understand exactly how she felt.

They were now the last two on the quad as the tardy bell

rang.

"Shit," Cal spat on the ground. "Fuck it." He looked around and spat again. "I fucking hate this place."

The school was still, and once again he heard the clanging of the flag catch as it banged against the pole. Cal squinted as he looked up at it and then lowered his gaze as he surveyed the school. "It's like we're on a boat," he said, but Henry missed that part, because he had already put his headphones back on and was listening again to "Bloodstains" as he walked to class, disappointed in himself and, perhaps even more upsetting, in barely conscious solidarity with the world.

*   *   *

The decision to drop acid was made in detention and perhaps a lot more easily than it should have been. It was two days after the episode in the cafeteria and they had both been sentenced to a three-day detention for the repeated offense of being tardy. It seemed a just, if not mysterious punishment, because although Henry knew what detention was from reading books like *Catcher in the Rye* and watching *The Breakfast Club* on cable over and over with his sister on Saturday mornings, he'd never known anyone who had actually ever served detention. Nor did he know that it existed as a variety of punishment at his school. Upon being informed of his fate, he imagined a dungeon somewhere deep under the administration building, the school's mascot, the fearsome porpoise, embossed on the heavy oak door, wearing not its customary cheerful grin, but instead a deep and angry scowl, its fins holding a medieval mace and morning star. You have broken the porpoise's trust, it was meant to convey. You have displeased the porpoise.

Instead, he was ordered to report to a classroom he had never been in before, one of the five or six classrooms that were reserved for students taking remedial versions of their subjects. He heard rumors about what went on in remedial classrooms: the atrocious behavior, the ridiculously simplistic subject matter, gym teachers giving instruction in mathematics, usually former remedial students themselves, conscripted into that duty by the arcane laws of the teacher's union that required they work a certain number of hours per week so that their tenure could remain inviolate. In the two years he had been at the school he had never actually been to the "R" building, which was the clever nickname given to this block of classrooms, so he was tentative about entering when he finally found the correct place. He poked his head in carefully and looked around. Coming from outside the room was dark, and as he waited for his eyes to adjust, a voice inside boomed out to him, "You here for detention, boy?"

He squinted into the darkness trying to make out who had just shouted at him.

"Yeah," he muttered, blindly obedient to the category-five voice.

"Then get in here." And before he had a chance to move, the voice crashed into him again. "NOW!!"

Laughter erupted from a corner of the room and as he walked in, blinking away the darkness, he saw a group of four black kids huddled together, laughing and pointing at him, slapping their desks, their knees, punching and clutching one another as if his confusion was the funniest thing they had ever seen. Maybe it was.

Sitting at the teacher's desk, dressed in a cheap tan suit, jerry-curled hair leeching toward his shoulders, was the school security guard, Mr. Neville. Henry had never had occasion to encounter Mr. Neville before; his duties kept him mostly busy breaking up fights, greeting the cops as they dropped off truants that they had picked up in the town center, admonishing certain clothing choices he deemed to be too "gangy," too provocative. "Levon, take that cap off," he had heard Neville yell at a kid in the hallway last week. Hats weren't allowed in school, not out of respect for decorum or greater aesthetic higher purpose, but because of the supposed connotations certain teams and colors had in regards to gang affiliation. Naturally, Henry had no idea what anything meant or was supposed to mean other than the obvious blue vs. red issues, which everyone in the civilized world implicitly understood to be nature's two most warlike colors, naturally at odds with one another, the rest of the rainbow doomed to be caught forever in the crossfire of their vitriol. The rest was a mystery to him. Why a Dodgers baseball hat versus a Raiders wool cap were deemed too controversial would, like advanced forms of mathematics and the way girls thought, be forever beyond him.

To that end, there were a lot of rumors about Neville, as well: that he was a former gang leader, ex-cop, that he was the football coach's brother, that he was illiterate. There was even a rumor that he carried a gun. Based on this quick interaction, Henry had no reason to doubt any of them. Perhaps they were all true. One thing he was sure of, like the subtle difference between gang signs and affiliations, he would never know for sure.

"Sign in," Neville said, pointing at a sheet of paper in front of him. Henry obediently bent over the page and signed his name.

"I'm He...," he started to say, unsure of the protocol.

"I know who you are. I can read the sheet. What? You think I can't read?"

The group of black kids, which he now thought of as a Greek

chorus of adolescent humiliation, howled with laughter again.

"No," Henry said. "I don't think you can't read."

"Sit down, do your homework, and don't fucking talk. Do you understand me?"

Henry nodded, turned, and seeing Cal at the back of the room, slid into the seat next to him.

He put his backpack down and pulled out his notebook and social studies textbook. He didn't want to look at Cal, because he knew if he did, he would start laughing, and if Neville heard him, he didn't want to even imagine what that wrath might feel like. They had been working on making maps of the Middle East in class and their assignment was to take them home and finish them for homework. Henry took out his paper and ruler and began to trace the borders of the Gulf states. He bent his head close to the paper so he could see his work. His eyes had adjusted a little to the dimness, but it was still way too dark in the room. He wondered if it was like this all day long.

"Maybe these remedial kids aren't that stupid and it's only because hey're forced to learn in total darkness that they don't do better in school," Cal whispered.

Henry stifled a laugh as he outlined the Kingdom of Saudi Arabia.

"Psst," Cal nudged him with his foot. "Check out the posters."

Elementary school level educational posters adorned the walls, promising among other things that "Reading is Fun" complete with a drawing of dog and an apple (with the words 'dog' and 'apple' spelled out beneath their corresponding pictures), and another stressing "Math is Easy," which had two worms, each stretched out to look like the number one, added together to make two worms. The worms, of course, were smiling. As was the apple and the dog. There was even the obligatory "Hang in there Kitty" poster on the wall behind Neville's head, showing a little tabby hanging precariously from a washing line. Some literary giant, clearly already possessed of the knowledge that reading is fun, had drawn a way too huge cock on the cat and re-written the slogan to say, "Well hung in there, Kitty."

Straining to see the map, he hunched even lower down over his desk until his nose was hovering just a few centimeters over the paper.

"Yo, cuz," one of the black kids shouted, either oblivious of Neville's presence or just not caring, "you doing lines on your desk?"

The rest of them busted up—he even heard Cal snicker—and when he looked up to protest his innocence, Neville was staring at him with arms crossed, shaking his head slowly back and forth.

"No, I'm not doing…," he began to protest, his nervous voice sounding like backfire sputtering from the tailpipe of an old, unreliable car.

They laughed again, cutting him off. It seemed that everything he said or did was going to be their entertainment for the afternoon, and he supposed there was something to be said for that sort of resourcefulness, the ability to find humor in even the most rueful of situations.

Without a word, Neville walked over to the row of transoms, twisting a rusted metal pole and in an instant flooding the room with steep shafts of light, silvery flecks of dust whirling in the luminescence like tiny organisms adrift in the palest of blue seas.

Neville glared at him again, as though the darkness had been his fault.

"Yo, man," one of them yelled across the room at Henry,

"Why you guys in here? Too much Monty Python and shit?"

They laughed again, and Henry almost said that he didn't even like Monty Python, but stopped himself. It was pointless. They probably didn't even know what Monty Python was. They'd probably heard some nerdy kids on the yard imitating sketches they had seen on TV—the silly walk or the dead parrot—and then he shivered thinking that's what they thought all white guys were into, the burning hot embarrassment of cultural divides.

"Seriously, dude," the kid went on, pronouncing dude as 'doyde', twisting the word into a fancy piece of garnish before plating it in the sentence, "why you here and shit?"

"Tardies," Henry answered. The word was barely out of his mouth when the smallest of the kids, who Henry assumed hadn't heard a word of what was being said given the enormous headphones his head was marinating in, began to howl with laughter.

"Tardies," he breathlessly repeated, "these motherfuckers got too many tardies and shit."

He held up his hand looking for a high-five but found only caustic glances instead.

"Shut up, Dwayne," the kid in the Raiders T-shirt said. "Keep listening to your tapes."

This cracked the rest of them up as Dwayne collapsed in on himself in some sort of shame implosion.

The guy in the Raiders T-shirt turned to Cal and Henry and said, "This motherfucker is so stupid," he pointed to Dwayne, who had suddenly sobered up as he steeled himself for the impending humiliation, "that when all them motherfuckas was rioting and shit in Westwood after that movie *Colors* came out..."

One of the other boys held his hand to his mouth as he pretended to stifle a laugh and then interrupted his friend as he pointed at his shoes,

"Check it out! I got these fresh Jordans, yo, and this motherfucker," he pointed at Dwayne, "this motherfucker stole tapes!" He turned to Dwayne, stood up, and threw his hands in the air. "Cassette tapes, motherfucker!"

With that the three of them collapsed into heaps on their desks banging their fists on the tables, struggling for air and jubilant in the victory of a perfect humiliation. Forcing a smile, Henry noticed as Dwayne's Adams apple bobbed up and down as he struggled to stifle whatever embarrassment he felt by the story.

Cal snorted and Henry looked at him and shrugged, "I don't get it."

"You don't? Jesus, Henry. That guy was saying that when all those kids rioted in Westwood last month most of them took sneakers and expensive shit like that. But this guy only took tapes. They're busting on him."

Henry looked at Dwayne again and immediately felt pity well up for the kid. He understood what Cal was saying about the expensive stuff being what he should have taken first, but he didn't see why they should care about who took what. If Henry had known about it, he probably would have taken tapes, too.

"Maybe he just likes music," Henry whispered to Cal.

"Yeah, but that's not the..."

He interrupted Cal.

"I know that's not the point," Henry said, feeling frustration begin to seep in, the frustration of having a point but knowing it's not going to be understood, "but why does everything have to be about what other people think? Shouldn't he just take tapes if that's what he wanted the most? Shouldn't he do what makes him happiest?"

"You're a good guy, dude," Cal whispered as he reached into his pocket for something, "but that's not the way high school works. And you know it. Don't pretend you don't."

Cal was right, of course, about that not being the way high school worked, but part of Henry had never wanted to admit to himself that hierarchies existed everywhere, even here, at the bottom of the barrel, in detention, where racking up a load of tardies was bad but evidently nothing compared to the ill-advised exploits of freewheeling larceny. Skirting the edges of school with Cal this past year, he had thought that they were somehow beyond the social order, operating just outside the lines of demarcation, but that was foolish, because clearly there was a social order to everything, even the smallest of associations, and maybe not being able to see that for what it was why he'd always be invisible in the eyes of his peers.

"Dude, check it out."

Cal held out his hand and showed him two small squares of paper, each one with the anarchy symbol on it. He popped one in his mouth and pushed the remaining one into Henry's hand.

"Wanna do some acid?"

Henry looked at the little square and then over at Dwayne again, who was still forcing a smile as his friends told each other stories about the day of the great riot: they burned whatever they wanted, they took whatever they wanted, and all this motherfucker could think to do was grab some tapes.

"I thought only hippies did acid," Henry said, already knowing that he would put the thing in his mouth, that there was no question that he wouldn't leave Cal alone, that he wouldn't violate the hierarchy.

"Yeah," Cal said, smiling broadly, "but this is anarchy acid."

"What's the difference?" Henry asked him as he placed the piece of paper on his tongue, letting it sit there in a small puddle of spit, before swallowing it quickly.

Cal seemed to think about it for a moment and then shrugged his shoulders as he waited for the drug to do its job.

*   *   *

The drugs came alive in him with what felt like one thread at a time, tying each of his senses to a new reality, gently at first, giving him a chance to ease into the languor of it all and then, just as soon as he thought this transition to another place was going to be a walk in the park, that was when the threads doubled down, became ropes and lashes, fastening him securely, and what felt like permanently, to a new set of rules, a new reality. But despite the quick descent, he was proud of himself that he had taken the plunge, done something that was irreversible and in a sense brave. Or at least brave for him. There was no going back from this. No safe word that would loosen the straps. He would just have to ride it out and take whatever shrapnel exploded his way.

The first of his senses to go was his vision. The lines on his map of the Middle East began to blur and bend, rivers flowed into borders, and borders became tangled filigree, elegant loops and nonsensical doodles that took the place of geographic demarcation, became infinitely more important than where and when. The real question was how. Had he said that out loud?

Glancing over at Cal, he wondered how he could delicately find corroboration that it was working, that it was the drugs that were making him see these things and not the heat or the boredom or the trauma of being institutionalized for the first time in his life. If Cal wasn't feeling this as well, and it was all in his head, then he was more fucked than he thought. Cal would use it against him forever. There'd be no end to Cal reminding him about the time he pretended he was tripping and the map of the Middle East turned into a cross between *Mad* magazine and an illuminated manuscript right before his very own bullshitting eyes. He decided to play it cool for now. Wait for Cal to do something first. Freak out somehow. See dogs urinating fire on Neville's desk. Chalk mysteriously levitating and writing jokes on the chalkboard that he would get blamed for by Dwayne and the rest of them. Shit, shit, shit. The more he thought about these things the more likely they were to happen. Fuck it. Keep cool, he told himself, breathing in deeply and gripping the sides of his desk, which even though he rationally knew were made of wood, now felt suspiciously like Jell-O. Or at least a little wet. Were they wet? Or was that him? After deliberating about it for what felt like half an hour, but in reality couldn't have been more than a second or two, he officially conceded the next of his senses to the great dominatrix in his brain. Touch was getting its comeuppance. Touch was going to get fisted.

There was no way to keep this away from Cal anymore. Whether or not Cal was feeling anything at all, Henry needed to say something. Shouldering the entire burden of the collective neurosis of the universe was getting to be a bit too much to handle on his own. If Cal thought he was a pussy or faking or whatever, fuck it. It was time to come clean.

It turned out, though, that he needn't have worried about it, because Cal was in far worse shape than him. Bent over so closely to his desk that his eyeballs were practically grazing the wooden desktop Cal was humming softly to himself as he used a fine-tipped pen to carefully draw something right onto the desk itself. Henry looked over trying to make out what the drawing was, but couldn't quite see it, and when Cal noticed him leaning over, he used his arm to shield his work as if it was the answers to the most important test he had ever taken.

"No peeking," he smiled and whispered loudly at Henry, "I'll show you when I'm done."

Henry waited a tense minute.

"Okay," Henry said, rubbing his maybe sweaty palms on his jeans, "are you done now?"

Cal sat up, surveyed his work, and then looked over at Henry with a horrified expression on his face.

"Uh-oh," he said, earnest as a repentant toddler convinced that he was just a witness to his own naughtiness, "I drew something bad."

"Oh, Jesus," Henry said as he leaned over and tried to make out the jumbled doodles. At first it looked like nothing. Just lines and scribbles. But as he looked closer he saw that it wasn't a random mess at all, but rather hundreds of tiny swastikas all linked together forming some kind of an ornate, albeit compulsive, tribute to Nazism.

Henry looked at him, his eyes wide with fright. "Oh, no!"

"I know," Cal said, shaking his head. "It was all I could think to draw."

Henry nodded. He understood. He took his map of the Middle East and put it on Cal's desk.

"I understand," he said in as kind of a voice as he could muster given the circumstances. "I broke the Middle East and I totally didn't mean it."

Cal looked at the map and nodded his sympathy. "Shit. I

know you didn't mean it. You're not that kind of a person. You'd never break the Middle East on purpose."

It was the sincerity of the comment that bled through, not the absurdity of it, and Henry felt a little bit touched. "Thanks."

"You're welcome," Cal answered, waving away an imaginary fly.

The next two senses to go were taste and smell, which both went suddenly and as one collective malfunctioning unit. He went from smelling and tasting nothing to suddenly becoming hyper aware of the calamitous colognes and hair gels the other kids in the room were wearing. Smells that ranged from a chemical spill to a burning garden, on their own, potentially viable odors, attractive even in certain social settings, but when taken together almost too much to bear.

"What's that smell?" he asked involuntarily, as if his nose had cried "uncle" and sent a message to his brain to surrender under whatever terms were being offered.

They looked at him and the kid who had led the charge against Dwayne called back, "You like that shit, huh? That's fucking Michael Jordan cologne. Bitches love that shit because it smells like pussy and then that makes them think that you're getting pussy so you must know what you're doing and shit. It's reverse psychology cologne."

Henry nodded as if the explanation made perfect sense to him. Next to him Cal muttered the word "Jesus" as if his mind had just been blown apart by the sheer logic of it all. Or maybe he was imagining Michael Jordan sitting in a room full of vagina-packed test tubes, sniffing each one, trying to decide which one best represented the essence of bitch psychology. Either way, the smell was revolting and he could begin to feel it metastasize in his mouth, becoming a dense and murky taste he could feel swishing around and sliding down his throat. He walked over to the door, cracked it an inch, and inhaled a gulp of blue air from outside.

"What the fuck do you think you're doing?" Neville asked him in such utter disbelief that Henry had to wonder if he didn't levitate over instead of walk.

"I was just getting a breath of fresh air. I'm not feeling that well."

"Sit your ass down, boy. This is detention. This isn't some kind of a..." he was at a loss for the word, which Cal supplied for him from somewhere in his vulgar depository of crooked thinking.

"Hootenanny?" Cal volunteered, innocently enough.

"What did you say?" Neville asked, his voice reaching truly incredulous heights.

Cal quickly spread his hands over the swastika tableau he had created on his desk as his eyes became wide and frightened ovals. There was no telling what monster he was seeing now.

Before he had to answer, though, the last bell of the day rang signaling the end of the school day. All four of the black kids got up at once to leave at the same exact moment as Neville yelled at them to sit back down. "Y'all are still in detention. Sit your asses down!" The four of them sat down as one groaning unit and Henry watched them, amazed and in something akin to awe of the sincerity of their disappointment. "Damn," Neville muttered as a postscript. "Stupid fucking kids," and he returned to his magazine, sparing Cal the need to further explain his strange comment.

The bell had startled Henry but not nearly so much as the noises that followed. All six of the kids stayed stock still and listened in a kind of reverence as the sounds of their peers getting out of school for the day flooded through the open transoms. It was a sound Henry had never really noticed before, never having had to stay late, but now, the sounds of kids laughing, celebrating the tiny victory of making it through another boring fucking day, the screaming challenges and invitations for pre-dinner mischief, and the flimsy tinny banging of locker doors being thrown open and slammed shut made him feel warm and grew in him as he wished for the first time since coming to this school that he could join them out there. The noises never ended but spiraled and began to intersect building a perfect honeycomb of echoing aggravation. He needed to get out.

He looked over at Cal to see if it was registering the same way with him, but Cal didn't seem to be aware that anything had changed, busy as he was licking the cuff of his filthy flannel shirt and using it to scrub away the drawings on his desk.

"I gotta get out of here," Henry whispered matter-of-factly and Cal looked over and nodded, his eyes wide and terror-stricken. It was clear to Henry that he was going to have to take control of this situation. Cal wasn't going to be any help.

He began to engineer an escape plan in his mind that became more and more elaborate as the noise from outside grew louder and louder. He was agitated and desperate. He imagined them causing a distraction and then shrinking themselves and crawling through the narrow crack of the open transom. It seemed plausible enough, but he kept getting caught on how they were going to become that small. He checked his pockets for an answer. Surely he hadn't left the house that morning without some kind of a shrinking pill or potion, but he couldn't find anything. Just his empty wallet and his house key, which he put on the desk. He stuck his hands back into his pocket but couldn't remember this time what it was he was looking for. A bullfrog? Slingshot? What was it again that boys were supposed to carry with them all the time? Syringes? Modeling glue? Aborted fetuses? Shit, that wasn't it. He'd keep looking, but he was becoming fairly certain that the answers weren't going to be in his pants.

Their prayers were answered, though, a moment later when Neville finished his magazine and stood up.

"Y'all can get out of here now. Get to class on time from now on," he pointed at the black kids. "All of you."

The four of them jumped up and ran from the room almost before the words were totally out of his mouth. Henry wanted to imagine that they had run so quickly because they were embarrassed that they had been in there for the same reason as him, nothing terribly insidious as he had imagined, but just being tardy too many times. But in his heart he knew that that wasn't it at all. They could not care less about what he thought and he couldn't blame them for that, either.

"Get out of here, you two," Neville said as he walked out the door. His ill-fitting suit made a swishing noise as the unidentifiable fabric rubbed together and then he, too, was gone.

Henry got up and realized after a few steps that Cal was still in his seat. He looked stuck and terrified. Henry went back to him and hoisted him up by his arm.

"Come on. I have an idea. I know what we're going to do today."

Cal nodded meekly as he let himself be led from the classroom and out into the real world.

Outside, the sun had flayed a layer of skin off the world, revealing beneath it bright and rich colors he had either never noticed before or had sincerely never before existed. He felt his pupils contract as they struggled to regulate the amount of light getting in, but once he was comfortable and secure in the feeling that his eyes wouldn't spontaneously combust, he let himself look around at the sparkling metal banisters, the richly green grass on the quad, the striking array of the colors of shirts and backpacks that his peers wore as they hurried with varying degrees of urgency toward the front gate of the school. It was difficult for him to believe that this was how the world was all the time, that this was how normal people walked around, the greyness he had always known and subscribed to nothing more than a feeble copout and excuse for a world view.

But if this was how everyone else saw things, and his view of the world was the exception rather than the norm, then maybe it wasn't that he was inconsequential, as he frequently worried, but that he was invisible, absolutely unable to be seen by the naked eye. Perhaps he was a ghost or one of those phantoms that people thought they saw out of the corner of their eye, but when they turned to look at it straight on, there was nothing actually there, and they convinced themselves that it had only been a trick of the light. Beginning to panic slightly, he ran his hands down the length of his narrow frame, the leanness of his arms, the feeble stubble on his cheeks that he would soon need to start shaving, trying to somehow substantiate his own existence. But that wasn't how it worked. You weren't the one who got to say if you were real or not. Someone else had to do that for you. So he turned to Cal with the intention of innocently asking his friend if he was really there, trying in his mind to figure out how to strike the right balance in tone between nonchalance and intellectual curiosity, when he saw Cal frozen in his tracks a few feet behind him, rooted to a spot near the door of the detention room.

"Cal? Are you okay, man?" Henry asked coming back for him. "Why'd you stop?"

Cal looked genuinely worried.

"I don't know. I want to go, but I can't. I'm...stuck."

"You're not stuck. Come on. We've gotta get out of here."

The tone had changed on a dime and as Henry grabbed Cal by his sleeve and yanked him forward, he felt like a seasoned soldier, finally finding that reserve of courage he knew he always had stored deep down inside of him but was waiting for just the right balance of pressure and circumstance to access it like a precious metal hiding below the surface of the earth. In his mind he could almost hear the whizzing of mortar shells and the screams of his comrades as they perished around him, their fate seemingly sealed the day they were boots on the ground. Not everyone had it, he would tell himself later once he was back from the war, not everyone had that extra little something that he had. But he would never say it out loud, that admission of invulnerability, because to actually vocalize it would immediately negate it. Besides, it was just an excuse. Survivor's guilt was a potent hallucinogen in and of itself, but self-trickery was not to be underestimated, especially given the fact that some memories stuck like shrapnel and were actually worse for the body if removed. The worst ones. The best ones. It was a good lesson to learn that there was no good way to remember and no right way to forget.

Henry continued to lead Cal through school, at various times pushing him from behind and sometimes pulling him along. "You can make it," he whispered to him as sincerely as the circumstances would allow him. "Don't give up." He heard Cal giggle when he said these things, but not once did he resist. It was clear to both of them that Henry was in charge and that if there was any chance of survival at all it would be him and him alone that would get them out of the shit.

More kids than he ever would have expected hung around school after the last bell had rung, and as he made his way through their impromptu drama rehearsals, games of Frisbee, and going over homework assignments with teachers, he wondered earnestly if this actually went on every day or was this some sort of special occasion, a pagan celebration, a ritualistic sacrifice to celebrate the leniency of spring or was it the clemency of fall? They weaved their way through the little cliques, faster and faster, dodging them as if they were landmines and only he had the map, and when they got to the front of the school they, without a word to one another, began to run at top speed up the canyon, sweat trickling down their soft teenage backs, their eyes focused on the line of bright blue sky that seemed to be teetering on top of the mountains in the distance. They were both laughing now, overjoyed at…what? Being out of school? The feeling of running? The cool breeze that would now and again force its way up the canyon from the beach, bathing them in sporadic bright blue bursts of salty air?

Henry stopped them at the bus stop on Sunset Blvd. and they both bent over, hands on knees, as they struggled to catch their breath. And maybe the running had sped up their metabolism, but Henry could feel the warmth of the acid as it transgressed…no, wrong word…dissolved (YES! That was it! Celebrate the easy victories!) even further into his body and he wished it would act even more slowly than that. Thirty-five or forty years ought to do the trick. Slow decay. His half-life was invincibility.

Traffic was a blur of noisy color stretching into an indefinite future, and they watched in silent awe as the cars went by, one after another, their trajectory making perfect lines that lingered steadfastly and hauntingly in the street. Soon, Sunset was flooded with these colored promises, and when the bus finally came along, Henry grabbed Cal again by the sleeve and tugged him on, resisting the urge to tell the driver to "follow those lines" like something out of a noir-ish nervous breakdown as he paid their fares.

The bus was blood pulsing its way through the circulatory system of the crowded streets. Each time it stopped to pick up a new passenger, its hydraulic doors bellowed open as it renewed itself by taking a giant breath before getting on its way again. Despite this seemingly perfect biological functioning, the mood on the bus was overwhelmingly somber and silent. No one smiled. No one spoke. It was mostly teenagers on the bus, kids just out of school who were on their way home, or to sports, or maybe an afternoon job, and they were altogether a joyless lot, or at least unaware, and Henry remembered that introspection was the ultimate teenage transgression and that maybe he was the one who had the wrong idea. Maybe he was the one who ought to be a little less ecstatic about the seamless biological functioning of LA traffic. He tried to distract himself, which, being high on LSD didn't in theory seem to be as difficult as it proved to be. He started to read the advertisements plastered up around the top of the bus: invitations to enroll in junior college, DUI attorneys, and exterminators who would come to your house and take care of your roach problems once and for all. On and on they went like that, practical solutions to worst case scenarios, and when he looked up again he saw that they were near the airport and a stupendously practical idea came to him that he thought might lift them out of this funk he felt they were in.

When the bus stopped Henry once again tugged Cal by the sleeve and led them into the Tom Bradley International Terminal. Luckily, Cal went along with it. He asked no questions, and Henry took it as one of those silent blessings and assumed that Cal had been bestowed with a certain type of second sight that let him see things as they really were, a roadmap to safely traverse the great narrowness of lonely days.

The terminal was beyond busy with a flood of people from

what, he assumed, must be every corner of the globe. They stumbled past Europeans wearing designer clothes that looked to be stitched together from the Goodwill pile at NASA, Indian men in dress shirts that were soaked through with sweat, a line of thirteen generations of Southeast Asians staggering along in single file order, a real-life exercise depicting the evolution of genuine disillusionment, their lives packed into half a dozen cardboard boxes stitched up tight with twine. An address printed on the boxes promised them a better life in a suburb Henry had only heard of in traffic reports as someplace that was always bottle-necked or jackknifed. That's not Los Angeles, he wanted to warn them, that place might not even exist. But he knew if he did that, it would be just the opening they needed, and the grandma of the family would come up to him and pinch his cheeks and tell him she'd been waiting eighty years to tell a white person that they have no idea what the fuck they were talking about. Leave them alone. That's what his soul told him to do. Leave them alone, because they deserved this anonymity they've waited for for all these years. The anonymity that doubtlessly took countless wars, ethnic cleansings, coups, and self-sacrifice the likes of which would shake Henry's very foundations to the core to learn. So, he just smiled at them and walked on, silently wishing them the best, envying them just a little for the obscurity they'd so diligently earned. He nodded to the grandma, the last of them in line, and she smiled back at him just a little, just enough to acknowledge that he was there, and as she passed, she too left a line, a fuzzy streak of light that hung in the air where she had just been and that followed her as she went to start this new and briefest chapter of her life. In fact, the terminal was full of these lines and although he knew he should chalk it up to the drugs, he decided to give the experience the benefit of the doubt and pretend they were something else, something more than a trick of the light. It was okay to do that, right? He wished Grace was there so he could ask her that question because he knew she would tell him, Yes, that it meant whatever he wanted it to mean. That people did that kind of thing all the time. That people cried and laughed for no reason. That they might hear a song or watch a movie or just hear a word and that would be it. Their soul would feel instantly like it belonged to that moment. Forever and ever. That was how he felt right at that moment; his skin had gone all gooseflesh from the air conditioning that blasted in from every corner of the large terminal, his pupils dilated beyond all measure of reasonable circumference, essentially two black holes from which no sliver of light could escape. Super powers. They had super powers and this was their base. Superheroes needed a place to hang out, a base where they could recharge their powers, hang out, hash out plans to stop the villains of the world, maybe grab a quick cigarette without having to worry about kids seeing them, a little grab ass with their buddies. Teenagers were supposed to have it, too. In books and movies it was always a reservoir they could escape to. Swim all day in the summer. Screw at night. The reservoir was where kids were always experiencing everything for the first time. Built by adults but somehow totally forgotten, as though they were never supposed to be functional at all but constructed merely as a functional monument to youth. Couldn't this be their reservoir?

He turned to ask Cal, but just as the words were almost out of his mouth he realized that Cal was no longer with him. Henry circled back, adrenaline kicking in, worst case scenarios running through his head as he imagined Cal commandeering a jumbo jet and demanding to be flown immediately to the nearest 7-Eleven, or worse, Cal commandeering a small Asian woman to be his wife, possibly kicking off an international situation because of his ultra-amorous leanings.

Circling back through the main terminal he was rushing by the duty free shop when he caught a glimpse of Cal's brown flannel shirt inside. He went inside and put a hand heavily on Cal's shoulder.

"I thought I lost you, man. Come on," Henry said, pulling Cal by the frayed sleeve of his shirt, "we've gotta go."

"Go?" Cal asked, his eyes fixed solidly on a broad wall of liquor and cigarettes, which, lit from behind and sitting on glass shelves, looked to be a gift from heaven. "Where do you want to go?"

"We've got a flight to catch," Henry explained, doing what he could to move his friend before something bad happened.

"We do?"

"Uh-huh, don't you remember?"

"No. I...I don't remember. Where are we going?" Cal was genuinely confused, and whereas ordinarily this confusion would have worried Henry, he had the fundamental realization that it wasn't his problem. Neither of them were responsible for the other. They were there as fucked-up equals and as such, it was every man's trip for himself.

"We're going home. Back to our own country," Henry explained, grinning at Cal to break the fourth wall as a goodwill tip of the hat to the reality that was currently just beyond the tips of his fingers.

Cal's eyes widened. He was at the peak of his trip, smothered in a smoldering hot, otherworldly, viscous liquid that clung greedily to his hold on reality and scorched his mind to a near burnt crisp roughly the size of a holy wafer.

Henry laughed and pulled Cal out of the store and down the way a little bit, weaving them expertly through the oncoming crush of foreign exuberance, and into a convenience store, where he searched the shelves until he found what it was he was looking for. He bought a child leash and quickly threaded it around Cal's waist and with the other side Velcroed to his wrist.

"There," Henry said to no one in particular, "now you're safe." Cal started to wander so he tugged firmly at the strap and giggled as Cal stumbled back to stand next to him.

The cashier watched this as he gave Henry his change.

"Is he your brother?" the man asked, deeply mystified, but showing altogether very little concern.

Seizing upon the moment to complete their metamorphosis, Henry looked blankly at the cashier and pointed at his own ear, "Strabble bon humdinger?" he said, yanking at the leash once again as Cal made his idiot's play for a box of rubber wonder balls. "Noey Englisheses."

"Oh," the cashier nodded. "Okay. Whatever," and closed the register drawer as he looked around Henry at the next customer in line.

The leash thing seemed to be working for both of them, and the confused stares that latched onto their arrangement only solidified that notion. It was a hell of a first impression they were making on the newcomers to their city, many of whom Henry saw quickly consult their Fodor's guide books, presumably searching for the section on teen-on-teen bondage week in Southern California, which they had presumably missed when first planning their family vacation. Cal made another leap, this time lunging at a nearby candy display and Henry yanked the leash back as hard as he could just as Cal was about to lay his mitts on an admittedly delicious-looking pack of Butter Rum Life Savers. There was a loud groan and then a thud as Cal landed heavily on his back, and for a moment

Henry imagined that he had made Cal paralyzed and that it would be his responsibility for the rest of his life to care for him and take him to Chuck E Cheese and Disneyland and to make sure his doody didn't fall out of his crap bag, and really he'd have to get one of those cat litter scoopers because they were willing to give you free shit and take you to cool places if you were a handicapped kid, but no one was going to put up with your feces falling all over the place, and that would be Henry's job. Henry's life for not letting Cal have a pack of Butter Rum Life Savers. Maybe they would call Cal the Butterscotch Kid, and people everywhere would write him letters telling him how brave he was and girls would send him their panties and tell him that they'd be the ones to make him feel something again, and then they'd make a TV movie out of his life and Ricky Schroeder would play Cal and they'd get someone terrible and tragic to play Henry. Someone like Gary Coleman. A person that the audience could hate and pity at the same time. After all, he was the reason the Butterscotch Kid was in this predicament in the first place, wasn't he? And then Lifesavers would do a special pack of candy in honor of Cal called Cal-Scotch or Butter-Cal or something that would test well in secret test group marketing sessions where they'd ask the participants, which one tastes sadder? Which one tastes more crippled? And they'd all point and then pick and then that candy would be the best-selling candy ever and the President would eat them, and so would the Pope, and ever supermodels and Kelly LeBrock, who never ate anything with sugar in it, would eat them all the time and it would all be Henry's stupid fucking fault. But that thought passed as soon as Cal started laughing hysterically, still flat on his back on the cold floor, and when it didn't look like he was going to be able to stop, Henry joined in, more in relief that he was not going to have to be Cal's servant for the rest of his life than that his tubercular laugh was contagious.

Even when Henry looked over and saw the cashier talking to an airport security guard and pointing at them, he didn't stop laughing. Couldn't stop laughing. This happiness was a brush fire in him, starting at his toes and quickly making ashy work of his insides as it consumed his nerve endings, his organs, the tissue that made his body wax and wane until it got to the tips of his hair. Even when 'CHUCK', which was the name on the guard's nametag, came over to them, let his line of vision dribble as slowly as yoke from an egg from Henry down the length of the leash to where Cal still genuflected like an autistic penitent before the great altar to Saint Hershey and Saint Mars.

"What's going on here?" Chuck's voice was slow and deep, authoritative only insofar as that's what Henry surmised he thought an authoritative voice was supposed to sound like from watching bad cop shows going on two decades and being told by an administrative worker that he didn't meet the minimum requirements to become a cop in this wretched city. "Are you kids supposed to be here? Where are your parents?" The words seemed to tumble from his lips like the first trickle of stones before an avalanche and Henry could almost see them roll down his chin and then the hilly slope of his stomach which stretched the fabric of his powder blue uniform to near bursting proportions. Chuck was a bona fide natural disaster.

Cal stopped laughing and looked at Henry, completely panic stricken. Uh oh, Henry thought to himself, the drugs have taken him to an entirely new reality. Gone are the days of shits and giggles. Now the drug was an evil architect, smashing down walls in his brain and converting his skull from a rumpus room into a panic room for his brain.

Before Cal could answer, Henry stepped up and let out a long stream of sincere gibberish. "*Narfle slurfin garble. Laben bin eich den hoofer."*

The guard looked at him carefully and then at Cal. The leash didn't compute, but somewhere he was trying to access the part of his memory that held his experiences in cultural diversity training that they made all new airport employees go through before starting work.

"Are...you...new...to...this...country?" Chuck asked slowly.

Henry did his best impression of utter confusion by blinking and then cocking his head to the side.

"Where...are...you...from?" Chuck asked again, his brain accessing protocols he thought he'd never have to use, but always prayed he would, simulating worst-case scenarios as quickly as his mind would allow. "Let me see your passports." With the word *passport* he let his hands trace an imaginary rectangle as if the shape was the universal provenance of official government documentation.

Henry stalled for time by sticking his hand into his jeans pocket, but a moment later the charade was up when Chuck shouted, "Hey!" and he turned around to see Cal running off, his bad boy leash trailing behind him, and without thinking, Henry turned and sprinted off after him, and because the spirit grabbed him, he tore through the duty free shop and screamed "Sanctuary! Sanctuary!" Chuck, who had been right on his tail, stopped long enough to look at him, trapped as he was behind a tall glass shelf filled with top-notch Scotches ,and looked at him, trying to remember the part of the training that dealt with the political neutrality of tax-free shopping locales, and as he decided that asylum was not guaranteed among the cartons of cigarettes and gallon containers of expensive perfumes, Cal came out of nowhere and pushed into Chuck with all his might, shoving the big man into a box of imported chocolates that tumbled down and fell open, tiling the floor with an assortment of delicious candies. The sight of the toppled chocolates reminded Henry of his favorite episode of the *I Love Lucy* show; the one where Lucy and Ethel were working on the assembly line at a chocolate factory and couldn't keep up with the chocolates as they came off the conveyor line, and instead of asking that the machine be slowed down, they did what they could to keep the candy off the floor, shoving pieces into their mouths, pockets, under their hats, anything but admit they couldn't do this impossible thing. He had watched that one with Grace one Saturday morning long ago as they waited for cartoons to start and they had both been hysterical over it; something about the way Lucy and Ethel refused to admit defeat even though they were clearly overmatched and outplayed, and the look on their faces that even though the odds were stacked against them it was still a mystery to them why they were losing. The memory made him smile, and he reached out gingerly to take one of the chocolates that had slid over by where he was standing. It was a chocolate-covered cherry, which was typically not his favorite, but this one tasted delicious.

It took Cal screaming his name to jar him from his reverie, and he followed him along the long echoey halls of the terminal, past monitors that gave a telethonic timetable for every possible outcome of their adventure, every place they could ever want to go but probably wouldn't. The possibilities were limitless, but life, he understood, wasn't, and the realization didn't upset him, but rather made him happy that their afternoon had turned out the way it had. Cal put an arm on his shoulder and he slowed down. There was no one behind them. They had outrun the airport's first line of defense.

"I like it here," Cal said to him as if the airport was a secret dive bar they had discovered by accident one rainy night. They were the first words in English either one had spoken since their immigrant experiment had begun, and the sound of his native tongue seemed strange to him now. But for the sake of international diplomacy, he nodded in agreement as they entered a large terminal space made entirely of enormous windows that allowed the afternoon sun's long and brawny arm to elbow its way across the faint brown hairs on his arm, activating pin pricks of sweat along his skin which quickly became gooseflesh from the omnipresent A/C.

He had no memory of having gone through the security scanner, of the conveyor belt that mulches your personal belongings with radioactive particles, or the X-ray machine that lets them see your hip bone connected to your vestigial tail bone, but they must have because here they were in an enormous hallway of departure gates, each one flashing another city, a red light district for destinations, winking times at them, mere minutes to something impossibly new and exciting. The possibilities were endless, it was almost too much to believe that from this point he could either go to Salt Lake City or take five steps to the right and be off to Jakarta.

When he looked up again, they were in the baggage claim area and he could see daylight percolating outside the noisy automatic doors. It was the end of their time at the airport, and Cal had taken the lead somewhere along the way and ushered them toward the exit. Henry wanted to stay, to somehow prolong the experience. He pulled out the watch set button on his crappy old Casio his grandfather had given him as a pretend heirloom and gave it a few wild spins. "Look," he held it up to Cal's face, "this is what time it is where I'm from. Take me to immigration! Take me to customs! I have everything to declare!" He was getting a little crazy, and Cal had to pat him on the head and on the shoulder, and hush him like a baby with too much gas. "Shh. It's okay. I know. I know. You're not from here. Shh. I know. Shh." It was patronizing, but he settled down and looked around, taking one last fond look at every possible permutation of excitement he'd ever imagined, and saw a small Indonesian family waiting patiently at the rotating luggage belt, their small patriarch pulling box after twine-tied box off the Lazy Susan of worldly possessions. The family was quiet, the kids unbelievably well-behaved. This was a holy moment for them, he realized, probably the culmination of many years of prayers, bribes, and other dehumanizing genuflections, sanctimonious graft and the careful calculations of tithing. A gentle ripple of worry broke over them and it took Henry only a few seconds to realize that they were missing a package. They looked around, quietly, careful not to make a fuss, used to disappointment, not understanding that being on American soil meant that you could raise hell about anything, the smaller the matter the louder you had the right to scream. He moved to talk to them but Cal caught him by the arm and led him toward the door. "I want to help them. I think they lost something…" Henry appealed to Cal, and in his own head his voice sounded a million miles away, coming through to him in static waves of extreme indifference that he didn't really mean. It was his intention to sound more insistent, but the drugs were breaking down in his system; he was leaving the high and starting to slide through the fog and obscurity of it toward the inevitable itchiness and mundane reentry into the civilian life that he was already starting to get flashes of, extreme blocks of flatness and the overall decompression of the senses. Already sounds and images were losing their brightness and corners. Reality was such a let-down.

"Comeoncomeoncomeon…" Cal grabbed him by the arm and tried to pull him out into the bustling disappointment of the world of first impressions. Henry knew the truth. Had seen it with his own eyes. There was no point in going out there if you didn't have to. It was just fine inside. The air conditioner was set to the perfect level of stasis, the exact temperature of the womb, so that the idea of leaving it made him feel like crying so hard he'd need to be whacked on the ass by a medical professional if he was ever to catch his breath again. An elderly janitor polished the floor with an enormous ancient electric buffer, the smell of the polish an essential blend of citrus and the kind of carcinogens that whispered sweet nothings to the ghosts in your veins, that made the poisoning feel okay, that it was the right thing to do because there would never be a trade-off as even as the feeling of well-being that was about to subsume everything else. He felt happy here, content, and then out of nowhere the overwhelming desire to be dipped and coated in sugar came and went. Henry pulled his arm back and searched for the leash he'd had earlier when he'd been on the business end of this expedition, the master of both of their fates in this upside-down wonderland. It wasn't there and then he remembered, with an epic sense of disappointment, towering disappointment the likes of which were only seen in history at the outset of lengthy diasporas where the natives knew they weren't coming back for a long time, and that their idols were probably going to be cheap erotica to the oncoming wave of heathen settlers, that he didn't have it anymore. They had gotten rid of the leash somewhere along the way, and when they had ditched it, he had lost the only few hours that he had been in control of anything in his life this entire year.

Cal continued to pull him, no longer using a mish-mosh of words to cajole, but simply relying on his sheer strength to move them both outside. Outside the spell was worse than broken. It was worse than what he imagined it being when he was looking through the window. A thick gag of car exhaust clung to his face, settled on his skin and gripped it roughly, closed all around him so he felt that the filth was actually abducting him, about to shove him into a windowless van and take him somewhere he'd never be heard from again. Before they left he took one last look at the small family inside the baggage claim still searching frantically for their missing bags. He had the notion to break away and run back to help them, to offer them money, lodging, a full and careful explanation of what Costco was and how they'd be able to build a better life if they'd just give it a chance. *Whatever you lost may have been in your family for fifteen generations, but at Price Club they have six whole aisles of false gods and deviant beliefs. Forget about what you were. Besides, the parking probably sucked where you were from. Just think of it: for $100-a-year membership you can be the chalice bearer in your very own neo-pagan institution. You'll look back on this one day and laugh and thank your new gods for the opportunity to disdain what you used to be.*

The boys made their way down the sidewalk, past cabbies offering them rides in a million different swarthy accents, accents covered in hair, accents so thick and degenerate their native languages should have been declared a crime against humanity years ago. Cal ignored them, but Henry couldn't resist staking his territory now that it was the only viable option. "Fuck you," he shouted, not actually looking at them but kind of barking it at the ground in a prototype homeless grumble.

"Ha!" Cal barked out a laugh to signal he appreciated the aggression that was seeping back in. Almost on cue a bus went by whisking up a thick cloud of black soot that settled over them like a blanket of pure filth. Henry coughed once, loud and hard, but it was no use and he felt the pollution go up his nose, into his mouth, invade his pores and in that split second, as he ingested the virus that was the out-of-doors, he was back to where he'd always been, lost among the living with the ghosts of recent memories still breathing heavily down his bony back.

The bus picked them up near where it had let them off, except this time he simply followed Cal, not really registering what he was doing or where they might be going. They found seats in the back by the windows and Henry immediately slouched low and pressed his forehead against the cool glass as he watched the streets go by, still unraveling in imaginary lines, although less colorful and pronounced than before. The effects were wearing off, but the lines were still there, thank God. There was still that. As soon as they appeared they began to fade giving credence to the sneaking suspicion that had been with him all day that moments were not moments fixed in time, but rather moments were memories that hadn't been processed yet, points of reference on a map. Hundreds of crisscrossing lines lingering in various stages of disintegration, the latitude and longitude of love and loss. A meridian of nerve endings. The here and now was a total farce. If he could get this down in the dumps in a matter of seconds, then the idea of living for the moment must be the biggest piece of bourgeois propaganda bullshit of all time. He pined for things that hadn't happened yet. A life worth living. People that would come and go, their long shadows the blood and guts of broken hearts and wrathful impulses. None of it was logical, but then there was nothing necessarily logical about getting all sentimental over an afternoon spent in the airport.

He turned to look at Cal, who was wrestling with the rusty window latch. He grunted and struggled with the latch, his muscles flexed, veins bulging on his neck. Being at public school reminded Henry that nothing owned by the city actually worked the way it was supposed to. It finally unlocked and the large pane of glass slid down quickly and dangerously, letting in a slice of wind that blew Cal's hair into a glamorous state of dishevelment. It reminded Henry of a guillotine and he smiled a little as he thought of Cal's head rolling off into a basket, his mouth still babbling some ridiculous diatribe as the last of his blood swished aimlessly around his skull.

"You laughing at my hair?" Cal asked him, noticing Henry's shit-eating grin.

"No," Henry said, waving him away. "It's not that... It's... nothing."

Cal struggled to push his wayward hair back into place, but it refused to budge. He frowned and then shoved Henry's shoulder.

"You're a dick."

It only made Henry laugh harder. Was this friendship? Was the ability to aggravate at will and one-upmanship the corner-stones of lifelong buddydom? If so, then fuck camaraderie. He'd rather go it alone and save himself the angst.

"Anyway," Cal said, changing the subject, "check it out."

He pulled a small bag out from behind his back. It was a black knapsack embroidered with red thread. Henry had never really seen anything like it, and he certainly had never seen Cal with anything like it, and then it dawned on him. This was the family's missing bag. Cal had stolen it.

"A little souvenir of our day on multiple planes of existence," Cal said as he unzipped the bag, turned it over and emptied out the contents.

Henry sat silent as Cal picked through the things that fell on the long bus seat they shared. He watched silently as the family's things spilled out, his stomach a hollow urn of shame. Cal kept shaking loose items into a pile: a carton of foreign cigarettes, a small folding knife, some kind of a woman's scarf he'd seen women wear in news stories about massacres where mothers and sisters stood around the aftermath in wounded circles wailing and ululating for the dead. Huge massacres. The numbers of dead and wounded were always just slightly beyond the realm of what he could comprehend like the distance of the nearest star to earth or the number of grains of sand on the beach. At a certain point your mind just shut off. Numbers too big to be real. A couple of envelopes tumbled out of the bag and Henry grabbed one and opened it, pulling out a letter of some sort written on the thinnest paper he had ever touched in his life. It was paper so thin that the words written on them—words written in an alphabet that bore little resemblance to anything he'd ever seen in his life—seemed to hover in thin air when he held them up, a cloud of words, correspondence on a puff of smoke. He turned the paper over and over in his hands trying to find some sort of address on it, something that would tell him where he could find them and give this stuff back, but there was nothing on it he recognized. It was completely foreign. And the more he handled the paper the more he felt like it would disintegrate in his hands like a relic from another age. He folded the paper up carefully, put it back in the envelope, and then began to put it and the rest of the contents back into the bag. Cal was playing with the folding knife when he noticed what Henry was doing.

"What are you doing?" Cal asked, folding the blade of the knife back into its mother-of-pearl handle.

Henry tried to keep his anger in check, but he could feel himself stiffen. "I'm putting this stuff back so we can take it back to the airport. You shouldn't have stolen this."

"What are you talking about? Are you still tripping? This shit is ours. I stole it for us."

Cal's innocence did little to assuage Henry's anger.

"Did you see the family you took this from?" He continued putting the stuff away—a handful of coins, an ordinary rock with a vein of bright blue running through it, a tea bag. They were the last of the comforts of home and it made him sick that his friend was the one responsible for stealing it, because even as he packed the bag back up with every intention of taking it to the airport's lost and found, and perhaps even leaving his name and number so the family could call him and let him explain that he was sorry and that if they needed any help he would be their friend, he knew deep down that it would never happen. He knew that Cal would argue and that he would eventually relent, not because he wasn't passionate about the outcome, but because he was predisposed to being talked out of his convictions. That they had never really been convictions in the first place, just the inklings of passions, ideas that he knew in his head should mean and be everything to him, but somehow weren't. He worried sometimes that there would never be anything like that in his life: an idea to die for. That's what was missing. His shot at the great war.

"You're fucking crazy," Cal said and then before he knew it they were fighting over the bag, pulling it back and forth between them, and rather than see it break, which was somehow too much for him to bear, he let go and turned back to the window to watch their slow progress through an unending clot of traffic.

"Half this stuff is yours," Cal said, trying to make amends.

"I don't want it," Henry told him, without turning around. His voice was near to breaking.

"You don't want this tea bag? How about a scarf?" Cal sniffed it and then held it quickly away from his nose. "Oh man, that fucking reeks." He tossed the black and white checkered scarf on the seat and when he had turned his head to fiddle with the window Henry snatched it and shoved it in his pocket.

A few minutes later he heard the flick of a lighter and turned his head just slightly enough to see Cal lighting one of the stolen cigarettes. He inhaled, assessed the flavor, and expelled the smoke out the window.

"Want a cigarette?" he shook the pack at Henry who feigned disgust.

"You're an idiot. And you don't smoke."

"I do now," Cal shrugged. "You've gotta start sometime."

He took another drag, hung his elbow out of the window, and relaxed back into the uncomfortable seat. He looked comfortable, easy with himself, and the sight was too much for Henry to bear. He almost wished he'd start hallucinating again just so he wouldn't have to see Cal acting like he'd been a smoker all his life, riding the bus all his life, stealing all his life. He had an easy indifference to all of it and Henry wished that once, just once, his actions would weigh him down the way they weighed Henry down. The way they should weigh anyone down. He'd had enough.

Gritting his teeth, he reached up and pulled the wire that signaled to the driver to stop at the next stop. He got off and walked toward the exit.

"Where are you going?" Cal asked him, sitting up in his seat.

Henry just shook his head. He didn't want to answer.

Cal yelled, "You're gonna have to explain to me why you're so mad, dude, because I don't fucking get it."

By this point the back half of the bus was staring at them, and he got the feeling, looking at the wary faces that looked back at him, that these were people not necessarily unaccustomed to conflict but were incredibly tuned in to it, living on a frequency especially and intricately attuned to alerting them to when evasive action was needed. A housekeeper with what seemed like ten armfuls of cleaning products clutched her things to her chest, embracing enough chemicals to render LA's public transportation ridership sterile for the next ten generations. Behind her a young Hispanic teenager put his arm around his girlfriend's shoulder, hugging her close, their skin colors almost a perfect matching shade of brown, as if the Pantone scale was a compatibility indicator. Even if all these faces staring at him, faces anticipating violence and accustomed to it (or expecting violence because they were accustomed to it), even if all these faces hadn't been turned to him, eyes waiting, he wouldn't have told Cal why he was so pissed. The truth was that there was no reason. Or maybe it was that there were too many reasons. The whole day was the reason. The year. The reasons were everywhere, too many to count. But even as he realized this, he couldn't summon one up that when articulated could explain his frustration, so when the doors closed, the heavy hydraulics sounding like an asthmatic grandmother's dying kiss, Henry simply turned and walked away, mass transit in Los Angeles for once reliable for at least letting him off the hook at having to answer someone just because they wanted him to. Besides, after today what did he really owe Cal anyway? Besides feeling like he owed him everything, for what? The gift of friendship? Fuck friendship. If Cal couldn't respect the reservoir, then fuck his friendship.

Henry wandered down a large street, unsure of where he was exactly, but happy to be off the bus. It was late afternoon, as benign a time as any, with kids of all ages huddled in their deeply conspiratorial yet happy scrums. The clothes they wore were nothing like what Henry and his classmates dressed in. Corduroys and polos festooned with the wear and tear of prolonged use, namely worn-out knees, the blooming ink blotter of pit stains, and a hint of chocolate milk splashed down the front. They eyed him warily as he walked past, trying without success to orient himself, his skin not dark enough to fit in, his clothes the wrong kind of faded. They stood beneath an RTD sign that boasted no less than a place to catch six or seven different bus lines. The 2, 7, 14, 34, 404, 576. It was a language he didn't even remotely begin to understand, a code for kids who never rode in carpools, their parents fugitives from their own children in the service of a level of responsibility he would probably never know. Or, as his parents might say to forgive themselves one day, wouldn't ever *have* to know.

A boy of about fourteen broke free from the group and sauntered over to Henry, who, without realizing it, had stopped walking and was staring at them from a distance of just a couple of yards.

"What do you want?" the kid asked him, matter-of-factly. The straps of his backpack were decorated with graffiti written in Liquid Paper. His clothes were loose hand-me-downs that he wasn't quite ready for yet, like fruit picked before its ripening, but consumed nonetheless, because hunger was what hunger was. "You wanna buy some weed? How much money you got?"

Henry stood there dumb, not so much surprised by the situation as he was taken aback. He'd actually love to buy some weed. It sounded outstanding, in fact. But he had no money, and even if he did, he wasn't sure how much you were supposed to ask for. This wasn't the walk home to his house after school when he and Cal would sometimes stop and have a couple of hits off of Cal's turquoise blue pipe. Cal was the one who always had it, so he wasn't sure how much a couple of hits off a pipe actually was. An ounce? A pound? A kilo? His drug lexicon was limited to the mass quantities bought and sold by the neon-suited Central American kingpins of *Miami Vice*. Maybe a sniper or two up in the building, the quick exchange of metallic suitcases; one full to bursting with sandbag-sized packages of cocaine, the other crammed with stacks of creaseless cash, all hundreds. Someone from one side would have a butterfly knife they'd pull from their boot and expertly flip open like a dayglow ninja. He'd stick the knife into one of the bags of coke and take a taste of the dope, nodding quickly and wordlessly to his boss letting him know that the shit was good. On the other side someone would fan one of the stacks of cash to make sure the bills were all hundreds and not stuffed in the middle with blanks or ones. He'd nod, too. No one spoke during these transactions. It was like a religious ceremony, all nuances and formalities. That was a drug deal. This...this was something else.

The kid turned to his friends who were all watching and shrugged his shoulders. As far as sales pitches went, this one was pretty straight-forward, and it dawned on Henry suddenly that he was fucking up the program, that he was the glitch in what was typically a well-oiled system. As the kid turned, Henry noticed that the backpack was an old He-Man bag, some vestige of youth he either hadn't or couldn't let go of. It reminded him of his own youthful allegiances: a *Star Wars* lunchbox, Spiderman Underoos, a Pac Man pencil case. His loyalties had always been claimed by something or someone as far back as he could remember.

The kid turned back with a clenched fist that Henry saw coming but could do nothing about. He was going to get hit. It was a foregone conclusion and as the punch came, landing squarely on his cheek, he felt his knees get weak and he sank to the ground. He'd only ever been punched in the face once before, the time he was suckerpunched on the quad, and he was surprised by the fact that there was no pain involved. It shocked him as the second blow came, this one striking him higher up on his face, just under his eye. No pain, but there were other reactions he hadn't ever anticipated: jellied legs, adrenaline running endless loops around his chest with nowhere to go, doubling back on itself over and over, making him shake all over as he never felt himself shake before. The third blow laid him out and he began to wonder, in a detached and idle way, whether it would ever end. How long had it been? It certainly felt like hours, but three punches? That couldn't be more than a few seconds, right? The kid's friends saw their chance and ran over and joined in kicking Henry all over and when he felt a shoe numbly strike his head, he knew he had better cover up, not because the pain was so bad, but because he knew at the very least that getting kicked over and over in the head couldn't be a good thing in the long run. More time went by, but it was impossible to tell how much exactly. His mind started to wander. He thought about the airport, about being lost, and finally how funny it was that he was getting his ass kicked by a kid wearing a He-Man backpack and his posse of superhero assistants. There was a certain irony in that. If all these superheroes were beating his ass, he must be the arch-criminal, right? Isn't that how it worked? He must have laughed, because the League of Justice stopped for a second to assess the damage, and in that split-second he jumped up, more as a channel for the chemistry of self-preservation that was swirling inside of him than for any specifically conscious reason, and took off down the street as fast he could run.

A series of bus rides later and he was back in familiar territory. None of the bus drivers he encountered had made him pay a fare. Somehow the bruises were enough. A wretched currency in their own right. He could only guess what he looked like, but he smiled as he walked to the back of each bus, something in him warming to the sheer Americanness of getting his ass kicked in by a prepubescent drug dealer in hand-me-down clothes. Later, when the numbness evolved into a tingle and the tingling exploded into pain and soreness, the likes of which he had never felt, he might ask himself why he didn't fight back. But that would be like asking why he didn't fight back against America. You just didn't. America was the one enemy you had to simply let kick your ass once in a while. This pound of flesh was the tithing that was required, the bare minimum that was expected from each person to keep the machine running smoothly. But these thoughts, these hard crystals begetting harder crystals, he realized, were proof that he was still high, that the rabbit hole had gone all calcified and he would keep going down it if he let himself, like a man near death going toward the light instead of resisting. He was definitely a "the light's just a little too far right now" kind of guy.

The bus let him off about a half mile from home into a different climate, the air here bustling with the dewy molecules people called the "marine layer," an expression that to him always brought to mind an amphibious assault rather than the precipitation brought on by their close proximity to the ocean. The mist reeled wildly in the headlights of commuters who were at the tail end of their drive home. It was an anxious time, as he knew from his father, who couldn't help but remark when he walked in the door at night that it had just taken him forty-five minutes to drive less than ten miles. The words would be barely out of his mouth as he grabbed a Coors out of the fridge and made a beeline for the TV to watch whatever sporting event would take his mind off things for a while. Until sleep. Henry, who once had the urge to please his dad, as all little boys do, would ask him at this point how his day was, and his dad would pop open the beer, suck down the foam with a noisy slurp, and briefly grumble the word, "Hectic," as if that alone was sufficient to sum up the cumulative experiences of his life until that point. Hectic. "What's that mean?" he had asked Grace once. "Is it bad?" "It means he was really busy today and now he's tired and just wants to rest. Also, it means that he doesn't hate us, even though his face looks like that, but he just wants a little time to be alone now." He looked at his father, already sunken into the couch, as he pulled the knot of his tie loose as though it was a fist that had been clenched tightly at his throat all day. "It means all that?" he asked her, wanting to be sure he understood correctly. "Look at him," Grace said, watching from the kitchen where she nibbled a cracker in tiny bird-like bites. "Don't you think that's what it means?"

It was not at all far-fetched to think that one of these cars might be his father's; glasses askance, a cigarette ignited between his fingers like a malignant afterthought, trapped in the silent netherworld of AM radio as he waited for the announcer to deliver the next salvo of sports scores.

Any one of these might be his father... It sounded like an orphan's lament.

His arms swung loosely at his sides, and when he pulled up the collar of his blue and white flannel shirt, he noticed that it had an enormous tear in it. Funny, but he didn't remember hearing a rip. *A tear this big you think you'd remember hearing*, he thought. It had begun to lightly rain and he pulled the shirt off and wrapped it around his head like a turban. The rain felt amazingly soothing on his skin and when he looked down at himself he saw that both of his arms had been skinned and bruised pretty badly. He was bleeding in spots and again was amazed that he couldn't remember at what point during the fight this had happened. Already the details were receding from his mind, and he closed his eyes as he walked, soaking in the rain that he imagined sizzled off him into whisps of smoke as soon as they hit his hot skin, and tried to remember, as though he had just woken up from a dream, what he had just been through. The recollections were vague, though, and when he did manage to bring up specifics they flashed before him like photographs instead of movies, heartfelt pictures that represented the experience instead of an actual reconstruction of the violence. Here are the pictures he saw:

The boy, dressed like an altar boy on a cigarette break, whirling around. The Wite-Out graffiti on his backpack straps. A look of terrific malice and effort on his face, eyes as wide as headlights, like the punch he's about to throw weighs 1,000 pounds.

Henry is on the ground with one hand on his nuts and the other covering his head. He cannot see himself, but he remembers feeling that these are the two most vulnerable spots and if he can just keep those two parts of himself covered forever, he will never die. The boy's foot is coming in toward his midriff. His shoes are black Chucks and the laces are untied. Someone's going to get hurt.

A girl is standing off to the side and she is in mid-cheer. Her face is a blister of happiness. She is ecstatic. At this moment Henry remembers hoping that his Walkman has not been broken. Also, he wonders if he should show them his wallet to prove that he has no money on him.

There are a sea of legs around him. Some are jeans, some black pants, some bare legs. They are in various states of coming at him and being pulled back to deliver the next blow. There is no order to it. Only the careless joy of children playing with a new toy.

He opened his eyes in time to run straight into the low hanging branch of a kumquat tree that hadn't been trimmed back in some time. He stuck out his hands and leaned to the side but he wasn't quick enough and the pointed end raked across his face leaving a bracing gash. Without touching it, he knew it was bleeding. Knew the cut was straight and clean. And with an overwhelming sense of déjà vu he couldn't place, he gritted his teeth, reached out, and tore the branch from the tree. The weight of the branch felt good, and the length reminded him of a rifle, of playing soldier when he was a child, when any object within arm's reach could be imagined as a weapon. Stooping down, rifle in hand, he imagined himself a soldier once again sent on a secret mission to infiltrate and destroy. But destroy what? It hardly mattered. There were plenty of bad guys out there. Finding an enemy, here, so close to home, was never the problem.

Shadows from the car's headlights fell across him and down the street in assembly line order creating texture where there was none, deep craters, the sporadic scarring of aircraft strafe fire. He was too exposed, so he quickly cut over onto the front lawn of a nearby house, staying low, always moving. That was the key. You should always be moving. Window curtains parted and a worried face peered out at him. *Run*, he wanted to say, *get out while you can*. But there was no time for that and he frantically waved his arms at the sky, hoping that whoever it was got the message that enemy aircraft were on its way. Bombs. Bombs would come and the night would punish them cruelly, once and for all.

Continuing on, he noticed the charred remains of a civilian lying dead, blown apart, in a trench, the victim of the enemy's new cruel incendiary bomb. The kind of bomb that stuck to you. That burned your flesh. That you never in a million years dreamed would even exist. Who would make something like this? What he didn't understand before this afternoon was suddenly clear to him, and if he wasn't so busy keeping his own ass alive, of trying to get back home and save his sister, then he would stop and tell them, explain to them as they lay burning in agony, wondering why they couldn't just die: *You can't die because they don't want you to die. They want to see you suffer. That's how they design their weapons. For you to suffer. For you to feel every second of their cruelty. To spite you for doubting it in the first place. We tried to warn you that the enemy is crueler than you ever knew. Than you ever believed was even possible. We warned you people, but you didn't believe us. Said it was hyperbole. Propaganda. I don't feel self-righteous now. I just feel sad. I feel sad for all of you.* He knelt by the corpse, which, as he got closer saw was a pile of community newspapers, fliers for dog walking services, housekeeping, babysitters, gardening, all the things that would make your children better people if they were to do it themselves outsourced instead to those that were desperate, at an incremental pace, to build a better life. He doffed an imaginary cap and bowed his head as he whispered a quick prayer. Something in Latin because Latin sounded like flowers and since he didn't have anything to leave than the least he could do was to leave those words, holy nonsense to wreathe the dead.

Everything looked different as he kept up the pace, but in a way that made these familiar surroundings seem more complete, as if the two loose ends of a thing had finally been connected. It was like seeing home again after a long journey, like he hadn't just gotten off the bus after a long strange day but had been away for many years, seen things, violence that had changed him, turned him inside out. He touched his face. Things were starting to swell, the skin spreading. Pulling away his finger he saw that it was wet with blood. No more stopping, he promised himself. No matter what he saw. No matter how bad it was. He had to keep moving and get home as fast as possible. Saving Grace was all that mattered now.

When he came to the intersection, he looked left and right before he ran across the street and dove behind an enormous eucalyptus tree for cover, his heart pounding wildly, his rifle pressed uncomfortably into his abdomen. Safe again. For the moment. A convoy of enemy luxury cars drove past, commuters returning home after long days at work, hectic days, seeking solace at home… If he had some C-4, he could plant a charge. Bomb them all to hell and back. But he didn't. His demolitions guy had been killed in an ambush earlier that day. He thought of Cal, riddled with bullets, or better yet, swinging from a noose that the enemy had made for him from his own belt.

As he turned the corner onto his street, still in stealth mode, he saw a group of younger kids playing a game of touch football in the last remaining dregs of daylight that strained to cover them, orange and yellow tendrils providing atmosphere more than illumination at this point. At that moment the streetlights came on with a dull fuzz of noise and a little cheer went up from the eight or nine of them. A last-minute reprieve, snuck in under the dinnertime wire. Now it would be harder for their moms to call them in since they couldn't use the "it's too dark to play" rule. It would take the fathers to get them in now. Booming voices that would rain down on them from above, trumping even the generosity of electricity.

He ducked behind a car and watched them play for a few minutes. The quarterback was a kid he vaguely recognized, an anonymous neighbor, but he was clearly the leader. His lean body flexed athletically as he dodged the outstretched hands of incoming linemen who were trying to sack him before he could get off another pass. He was probably at the front when the gang of them rode their bikes to the corner store to get some candy and play the arcade games. He probably chose the games they would play, dictating whether it was going to be basketball or football or once in a while, when they could get enough kids, a neighborhood-wide capture the flag free-for-all.

Henry partook of these games when he was a kid, occasionally, too, when the numbers were uneven and they needed another body to balance things out. He was recreational ballast. That was why he'd been able to pick out the leader so quickly. The kid who rallied all the others. The biggest, most athletic. The leader kid was the first one who came to know a little bit of self-confidence, discovering it like buried treasure on the basketball court or in a schoolyard fight. Buried treasure because it was beyond value. Buried treasure because it was more than he could ever hope for. Riches beyond his wildest dreams.

Somewhere on the next block Henry heard the pitched voices of smaller kids engaged in another type of game. Too young to join this one, they had their own versions of competition, where the stage was set for their matriculation to the next category of growing up. Theirs was an innocent phase, maybe the last one there would ever be. He wished he could tell them to enjoy it, but it wouldn't do any good. No one ever enjoyed what they had while they had it. Not really. That wasn't how people worked.

He watched the quarterback fade back for another pass, his lean muscles straining as he leaned this way and that, taking his time to scan downfield for an open receiver. He easily dodged the incoming rushers. It wasn't even fair. And it never would be. Not for a long time. His DNA was enough to invoke the slaughter rule.

The ball sailed toward a receiver near Henry in a long, tall arc, went through the boy's hands and bumped along landing next to Henry's feet. The kids, having not noticed him until then, went silent as they waited for him to throw the ball back, but he just stood there, the thoughts of the day coagulating in his mind: of Cal and the airport, the kids who had beat him up, and how coming back to his side of town had put him in the mood of being ensconced in a battle that somehow made more sense to him than it ever had before: it was that he finally understood his responsibility in the grand of scheme of things. The responsibility to rebel. The responsibility to violence.

He picked up the ball and looked at the hard brown leather. Scuffed black in places, its scaly exterior reminded him of the skin of some exotic lizards he had seen at the zoo once when he was a kid. They had brought these gigantic green monsters out for the kids to touch and he had been petrified by their size and their cool demeanor. How they blinked only occasionally and barely moved except to scour the air with a quick flick of the tongue. Nothing moved that slowly that wasn't terribly dangerous, he remembered thinking, as he turned the ball over in his hands, idly looking for the thing's mouth and eyes.

Without noticing it the quarterback kid had walked over and was standing in front of Henry with his hand out for the ball. They were almost the same height, but the kid, who had to be a good four or five years younger than Henry, was clearly the stronger of the two of them. He pushed his Dodgers baseball cap to the back of his head and cleared his throat.

"Excuse me," he said politely, probably wishing at this moment that he wasn't the automatic delegate to handle situations like this. "Can we have our ball back please?"

A car drove by, a new Mercedes, and the kids automatically wandered to the side of the street. The man driving the car gave his horn a little beep and waved generally at the kids who waved in unison back to him. There was so much understanding here between everyone, so much corroboration, and just as he held the ball out he pulled it back again as the quarterback reached for it, giving him a puzzled look.

You have it too easy, you fucking collaborators, he thought, as a kind of mania overtook him, an anger at not only the easy life he knew they would have just by continuing to be who they were, but an anger that here was this new thing he had learned today, this violence, and like any kid with a new toy, there was no way for him to experiment with it that wouldn't land him in a world of shit.

The quarterback reached out for the ball again. "Hey dude," he said, beginning to lose his patience. "Give us our ball." The rest of the kids began to crowd in a little closer, not exactly engaging, but showing their support for their leader by closing off Henry's possible routes of escape. The adolescent muscle was flexing, and it was the power of the mob.

He let the ball drop from his hands and it bounced awkwardly away from them. He could see the quarterback's jaw line tense as the boy clenched his teeth, glared at him, and bent over to pick up the ball. As he bent down, Henry, almost without thinking, lifted his knee into the boy's face as hard as he could, turned, and began to run in the direction of his house. Behind him he heard the crowd of boys react in shock as they crowded around their friend. He couldn't tell if anyone was behind him. There was a sound, but he couldn't be sure if it was them chasing him or merely the desperate machinery of his heart setting the pace for his quick retreat. There was no way to be sure without stopping and turning around, and that seemed like the worst idea of a day that was already record setting when it came to poor judgment and rash decision-making. He sprinted until there was a searing pain in his lungs, not to mention in one of his knees. It was the knee he had used to hurt the quarterback with, and for it to be hurting him, he knew that he must have done some serious damage to the boy. It had been a solid connection and there had definitely been the sound, no, more like a feeling, of something crunching, the beautiful feeling of soft flesh making room for harder flesh. There had also been something warm, too, which he assumed was blood. Again, there was no time to stop and find out. Violence had a certain momentum all of its own, and besides, it was dark now and blood would be hard to see against the dark blue of his jeans.

When he finally stopped, about a block away from his house, he turned and braced himself, ready for the counterattack, but the street was clear. Only the occasional station wagon swishing by and a frantically barking dog in the distance protecting its territory against the night's shadows. Little had changed. He patted himself down looking for evidence that it had actually happened; that he had actually smashed that boy's face, that his own face was beaten and swelling, that he had been at the airport and seen a family lose everything that ever meant anything to them. The drugs were still there, albeit ebbing, and at this stage of the journey a reality check was more muscle memory than anything. When he was a kid, he would have these out of body experiences when the house was empty—Grace and his mom at ballet class, Dad perpetually at work—and he would say something, a bad word, say, that he wouldn't dare say if anyone was around, and he'd feel the house take the word, absorb it into the walls and the carpet, metastasize it so quickly that he couldn't be sure he had actually said it in the first place. So, he'd say it again. And again. And again. And he would get caught in a loop of saying it until he heard the garage door grumble open and force himself to stop and when his mother came in and gave him a kiss on the head and asked him what he'd done with himself all day, all he could say was "nothing," and even though it wasn't what she wanted to hear, it would be the truth. There would be no repercussions for what he'd done.

There never were, because the house, or the neighborhood in this case, took everything in and held it like a sponge that was never squeezed.

The sun gone, he came upon his house not entirely sure that it was actually his house. The night had made everything tenuous, or maybe it was the drugs, or maybe it was a concussion, or maybe it was all these things put together, finally the secret formula he'd been searching for his entire life. In fact, the only way he knew for sure that it was his house was the blotch of yellow paint on the wall near the front door that he had painted on when he was ten. It was the summer of the Night Stalker and theories were everywhere about what type of house attracted the serial killer. One popular notion was that he skipped yellow houses, so Henry, who had been kept up nights worried sick about falling victim to the knife that seemed to arbitrarily carve up its victims, had gone down to the hardware store and used his allowance to buy a can of yellow house paint. He had been painting for about fifteen minutes before he felt his father's hand grab him by the back of the shirt and yank him back, hard, making him spill the paint on the lawn. They both cursed, but for different reasons: his father's "Goddammit!" was pure frustration, the penultimate pressure valve on a mechanism that might otherwise lash out and do something to someone, and Henry's "Fuck!" simultaneous but completely different, was pure despair. The sound that hope makes leaving a vacuum. They were both exhausted noises and the two sat glaring at one another for a minute and then, suddenly, and for no apparent reason, smiled. Henry liked to think that the moment was their first bonding experience.

Inside the house, nothing. Darkness had erased all distinguishing features, dumped a bucket of gray paint over family photos taken at Penney's, leached all of the color out of poorly made Father's Day ashtrays and all the other domestic artifacts they'd all been so proud of once. They were the things that were beyond utility. Egalitarianism at its purest. He let his fingers brush over the objects, as fragile-seeming as relics at a museum. Everything was bound for dust and he understood that reverence was due not to the objects themselves, but to the light that, through its conjurers quality, got it there sooner.

"Hello," he called out, testing his voice against the dead space of the house. Expecting nothing back, he continued up the stairs and at the top stopped when he heard something rustling from his sister's room. His first thought was that Cal had broken into his house and was murdering Grace. He saw it so clearly in his head, the motive, the argument, the action. He picked up his pace, blaming himself for their argument earlier in the day, the brutal rape and murder of his sister the inevitable consequence of his having stood up for himself even that little bit.

He crept silently to the door, which was open a crack, and on the precipice of hallucination, albeit the backing away from the precipice part of it, peered nervously into the room. It should have relieved him to see what was happening, that it wasn't what he imagined just a moment ago, but it wasn't relief or thankfulness that he felt, but surprise, the distinct wash of wonderment that the worst had not happened when the worst possible scenario always seemed the most likely. So he was startled when he looked in and saw his sister, her back toward him, not being savagely attacked by his best friend, but dancing wildly to what at first appeared to be no music, but then when he looked closer, realized she had on her Walkman, wearing only a long men's shirt that hung down over her butt to the tops of her legs. She was ecstatic as she jumped around and flailed her arms, the rhythm of what she was listening to completely indiscernible to him, but clearly in sync with something divine.

"Grace," he muttered softly as he tiptoed into her room. He didn't want to scare her and he had the feeling that if he shook her shoulder as he was tempted to do, it would be like shaking a sleepwalker, which, like swimming after eating and not flossing every night, his parents had always warned him not to do.

He tiptoed closer and noticed some ripped up paper on the floor. A trail of confetti led to her bed where he saw a stack of papers, and he instantly knew that this had something to do with her mood. He sat on her bed and picked up the top sheet. It was a letter adorned with the deep red logo of BROWN UNIVERSITY and it read, *Dear Ms. Colmes, On behalf of the Admissions Committee of Brown University I am pleased to offer you a spot in the freshman class of 1990. If you choose to accept this offer...*

He had no idea where Brown was, but it sounded far away. Nothing with a simple name like that was ever in California. Everything out here was new or Spanish or sun-drenched, nomenclature that promised something better. The return address on the envelope said Rhode Island and he tried to picture it in his mind. Grey days and a perpetual mist that hung over ivy-covered brick buildings like atmospheric camouflage. Weather that was easy to lose oneself in. Anonymity behind wool scarves and heavy coats with the collars turned up. How lovely it sounded. People everywhere all bundled up and confident in their no-frills lifestyle. Maybe she would let him come with her, he thought. They could get an apartment together and he could finish high school while she went to college. He could reinvent himself there, become the person he felt like he had the potential to be, as if the perception of his peers was the only thing holding him back from self-actualization.

She turned, caught sight of him and squealed a shrill little alarm of surprise.

"Jesus," she said, her hand going instinctively to her chest, "doesn't anyone in this family knock?"

She took her headphones off and Henry could hear a Stiff Little Fingers song blasting through the headset. It was the mixtape he had made for her months ago. He had always wondered if she ever listened to it and here she was, dancing and singing along, as comfortable with the music as she was with everything and everyone. She clicked the stop button and tossed the Walkman onto the bed.

"That's the tape you made for me. Do you remember? I love it. I think I'm going to be a punk rocker. Can you see me with my hair spiked up and a safety pin through my nose? Think I could pull it off?"

He pictured her that way for a second and could see it clearly. She would always be comfortable no matter what she wore, what identity she tried on. Some people had that luxury. Not many, but she was certainly one of them. She walked to her desk and switched the light on, turned back toward him, and let out a genuine scream of alarm. The instant the lights came on whatever was left of being high vanished from his body as if vacuumed out by the light and was replaced instantly by a searing rush of pain that started in his face and at the back of his head, and then radiated throughout the rest of him, a pulsing ache that had the decency to keep time with the pace of his heartbeat, allowing him the small favor of reliability and consistency so that he could brace himself each time a wave of it came.

"Oh, my God, Henry! What's wrong with you?" And then, "What happened to your face?"

She covered her own face with her hands and ran downstairs

to get the first aid kit and an ice pack as he wandered over to the mirror above her bureau. She was right to yell at him. His face was a black and blue mess, swollen in places he didn't even remember getting hit or kicked. Dried blood criss-crossed his face in random lines and he began to scratch if off with unhurried scrapes of his fingernails letting the red flakes sprinkle to the bureau. Grace came back and threw the supplies on her bed as she pulled him away.

"Gross, Henry. That's my stuff. What's wrong with you?"

He looked down and saw that the dried blood had settled over all her stuff, her books and makeup and pictures of friends, like a recent snowstorm.

"Sorry," he mumbled, as he absently tried to wipe it away.

"Just forget it," she said, pulling him to the edge of her bed where she methodically went to work rubbing antiseptic on his wounds and using large Band Aids to cover what she could. She gave him the ice pack to hold to the back of his head, but he couldn't make his arm work, so she slapped the thing on his head and lifted his hand and roughly placed it on the pack. "Hold it there. Don't move."

"I'm sorry," he said again, although he didn't know exactly what he was apologizing for.

"Stop saying that," she said without looking at him. "It doesn't do anything to say you're sorry all the time. It just makes it mean nothing."

"Sorry."

She glared at him as though he were teasing her, but he wasn't. Apologies were nothing more than a reflexive action to him.

"What happened to you, Henry?"

"It's hard to explain," he began as he tried to sketch out his day from detention until now. He left nothing out, except for the part about hitting the boy with the football, and at the end of the telling he came to the conclusion, "I don't want to be friends with Cal anymore."

"Good," she answered, dabbing Bactine here and there, blowing on it as she put it on his wounds so it wouldn't sting too much. "He's an asshole."

"But he's my only friend."

"That's not true."

"Yes, it is. He was my only friend, so I guess that made him my best friend, and the thing is, even when he was my best friend I didn't like him that much."

"Then why did you hang out with him?"

He laughed. "If you have to ask that question, then you'll never understand."

She became silent as she continued to nurse his wounds.

"Where are Mom and Dad?" he asked her, trying to engage her somehow in something other than his injuries.

"Therapy," she said, as if it needed no further explanation.

"What kind of therapy?"

"Marriage therapy, dummy."

"Why?"

She looked at him searching his face to see if he was testing her or not.

"Are you kidding me?"

He shook his head.

"You can't tell how unhappy they are together?"

"No."

"Henry," she stopped dabbing his face, "when's the last

time you remember them ever kissing one another or even hugging? Can you remember it at all? I can't."

He thought about it for a second and remembered standing outside his parents' bedroom door, eavesdropping, as they bonded almost romantically over their shared misgivings about their son. He'd never told Grace about that and now he never would.

"They're gonna split up, Henry. It's just a matter of time. Did you really not know this was going on? You really had no clue?"

He shook his head and wondered how he could have missed what was so obvious to her. It wasn't like they lived in separate houses or had two separate sets of parents. All this time he thought they were living the same kind of life together, sharing the same experiences, building up a set of memories they would one day share and shake their heads over in mock amazement that they'd ever made it through all the madness. But it wasn't the case. Their memories would be entirely different because they weren't really living in the same world together, after all. Her room was littered with books, novels she read, one after another, everything from the classics to modern things, some by authors he'd heard of: Dickens, Dostoevsky, Kerouac, others he hadn't heard of but felt like he should have. In her room she devoured these stories, hour after hour, day after day, and he wondered if that was why she could see what he couldn't when it came to their parents' marriage falling apart. She read enough that she should know the ending to everything by now.

He threw the ice pack down and stormed into his room. A few minutes later she came in. He could hear her contrite steps move across his floor. His face was buried in the old book, *Jane's*, solace once again found in the old promise of battle. The reliability of a fight. He was going through the section on Vietnam, his favorite. The M16, the Claymore, the Phantom; weapons that were now outdated, but at one time represented an entire generation, bound men together in a common purpose. Straightforward? No. But common. There was nothing like this in his world. No collective context. Just pain and confusion, the sense that life was happening faster than he could ever hope to keep up. He missed what he didn't have. What he never had. A diagnosis for the disease that ailed them all.

Grace's steps were slow as she approached his bed. She sat down and pulled the book out of his hands, replacing it with the ice pack. He let her make the switch and pressed the cool blue bag to his face.

"I remember this old book. I can't believe you still have it." She flipped absently through the pages and he wanted to know what she saw there. She put the book down and took his hand in hers. "I'm sorry, Henry. I had no right to get mad at you like that. I'm just so frustrated by everything right now. Nothing has been feeling the way it should, if that makes any sense. Not just Mom and Dad, either. I'm sick of my friends. I'm sick of how stupid and shallow they are and how little it bothered me until just recently. I'm pissed at myself for that. I'm sick of school. And I'm sick of this house," she paused as she glanced around appearing to wait for the house to answer her insult. "I broke up with Peter today. I got the letter from Brown and the first thing I did was call him up and tell him that it's over. And now I can't even give you one good reason why I went out with him in the first place."

"Why did you?" he asked, hiding his face beneath the ice pack.

She shrugged. "Something to do? No, more than that. The right thing to do."

"Are you sick of me, too?" he asked, a lump forming in his throat.

"No!" she almost yelled it. "Not at all. Not even a little bit. You're the only thing I'm going to miss when I go. You're a good guy, Henry. A really good guy. You're funny and mysterious…" He snorted and she slapped him gently on the shoulder. "I'm serious. You're mysterious. I never know what you're thinking or what you're going to do next. I like that. My friends, I always know what they're going to do, what they're going to say. But not you. That's something special. And you're going to find out that lots of girls are going to love that, too."

He took a deep breath and when he exhaled it came out all ragged as he started to cry.

"You just need to stop letting people tell you how you should feel. Mom and Dad shouldn't do it. I shouldn't do it. Cal shouldn't do it. You deserve to live the way you want to live. I think that's why you've been having all these problems and getting into trouble. No one is letting you feel the way you…" she paused as she searched for the right word, "… deserve to feel."

He took the ice pack away from his face and looked at her. The blues of her eyes trembled behind tears that wouldn't fall, a smile that showed the small pits of dimples that sat in her cheeks, a feature he'd heard her complimented on his entire life by relatives and friends of his parents. Another thing that made her perfect.

Just then they felt the rumble of the garage door opening signaling that their parents were home. In another minute the back door would open and his mother would call to them as she always did first thing when she got home from being out. *Grace! Henry!* When they were little they would shriek back, *Mommy!* and then as they got older it was, *Hi Mom*, and then, *Yeah?* Tonight it would be nothing. Tonight they'd let their names ring hollow in the space that was no longer theirs. The space that no longer belonged to either of them in the way it once had.

"Hey," she said, grabbing his leg and shaking him. "Should we go up to the attic like we used to when we were little? Do you remember that?" The mischief in her eyes was genuine, and he appreciated it more than anything she could have said or done, but he wasn't interested in hiding anymore.

"No," he said, gently taking the book back from her and sliding it beneath his bed. "I want to stay right here."

Chapter 11

THE APARTMENT BUILDING was falling further and further into chaos every day, and Henry started to think very seriously about finding a new place to live when he wasn't obsessing over his Potter story. It would be hard, though, since he might be getting fired at any moment and had very little money put aside for a "rainy day." All his days seemed rainy now. Tenuous. Temporal comb-overs to hide his thinning existential pate.

Although, from what he'd observed, a lack of money didn't seem to stop most people from getting what they wanted in LA. Deciding whether or not to appear wealthy was nothing but a social construct to most folks, a glib afterthought or affectation, like whether to match your belt with your socks or paper or plastic.

He awoke, as usual, to the din of pathos. Stretching in his sleeping bag on Truman's floor, he coughed and drank a full glass of water while still lying prone. An old drunk at a bar had once recommended the practice to him around closing time as a good way to "flush the liver," and while he doubted that there was any medical veracity to the idea, it had become a sort of habit for him, which, psychologically, was at least as important as any scientific evidence.

He dressed quickly, afraid that one of the neo-Pagans might

accidentally barge in on him, which was what happened a few days earlier when one had busted in to ask Truman if he was allowed to plant fruit trees in the den. "I'm pretty sure he'd say yes," Henry told the guy, hiding himself behind his hands. The guy didn't even register that Henry was naked. Modesty had no place in this morass. It was niche, fetishistic even, as abhorrent a pastime as child pornography or Republicanism. The idea of impolite company was a moving target these days and so, Henry thought to himself, it was probably better not to even put up a fight.

Leaving the bedroom and stepping into the living room he was quickly asphyxiated by a variety of odors he prided himself, like someone with perfect pitch being able to hear and identify the notes being played on the individual instruments of a song, on being able to pick apart and identify from the ghastly whole. One of the freaks had splashed on a generous helping of sandalwood (a smell that always reminded him of having sex with sad women). Underneath that he caught a whiff of sour milk. And below that the unmistakably acrid stab of used rubbers. Dante's circles of hell couldn't do justice to the sensory overload. And that didn't even take into account the smoke, which he put into another category altogether. Cigarette smoke drifted in the air. Pot too. Maybe some hash. Bilious clouds of paranoid premonitions hung over everything, densely, like a shroud. And in a way it was a religious experience because they lingered, these men, in the long shadows of nihilistic servitude. They were slaves to a cause now and that cause was doom. He tried to ignore their sideways glances as he went into the bathroom to brush his teeth and then into the kitchen on the off chance someone had made a pot of coffee. He didn't judge them. He just didn't want to engage. He recognized that everyone was desperate for something, that fact evident by the six or eight guys he saw huddled around a laptop watching videos on YouTube of children having their cochlear implants switched on for the first time. Sometimes the first thing they'd hear would be music, or clapping, and sometimes it was the sound of their mother's voice. The men were enraptured, and some were even crying. The videos were an anti-catharsis, he realized. Exposure therapy as a cure for their collective numbness. They were desperate for anything.

He paused by the door and listened to a conversation going on at the kitchen table. Not sure if it was the neo-neocons (who, as far as he could tell, were the children of Republicans who'd rebelled when they were younger, found Jesus at some point, and were now doubting their faith because Jesus wasn't authoritarian enough) or the California separatists. He listened as they talked about writing up some sort of organizational manifesto.

"We should include a question that really gets in people's heads. Makes them think about themselves in a way they never have before," a man with greying, curly hair said. He tapped a pencil nervously on the table as he let the thought percolate through him. "I don't want just anyone with us. I want someone who's really thought about it. Or at least someone who has the ability to think about it. And would if push came to shove."

"I thought," said another guy wearing a checked bow tie and who looked a hell of a lot like Henry's dentist, "the idea was to get as many people to join as possible. Isn't it?" He looked around at the rest of the faces at the table for confirmation.

"Yes, Charles, I agree," said the guy with the pencil. Henry wondered if this was the beginning of a power struggle. "But at the beginning we need the elite. The followers will come later once the elite have developed the structure." He paused. "You see?"

They all nodded and then fell silent again as a group.

"I was in a job interview once," another of the "elite" piped up, "and the guy interviewing me asked me if I was a tree, what kind of a tree would I be. Maybe we could use something like that?" His voice went up at the end giving away the fact that he didn't know if this was going to be accepted as a great idea or the stupidest thing ever uttered.

"I like that," pencil guy said. "What did you say when he asked you that?"

The interviewee's face turned red. "Weeping willow. I felt like it would show I had a sensitive side in addition to being large and substantial. And slightly droopy."

"Did you get the job?"

He shook his head no and let his eyes drift lazily to the floor.

"Well, I for one like it," the guy with the pencil said as he began scribbling furiously on the piece of paper, "but I think we need to have our own spin on it. Trees are nice, but we're talking about a new world order here. Right, guys? We need probing. We need to get to the heart of the matter with these people. Really see into their souls." He looked around the table. "Ideas?"

The table was silent. One of the guys unzipped a fanny pack and dumped a small packet of Crystal Light into his cup of water, stirred it with his finger, and then drank the whole thing down in a couple of mammoth swallows.

"Another glass of Crystal Light, Eddie? Really? That's all you have to add to these proceedings?" The pencil guy's voice began to rise. "Whoever's taking minutes, I want this in there. I want it noted how many glasses of Crystal Light Eddie has drunk and how that's all he's done so far. Let the record show…" He looked around. "Who is taking minutes? Guys, don't tell me no one is taking minutes." He threw the pencil down onto the table disgustedly.

Eddie looked at the empty glass and grinned.

"How about we ask people, 'if you had to be a flavor of Crystal Light what flavor would you be?'"

"That's ridiculous. You're not taking this seriously at all! Why are you even here, Eddie?"

"Same reasons as you, Jack," he spat. "I'll list them all if you want, but I don't think either one of us has the time or stomach for that kind of reflection right now."

Jack took off his wire-rimmed glasses and rubbed his tired eyes. It appeared that even manufactured surrealism had its breaking point.

Jack, his voice exhausted, his fingers rubbing his eyes a little too vigorously for Henry's taste, said in a tired voice, "Why don't we just ask people if they had to fuck a musical instrument, which one would they fuck?"

He had said it as a joke, but it seemed to resonate with the rest of them. Eddie nodded thoughtfully as he arched his eyebrows.

"I like it," he said. "It kind of gets to the heart of everything. The arts. Sexuality. Even politics if you think about the French horn."

They were silent again as they considered it, and after a few moments Charles asked, "And why?"

"What?" Jack asked him.

"Well," Charles said, looking around the table for support, "do we ask 'If you had to fuck a musical instrument, which one would you fuck?' or do we ask 'If you had to fuck a musical instrument, which one would you fuck *and why*?'"

Henry left before he heard the answer. He had to get to the office, put in an appearance so that Ken knew he was at least trying, despite the temptation to stay and watch the proceedings, because it was undeniable that the gravity of their meeting was palpable. In their minds the future would remember this moment as historically significant. The birth of a society that superseded everything that came before it. For some people one Big Bang would never be enough. One superstition could never provide enough parameters to lead a normal life. And this was why these people had come to the apartment, he had suddenly realized; to indulge their need for context the way addicts stayed in shooting galleries from dawn to dusk to satisfy what? Addiction? Sure, but that was just part of it. The rest of it was knowing where you belonged.

*   *   *

The office was busy, humming the way large rooms with lots of people busy doing their own thing bristled. He tried to figure out how to plug into it, but there was no clear way in. He rearranged the few knick-knacks he had on his desk and then got a coffee from the dirty communal kitchen, but neither thing made him feel more centered. He made sure Ken saw him as he walked back to his desk but didn't stop once their eyes locked. That would be putting too fine a point on it.

He was four hours into an internet search about Potter with nothing much to show for it but a ringing headache and a debilitating neck cramp worthy of an Oxycontin addiction when an email came in from Oscar telling him to meet him at the West Valley Gun Club in an hour. This after four hours of surfing the internet that had led him to websites claiming to sell pieces of the original flowers' dresses that were a "must" for any real "suicide aficionado" and conspiracy theorists who alleged the raid on the compound in '84 was actually perpe-trated by rival networks trying to draw viewers away from NBC's coverage of the Olympics. He didn't know if he was in the Dark Web or not, but it sure as hell felt like it.

Closing his eyes, he rubbed his temples and had a quick flash of himself waist deep in a grave of his own digging. He laughed and when he opened his eyes was startled to see Ken standing over him reading his screen.

"Gun club with Oscar, huh? Good luck with that. You should check with HR, but I'm pretty sure workers' comp doesn't cover gutshots or pistol whippings." He laughed and then cleared his throat, embarrassedly, as if instead of laughing he'd ripped a loud fart. "Is he helping you find a way in to Potter?"

"No, but I'm working on him. Inch by inch." Henry replied with a smile he hoped emitted more confidence than he actually felt.

"Remind that shell-shocked asshole that his notes and contacts from that story are the newspaper's property. Not his."

Ken sounded annoyed and Henry hoped it had more to do with Oscar not being forthcoming than it did with Henry's progress on the story.

In a few minutes he was in his car speeding north on the 101 toward the Valley. Most people who lived in LA hated having to go to the Valley and talked about it, and the people who lived there, as though it were an internment camp for asthmatics. Henry didn't feel that way. He liked the openness of it, the reliable heat, the stippled strip malls that were an endless ellipses of commercial opportunities.

The West Valley Gun Club was in a gigantic office park out by the Van Nuys Airport, and when he finally got there and parked it was amid a sea of oversized pickup trucks and gas-guzzling SUVs. The cars all seemed to have American flags waving from their antennae and the display of patriotism reminded him of a military cemetery decorated by Boy Scouts for Veteran's Day.

Inside, Oscar was waiting for him at the check-in desk. He was chewing a piece of straw and making small talk with the clerk, who seemed to know him. Just when Henry was almost next to him Oscar swung around with surprising speed and yelled, "Bang!" Henry felt his heart take a leap into his stomach as he clutched his chest.

"Whoa," Oscar laughed, "you've gotta relax, buddy. All that tension is gonna kill you one of these days. Forget about guns. Your heart, that's the real killer."

"Jesus, Oscar," the guy at the counter said with a complicit smile, "you're a real son of a bitch."

"We're gonna have a great time today," Oscar went on in his fast mumbling way, the space between his words being eaten by the words themselves. "I'm so glad you could make it. Do you like guns, Henry? Would you say you're a gun guy?"

Henry could still feel his heart buzzing inside him like a fly bouncing against a closed window trying to find a way out.

"No, I wouldn't say that."

"Not a gun nut, huh?" Oscar sighed and put his hands on the counter. "Too bad. I like gun nuts. They're reliable. They're the only people you can trust to tell you the truth all the time. It's a Constitution thing. They think if they lie, God will send Communists to rape their daughters. They operate from this place of really violent fear and profound paranoia that I deeply appreciate. It's kind of glorious to behold."

The guy at the desk laid two pistols and a couple of boxes of ammo on the counter.

"No thanks," Henry said politely.

"What do you mean 'no thanks'?" Oscar shot back. "These aren't Brussel sprouts. Pick up the gun."

"I'm not going to shoot," Henry said.

"Oh, come on," Oscar said, sounding genuinely disappointed. "Don't tell me you're one of those liberal gun-hating types."

"No," Henry said, stuffing his hands in his pockets. "I just don't want to shoot."

"Have you ever held a gun before?" Oscar asked taunting him a little. "Do you know anything about them?"

"I know enough to know that I don't want to shoot one, let alone hold one."

"Well that's an awful lot of knowledge for someone who just admitted to being willfully ignorant."

"I'm not ignorant," Henry said, trying to swallow the lump he felt swelling in his throat. "I'm the opposite of ignorant."

Oscar laughed. He crossed his arms and shot Henry a look that made him feel small.

"And why's that?"

Henry took a deep breath before he started. He didn't like the idea of talking about Grace to prove a point. She wasn't currency and he didn't owe Oscar anything, but he did want something from the man, and if this is what it was going to take to get it, then so be it.

"My sister was murdered. A long time ago. She was shot, and ever since then I guess you could say I've had a little bit of a thing about guns." He turned to look at the guy behind the counter and then turned back to Oscar. "Is that the opposite of ignorance enough for you?"

Oscar said something that he could tell by the tone was contrite, which Henry only slightly heard, because underneath it all he was concentrating on the irregular spatter of gunshots ringing out from the next room, the eerie pauses as people reloaded, the anticipation of not knowing when it would begin again but knowing that it would, that it was as inevitable as the next breath.

He put on the oversized earmuffs he was handed and followed Oscar into the main room, a dark cavern of a place that was infused to the rafters and in every corner with the rich sweet smell of gunpowder and the eddying pinwheels of smoke drifting stoically in the air, giving it the look of something alive and prehistoric, a single-celled organism out for a midnight stroll. As Oscar started loading one of the guns a few large men came over to say hello. One by one they clapped him on the back and then folded their gigantic arms in front of T-shirts bearing reference to particular Marine units and divisions. They exchanged words for a few minutes, and once or twice all four of them looked over at Henry before turning back to one another and continuing their quiet conversations.

When they'd finished talking, each of the guys nodded at Henry before walking back to where their guns were waiting to take more target practice.

For the next ten minutes Oscar wordlessly emptied his gun into the man-shaped targets down at the end of the range, switching between the two guns now and then, reloading, shooting again. It was hypnotizing to watch and before too long Henry found himself imagining being at the other end, behind the targets, watching the muzzle flashes and the grim looks of determination on all the shooters' faces, feeling the dull thuds of the slugs entering his flesh, manipulating it unkindly, and then his breath, the last simple thing he'd ever know, and then that too dissipating in awful, slow gasps.

Oscar finished his last few shots and when he turned around, Henry flinched.

"Whoa," Oscar said, holding up his hands in mock concern, "jumpy much?"

Oscar reached in his back pocket and took out a hip flask from which he drank for several seconds before proferring it to Henry.

"No thanks," Henry murmured softly, still unsure what the hell he was doing here and what it would take for Oscar to tell him what he wanted to know.

"Right, of course you don't drink," Oscar said, taking another sip. "That would be absurd."

Oscar took another long pull from the flask and held it out meekly once again to Henry.

"Come on. There's tons to drink to."

"Like what?" Henry asked, his eyes darting this way and that, making unconscious notes of the various exits, the location of Oscar's friends, where the guns were. Worry was an exhausting chore; he could barely imagine the effort that genuine paranoia took.

Oscar smiled at the crack that had opened.

"I like to drink to the men we could have been but aren't. You know, giving yourself a little credit for what you could have done but didn't. That's my superpower. I walk around silently lording all the shit I could be doing to people over them but don't."

Without thinking Henry looked him in the eyes and asked, "If I drink, will you let me hear the tapes you have, and tell me how to find Potter?"

"Is that what Ken told you? That I knew how to find Potter? Like he was my personal snake handler, on call to answer my questions whenever I have a nightmare or get into some existential funk. Does that sound right to you, Henry? Does that sound like something a guy like me would know how to do?"

Oscar's voice was almost pitying and Henry felt, for a moment, like he was being consoled after finding out too late that the money he just invested had gone into a pyramid scheme. The flask was offered again and in one continuous movement Henry grabbed it, pressed the cold metal to his lips, tilted it up, and drank for several long seconds.

"Wow," Oscar said, impressed by the gusto with which Henry drank, "I guess I don't need to ask what your superpower is."

Henry shrugged and handed back the flask while the tequila he'd just drunk worked its way along his bloodstream to the muscles in his neck, which immediately bunched up into painful little bouquets as they always did when he drank the stuff.

"Tequila gets into my negative spaces," he said gently massaging his neck. "Also, that's not my superpower. My superpower is the ability to feel guilty about anything."

Oscar nodded. "Good to know."

Henry swung his neck around in an effort to unlock his cramping muscles.

"So," he said, not feeling like being there anymore, "what am I supposed to do?"

"What did Ken tell you exactly? Did he tell you to say that the paper owned my memories? Or did he tell you that he kicked me out of my office last week, didn't fire me exactly, but took away my desk, had me clear out my things. I'm not sure where he expects me to go, but that's probably the point, right? Doomed to haunt the halls forever like a ridiculous rumor, looking for an outlet to plug in my electric typewriter and the forehead of some young worshipping newbie to hang my Pulitzer. Now tell me, does that sound like a life to you?"

Henry said nothing as around them the sound of guns firing filled in the uncomfortable silence. Gone now was the fun-loving lout, he thought, as he looked into Oscar's eyes that suddenly had the seriousness of narrowed grooves cut into marble.

"Feeling guilty yet?"

Henry shrugged. "I feel something, but it's hard to tell if it's the tequila or the guilt."

"That's okay," Oscar said, "one usually precedes the other. We'll get there eventually."

Now he wanted to leave. He didn't even want to talk about Potter anymore. He wanted to be in his car, tucked safely into traffic somewhere, anonymous as he'd been as a kid when to crave being noticed felt like the most decadent wish there ever was or ever could be.

"I don't..." he began but as soon as Oscar interrupted the words just felt like a vain attempt at remembering a safe word.

"A few days ago I heard that prick, Jeff, and that other prick, Ken, talking in Ken's office about an apartment building your friends have turned into a nation state. Apparently no one knows these guys but you."

Henry was confused. "You want the story?"

"Not exactly."

"Then what?"

"Me and my friends," Oscar said, indicating the men he'd introduced Henry to when they first came in, "want to go there."

"And do what?" Henry asked, still not understanding.

"What do you think I'm talking about, Henry? Stop being so fucking obtuse. We want in. We want to be there. We're offering ourselves up to the cause."

"Race war?"

Oscar laughed. "Not race war, you fucking weirdo. The

'Cause'." He threw up air quotes as he said the word 'cause'.

Suddenly, Henry understood what he was talking about and the prospect frightened the hell out of him.

"No, you don't want to go there. You guys would...I mean, they're just a bunch of confused dads and weirdos looking for an excuse to get out of their sad lives for a little while. They're not serious about it."

"That's not what I hear."

"What do you mean?" Dread was starting to inflate in him like a balloon.

"Your friend...Truman...Is that his name? Funny. Anyway, Truman called the paper trying to get someone to come down and interview him about it all. He was talking about urban warfare and armed resistance. He was talking about property rights and Existentialism. These are enticing subjects to me and my friends."

"Sounds like a bunch of bullshit to me," Henry replied. Since when had free speech become such a fucking nuisance? "So why do you need me?"

"Because, we want to join him and we need an introduction. You can give us entree. How's that feel, buddy, to have all this juice?"

A few of the ex-soldiers were gathered around them now, listening in on their conversation.

"I think it's a bad idea. You're too...Someone's going to get hurt."

"Don't mistake bloodlust for gumption, Henry." He smiled and patted Henry on the shoulder. "Why don't you go away and think about it. I'll tell you everything you want to know about Potter and the COL. In fact, I'll do you one better. I'll introduce you to one of the Flowers. All you have to do is take us to the building and get us in. That's it. Simple syrup."

"The Flowers?" Again he felt like he was one step behind. "There are no flowers. The ones that didn't die left. They're all gone."

Oscar shook his head matter-of-factly. "No, they're not. They're still very much around. Just waiting."

"Waiting for what?"

Oscar raised an eyebrow at him. "What do you think?"

The saliva in his mouth, he realized, had evaporated. It was happening. He was becoming a desert.

"How do you know her?"

He shrugged. "I met a lot of those people when I did my Potter story. It's a pretty small world, that whole end-of-the-world scene. Also," and this time Henry detected a little empathy in his voice, "they never really leave. It doesn't work like that."

Oscar was all smiles again as he walked Henry out through the lobby and back into the parking lot. Far off in the distance the sun was setting over the ocean, spilling its secrets that were a million shades of red and orange. They stood next to one another, appreciating it for a moment, before Oscar turned to him and said, "All we want is to be moved, Henry. Forget everything else and focus on that. We're lucky men. We know what it is that moves us. Do you know how rare that is?"

Driving away, he looked back in his rearview mirror and saw Oscar still standing in the parking lot watching the setting sun and he thought to himself, as his stomach bobbed on the rising and falling tides of panic, that it was no coincidence that LA was at its most beautiful when it looked like it was on fire.

Chapter 12

THE NEXT MORNING he awoke on Grace's floor, her toe gently prodding his shoulder as she whispered his name. "Henry. Henry. Time to get up, Henry."

It was Saturday. He knew that much. He also knew that yesterday wasn't a dream as pain began to reveal itself to him from nearly every corner of his body, pain within pain, like a Russian stacking doll with a mean streak.

"Mom's got a migraine," she went on as she pulled her shades open, letting in a flood of light that nearly drowned him in its brightness, "so Dad's going to take us to see Grandma. I already ate. You get to have McDonald's."

Struggling against the light, he finally placed her and was jealous that she was already showered, dressed, and ready for the day. Getting from where he was to where she was seemed like an impossibility, but his mother's migraines, when she got them, which, as she drew nearer to menopause, seemed to be more and more often, trumped any other problem no matter how big or serious.

"You don't really have any bruises, but you must feel like shit. Am I right?"

"Right you are," he grinned, and the words, his first of the day felt like a slurry in his mouth.

Finally, she began to materialize as something more than

a silhouette, and he could see her standing there, hands on hips, a white T-shirt tucked into pink jeans, black combat boots, a black belt.

"What's with the no-bra thing?" he asked her as he rubbed absent-mindedly at an especially tender spot on his thigh. He peeked under the covers and saw an enormous purple bruise spreading out like an oil slick. "Is that a college girl thing?"

"Jesus," she said, pulling the light blue comforter off him. "You're disgusting. And by the way, I haven't told Mom and Dad about college, so please don't say anything, okay?"

"Fine," he said, getting up, stretching, scratching, performing all of the calisthenics of recovery.

He shuffled past her, down the hall, and into his own room, where he slowly got dressed, gingerly pulling on a pair of faded Levi's and a Circle Jerks shirt. He took his time putting his clothes on, bracing himself for any quick flashes of pain that might decide to ambush him from out of nowhere. Catching a glance of himself in the mirror he smirked and couldn't help thinking that he looked like an astronaut going about his everyday life in zero-g's. Every movement was a patriotic event.

"That's one small step..." he muttered to himself when he was finally done. The last bit, when he was leaning over to lace up his Converse, confirmed his suspicion that he had at least one broken rib.

Before heading downstairs he quietly pushed the door to his parents' room open and went straight to their bathroom where he turned on the sink and let the water get as hot as it would go. When it was finally almost too hot to touch, he took a washcloth and dropped it in the sink, letting it get completely wet, and then turned off the faucet. He gritted his teeth as he squeezed the excess water out, wringing it over and over until it was just barely damp and then brought it to his mother, a simple act of relief he'd been doing for her for as long as he could remember. When he was a kid, his mother would send him back sometimes if the cloth wasn't hot enough.

"It's got to be real hot, Henry. As hot as you can make it. Do you understand?"

He'd go back and do it again for her, inevitably scalding himself, but understanding that it must be nothing compared to the pain of one of her migraines, because it would have to be the worst for her to have to ask him to hurt himself like that for her.

He crept to her bed and put the washcloth on her face that looked glazed in pain so that it covered her eyes and the bridge of her nose, and as soon as she felt it she let out a huge sigh of relief and reached around for his hand. He gave it to her and she pulled it to her chest, clutching it tightly, and began to softly stroke his arm with the tips of her fingernails. Fingertips like flashbacks. It was a lovely, lonely feeling, something she would do when he was little to get him to calm down. It instantly put him at ease, froze him, and she would tease him that he was hypnotized and couldn't do anything until she let him go. He'd protest, but she was right, and as hard as he tried he wouldn't be able to pull his arm away from that adoring electricity.

"Thank you, Henry," she moaned, the room nearly black in the daylight, but with just enough light edging its way in to show the outlines of the objects in the room; the bed, the desk in the corner, a floor lamp, all of it a dim apparition as though that reality had all been purloined and the only real thing was his mother and the pain throbbing in the front of her head. She kissed his hand, and it brought to mind the anointment of a saint, a true savior, but that was too much, because he knew what he did for her was the least he could do and that actions like these were far and few between. He took his hand away, embarrassed, and stuck it in his pocket.

"Henry?" she spoke to him, her voice impossibly light and airy, a thing that might float away if not moored to the ears that bent to hear it, "I just want you to know that I love you very much, okay? You know that, right?"

"Right," he said, swallowing hard, wondering where she was going with this.

"Are you sure you know that? Sometimes..." she paused as she pressed the cloth harder to her face as though she was trying to press it into her head, crush the headache from the outside in, "sometimes I'm not sure that you do, and I get frustrated because I'm not sure that that's my fault or yours, but today I want you to know it. Today I want to make sure that there's no room for doubt," and here she laughed, maybe, thought Henry, because it occurred to her then just how much like a business deal what she said sounded like, a gentlemen's agreement. Not quite the type of thing to need a signature, but a handshake...a handshake would more than suffice. He leaned over and softly kissed the top of her head in answer and when he turned to leave, Grace was standing at the doorway watching him, smiling knowingly, and when he was next to her she threw an arm around his shoulder as they walked to the garage, matching one another's steps so that by the time they had made it to the garage, they were in perfect lockstep, giggling like a couple of mischievous Rockettes.

*　　*　　*

The ride to their grandmother's house was inordinately silent both inside and outside the car. It was Saturday morning and the roads were empty save the unlucky few who had drawn weekend shifts and parents chauffeuring their children from one activity to the next, killing time until Monday morning, which, when you were a parent, was the new Friday night. Inside their car it was quiet as well. None of them spoke. The radio was off. Each of them stared, hypnotized by something outside the window, something enchanting, and it took him a moment to put his finger on it, but after they had stopped at the McDonald's drive-through and he had his food in hand, he understood that it was nothing in particular that was holding their attention, making them each feel so at ease, but rather it was the day itself, a perfectly blue endlessness brought on by the strong winds of the night before that had blown all of the smog away. Clarity. It was clarity that was remarkable to them, and they drank it in, thirstily, each lost in a captivated state that was all their own, private kingdoms of utter peace. It took days like this, Henry realized, chewing happily, to make sense of the other 99 percent of the time when it was all smog and grit. Perfect perspective was the result of an extraordinary set of circumstances all occurring at the same time. It took weather conditions, people's moods, the traffic, time of day. Nothing could be left to chance on a day like this. Every particle had to be in its perfect place. Every atom centered.

He thought he had dreamt the wind the night before and was about to ask if it had woken anyone else up, and then stopped himself. He didn't want to be the one to ruin the moment with small talk. Small talk was for filling in the gaps, for collapsing oppressive silences. This was anything but that. This was freedom.

But as they got closer to their grandmother's little house in Westwood, the house their dad had grown up in, Henry and Grace grew suspicious and looked at one another worriedly. This was the point in the drive where their dad would invariably begin pointing out the landmarks of his youth, relating stories they had heard time and again, yarns so familiar they often wondered if they had not lived through them themselves. Nate Costa's house at the end of the block where they would all gather for the daily street football games. Across the street and a few houses down from that a huge spiraling oak that Morgan Hendrick had fallen from and lain in a coma at UCLA hospital for almost a week and when he finally came back to school a month later he was never quite the same. And finally another hundred feet on to his own house with the lawn jockey out front and how this wasn't the original little cement man, but more like the fifth or sixth one since stealing it had become a pledge class tradition of one of the nearby UCLA frat houses. Not only were these kids part of Henry and Grace's collective consciousness, but there was also the second part of the tour that always struck him as the sad part, when their dad would tell them what each of these boys and girls had grown up to become. He detailed for them their divorces, their careers, their untimely deaths, and in that way he could build and destroy an idyllic childhood before the car was ever put into park. And when he talked about the boys that had gone on to have great success his voice got low and disbelieving. It was more than he could bear, Henry understood, worse to him than the ones who had died in auto accidents or developed rare forms of cancer. Jealousy for him was a profound state of disbelief. Incredulousness. He gave away the ending to their own lives in this way, laid out all the possible permutations for them, the finite variables. He probably thought he was doing them a favor by doing this, by bending their expectations to fit into the insanely narrow slots of his experiences.

But not this time. There were no stories. No reminders. He parked the car directly in front of their grandmother's house and sat there, stonily, the only sound to be heard was the engine making its little clicking sounds as it worked to cool itself off. Henry and Grace stayed still because by now it was more than evident that something was amiss and Henry felt a quick surge of electric panic at the idea that something had happened to their grandmother. She was old and unwell, but she had always seemed that way to him, and the notion that that wasn't an indefinite state had never really occurred to him.

Henry asked, "Did something happen to Grandma?"

Grace looked at him, shocked, and then looked at their father as the electricity of Henry's panic spread to her.

Their father sat still for another moment and then adjusted the rearview mirror so that he could see both of them and they could both see his eyes.

"You guys are aware that things between me and your mom haven't been great for some time. We've tried to make things work, mostly for you two," his eyes stayed fixed on them, his voice a thick lawyerly thing, "but we both feel that it'd be best for everyone if we split up for now. Took a break. It doesn't mean we don't love you, or don't love each other for that matter, but this has been coming for some time now. I can't really see it being much of a surprise for either of you."

The engine continued to click as a couple of kids went by on skateboards. This was a young person's street now. No one from his father's day lived here anymore, having moved on to their inevitable destinies. It was all new young families and Henry could only imagine how much they wished his grandmother would get put into a home or just die so that another one of their type could come in and fix the place up, get rid of the lawn jockey and the flagpole, strange holdovers of patriotism and fashion that had long passed their expiration dates. This house, his memories. Nostalgia sat on him like water weight. They were the last obstacles to a picaresque existence for the new neighbors but were all their father had left of the picaresque for himself. It was greedy to hang on the way he did, Henry thought, as he let sink in the surreal news his father had just told them.

"Do you have any questions?" he asked, eager to move on to something else.

Neither Henry nor Grace said anything for a minute. It was hard to know where to begin, what to say, especially since the way he had told them made it seem like the most obvious thing in the world. It would almost be embarrassing to ask a question.

"Is Mom okay? Was she really not feeling well enough to come with us or was it because of this?"

"Henry, this isn't a conspiracy. Of course she has a migraine."

"So, if she didn't," Henry went on, panic rising in him like adrenaline, "she'd be here with us?"

Grace reached across the seat and took his hand. He was trying to cope with this the only way he knew how to cope with anything. Understand the mechanics of the problem. If he could just fathom the new rules, then things wouldn't seem so strange.

"Henry..." his father began to answer but then stopped himself. It was hard to tell if the fight had suddenly gone out of him or if it was just that empathy had gotten into him. "Let's go see Grandma."

Their dad used his key to let himself into the house, and Henry and Grace followed closely behind and straight to the back of the house where their grandma's bedroom was. Familiar smells overwhelmed him, the feeling of the plush pale blue carpet beneath his feet, associations with foods he only ever ate when he was here like Tropicana Orange

Juice their mother would never buy for them because it was "pure junk." Glancing into the living room he noticed stale candy decaying in a dish on the coffee table, oil paintings that depicted European cities in such abstract forms it was hard to tell what century they belonged to. Everything was on the verge of being classy, but not quite there. It had been their grandmother's aspiration her whole life to be a rich woman, but it had never quite happened. Comfort hadn't been enough for her, and she had worked their poor grandfather into an early death trying to make something more of their lives. Something bigger. Now she was old and ill, light as tissue paper, commanding her full-time Filipina nurse from a hospital bed that occupied a large portion of her bedroom.

Their father leaned over and kissed her papery cheek and the two of them spoke in a hushed whisper for a few moments before he walked off to the kitchen where the door to the basement was to undoubtedly once again look for a fabled trove of baseball cards he was sure had to be there somewhere. Ever since Henry could remember his father had spent all his time at the house in the basement going through old boxes, moving around dusty artifacts, once or twice even using a shovel to dig into the earthy floor.

Henry and Grace leaned over to kiss her and she smiled broadly at the sight of them.

"He's going to look for those stupid baseball cards again," she started laughing, a half snort that always brought a smile to Henry's face. "I've told him a million times that I threw those things away when he was at summer camp a long time ago. You can't tell your father anything."

She had been a very vain woman once but that was long ago. They each took a bony hand and gazed down at her face that was dotted with brown age spots, her skin so pale it was almost translucent. A thin, light blue nightgown covered her the way a slipcover is used to cover nice furniture.

"I asked your dad to bring you here because I want to make sure you both get something from me after I die. Of course you're both going to get a little money, although," and here she snorted again, "there isn't much left. Your grandfather was sweet but lazy. You know." They didn't, but they nodded their heads. All they knew was the sweet old man who took them bowling and out for ice cream, who took them for walks through the backyard and hung a sign in the garden that said "Camellia Canyon," which, when they were small loomed like a forest of the perfumey flowers their grandmother loved to have around and kept freshly cut in vases in her bedroom, the kitchen, even in the bathroom. "Anyway," she went on, rolling her eyes, giving them a sly smile to suggest they knew exactly what she was talking about, "I want you to each take one of these pads and stick your name on whatever you want, and I'll make sure you get it one day. Okay?" She nodded at two pads of Post-it Notes and pens on the little table where she kept her magazines, Danielle Steele novels, and the TV remote.

Neither of them moved or said anything. It was a reasonable request, pragmatic even, to make sure your family got what they wanted instead of the junk you thought they should have, and it touched Henry in a way he didn't expect she thought it would.

"Nana," Grace began, but really didn't have anything else, because to do it this way made perfect sense.

"Come on," she said, slapping the table impatiently with her frail fingers. "I'm not saying I'm going to die today. But let's face it…" She snorted again and Henry and Grace both started laughing because in a way it was so morbid that the alternative was not an option. Neither had said a word yet to the other about their parent's bombshell, and now, suddenly, it didn't seem to matter much. Maybe their father knew that would be the case and that's why he had brought them here, to let their grandmother give them the relief and comedy he wasn't able to.

"Do you kids want some orange juice?" And before they could answer she was yelling at the top of her lungs, "Leticia, get my kids some orange juice, will ya?" She looked at them and rolled her eyes, "Lazy thing." She had barely lowered her voice, and they were sure the nurse had heard it, but their grandmother could hardly seem to care less and Henry smiled at her obliviousness. He couldn't believe that she would treat someone so shitty who had her very well-being in the palm of their hands. Ignorance was indeed the epitome of living fearlessly.

The nurse brought the orange juice in, and their grand-mother nodded as they each took a sip.

"Thank you, dear," she said kindly to the nurse. She couldn't help the way she was. Nobody could.

They each took a pad, tentatively, as though the very act would somehow kill their grandmother instantly. She smiled, nodded, and then turned her attention back to the television, which looked possessed with some kind of TV awards show. It was the kind of overflowing colostomy bag of entertain-ment she loved. All flash and beauty. It put her at ease.

Walking around the house, it took only a few minutes to realize that there was nothing here he really wanted. Trying to generate some sentimentality he closed his eyes and pictured the kind of house he wanted to live in when he grew up, the type of family he'd have surrounding himself, and none of his grandparents' gaudy and overwrought mementos really fit into the picture. In his grandfather's closet he found an old beige trench coat, the lining torn, but overall it was in pretty good shape. He wrote his name on a Post-it and slipped it into the jacket pocket. There was a cool old card table and chairs by the bay window in the living room that he could picture himself sitting around when he was older. Maybe he would learn to play bridge like his father, uncle, and grandparents used to do when they all got together at holidays. It seemed a reasonable way to pass the time when there was nothing to say to one another, and although he didn't want to think about that right now, not with his parent's situation on the top of his mind, he knew that silence was an inevitable by-product of love. He stuck a Post-it on the table.

The dining room. They had spent countless holidays in this room with its imperial-looking chairs and monolithic white table. It was a monstrous thing and it looked more like something one would worship or circumambulate rather than eat off. A small oil painting hung at one end of the room, and although he'd seen the thing a thousand times he had never really stopped to study it. The painting showed a horse-driven carriage on a shady lane, leaves of every color sprinkled around, as though the artist couldn't decide what season he wanted it to be. A man in black with a top hat held an elegant woman's hand as she stepped onto the carriage. Neither of their faces were clear, so it was difficult to say whether they were going somewhere for fun or if it was to be a sad outing. He went to put a Post-it on the painting and was surprised that his sister had already claimed it for her own.

He took another tour around the house and finally entered the last room, which was his father's old bedroom. It had been made into a guest room ages ago, but there were still traces of the old man here and there. A lamp that had a baseball player in a batting stance as its base, crumbling paperbacks copies of *Catcher in the Rye*, *The Old Man and the Sea*, and *The Lion, the Witch, and the Wardrobe*. It was hard to picture his father getting into any of these books. Rebellion and curiosity weren't exactly the first two adjectives that sprung into mind when he thought about him. He put a Post-it on each of the books.

Grace was sitting on the edge of the bed leafing through an old photo album. A box of keepsakes sat open at her feet with more albums and paperwork inside.

"You took my painting," he said, nudging her a little with his elbow.

"Huh?" She was barely listening.

"I said you took my painting. The one in the dining room. I wanted it. Whose *Showcase Showdown* is this anyway?"

She ignored him.

"Do you know what's weird?" she asked, her eyes continued to study the pages of the photo album. She put it down and picked up another at random.

"That we're picking through a dead person's belongings who isn't dead yet and our father is in the basement digging through the floor with a shovel? I feel like we've just broken in and murdered Nana."

"No," she said, not even giving him the courtesy of a polite laugh. "I've been going through these photo albums and they start with Dad when he was a baby, okay? He lived here until college and then went to UCLA, which is basically two blocks away. After that he lived in Nana and Papa's guest house while he was in law school and then met Mom just as he was about to graduate. They moved in together after graduation and now..."

"What?" he shrugged his shoulders. The mystery was lost on him.

"Henry, he's never lived without a woman around to take care of him. Isn't that weird? Can he even do anything on his own? Can he wash the dishes? Can he do his laundry?"

"Maybe he's planning on moving back in here," Henry said, picking up a stack of papers from the bottom of the box.

"That," she answered, closing the book, "or he already has someone else."

The remark startled Henry and he looked up at her quickly and sternly.

"What?" she said, finally making eye contact. "Would that be so weird? If you really think about it, the opposite would be weirder. If he didn't have someone else."

As she left the room, she stopped at the door and called back to him. "You can have that painting if you want it. I don't really care. I was just picking stuff out to be polite. There's nothing here I need."

He sat for a moment, taking in the possibility that their father was having an affair. Grace was right. Why was that so hard to believe? Because it was happening to him? What a stupid way to think about things. If that was the case, did it mean that cancer and miscarriages and alcoholism didn't really exist because they'd never happened to anyone in his family?

Barely registering what he was looking at, he began to glance through the stack of papers in his hands, letting each one glide back into the box as he quickly scanned them. The smell of dust and mold wafted up at him as he leafed through these old things. Ambience, he told himself. This is what the fifties smelled like. What he saw was old report cards, a certificate of bar mitzvah, even a college acceptance letter. Jesus, his grandmother kept everything. Outwardly she didn't seem the sentimental type. Probably just negligence. The whole house was bulging at the seams with old junk. What was the point?

The next piece of paper, though, stopped him in his tracks.

It was a certificate of honorable discharge dated 1971 and the name at the bottom was his father's.

He took the paper and ran into his grandma's room. Grace was bent over the bed and the two of them were speaking in low tones to one another, and when they saw him, they both looked at him for a second with a glance that said "this is none of your business" and went back to their conversation. It was over in a minute and Henry saw Grace walk away from the bed with a small plastic bag in her hand. She raised her eyebrows at him as she walked by and he couldn't tell from the look if he was about to be let in on the joke or if he was the joke.

Never mind. He rushed to his grandma's bedside with the yellowing piece of paper and held it out for her to see.

"Nana, what is this? Dad was in the army?"

The paper shook as she took it and held it up close to her eyes. She squinted her eyes behind thick glasses and then lowered her head so that she could see over the rims.

"Where did you get this?" she finally asked with a snort.

"In a box in Dad's room."

She put the paper down on her table and looked up at him.

"Your dad was in the army all right. The National Guard over here in Westwood. He'd go there one weekend a month and play poker and drink with a bunch of other 'soldiers.'" Almost every sense of hers had been dulled except sarcasm.

"You know," she went on, "I didn't agree with the war in Vietnam. I never thought it was a good idea. Papa, though, oy," she threw up her hands as though she were in the middle of an argument with her late husband now, "he was so gung-ho. Another great soldier, by the way. Spent World War II in Long Beach helping resupply naval ships or something. They made him an officer. What a joke!" Laughter turned into a cough and she held his arm with one hand as she pressed a Kleenex to her mouth with the other. "His bunkmate was Clark Gable. Did you know that?"

Henry nodded. He knew it. It was an important piece of family lore that his grandfather had lived in the same barracks as Clark Gable for a year during World War II. The rabbi at his funeral had mentioned it in the eulogy right up along with all of his other accomplishments, and Henry remembered it seeming odd that the mention of it should be so important as to bring it up at the man's burial. How was a roommate assignment an accomplishment? He resolved to never be remembered for his proximity to greatness, let alone fame, which he thought of as greatness' juvenile delinquent younger brother.

"I also didn't vote for Reagan. Did you know that?" Another accomplishment. "Your grandfather hated Carter so much that if I had told him I was going to vote for him again, I don't know what he would have done. Still," she grinned deviously, "I didn't." It's the little things.

He found Grace at the kitchen table sipping a glass of orange juice and staring out at the empty street. He wasn't sure if she had heard him walk in, but then she started talking and it was clear she was trying to work something out in her head.

"It's weird that Dad grew up here. That he sat at this table and had breakfast and dinner every night, that this is where Nana sat, and Papa sat there," she nodded at the chair at the head of table. "He was so happy then. So much happier than he is now. I wonder how that happened."

"He loves us," Henry said, taking a seat at the table.

"I know he does," she said, her eyes back on the street where a mom was holding her little girl's hand as the kid struggled down the sidewalk on roller skates. The little girl squealed as she went over a bump and the mom's laughter rang out, a call and response of pure happiness. "But I think he was happier then. Happier here."

"Do you really think he's been cheating on Mom?"

She shrugged.

"I think anything's possible when you're trying to feel something you've lost."

He put the discharge paper on the table in front of her and said, "Did you know Dad was in the army?"

She looked at the paper and then up at him, a smile decorating her thinly beautiful face.

"Poker and beers? Yeah, I knew that. Me and Nana talk."

A hole opened up in him. How long had she known? What did they talk about? What else did she know that he didn't?

"Not about you, Henry, don't worry," she went on, misunderstanding the concern that must have shown on his face. "You know what you need to do with Dad? What works for me is you have to stop putting yourself in the position for him to judge you. I know why you do it. You want to be nice and accommodating and that's why I love you so much. Because you are nice and accommodating. But really, he's never going to respect you as long as you're like that. He comes from such an easy place," she said, inclining her head toward the street and then the house, "and if you don't make it hard for him, he'll just walk all over you like he does to everyone else. Do you understand?"

Swallowing hard, he nodded.

"Do you want a sip?" she asked him, indicating the glass of juice.

Without a word he grabbed it and took a big swallow.

From down in the basement they heard the sound of metal on metal and then their father's voice. "Shit!" Then the stomp of his feet as he ascended the wooden steps and emerged into the kitchen. He went to the sink, took off his glasses, and splashed some water on his face. Washed his hands. He looked so young, then, Henry thought, like a little boy washing up before dinner after a long day spent looking for pirate's treasure.

He turned and noticed them both staring at him and, smiling asked, "What?" It almost broke Henry's heart.

Neither of them answered and he put his glasses back on and suddenly he was their dad again. Stern, uptight, wrongly persecuted. He told them to get ready to go. That he was going to say goodbye to his mother and then take them home.

When he left, Grace got up and Henry saw that she was holding onto the bag their grandmother had given her earlier.

"What's in the bag?" he asked her.

She smiled and held it open for him to see. Inside was a bunch of jewelry—rings, necklaces, brooches—and he recognized every piece as things he used to see his grandmother wear. On her these things had always impressed him, made her seem as though she herself sparkled when she walked into a room. Now, though, laying together all tangled up in a bag they had no luster, as though their proximity to one another cancelled out their effect. Or maybe, he thought, she was the one who sparkled and shined and gave life to these trinkets and not the other way around. Baubles. She called them baubles as if to downplay their obvious significance.

"She gave you all that?" he asked, a little bit in awe of an heirloom that might be a superpower.

"It's not for me," she answered, closing the bag. "It's for Mom. She wants her to have the good stuff. But don't tell

Dad, okay? She doesn't want him to know."

*   *   *

The rest of the weekend was spent in unfamiliar orbits as their mother and father began to pack up his father's things into boxes someone had evidently procured from the local grocery store. They smelled faintly of rotten produce and Henry wondered if that was the smell his father would have to deal with in his new place. His mother was still in her nightgown when they got back, which meant she wasn't feeling totally well yet, but she moved with purpose and with a smile on her face when they came back in walking from room to room filling boxes with books, clothes, and anything else that was distinctly their father's.

"How did it go?" she asked them with a smile when they walked back in. Grace gave her a huge hug and Henry shrugged his shoulders. "Good," she said. Her eyes were slits, her face still lustrous with pain. She turned to go back to packing. There would be time for talk later.

For the rest of the weekend Grace and Henry took up position on the fluffy couch in the family room and watched movie after movie on TV. Whatever was on they watched. *The Great Escape. Saturday Night Fever. Crocodile Dundee.* Everything seemed excruciatingly relevant to their situation. Junk food fueled them: Hot Pockets, cereal, can after can of Coke, near lethal doses of sugar and sodium were evidently what their bodies needed to survive, preservatives the long-sought answer to the question: What is the meaning of life?

Their parents continued to pack, and Henry watched them with interest as they moved in wide arcs around one another, keeping their distance but not so overtly as to insult one other. It was not how two people who belonged together occupied a similar space, overly cautious that their latitude and longitudes of affection never pinned them down to a specific location. Refugees, drifting boats, that's what they looked like to Henry now, thoughtful landslides that did their best not to hinder the flow of traffic. At one point his father went up into the attic to have a look around and Henry thought about the times he and his sister would stay up there, hiding from their parents as they fought, not afraid of anyone's wrath necessarily, just not wanting to see and hear the complaints that seemed so personal, things between husbands and wives that had nothing to do with their children, nothing that seemed to have anything to do with the family at all for that matter. Was it possible to divide things up like that? Take one without the other? Sugar and salt. Preservatives.

Later that night their mom surprised them with take-out Chinese food. She spread a beach towel on the carpet and laid out plates for each of them, scooping a bit of each thing onto their plates. It had become night and he hadn't even realized it. Darkness was the absence of birds, the steady droning song of crickets, the occasional wash of headlights sneaking in under the shades like a wintery draft. The house was cold and felt empty and it took him a minute to realize it was because his parents had been packing all day and lots of things were already in boxes, ready to go where? Some of the kids he knew whose parents were divorced went to their dad's places in the Marina on the weekends, sometimes to smaller unkempt houses, not very good replicas of what they'd left behind, like a little model train version of normalcy.

"Is Dad going to eat with us?" Henry asked. Innocence was his intention, but as soon as he said it he wished he hadn't. It suddenly seemed provocative and rude.

"What are you guys watching?" his mother asked, ignoring the question.

"*Raiders of the Lost Ark,*" his sister answered, shooting Henry a look as she did so.

"It's a good one," she said, taking a small bite of her sweet and sour shrimp. It was pretty obvious she wasn't hungry, that she was eating for their sake, like a mother penguin storing energy for her young and the tough times that lay ahead.

The part of the movie where Indy cavalierly pulls out his gun and shoots the sword-wielding bad guy came on and they all laughed and it suddenly struck Henry that this was it, this was their new unit. They didn't have to pick sides, because their father and mother had already done it for them, and it made him wonder if it'd been hard for his father, that moment of realizing they would stick with her, that she was the natural choice.

After the movie was over, and everyone else had gone to sleep, he took a tiptoeing walk around the house exploring the new emptiness, trying to remember what had been where only hours earlier, surprised at himself at how easily and quickly he had forgotten things he had lived with his whole life. What had been in that space in the corner by the front door? Had it been a coat stand? It was the opposite of exploration, really, this attempt to piece together the meaning of negative space, and it startled him more than a little, as he wandered from room to room, feeling more and more like he had broken-in with every guilty step he took, at how effectively the change had made him feel like a visitor. What picture had hung in the now empty space on the wall, the square patch of wall behind it a brighter shade of white than the rest of it. The grandfather clock that kept his friends awake at night when he was younger and used to have sleepovers, but that he didn't even notice anymore, the religious dedication of its steady ticking suddenly absent. Would he be able to sleep without the noise? he wondered. Would the emptiness change the air currents so the climate wouldn't be what it used to be, that certain parts of the house would be warmer or colder than before, that the pitch of new echoes would dangle restlessness before his weary eyes like the pocket watch of a master hypnotist.

He stopped outside his parents' room, took a breath, and then pushed his head in through the crack of the door. There they were, asleep, side-by-side, as if nothing had happened, his father's usual snoring coming in low rumbling waves, his mother still, the gap between them as wide as a California King would permit.

Back in the TV room he flipped around until he found something that was just starting. It was *Deliverance*, a movie he'd never seen, but it had Burt Reynolds in it, so how bad could it be? After it was over he could barely move. It wasn't so much the violence of it that shook him to his core but the realness of it that got to him. It was the inbred boy's face as he played the banjo and how he turned away after Ronny Cox tried to shake his hand when their duel was done, the haunting image of the boy on the suspension bridge as their raft traveled beneath it, his arm hanging carelessly down, the banjo swinging in his hand. And of course the rape and Ned Beatty being made to squeal like a pig for the enjoyment of his attackers. All of it was too real seeming, and it chilled him to the bone. He was speechless as the end credits rolled and he looked around, wishing there was someone nearby who could confirm for him what he'd just seen, that he hadn't imagined it.

It was after one a.m. and the next day was Monday. Forcing himself from the room he ran back to his room, threw himself into his bed, and pulled the covers tightly up over his head.

*   *   *

The next day, Monday, was wildly windy and slightly chilly,

the perfect conditions, he thought, for becoming invisible. It was the ideal kind of misery for what he needed to do, just a small taste of adversity, the wind leaping up to sting the eyes forcing students to keep their faces tilted earthward, hands pressed to the body to control hats and skirts that would otherwise leap up and away like untrained animals escaping from their owners. No one had gone surfing that morning, either, that was for sure. Henry knew enough about it to understand that high winds were terrible for catching waves, worse even than when it was raining, because the waves didn't form the way they were supposed to, coming in all choppy and irregularly instead of smoothly and in sets. It was days like this one that he and Cal were the happiest, when conditions weren't at their most optimal and there was a little hint of struggle in the air. Just a touch. Enough to remind their peers that not every day belonged to them, that the perfection they had become used to wasn't an inalienable right but the exception. They were hard-headed, though, this student body, and it would take more than chilly winds and the hint of rain to get them to change their ways, how they dressed, to put the tops up on their convertibles. So instead of conceding to the conditions, they fought them, went about their lives the way they always did, innocently obstinate, not too unlike the seagulls above them that banked uselessly this way and that in the sky, gliding headlong into a wall of rushing air, getting nowhere fast.

He knew that Cal didn't understand how angry he was about what had happened at the airport and everything leading up to it. That he was tired of being led around by the nose. Tired of feeling like the sponge, like the wide-eyed loser with nothing to contribute. That wasn't a real friendship. Friendship wasn't wanting to play whack-a-mole with every word coming out of your buddy's mouth, was it? What had Grace asked him that weekend? Why was he always putting himself in the position for people to judge him? It was a fair question and it made him sad that he didn't have a good answer for it.

The rest of that day was spent avoiding his usual routes and hangout spots around school. They were simple deviations, taking the long way around a building to get from one class to another, choosing a different bathroom than the one he usually went to for his morning piss between first and second periods, but they did the trick and he was able to avoid running into Cal the entire morning. He'd see him, though, from time to time, Cal craning his neck around as he walked the halls to see if he could catch sight of Henry, a slightly puzzled look on his face, and Henry couldn't help but notice how small he looked, how lost he seemed by himself as crowds of kids moved confidently between classes, laughing at and speaking loudly to one another. He watched as Cal stopped in his tracks and massaged his eyes with his thumb and forefinger, heave a deep breath, kids simply moving around him as they continued to laugh at and talk to one another. They'd been studying erosion in biology recently and seeing Cal like this he couldn't help but think of him as something that would wear away over time, diminished slowly but surely by the elements until one day when there would be absolutely nothing left of him. It happened in rivers and in deserts, even in the tundra. No climate was immune to apathy. Nothing left of him at all. Not even a nub.

He ate his lunch at the far end of school where he knew Cal would never look for him and plunked himself down near a group of Goth girls as he pulled out a turkey sandwich, the packaged kind of meat he saw to his dismay, not the good kind his mom sometimes surprised him with from the deli counter. He took a bite and quickly put it away. The thing tasted like rancid salt. He ate bits and pieces of the rest of it; carrot sticks, chips, a Girl Scout cookie, and finally gave up on sustenance and cracked the top on a can of Coke that was at the bottom of the sack. It made a loud 'hiss' sound as it foamed up and he stuck his mouth on the edge and began to slurp at the overflow. When he looked at the circle of girls near him he saw that they had all turned and were staring at him with, if you believed in the power of gender-based magic, no little bit of obvious disdain. "Sorry," he mumbled, his face hot with shame, as whatever pride he had left foamed up and out of him like the can of shaken soda he sipped at. They scowled a moment longer and then turned back to whatever business his carbonated insolence had so rudely interrupted. He imagined them creating spells that would make boys like them or hexes to put on their enemies for unremembered playground slights. It was funny, because he knew the names of every single one of these girls, had known them all since kindergarten, but now, all these years later, they had gone in one direction and he had gone in another, and here they were, perfect strangers to one another, a coven of peanut butter-and-jelly-eating brooding teenagers who saw him as what? The time between then and now had to have gone somewhere, he thought. It didn't just disappear. You didn't just go from swinging on the monkey bars with someone to utter disdain without a middle act, did you?

"Hi, Debbie," he called over to one of the girls who he used to play with when they were little. The whole group swiveled their heads back around and stared at him with uniform disdain. Debbie fished a cigarette out of her purse, lit the thing, took a single long drag, and then flicked it, lit, at him. Henry reared back as the Goths sniggered. He grabbed his things and moved away as fast as he could.

By the end of the day he was exhausted by all the subterfuge. Between running every time he caught a glimpse of

Cal and running from the Goths who he was now sure had a lesbian/moon/blood vendetta thing against him, he could barely wait for geometry, his worst subject, but his last class of the day. It would also be the trickiest because it was the only class he and Cal had together, and they usually set next to one another.

He hid around the corner from the door as the kids filed in and when he was sure everyone had gone inside he slipped in and looked for an open seat. Cal, who had been watching for him, perked up as he entered and patted the back of the open seat next to him. They locked eyes for a second before Henry quickly looked away and slid into the first open seat he could find, which was just inside the door. He resisted looking over at Cal, but after the tardy bell rang he stole a quick glance. Cal was unabashedly staring at him, the quizzical look he had on his face when Henry first came into the room now substituted by one of red anger. Henry pretended not to notice as he took his geometry book and notebook from his backpack. He searched in vain for a pencil, and failing that, a pen, and finding neither tapped the shoulder of the short Hispanic girl in front of him. "Lily, do you have a pencil I can borrow?" The girl snapped open her small Hello Kitty pencil case and passed him back a sharpened pencil without ever once turning around to look at him.

"I want that back at the end of class," she said with irritation in her voice.

"Yeah," he said. "Sure. No problem."

Class started with Ms. Garcia taking roll. Even though he sucked at geometry she was his favorite teacher. She was young and pretty and she smiled a lot. She could even make their shitty public high school classroom not seem so dreary with its fucked-up acoustic tiling on the ceiling, walls painted the color of the insides of your eyeballs, broken blinds that rattled when the wind came in and fluorescent lighting that buzzed incessantly, giving off the unnerving feeling that they were completely surrounded by unseen predators. Unlike most of the other teachers at school, Ms. Garcia didn't get mad at them all the time. Not everything her students did irritated and infuriated her. She was more patient than they deserved, and he wished he could do better at her class, even though she never rode him or hassled him about his performance. They had spoken about it once, after school, when she told him that he should expect to see a D on his report card.

"I'm sorry, Henry. I just can't justify giving you a higher grade given your test performance."

"I know," he said, wanting to comfort her, to make her understand that he didn't blame her for what she had to do. "It's not your fault."

They had tried to get down to the bottom of the problem, and Henry had finally been able to tell her that it was the memorization of the rules he couldn't get his head around.

"Well, that's just it," she said patiently, trying to coax him into accepting the inevitability of it, "it doesn't have to make any sense. You just have to learn it."

He had shaken his head more mystified by his inability than she was. "I can't do it. I don't know why, but I can't do that."

She had put her hand on his arm and given him a friendly squeeze and even after she took it off he could still feel the spot tingle where she had touched him, it was radioactive now and he thought it always would be given the half-life of genuine affection mixed with teenage hormones.

Earlier in the year she had begun showing and even after she started wearing flowing dresses and cavernous poncho type shirts, it was obvious she was very pregnant. Henry would watch her in class, loving her even more somehow after he found out that she was going to have a baby, as though it made her seem more kind, even that much easier to adore, and once, as she flipped her long dark hair back from her eyes as she went to draw a diagram on the overhead projector, he had turned and whispered to Cal when he just about couldn't take it anymore, "She's so pretty. I'm not surprised she's pregnant."

As soon as he had said it, he knew it hadn't come out the way he intended. He had just felt such an overwhelming affection for her at that moment as she clumsily pushed her hair back, smiled down at her herself as she illustrated some kind of right angle or other, and he thought that that smile was for her baby, for her husband, for all the happiness. He'd been so overwhelmed by it that he felt the need to say something, but he hadn't meant it to sound the way it had. It was the first time he had ever said anything like that about a woman, hinting at the sexual, and of course Cal had taken it the wrong way and busted up laughing.

"That's the most fucked-up thing I've ever heard anyone say," Cal had finally said when he was able to compose himself enough to speak and held up a hand for Henry to high five. "Come on, man, slap it." Henry just looked at him blankly. There was no point in even trying to make himself understood. That's when really bad things happened. When you tried too hard to make someone understand you.

Ms. Garcia took roll and looked up when she said Henry's name.

"New seat, Henry?" He smiled embarrassedly and kept his eyes focused straight ahead. "New perspectives are a good thing," she said and went on with attendance.

He kept his head down throughout class, even after Ms. Garcia turned toward them after writing on the board and he noticed a major chalk stain marking her belly where it had slid across the board. Normally he wouldn't be able to take his eyes off something like that, but he was so afraid of accidentally locking eyes with Cal again that he didn't dare look up. Toward the end of class a group of kids in the back of the room began to laugh over some private joke or another and one of them let out a high-pitched laugh that literally made him flinch.

"Jesus," Henry muttered, "squeal like a fucking pig, why don't you?"

"What did you say?" a voice next to him asked.

He froze, afraid that he'd said the wrong thing within earshot of the wrong person, and it was only after the voice asked again, "What did you say?" that he turned his head and locked eyes with Sonny Armour, a kid his own age that he'd known for more than ten years and during that entire time probably said less than five words.

"Sorry," Henry said, reflexively.

"No, I'm asking what you said. Did you say, 'squeal like a fucking pig, why don't you'?"

Henry shrugged.

"Did you see that in a movie last night on TV? That's all I want to know."

Henry nodded. "Yeah, a really weird movie."

"Yeah," Sonny was nodding vigorously now, "where they rape that guy and there was this retarded-looking kid playing the banjo?"

"Uh-huh," Henry replied. "It was weird."

"Weird?" Sonny was ecstatic. "It was so fucked-up. I thought I had imagined the whole thing it was so late at night. I'm so glad someone else saw it, too. Do you know what it was called?"

Henry smiled. "*Deliverance.*"

"*Deliverance,*" Sonny repeated the word with wonder like it was the lost name of god. "So fucked-up, right?" He laughed again and punched Henry playfully on the shoulder.

He tried not to look over at Cal but couldn't help himself and when he did he saw him scowling angrily back at them.

"We should watch that again sometime," Sonny said. Was he inviting him to hang out? Henry couldn't be sure if it was just a flip comment or an actual invitation.

"Do you want to?" Sonny asked him again, looking him dead in the eyes this time, and Henry, without really knowing what he was doing said, "Yeah. Totally. Whatever." And just like that Henry had his second friend.

Chapter 13

WHEN HE GOT back to the apartment that afternoon after the shooting range Henry was greeted by an enormous crowd of onlookers, media, and law enforcement and, for a moment, before even finding out what was going on, thought seriously about getting back into his car and driving as far as he could on whatever gas was in the tank. Wherever he stopped, he would stay. Set up a life there in that random spot, believing with his heart and soul that leaving everything to chance had to be better than what was going on here. But he had been down that road before—arrived at moments of self-realization because he felt backed into a corner, made promises the color of night and then found himself caught for years in the resulting far-flung diasporas of reason. True, they were of his own making, but nonetheless... Well... nonetheless. Fight or flight. Fight or flight. His body tried to tell him what to do, to counsel him, pumped adrenaline into parts of his flesh that had been fallow for years, a dose of Mother Nature's tough love that made his heart beat like a runaway truck and the skin on his arms come alive to the touch, an open-ended chemical reaction that had no practical applications. Science for science's sake. The origins of profound mischief.

It was a genuine clusterfuck and the natives were eating it up. Some of the faces he recognized as neighbors, people he had often seen walking their dogs at night and leaving unclaimed shit on one another's lawns, a simple act of civil disobedience, which when he caught someone doing it, he could never understand, but now, watching them, their open faces hoping to recognize a disaster the way long-lost lovers craned their necks at airport arrival gates searching for the faces that would finally complete them, he understood their need for spectacle, that the possibility and inevitability of conflict was built into everyone.

For the first time he noticed the sheer number of damp notices that hung limply from trees and telephone poles all around him. People were looking for lost dogs (answers to Stu), missing brothers (also answers to Stu), a maid service that will do things to your house for $40 that you'd never in a hundred years get your wife to do. The few square blocks around the apartment building were nothing but a canvas of need.

A taco truck arrived and flung open its windows, ready for business. And not to be outdone, a couple of pushcart vendors selling bacon-wrapped hot dogs appeared out of nowhere to peddle their sizzling wares. With the smell of grease everywhere there was now an undeniable ambience to the evening, something that could never happen by design. It had to be spontaneous like this or else it wasn't real. And if as on cue, someone in a nearby apartment building turned their stereo on, cranking the volume all the way up so that Kool and the Gang's "Celebration," like a message from god, rang out everywhere and nowhere at once. Now it was a party, but that was okay, Henry told himself, party...disaster... what was the difference, really, when there was this much enthusiasm for a thing?

While trying to put together the pieces of the shit puzzle before him, a face he vaguely recognized but couldn't immediately place materialized and spoke his name. "Henry? It's Henry, right?"

Henry looked at the guy blankly as a puff of smoke rose off the grill and hovered over them like a raincloud threatening to deluge them in a torrent of pork fat. He coughed, trying to somehow dislodge the thick odor he was sure was already coagulating inside of him, metastasizing into a tasty cancer.

"You don't know who I am, do you?" the man asked. He sighed and turned to face the hot dog seller. "What is this?" he asked the dark-skinned vendor.

"Bacon-wrapped hot dog," she replied, moving the dogs around with a fork, oblivious to the sparkling hot grease that popped off the meat and onto her hands.

"What about that?" he said, pointing at some onions and peppers grilling on the side.

"Onions and peppers," she replied. If she was suspicious that he was somehow fucking with her, she didn't show it at all. Her face was a constant mask of unflappable servility.

"Do you put the onions and peppers on the hot dog, or are they meant as a side?" he wondered.

Henry watched, fascinated. There was no irony here, no hidden agenda. This was a real conversation.

"You can," she told him. "They are no extra." Her hair was tied back in a high ponytail. She was pretty. Very pretty. There was no way the man noticed, being the physical manifestation of brunch that he was.

"Hmmm," he said aloud. He tapped his chin and scrunched up his face. After a minute or two of consideration he put his hands down and shook his head. "No," he said, and turned around and walked back to Henry.

"I just can't eat normal food, anymore," he told Henry when

he was standing in front of him again. "Know what I mean?"

Henry shook his head.

"Yeah, well…doesn't matter," he replied. "The real question is: what are you doing here, Henry? You think you can swoop in and grab this story away from me? Is that it? I know for damn sure that Ken didn't send you here. You can't even get a fucking obituary done. That's a piece of cake compared to a moving target like this. Out of your league, buddy."

Of course. It was the hot-shot reporter from his paper, the dick who had led the charge in his humiliation during the editorial meeting the other day. Jeff Schofield was his name, Henry remembered. As he sought to process all of this, Jeff grabbed his iPhone from his belt clip, scrolled urgently through whatever messages he had just received, and then replaced the phone quickly and efficiently.

"So," he said, his attention once again focused on Henry, "did Ken send you or didn't he?"

"I have no idea what you're talking about, Jeff. Ken didn't send me. I live here."

"Wait," Jeff said, flipping open his small reporter's notebook and pulling a pencil out of, what seemed to Henry, thin air. "You live here? In this neighborhood?"

"Yeah," Henry replied, getting incrementally more worried by Jeff's piqued curiosity.

"Where?" Jeff pressed him. "Which building?"

"This one," Henry pointed to the building across the street, which also appeared to be the one where most of the attention was being focused.

Jeff smiled and draped a snaky arm over Henry's shoulder.

"I am so glad that you're here, Henry. Honestly. I know we've had our differences in the past, but the important thing is that we're colleagues and there's a professional courtesy that colleagues offer to one another. Am I right? A code. Are you with me, Henry?"

"What do you want from me?"

"It's not like that, okay? You shouldn't be such a pessimist." Jeff ripped the iPhone from his belt again, entered a few firm keystrokes on whatever social networking app Hitler's Youth were using these days, and replaced it just as quickly. Amazingly, Henry couldn't be sure that Jeff's arm had ever actually left his shoulders. "Listen, there was a building inspector who went into that building today and he hasn't come out yet. Also, the guy called his office and told the supervisor on duty that he was quitting and also renouncing his US citizenship. They sent a truck to come get the guy, because apparently this isn't all that rare of an occurrence, city workers freaking out and making unilateral political declarations." Things had clearly escalated since the morning. He could picture Truman rubbing his hands together deliciously, savoring a kind of linchpin moment, the tipping point of idiocy, when the thing would continue through to the end on its own volition. No more pushing uphill. It was all smooth sailing from here on in, and Henry imagined the pride Truman and Alberto were taking that it now had a life of its own, like proud parents of a very disturbed child.

"Anyway," Jeff went on, "they sent some guys to come get the other guy, but he won't leave. So the cops got called and now they're waiting for a warrant so they can go in there and figure out what the fuck is going on. But," he said, removing his arm from Henry's shoulder and turning around to face him, "since you live here, you can still get in. You can get us both in, and we can take a look around and get a story together before anyone else. We can scoop this shit. You and me together. Whaddaya say, buddy?" He made his eyes go big and innocent like Henry had his life in his hands. "Wanna go get this story?"

The screech of a murder of crows who had made a home of the tree on the sidewalk in front of the apartment building competed for air time with the general clamor; police walkie-talkies producing unintelligible white noise, parents screaming for their children to come inside, the general din of gossip and speculation spreading round and round like a glorious hosanna, a group prayer beseeching a higher power for the truth of the situation. If there were snakes around, he had no doubt that they'd be being handled right about now. Cops were putting up barriers in front of the street, a combination of yellow traffic cones, roadside flares, and yellow and black plastic tape warned people to stay away with the admonishment of a "Police Line—Do Not Cross." A traffic jam materialized almost instantaneously and drivers began to honk their horns and stick their heads out of their windows, angrily asking where they were supposed to go. It was a rhetorical question, which is what made it excruciatingly pertinent. Some just gave in and turned their cars off where they were and came to join the fray, get a hot dog, settle in for the evening. It was an organic thing, multiplying with the slow menace of a lethargic pervert. All the while the crows bellowed louder and louder, trying to be heard, until they finally couldn't take it anymore and flew off, as one, to saner quarters.

Shoving past Jeff without answering his question, Henry crossed the street and found a quiet patch of sidewalk. He pulled out his phone, dialed Oscar's number and used his free to hand to cover his other ear.

Oscar answered the phone on the first ring. "Miss me already?"

"Ha ha. Yeah."

In the background Henry could hear the sound of guns being fired and in front of him an ambulance crept by slowly, its siren doing nothing to move the crowd that was now taking up a large part of the street. Inside his chest he could feel something like panic creeping up and for a moment he considered jumping into the back of the ambulance and demanding to be taken to the nearest neutral country.

"I know we just talked, but I'm back at the building and there's been some kind of...incident."

"Ooh," Oscar said, his voice a perky bag of nails. "Do tell."

"I think you should come down here and see for yourself. I'll get you in and introduce you to the two crackpots running this thing, but I want you to understand something."

"Lay it on me, man. I'm the king of understanding. You're talking to the guy who once wrote three thousand words on the benefits of urophagia. Know what that is? It's the consumption of urine. Get your mushy Gen-X head around that. I fucking own objectivity." He was panting lasciviously. "I'm riddled with understanding. It's like a cancer in me."

Henry took a deep breath and explained the situation, the police, the crowd, how the whole thing had seemed to escalate from worrisome to apocalyptic in an alarmingly short amount of time. Across the street Jeff was watching him, his eyes narrowed into suspicious slits, and Henry had that old urge to smash his head wide open, a youthful impulse he hadn't felt in years. He turned so he wouldn't have to look at him.

He was about to tell Oscar the thing he had to understand was that he was making the introduction because he was worried about everyone at the building, that he could sense the end was not far away, and that it wouldn't be good. Not for anyone. He would explain that he thought Oscar and his friends might be just what the doctor ordered: a strong hand to supervise and make sure the children didn't do anything stupid. But he didn't believe that. Not really. He was doing this so he could get the introduction to Oscar's person in the COL and get his story. That was all that mattered now. Everything else was a wreck. Irredeemable. The story, that was the thing. The story was the only thing worth saving.

He looked over his shoulder again and saw Jeff still staring. Fuck Jeff, he thought. Everyone else did what they needed to do to get what they wanted. Why shouldn't he?

"So what is it you wanted me to understand?" Oscar asked after Henry had given him Truman's number with instructions to say that Henry thought the two of them should meet.

"It was nothing," Henry replied, shaking his head. The sun had set and the lights from the police cars and ambulances gave the street a carnival atmosphere. A few more vendors had shown up and were selling glow sticks to the kids. Commerce could not be stopped.

"You may want to stay away from the building for a day or two. Do you have somewhere to go? I'd tell you to crash at my old office, but Ken's probably already turned it into a primal scream therapy retreat."

He imagined Oscar already signaling his junta, waving frantically at the men to saddle up, grab their gear, that he'd deputize them in the car on the way over to the building. He hoped he wasn't making a huge mistake.

"No," he started to say, but then had an idea. "Yeah. Actually, yeah, I do."

"Atta boy," Oscar replied. Henry could hear the evil smile shaping his words. "Come back tomorrow and I'll have a contact for you. Twenty-four hours. Does that work?"

The story was due in three days. He'd need at least a day to write the rest of it, edit, get the thing in good enough shape so Ken wouldn't laugh in his face.

"Fine." He heard Oscar start to hang up and shouted, "Wait! What about the tapes? What about your conversations with Potter?"

Oscar laughed. "Wanna hear something really funny?"

"What's that?."

"I never met the guy. I went to the compound but they never let me see him. I talked to some of the other people, met some of the girls, the Flowers. I kept in touch with one of the ones who made it out. Iris I think her name was. She usually gets back to me pretty quickly. I'll tell her it's an emergency. It is, right?"

"What?" asked Henry, his head spinning.

"An emergency?"

*   *   *

He wasn't sure why he chose the old neighborhood library as the place to spend the night, but as soon as Oscar had asked him if he had a place to go it was the first thing that occurred to him. The more he felt his life slipping out of his control the more he found himself retreating further and further into himself, circumstances sending him careening into the past, memories he couldn't help but take refuge within as though each one was a private panic room built just for him. It didn't take much to make him feel nostalgic these days. Now the right combination of sounds, smells, and color could channel urges to revisit the past, their intensity as riveting as puberty's denouement.

He wasn't shocked by Oscar's confession that he'd lied about having a conversation with Potter, nor was he shocked by how blasé Oscar was in revealing it. The fact that he never talked to the man seemed beyond the point. The story, after all, wasn't about him. It was about the people that made up the Children of Light, the decisions that led them there, the escalation of their dedication until everything else in their lives seemed petty in comparison. Oscar's story, which he'd read many times since getting the assignment, reflected all that beautifully. Potter's quotes were just window dressing. The real dread was that they all knew what was coming, that they'd accepted it, that they were anxious for it.

For a brief moment he toyed with the thought of doing the same thing. It would be so easy to say he'd met with Potter, produce a transcript of a conversation he could concoct with little trouble given the amount of time he'd thought about the man in the past couple of weeks. He'd thought of how the conversation would go a thousand times. In his mind he saw Potter sitting across from him dressed in overalls and a straw hat, his thin old skin sagging from his face. Potter's voice would be cheerful and his speech would be plain and slow. He'd indulge Henry's questions with patience and treat his skepticism the way a parent of a small child might overdo sympathy for a skinned knee or some other inconsequential boo-boo. In his mind there'd be iced tea. There'd be civility. Somewhere someone would be strumming a guitar, a lonely folk song that would make him feel like, under different circumstances, he could see himself living in a place like this. Objectivity didn't come naturally to him. He really had to work at it. Always had. It was the lasting curse of being too trusting as a child.

As he pulled out of his parking space, he looked in the rearview mirror and saw Jeff still standing on the sidewalk, watching him. The panicked strobes of cop cars and ambulances clambered for his attention, tantrums of color, and in the distance two enormous lights suddenly appeared in the sky and began to churn the night air slowly; spotlights up on

Hollywood Boulevard no doubt, the celebration machine doing its thing no matter the merits of the object of its adoration.

At the old library he made himself comfortable at a small table deep in the stacks. He unloaded his laptop, his notes, connected to the Wi-Fi, and sat there without a clue of what to do next. He wandered over to the old card catalogue, which was as antiquated a concept as libraries themselves, it occurred to him, opened a drawer at random, and began to leaf through the moldy old cards. The smell of the place embraced him, the dust, the old paper, fresh pencil shavings laying like potpourri in the waste baskets. It was the smell of decay, sure, but it was a wise decay, a self-conscious decay. Above him fluorescent light bulbs buzzed softly, just enough to suggest a healthy dose of radiation was in the process of being doled out. It wasn't so much light these fixtures provided, as the absence of dark. Just enough illumination to tease reality into being.

A thought occurred to him and he raced through the library suddenly on a mission. "Walk!" A stern librarian hissed at him, but he was already around the corner headed into the bowels of the place; past bored nannies scanning their Facebook feeds while their charges systematically dismantled the children's area like militia commanders turning a blind eye to the rape and plunder of the enlisted men, past row after row of books that would never be plucked from the shelf again, that would one day turn to dust and become an entirely different kind of wisdom.

Finally he found the reference section and used his finger to scan the titles. Lots of *World Almanacs* and *Guiness Book of World Records*, which they used to fight over when they were in elementary school. There was something undeniable about kids and facts. As they got older, of course, the charm of facts wore off and they began to search out the more rebellious offerings; *Catcher in the Rye* (which Henry had read as *Catheter in the Rye* for years), *Siddhartha*, *All Quiet on the Western Front*. Maybe it coincided with puberty, which coincided with the realization of the notion of mortality, which precipitated the inevitable freefall into self-exploration and all that other shit you needed to do to "grow as a person." Leaving these books was essentially the birth of selfishness, the emergence of the ego, which didn't come on slowly, but rather made itself known in a dramatic and sudden way like the alien popping out of John Hurt's chest in *Alien*.

Finally he found what he was looking for and plucked the enormous and familiar copy of *Jane's* from the shelf. Its weight felt familiar in his hands, as did the smell when he flipped it open and inhaled the scent of its long-neglected pages. This was the library's second copy of the book. He'd stolen the first one decades before in a rare fit of avarice. He had never been one of those kids who, when he wanted something, would hold his breath until he got it. Stealing the book was the only time he had ever had to have something so badly that he felt he would have exploded if he couldn't take it home at that exact moment. It wasn't petulance, he reflected, it was need. Pure and simple need.

Back at his little desk deep in the stacks, he flipped the book open and began to read at random. Weapon types, ammo capacity, range and usage. Basically, who shot who, where, and how. What was missing, he realized now, all these years later, was the why of it. The weapons, he noticed, were presented as a separate entity, like they were another actor in the conflict. Like they had their own side in the conflict and nobody needed to pull their trigger to make them fire. They just were. But that wasn't true at all. The binding moaned as he quickly flipped the pages, going from conflict to conflict, chart after chart.

Flipping to the beginning, he pulled the borrow card out of its pocket in the front cover and scanned the names written there. Written in fuzzy pencil his was the last name on the card. 12-9-85. Since then it appeared no one had ever checked it out. He wanted to believe that it wasn't possible. That in twenty-five years (a quarter of a fucking century!), even if it had been a mistake, or someone had been assigned a random term paper project, this book hadn't left the library since he last took it out. Had it even left the shelf? He blew at the light film of dust, but that was no way to be sure of anything. Everything in this place had a light film of dust on it, dust that would collect and grow thicker and thicker over time until the building itself was buried completely underneath it all, little by little, not all at once. Little by little the way things disappeared without anyone noticing they were gone.

He needed fresh air and also something to drink and when he passed the multi-purpose room, he stopped long enough to peek through the little window in the door. A group of about six or seven kids were gathered around a table playing Dungeons and Dragons. He could tell by the fact that the players were laughing and that the kid who was the Dungeon Master, shrouded behind a cheap cardboard screen, scowled back at them, wishing he was a sorcerer just long enough to enchant them into paying attention, that it was a good game. Before he could walk away, though, they looked up as one and saw him staring and their faces went cold. He wasn't welcome and could only imagine what they were thinking. That he was old and could never understand. Or worse than that, he had never been young. What he thought of as his youth was just a dream. Old people like him were born old, born with responsibilities, born with unhappiness. Youth belonged to the young and it was theirs alone to bestow unto others. For a moment he thought about getting the *Jane's* book and bringing it back to show them his name in the card. *See?* he'd say. *1985. That wasn't that long ago. I was a kid once, too.*

He walked to the convenience store next to the library and bought a large cup of piping hot coffee and a pack of grape Now and Later. He added a long stream of clotted sugar to the coffee and stirred it until he could feel a sludge form on the bottom. He took the drink and the candy back to the library and sat on a bench out front while he sipped slowly at the scorching concoction. It was finally beginning to feel a bit like fall, he realized, as a cool wind used its bony fingers to caress his face, sending a chill of pleasure down his spine. A small sparrow hopped toward him and cocked its head fearlessly in his direction. "Sorry," he told it, sincerely. "Just coffee, buddy. And not very good coffee, either." The bird cocked its head the other way, took another hop toward him as if to give him a piece of its mind, and then flew away, barely missing Henry's head as it went.

He got up and was about to walk back in the library when he noticed the "No Food or Drink" sign on the front door. He turned, and as he was trying to figure out how he was going to put the coffee under his shirt without burning his nipples off, looked up to see an old woman watching him. She smoked a long thin cigarette, savoring every inhalation with a grim satisfaction that suggested she took great pride in having beaten smoking at its own game. Every puff was a bonus puff at this point, her curved body indicated, pure gravy. Her lips were a hideously overpainted shade of orange, and when she parted them to insert the cigarette he imagined he could hear them, forever damp, coming sickeningly apart like sweaty skin peeling away from leather on a hot day.

"Oh my God," she said exasperatedly, her gravelly voice the sonic equivalent of a fog machine. "Just take it in with you." She paused to take a pull off the cigarette as though it were a respirator and not the opposite. "No one's going to see you."

He looked around, not sure if she was actually addressing him or simply in the thralls of a vivid Alzheimer's hallucination.

"Just take the coffee in. What's that old bitch going to do? Tell you no? Hahahahahaha." Her laugh rolled on and on like an evil landslide.

"Yeah," he answered, assuming she was talking about the librarian on whom she had at least a dozen years.

"So? If she does that, you just go right in anyway. She's just a librarian. That's what my husband would have done." To put a not so fine point on it she nodded decisively as she said the last part, and as she did so he could have sworn he heard the bones in her neck crack and crumble into dust.

He turned quickly and just before he walked inside he heard her call out to him one last time, "I spend my time in the record room. They have everything back there. Sinatra. Big band. You name it. You can join me if you care to."

"Thanks," he hollered back, feeling, for the first time in his life, profoundly afraid of lust.

He wasn't two steps into the library before the librarian's harsh whisper came at him from behind the check-out desk.

"You can't have that in here. You'll have to throw it out or go back outside and finish it."

Half of him wanted to report the sexual predator right outside the doors and part of him wanted to point at the sagging and stained acoustic tiles that hung from the ceiling. *So much decay* was what he wanted to shout, *and you're going to say no to a cup of fucking coffee?*

Back at his desk he took out the Now and Laters and popped one rebelliously into his mouth. It tasted just like he remembered, like he thought it would, and he closed his eyes and sucked deliriously on the medicine-tasting candy. It was flavors like these that ruined his generation for the real thing. Real grapes could never compare with this. Nature came in a distant second when compared with such rich, bold tastes. He quickly popped the rest of the candies into his mouth one after another and sat back as his salivary glands went into overdrive. It was almost too much pleasure. His third eye opened as lines of purple drool parachuted out of his mouth.

He let the caffeine and sugar do its work while he opened his computer and logged once again into the library's Wi-Fi. To his surprise the Children of Light website was not one of the many sites the library's network blocked. Accessing hate sites was forbidden, even though he could barely think of a place less conducive to masterminding the rise of an all-white nation than the public library. But how did they rationalize blocking that while allowing people to access the website of a cult whose members were convicted of sexually abusing children and encouraging them to commit suicide? *Lord, forgive us our bureaucratic oversights*, he prayed silently, scoffing at the notion of how little it took to be a holy man. *We know not how these things get lost in the shuffle.*

He went to the section of the Children of Light website where someone had archived hundreds of hours of recorded video of Potter speaking, as far as Henry could tell, about every last thought that had ever entered the crazy man's head. Henry had gone through a lot of these recordings over the past few weeks looking for clues. At first he'd had the notion that he would start at the beginning and work his way through the recordings chronologically. But after a week of watching he'd realized he was never going to get through them all and as interesting as it was to hear Potter's thoughts on the Soviet boycott of the '84 Olympics, or how Michael Jackson might or might not be the Antichrist, he was going to have to figure out another way to go through them all. So, he started skipping around, picking videos at random, so that one moment he'd see a young Potter, a lean man with a gleaming head of thick black hair, confidently staring into the camera's lens, his thumbs hooked in the pockets of a worn pair of overalls. The next video, however, might be Potter thirty years in the future, his face a thin mask of anxiety lined with wrinkles, his grey hair combed over a bald spot dotted with age spots. What never changed was his voice. As much as everything else deteriorated over time his voice always remained the same strong vibrant tremor, an electric current that was his essence, the body through which it traveled merely a conductor for its wattage.

Not sure how much later he awoke with a start. He lifted his heavy head from the desk and looked around, unsure at first not only where he was but when it was. It was one of those sleeps that could have lasted minutes, hours or days. Dreamless. Senseless.

He stretched and looked around, and it quickly dawned on him that the library was dark and there was absolutely no sound to be heard, not the scrape of a chair being backed away from a table nor the quick loud cough emanating from an anonymous student, normally innocuous noises that took on the weight of seismic occurrences when they happened without warning against the background of nothingness. Clicking the space bar of his computer the screen came to life and he squinted down at the little clock in the upper corner: 1:43 a.m. Seven hours! Holy fucking shit. He hadn't planned on spending the entire night there, but it was better than sleeping in his car in front of his old office, which is what he had planned to do. How had he not had to go to the bathroom? How had the librarian, for whom vigilance was an aphrodisiac, failed to find him when closing up and not shaken him violently, admonishing him that "this was a library and not a refugee camp"? Maybe he had been drugged. Maybe the old woman out front had slipped a lethal combination of estrogen and arthritis pills into his coffee when he wasn't looking and then taken advantage of him while he lay comatose deep in the stacks. He felt his body for bruises and violations, but there was nothing. An older Potter was frozen on the video player, and he closed the top of the computer, sighing lightly to himself. Nothing learned. Not even dreams. Seven hours of nothingness. It hardly seemed possible.

He got up and stretched. A dull pain in his lower back blossomed suddenly, and strangely, an ache on the heel of his left foot. Old age was graceless and random, he thought to himself, taking off his shoe and rubbing his foot, considering whether he should write down that today was the day his heel started to hurt in case it was something he was going to be living with the rest of his life. Some point of reference he could point to in fifty years when sitting with his grandchildren, telling them his war stories, like about the day his heel started hurting or about the time he got locked in the public library overnight. Milestones? Sure. Highlights? Fuck that.

He flicked on a light switch and began to walk around the library. It wasn't as strange to be in a deserted library at night as he might have thought, since, by its very nature, it was designed to convey a kind of deserted feeling anyway. Or was it a deserted ambience? Could isolation be an aesthetic? He tried the front door. Locked. He peered out and saw nothing but quiet streets and a flickering street lamp. This was the suburbs: no random group of teenagers bunched together like amoebae looking for something to spray paint, no car going by with its tailpipe scraping against the street as bass bellowed from its innards, no nothing but the wind and the occasional cat scampering happily down the sidewalk, oblivious to just how good it had it.

After hitting the bathroom, he wandered back to the reference section when another familiar tome caught his eye. *The Prophecies of Nostradamus* never used to be in reference, but where it was shelved when he was a kid he couldn't remember now. Wherever it was had made perfect sense back then. When he was a kid it was pertinent information, useful to the utmost degree. Predictions about the end of the world and assassinations were as important to any twelve-year-old as a history textbook. That was information worth knowing, because it was worth sharing with friends. Those predictions were playground currency, a chance to shock and awe even the coolest of the cool kids. "Nuh-uh," they'd say. "That's not true." "Yes, it is," Henry would reply, steadfast. "He predicted the Kennedy assassination six hundred years ago. Next, he said a great dictator is going to rise up in the Middle East and bring about the end of the world in 1994. That's nine years away," he'd say, worriedly, as if nine years was just around the corner. "Who cares?" The kid would say, scampering away. "That's forever." And Henry would be left wondering why no one else was as worried about this as he was. How did everyone get to be so carefree but him?

He replaced the book and went into the record room the lustful woman outside had so highly recommended. Looking at the large cache of LPs, he saw that there was a 'punk' section and began to aimlessly flip through them. The library had everything. An index of his teenage years in alphabetical order. He took out the blue Adolescents record, put it on the turntable, and placed the oversized headphones over his head. The first song, "I Hate Children," leapt into his ears and he began to dance around, slowly at first, and then faster and faster, whipping his arms and legs in all directions. He caught sight of his reflection in a darkened window, and though he looked ridiculous, he couldn't help dancing and singing along.

As he moved, he began to think about the piece he had to write. There was nothing stopping him from making up a few quotes from Daisy, a few innocuous tidbits that would fill in the spaces and round the piece out, give Ken what he wanted, which was a little first-hand perspective. What was she really going to say that he couldn't make up? That he was charismatic? That she had no idea he was such a monster until later on? Ken would say that he needed to get something that got to the heart of the man, but what was there to say besides "you had to be there"? "You had to see him with your own eyes to know." "Know what?" he'd ask her, innocently. "Just…know." How could he write that? Maybe a few juicy made-up tidbits would make up for the fact that he never managed to get an interview with Potter. He sighed. None of it would be good enough. He was stuck.

The Nostradamus book sat on the table next to the record player. What an idiot he'd been to have wasted so much time leafing through its pages, looking for answers about a future he didn't have the guts to blindly wade into like all his class-mates. No wonder no one wanted to be his friend.

The first side of the record ended, and he flipped it over, placing the needle down as gently as he could. When the music started again he picked up his dancing right where he had left off, flailing around like a crazy person, waiting for the morning to come.

In the morning he left the library, just walked right by the librarian as she unlocked the front door, her face registering as much shock as a person can actually feel first thing in the morning.

*   *   *

Back at the apartment building the circus had hardly dissipated. In fact, if anything it'd gotten worse. The carnival element was still there, but now it was an exhausted carnival and, sometime during the night, the religious and political nuts had come out to join the fray. The thinking there being that if society was going to fall apart they had as much right as anyone to a front-row seat.

It took a few minutes to get inside the building; he first had to get past the phalanx of onlookers who constituted the outer circle of this scrum of insanity, and then the fanatics whose idea of personal space was who wanted in, wanted to be a part of it even if they didn't know exactly what "it" was, and then finally to the most inner circle of hell, the cops, to whom he explained, "I live here."

The young cop, square-jawed and bored, looked at him and then to his partner standing nearby.

"Says he lives here," he said.

The other cop shrugged. "Can he prove it?"

"Prove it," the cop said childishly.

Henry sighed. "How?"

"I don't know. ID?"

"My license has an old address. Listen, why the hell would I want to come in if I didn't absolutely have to be here?"

The cop looked around and then leaned in to whisper, "I know. That's what I keep thinking. But look at all these people trying to get inside. Weird, right?"

He couldn't disagree.

"Wait a minute. I have a key." Henry announced a little too excitedly. He felt someone push into his back. He took the key from his pocket and handed it to the cop, who slid it into the front door lock, fiddled with it for a minute, and then came back to him.

"Okay," he said, lifting up the strip of yellow tape. "You can go in."

Henry ducked, and as he walked toward the door, felt the crowd swell with excitement behind him. For an instant he felt like Charlie walking up to the front door of the Chocolate Factory.

Despite the excitement outside, very little inside the lobby had changed. Suspicious residents, some now wearing face paint and ripped white T-shirts that revealed their stomachs which he took to be uniforms, eyed him as he waited for the elevator; when it opened, he saw that someone had written the words *MEXICAN SPACE SHUTTLE* across the entire back wall. That was new.

On the third floor he knocked on the door of the apartment he'd been sharing with Truman and the other nuts. Mark, one of the California Separatists answered, and looked at him quizzically.

"Can I help you?"

He thought of making a joke about being from Publishers Clearing House but then thought better of it, not being able to be absolutely certain whether or not memories of Ed McMahon might trigger some long-dormant psychopathic impulses.

"Yeah, uh, I live here," he said tentatively more than a little aware how loaded of a statement that was.

"You do?" Mark let the door open a crack more. "Where? Are you the guy that sleeps in the tub?"

"No, I think that's the Freegan. I'm Henry. Truman's friend."

"I don't remember you. What's your..."

"Problem?" Henry spoke too soon.

"Problem? No, that's not what I was going to say. I was going to ask what your cause was. What brought you here?"

Mark pulled down the brim of the John Deere cap he was wearing. His face had wrinkles that made it look like aliens had landed on it and carved elaborate crop circle into his flesh.

"Necessity," Henry said after thinking for a moment. "My house blew up."

Mark nodded and pulled down his hat again. Must be a tic, Henry thought, a subconscious need to disappear that he immediately identified with.

"Oh, yeah," he said scrunching his face up so completely it looked like it was being swallowed whole by his head. "I think I heard something about that. ISIS?"

"Close. Cultists."

"Mm-hmm," Mark muttered.

An awkward silence, which Henry felt compelled to fill, quickly ballooned between them. "Seems quieter in there than usual," he said.

Mark looked behind him anxiously as though silence were a slobbering monster closing in on him fast.

"Change in leadership," he whispered. "There's been some turnover at the top."

"What do you mean?" Henry asked, instantly worried.

"Truman left and this new guy came in. Had a group of about six of the roughest looking dudes I've ever seen with him. Not sure if they're Marines or what, but they definitely look like they've seen some shit. Know what I mean?" His voice got even softer. "Like they've been broken and rebuilt."

Henry nodded. He knew exactly what he meant.

"Where's this guy now?"

"They're out patrolling the halls. He said they're putting an end to all this fake race war bullshit. Time for us to pull together, he says. One mission." Mark laughed. "Like that's ever going to happen."

Mark pulled a canteen from his belt and took a long, exhausted swig of water. Henry grimaced as liquid ran from the sides of his mouth and down his shirt and without seeming to realize that he'd spilled, Mark put the cap back on and put the canteen back on his belt.

"Anyway, Truman moved out. Took an apartment a floor up with that Mexican guy. One floor up. Last door on the righthand side." He looked around suspiciously. "But don't tell anyone I told you, okay? Commander Oscar says 'Snitches get stitches'."

"Commander Oscar?" Henry asked, but he didn't really need an answer. It all made sense to him now. Destinies were playing out left, right, and center, and although he'd willingly fed these poor souls to Oscar to get to Potter, he couldn't help but feel worried about the morass he'd enabled. After all, what Oscar had in mind was nothing less than whole-sale nation-building. One thing he knew was that people were going to get hurt and that their blood would be at least partially on his hands.

"Listen, don't worry too much about it, okay? I know this guy. He doesn't want to hurt anyone. He just misses being in control of his own life."

Mark lifted his cap and ran a hand over his bumpy scalp.

"I don't know," he said worriedly. "They already frog-marched some people out of here. 'Dissenters' they called them. I hear they've got a prison camp set up in the laundry room."

Fuck, Henry thought. He hoped whatever information he got about Potter would be worth the cost of inflicting this trigger-happy junta on a bunch of lonely old Libertarians. Could be the best thing that ever happened to them, he tried to tell himself. Only time and a run on PTSD medicine would tell.

On his way up the stairs to the next floor, he was surprised when he ran into Oscar, who was accompanied by six of the largest men Henry had ever seen in his entire life. Oscar, wearing a crisp black T-shirt tucked into olive green pants, smiled broadly and threw his arms around Henry. He pulled off his Aviators and put his hands on his hips.

"Henry, Henry, Henry!" He was wall-to-wall smiles, and Henry noticed a revolver sitting in a holster at his hip. "Boys, it's the hero of the revolution. Henry Colmes. All hail, Henry, huh?"

The men, who were all dressed the same as Oscar except for brown shirts instead of black, bellowed back, "All hail, Henry!" Their voices were beyond enthusiastic. Genetically engineered to suppress their own will, they were clearly happy to be back in their sweet spot of incestuous amplification.

"So, what do you think?" Oscar asked. He looked as proud as a new parent.

"So far, so good?" Henry half-asked, hoping it would suffice as an answer.

"I like how you answered a question with a question. That's very smart." Oscar put his hands on his hips and inhaled deeply. A satisfied grin spread over his face, like a shadow at noon, as though he had just inhaled a double lungful of cordite or Napalm instead of an overflowing septic tank and, from somewhere further away, the smell of a campfire. "There's a place for you here, you know, if you want to stay. I could use a guy like you to run my propaganda machine."

To a certain sad extent, he was honored to be thought of

for such a prestigious role in the dictatorship, but he shook his head.

"That's okay. I've got the story to finish and everything. Also, pretty sure I'd be 4F." He pointed down at his feet. "Flat feet."

Oscar patted his shoulder.

"That's okay. We can't all be soldiers, can we?"

"Absolutely not," Henry answered.

He put a hand on Henry's shoulder and then leaned in to whisper. "Thank you for this. For making the introduction to those guys and getting us in here." His breath was a bright plume of stale cigarettes and cut-rate liquor and Henry tried not to gag as he spoke. "I know you only did it because of the Potter thing, but still. Go upstairs and see your friends. They'll tell you where to get the information for your story. Good luck with it, Henry. I hope it's everything you think it's going to be. Or not. You are kind of a weirdo, after all."

It was a strange feeling, getting what he wanted after all this time, and as Oscar leaned back, smug and resilient again as he posed like Douglas MacArthur, surveying the stairwell as though it were the 38th Parallel, Henry felt a sudden onset of buyer's remorse he promised himself he wouldn't have if he went through with this.

"Oscar, I don't know when you last looked out the window, but there's a ton of police out there. News crews. Onlookers. How long do you think this is going to last before it all comes crashing down? Before people get seriously hurt?"

The smile Oscar flashed him was unexpected, and it struck him that it was the consolation prize you win for doing too little too late.

"You're a sweet man, Henry. A sweet, sweet man. Now," he

said, with what seemed like the last vestiges of sympathy and pathos he could muster said, "get out of here before someone kills you."

He squeezed Henry's shoulder and, together with his troupe of middle-aged ennui players, continued down the stairs toward whatever battle he felt he couldn't live without.

The door at the top of the stairwell opened with a heavy yawn onto an unfinished hallway where a bare light bulb showed off patches of off-colored plaster that covered blemishes in the drywall. Carpet scraps lay on the floor like tumbleweed in an old west street and everywhere was the chemical smell of unfinished business. Just a little paint, a last-minute vacuuming, a light fixture or two and it would be ready to go, ready to welcome home families who were eager to start their lives in a place like this, a place that was also just starting out.

He imagined the kind of people who might live here one day, and he saw in his mind's eye young fathers and mothers either very pregnant or already with small children, early in their careers, conscious that an apartment was just a first stop on the road toward domestic bliss. Somewhere down the line there would be a house, a better car, a bigger job. This was just the beginning of things, and the beginning didn't really count, did it? Not if you didn't want it to count, it didn't.

But Henry thought of the kids who would call this home, remembered back to when he was a child and how much movies and books and art had meant to him then and how those things had steadily lost their impact over the years, as though you hit your threshold for amazement just as puberty began to set in, and when biology finally won out, as it inevitably had to, all the ideas you had left were the ones you had come into the battle with in the first place. Music never meant the same thing again. Movies were a distraction if you were lucky. Books, fleetingly moving at best. He closed his eyes and took a deep breath, trying to tamp down the desperate feeling that was climbing in him that he'd do anything to feel that way again, if even for a moment. But that wasn't a bargain anyone had the capacity to negotiate and if that was what he really wanted he would have to create the opportunity like Truman and Arturo had done, like Oscar had stumbled onto with what seemed like perfectly exquisite dumb luck.

At the end of the hall he stopped and knocked on the door of Truman's apartment.

He heard someone fumble with the lock for a few seconds and he was only slightly surprised to see Truman peering at him from behind the narrow gap the chain provided.

"Henry!" Truman yelled, closing the door to undo the chain. "Alberto, Henry's home!" Before Henry could say anything, Truman had him in a giant bear hug, and when it felt like it had gone on as long as it should and he tried to pull away, Truman tightened his grip, and it became like quicksand where the more he struggled the more he felt himself getting trapped, so he finally just let his body go limp until Truman had exhausted himself and let go, panting, his hands on his knees.

"It's so...*pant*...good to...*pant*...see you...*pant pant pant*... Henry."

Henry walked past him into the apartment, which was furnished quite normally, the way it might be for the kind of family he'd just been imagining.

"Truman," he heard Alberto's voice from the living room, "the phone."

"Right, right," Truman said. He was wall-to-wall smiles as he bounced giddily into the kitchen. Henry couldn't believe how different he looked since the last time he had seen him which was just a couple of days before. He had on a pair of clean jeans and a green T-shirt with the *LA Daily Ledger* logo on it. His hair was combed, his face shaved. He looked like he had just come out of suspended animation. "I've just got to finish this call. Make yourself at home. Go say hi to Alberto. Want a drink? Are you too hot?"

"You're smothering me, Mom. I'm fine," Henry said, waving him away. "I really need to talk to you, though, Truman. Seriously. Truman?"

But Truman was already gone, he had taken the phone into one of the bedrooms and closed the door, behind which he could hear the strange pitch changes of an impassioned muffled conversation.

He wandered slowly from the kitchen to the TV room taking in the décor, the art on the walls, the disarming ordinariness of it all. At first glance there was no particular style to be discerned, but no, that wasn't true. There was a style, he realized, as he glanced at the framed French café poster that hung slightly askew over the couch in the living room, the perfunctory orchid on the prefab hallway side table, the ironic, oversized light fixture that played host to one of those old-fashioned bulbs that was all filament and probably buzzed like a premonition when it was switched on, and ironic because it barely gave off enough light to read the labels of the medicine bottles he was sure they were abusing, the only rational explanation he could conceive of to explain what he was seeing. It all added up to a perfectly curated experience in banality, a place so benign and generically familiar it looked like it had been staged to prevent an unhinged inhabitant from having a relapse of a psychotic episode. The overwhelming sense he had of déjà vu was disarming and he was pretty sure that if he made that point with Truman, he would get a smile back, a pat on the shoulder, and be told,

Good, that's what we were going for.

An enormous flatscreen TV loomed on one of the walls of the living room, its dimensions so massive Henry imagined a unit of measurement other than inches would be needed to assess its mass, something that could simultaneously express girth, radiation, and entropy. The movie *Gladiator* boomed to an empty room. Russell Crowe's character was in the middle of one of his overwrought speeches about honor and individualism.

"Can you move over, Henry?" A voice he recognized instantly as Alberto's politely asked him. "This is my favorite part."

It took him a moment to see where Alberto was speaking from, camouflaged as he was at one end of an overly cushy-looking purple sofa ensconced in what looked like a terrycloth poncho from which only his face protruded.

"Jesus, Alberto, I didn't see you there. You scared the shit out of me."

"Sorry," Alberto said as he shifted his mass a little, generating a small landslide of pillows. "Have a seat. Have a drink. I want to talk to you, but I just really love this scene. When you're in the right mood, there are parts of *Gladiator* that seem more important than the Bible."

Although a bundle of nerves, Henry plopped himself down on the couch and watched the movie until the scene ended and Alberto finally clicked the 'mute' button.

"Sorry about that," Alberto said, sitting up, causing the rest of the pillows he had stacked around him to fall. Henry saw that his suspicions about the poncho were correct, except that it wasn't a poncho, but one of those giant blankets you could zip yourself into, with holes for the head, arms, and legs, that were sold on late night TV that cloaked your whole body in snuggly comfort. "It's good to see you, Henry. So good to see you. How long's it been?"

"Two days," Henry answered matter-of-factly, but he knew what Alberto meant, because time seemed to be stretching in strange ways the last week or so, more of a moving target than an actual yardstick.

"Alberto," he forced himself to stay as calm as possible, remembering that Alberto and Truman fed off hysteria, but his in particular, like it was a special vintage of panic they had socked away years earlier, only to be opened on the most special of occasions, "what is going on here? I need you to explain this to me. I'm very worried about..." he looked for a word that wouldn't necessarily give away his feeling of complete helplessness but finally settled on, "everything."

"Shhh," Alberto's hands escaped efficiently out of the arm holes in the blanket sack and patted Henry's shoulders. "It's okay. You've got to slow down, though. You've got to breathe. Do you want me to breathe with you?"

"What are you talking about?" Henry asked with more indignation in his voice than he intended.

"Don't be offended, Henry. Lots of people don't know the right way to breathe. It takes practice to bring in the blue energy and expel the red. We aren't born knowing how to do these things."

"Alberto, can you even hear yourself anymore? You just told me that people aren't born knowing how to breathe. Are you nuts?"

Alberto laughed, brought his hands back inside the sack, and then brought them out again this time bearing a can of Coke and a bag of Fritos.

"You're right. God, you're funny, Henry. I've missed you."

"Just tell me what's going on? Is this real? Is it fucking

performance art? That, I might be able to get my head around. But this…" he waved his arms around, which were now trembling, ever so slightly, "this I don't know…"

Alberto studied him through tortoise-shell glasses perpetually glazed with a thin layer of dappled fog. Henry felt like he was being evaluated as to whether or not he deserved the truth. No, not the truth exactly. That wasn't quite right. He could always count on the truth from Alberto and Truman, their honesty was reflexive, another demarcation of their dizzying innocence. It was their motives that were the problem, grounded as they were not in reality, but rather in Alberto and Truman's approximation of reality, one that led them to instigate racial unrest to achieve domestic stability. *That couldn't be reality, could it?* Henry wondered.

"First," Alberto began, his voice an overwhelming source of calmness like a sonic scented candle, "no one is going to get hurt. No one's been hurt. This is playing out exactly the way we intended it to and everyone is getting exactly what they want."

"What do you mean?"

"I mean that the people who came to fight for something are fighting, and the people who came to subvert something are subverting, and the people," and here his arms came snaking out of their holes again as he pointed at himself and at the room Truman had disappeared into, "who came to have a nice middle-class existence and put down roots are doing just that." His chubby hands disappeared once more into the blanket like two scared burrowing animals.

"But what about those ex-soldier guys with Oscar? Have you seen them?"

"Henry…" Alberto shook his decapitated looking head. "They're soldiers if they want to be soldiers. If they say they're

soldiers. And we're middle class if we say we're middle class."
He nodded at the TV, the couch, the pile of empty IKEA
boxes that cluttered a corner of the room like a cardboard
monument to social mobility.

Henry stood up and walked to the kitchen. He took out a
glass and a bottle of something clear and drank a quick shot
of something that tasted like chlamydia. Then another. He
hoped it would clear his head, maybe steady his nerves, but
instead all it did was made him want more. He wanted to
drown himself.

"What about Oscar?"

"After you put him in touch with Truman they started
talking, about you at first, and then, well, one thing led to
another. Oscar was kind of interested in it as a story at first,
or least that's what he said, but once he came and saw what
was going on, there was no going back for him. He was in.
He told Truman that he'd been trying to create this kind of
aesthetic for three decades. After that he took over, brought
some of his friends in, and we were able to move up here.
Win-win."

"Win-win?" Henry slammed the glass down on the kitchen
counter and stormed back into the living room. "These guys
think they're in a war! There's going to be a huge amount of
violence here, Alberto. Can't you see that? Can't you understand that people are going to get hurt? Seriously hurt? Maybe
even killed?" He took a deep breath and begrudgingly decided
to give reason another try. "Say you're right. Say this is one
big fantasy land. One big commune dedicated to wish fulfillment. If that's the case, then how long do you think this is
going to go on for? I know you don't stand up that often, but
the police are already outside. Did you know that? It's only
a matter of time before they come in here and arrest you all.
Forget about the great bourgeois daydream. You're going to

wind up in jail. Don't you care about that?"

Alberto was silent, his eyes trained on the TV where Russell Crowe was doing more slaughtering in the name of freedom. The quiet went on, an enduring answer to his last question, and Henry realized that Alberto was not going to tell him anything, because there was nothing to say. He wasn't arguing, because there was nothing to argue about. Of course Henry was right, the outcome was truly inevitable, and to deny it was not part of the calculus of this experiment. They merely chose not to consider it. They accepted the inevitable conclusion, no matter what that was, and that was all there was to it.

Just then the door opened, and Truman walked into the room carrying his phone and flashing a huge smile at both of them.

"Did Alberto tell you that I'm doing the relationship thing again? I put an ad on Craigslist last night offering to write people's dating profiles for them and I've had like fifty calls since then. I'm a fucking machine. I don't mean to brag," he went on, rocking backing on his heels a little, "but I just basically talked some guy's dick off a ledge. How does it get any better than that? How does it get any better than saving someone's dick from loneliness and isolation?"

Neither Alberto nor Henry said anything, and Truman pulled his smile back in like a turtle disappearing into its shell. "What'd I miss?"

"Henry's worried," Alberto said plainly and without a little disdain, suggesting that Henry was the one being irrational.

"Henry, Henry," Truman approached him with a smile and Henry backed away from him as though he were holding a gun.

"Don't get near me right now. I'm not in the mood."

Truman shook his head sadly and the smile disappeared. "You're acting really crazy right now. I wish you could see yourself."

"You need to stop posting things on Craigslist," Henry said, looking down at the street that was even more crowded with people then it had been just an hour or so before. "It's gonna be the death of you." When he turned back, Truman was smiling at him and he felt the tension he had been nursing for so long suddenly extinguished, could actually feel it disappear into near perfect wisps of forgetful sentimentality. He shouldered his bag and walked to the door.

"Where are you going?" Truman asked.

"I'm going to try and finish this story with what I have," he answered, not in a resigned way, but matter-of-factly. It felt amazing to be dwelling in the land of circumspect for a change. "It's not enough, but I'll write it up anyway and hand it into Ken. He'll either like it the way it is or he won't. I can't really worry about it anymore, can I? In any case, it'll be someone's obituary."

"What do you mean?" Alberto asked from the couch.

"It will work or it won't so in a way it'll be Potter's farewell or mine."

Turning to leave he heard Truman snap his fingers.

"Oh shit, I forgot to tell you," his brown eyes went wide, and Henry noticed heavy bags of weariness embedded beneath them. It reminded him that all of this had taken its toll on all of them, that no one was immune from a battlefield's bells and whistles, "a girl came by earlier looking for you. Before the police and all that. She said she needed to talk to you. That it was important."

For a quick second his mind went immediately to Grace. That she had somehow found her way back to him and was anxious to make up for lost time. He imagined…no…he *felt* her kindness surge through him. But, no, he quickly reminded himself. That wasn't possible. Not anymore.

"What did you tell her?" he asked.

"I told her that if it was really important that she should feel free to wait. That you would be home soon."

"What'd she say?"

"She said she'd wait." And with that Truman pointed to what Henry assumed was the second bedroom. The door was closed, and he again, and not unfamiliarly, felt his heart begin to beat faster and faster, the old tension coming back like a kaleidoscope of butterflies. "And Henry," Truman added with a grin, forcing his eyebrows up and down in a pale imitation of a pervert, "she's pretty cute, too."

*　　*　　*

It took a moment for his eyes to adjust to the sympathetic light once he stepped into the bedroom. Indigo drapes were drawn over the windows, synthesizing a peaceful violet hue inside that bathed the bed, walls, and the sleeping girl. Slashes of sunlight found their way in around the sides of the curtains and fell across her in perfect lines of white light, suggesting segmentation of random areas of her body. So straight were the lines he thought for a moment that Truman and Alberto had drawn them there as a joke, like the dotted lines plastic surgeons made on the bodies of their patients reminding them where to make their incisions. Evidently Truman had brought all of Henry's things up from downstairs because she had plugged his old iPod into a pair of small Bose speakers and had selected what he assumed was his 'Sleep' mix because Marvin Gaye could be heard at a low volume, his voice soft and diffuse like the sound of cotton balls being pulled apart. Light as air the music landed on his skin like little bubbles, sitting for a second on the surface of his flesh before lightly exploding, raising the hair on his arms with pinpricks of the world's most delightful energy.

She moved slightly as he sat on the edge of the bed unsure of what he was supposed to do. Was he supposed to wake her? Wait for her to wake up on her own? Or was he simply supposed to lie down next to her, find her current of breath and match its pace, dissolve into the waters of sleep himself and wake up sometime in the far future, after his story was due, after the war downstairs had commenced and ended. It would be easy to be Rip Van Winkle, preferable even to the responsibility of consciousness. There was a burden to being a passive observer, he thought as she shifted again, a weight that wasn't felt by the doers who had the benefit of constant motion. He noticed a bruise on her thigh that disappeared beneath the leg of her jean shorts. He couldn't help but wonder how far up it went and how it may have gotten there and as he continued to wonder at its provenience her toe nudged him and he leapt a little in surprise. When he looked up at her, she had her eyes open and was smiling groggily at him.

"I've been waiting for you," she said in a foggy far away voice.

"That's what I hear," he said. "Am I in trouble?"

"Do you think you're in trouble?"

"I've got to admit that it's always my first reaction."

"You have a guilty conscious, don't you? You shouldn't."

He shrugged in response, afraid that if he spoke his voice would split apart like a piece of wet tissue paper. If he could have found his voice he would have said to her *But you don't know what I've done, Daisy.*

As she pushed herself up on her elbows the hem of her gray tank top rose up and revealed the tan skin of her waist and stomach.

"I found your sleep mix on your iPod. It worked really well. I was out by the second song. Maybe that's your calling"

"What?"

"Curating moods. Creating the perfect soundtrack for situations."

"Like what?"

"I don't know," she said, looking around, as though the answer lay on the walls or on the floor under that thin veneer of purple. "Like if you're caught in traffic or you're waiting for the results of an AIDS test or something like that. You can use it to build tension or diffuse it. Music's pretty powerful, really. Highly suggestive."

"Something for sex?" He was surprised the words had come out of his mouth. It had been a long time since he had flirted with anyone and she was so much more beautiful than the type of girl he'd usually allow himself to fantasize being with. But she was in his bed waiting for him.

"No, sex is too obvious. You'd need to do different ones for different fetishes. Like country music for the bestiality set or electronica for the emetophiles."

"What's that?"

"Emetophilia? It's when you can only get sexually aroused by throwing up or getting puked on."

"That's a real fetish?"

"Apparently so."

It felt so strange discussing fetishes in this room, which hadn't been neglected by Truman and Arturo's banal aesthetic. He let his eye wander to a bouquet of plastic tulips that sat up perkily in a faux Victorian vase on the bedside table and various stock photos of newly married couples radiating supreme happiness all to sell the burnished silver frames in which they arrived. Maybe this could be a fetish, too, he thought, the normal life fetish. It had to be a thing because everything was a thing, wasn't it? He wondered what kind of thing a girl like Daisy would have to be afflicted with to want a guy like him. What kind of fetish drove the ladies crazy for a guilt-ridden neurotic with hyperhidrosis and a flair for failing at the simplest of tasks? If it wasn't already a diagnosed perversion maybe he could name it. Henryphilia. He would give almost anything for her to be the first recorded Henryphiliac, the two of them parlaying a research grant into a debauched weekend of therapeutic role-playing in Mexico replete with Prozac-flavored margaritas and long bilingual therapy sessions. *Anything and everything for science* would be his personal motto from hereon in.

"I love that you still have that old iPod, by the way." She changed subjects with reckless abandon, which was the prerogative of attractive young women. One of the straps of her gray tank-top slid off her shoulder, and she let it dangle there for a moment before hoisting it back up with her thumb, suggesting that from time to time things slip away and there was very little one could do to prevent it.

"Why are you here, Daisy?" he asked in a small voice.

"Noooo," she winced as she said it. "Not yet. Ask me later. Okay?" She smiled hopefully at him, the smile of a little girl asking for a pony.

"Okay," he answered.

She picked up the iPod and turned it over in her hands, examining it as though it were a rare and dusty relic.

"Want to hear something weird?" She didn't wait for an answer because she was transfixed by some memory that made her eyes glaze over and the corners of her mouth go soft, her muscles relaxing into the easy reverie of sentimentality. "When I was a kid, I had this fear of letting objects go. When my mother would try to throw out an old vacuum or a toaster, or even a stuffed animal that had gone all moldy, or 'unloved' as she'd try to rationalize it to me, I would cry and scream until she promised she wouldn't. And when I found something in the garbage cans out in the cul-de-sac, I would pull it out and try to put it back where it had been, hoping she wouldn't notice I'd done it," she chuckled lightly to herself. "As if she wouldn't notice we had two vacuum cleaners all of a sudden or the toaster had somehow sponta- neously reproduced."

"That's sweet," Henry said after thinking about it for a moment. "You had an attachment to the things in your house, the things that belonged to your family. I don't think it's that unusual to assign meaning to objects that others may find meaningless. Might be the only thing that actually separates us from the animals."

"No," she said, shaking her head, "it wasn't that, because I felt the same thing about other people's things, too. I figured it out later. Want to know what it was?"

"Of course," he said, resisting the urge to add the words: *I want to know everything you want to tell me.*

"I was jealous of these things."

"Jealous?"

She nodded. "Yeah, jealous. Because they had this function that I found amazingly straightforward. They were built to do a thing, usually a really specific thing, and that's what they did. No questions asked. No wondering. No searching. And they'd always be here. I mean they were built to last. After you and I are gone, and our skin is gone, and our bones are gone this thing," she held the iPod up, "will still be here. It may not be working, but it will still be here. That's kind of amazing, isn't it?"

It sounded like something a stoned person would say, but he was pretty sure she wasn't high, she was just expressive, assimilating emotions that she'd probably had driven out of her when she was with Potter, relearning what it was to be astonished and sound stupid if that's what she wanted to do. And besides, if she was jealous of these things, then he was jealous of her innocence. He couldn't decide which was more absurd.

She stretched a cat's stretch and her shirt's strap fell again and this time he let his eyes linger on her skin, the light fuzz of blonde hair on her arm that caught the purple light and exploded along her arm like the spent fluff of a dandelion. There was another bruise, this one at the top of her ribs right near her armpit and his mind did some quick calculations as to how one gets injured there. It didn't seem like a spot for an accidental injury. Hard to imagine falling and landing on the spot just under your armpit.

"Are you looking at my bruises?" she asked him, letting the shirt strap stay down this time.

"Yes," he said, resisting the urge to touch it, trace it with his finger, map the coordinates between that one and the one on her thigh as though it would lead him to some yet to be discovered tropical island.

"I've got more," she said as she turned over and pulled up her shorts. "There are those two and this one," she went on with the tour pointing out the landmarks to him as if he were a visitor to a new place. He winced in commiseration, and when she saw his face she just smiled and he realized that this wasn't a registry of sympathy, but points of pride, skin worth flaunting.

"Where are you from?" he asked her, not out of politeness

but as a way to clear his throat.

She pulled her shirt down and formed her lips into a little girl's pout. The flirtiness was gone, and it was obvious to him that she was disappointed she wasn't getting her way. Still, she was patient.

"I'm from the Midwest," she said, waving her hand toward the far corner of the room as if to indicate the exact direction and location were inconsequential, that it wasn't a place so much as it was a state of mind that was as easy to dismiss as one's entire childhood.

"What's it like?"

"Oh, you know, big trees, wide roads, snow in the winter and colors in the fall. Whatever you're thinking right now is exactly what it was like."

He let his mind wander there for a moment, took a stroll down her block, kids playing football in the street, dads on the porch in argyle sweaters smoking pipes, moms calling their broods in for dinner, the smells emanating from the perfect homes perfectly rapturous. The bliss of it must have registered on his face, because she was quick to interject.

"Don't get too dreamy, mister, with your Midwest envy. It wasn't that great. Just another place. My parents were neurotic freaks, 'tyrants of indecision' is what an old shrink of mine used to call them. It was stifling there, Henry, really. Fucked-up kids by the scores. I had a friend who got caught stealing her own mother's chemo pills she was taking for her breast cancer because she saw her mom losing weight and thought it would do the same for her. Bad decisions everywhere. Look at me," She stood up and spread her arms out as if measuring the distance of an error. If there was something broken there, he didn't see it. What he saw was a girl for whom summer would always come when called, for whom the sun would always shine, for whom men would always subject themselves to guilty breezy thoughts.

"So you left? Is it as easy as that?" He was asking more for himself than for her.

"I did, but it didn't feel like that at the time. I felt like I was always on the cusp of something greater, you know? Like I was being pushed. Yeah, that's it. I didn't leave, I was pushed."

"Now," she said with the sigh of an interrogated prisoner who'd just told her inquisitor everything there was to tell, "will you kiss me?"

Without hesitating, he leapt into her arms like an action hero and planted his mouth on hers. Their kissing was urgent, yearning beyond yearning, and they stopped at the same moment to struggle their way out of their clothes like unpracticed synchronized swimmers.

"What mix do you have for this?" she asked, laying back on the bed.

"I don't know," he answered as nonchalantly as possible, "what do you like?" He thought he was being sexy.

"Shopping," she said, deadpanned, and then burst into laughter. "I don't care. Play something soft. Something hopeless."

"You want sad?" he asked her, a little disappointed.

"Yes, but only because in a few minutes we're going to be more than that. Something better. Don't you want to win for a change, Henry?"

It was the million-dollar question for which he'd only ever been able to respond with a ten-dollar answer. What was the saying? Ten pounds of shit in a five-pound bag? If she could divide the world as simply as that, into winners and losers, then who was he to resist that kind of simplicity, the alluring objectivity of it. She opened her arms wide to him, and then her legs, her mouth, and as he fell into her, softly toppling for what felt like forever, he realized that he wouldn't have to answer because falling was an answer in and of itself. But not just the falling, the letting go.

*　　*　　*

Their lovemaking was crucial and vivid, and when it was at its best they were a shared silhouette, the outline of something better than they could ever be apart. At its worst it was the feeling of drowning, of not being able to make it back to shore, his lungs filling up with the impulse to howl a pretty picture, like being waterboarded in truth serum.

Exhausted afterwards, they slept and dreams came upon him in great unrecognizable clots, amalgamations of people and experiences, no credence given to chronology or the actual space of things. He dreamt of Cal and Daisy together at his high school, the perfect teenage couple. He dreamt of Grace and Potter at the library researching his life and finding nothing on the shelves but thousands of volumes of the same *Jane's* book. He dreamt of his mother and father, a couple again, living happily in the heat of Pottersville, tending a nameless garden of souls. He himself didn't exist in these dreams.

When they woke, the sun had shifted and the drape was a dam that had burst, letting great pools and washes of violet flood their room. They sat up, looked at one another, and giggled. It wasn't an embarrassed thing, just a way to acknowledge that they recognized one another, that they both belonged in this room and in this bed.

"How about you?" They were the first words she spoke since waking.

"How about me what?" He was groggy and wanted to sleep

some more. Sleep until all the sleep was out of him.

"Where are you from?"

"Here," he said, running his fingers through his hair. "The beach."

"What was it like growing up by the beach? Must have been sort of wonderful."

"Not really," he replied, unusually focused. "Beach culture was kind of traumatizing for me. Everyone had this frightening glow all the time, kind of a health inertia, and it was like all that happiness and sunshine and laziness and all those vibes could erupt at any moment and what would come out would be worse than anyone could imagine."

"Because no one expected it?"

"Yes," he said, "it would be the worst because no one expected it."

By now, he thought, his classmates would have all dissolved into degrees of professionalism and taken on the form of women who looked too confident in casual clothes and men with significant, but fixable, reproductive problems.

"Sounds pretty amazing to me," she sighed. He dropped it there. There was an insignificance that was felt in the presence of the sea that had nothing to do with one's infinitesimally small place in the world. What he was talking about was more direct than that. The insignificance he was trying to convey was more immediate, like picking up a seashell and hearing not the lush thrum of the ocean but a low gravelly voice that pointed out all your flaws, or how the gentle swaying of palm trees reminded him of a murderer's row of bullies imitating the way he walked, sort of crookedly loping along the way teenagers did, as though self-esteem and muscle tone were directly related to one another.

"What did you want to be when you grew up back then?"

"Nothing. Well, not nothing. It wasn't a thing," he began to tell her, conscious of the fact that he was being interviewed, that at some point he would have to ask her again why she was here. "My father was a lawyer and I knew you could be that if you went to school long enough. Or you could be a doctor. I saw teachers and knew that was a thing, but besides that I didn't know what else there was. I didn't know there was such a thing as an investment banker or a hedge fund manager. I didn't know I could be a screenwriter or even a journalist. Those things didn't seem real to me. They felt like preordained professions, the kinds of things people other than me were fated for."

"So what was it?"

"It's hard to put into words exactly, but where I saw the space for me was in what no one else wanted to do. I would be the thing that was left over."

"Which was what?"

Her voice was earnest, and he decided it would be worth explaining the truth to her because she seemed to be genuinely interested.

"I don't know about you, but I remember history class being one description of injustice after another. Whether it was the Holocaust or this race massacring that race, or slavery, those things were the commas in history, the places where you were supposed to pause and think about it, but I felt like no one did. Back then I felt like no one reading this stuff cared about any of it and that certainly no one cared about it as much as I did, no one could be as outraged as the outrage I could conjure up in my brain and my throat, outrage that could make my stomach twirl like a roller coaster. I remember it. I remember feeling that sick about it all. And the funny part of it was that I felt responsible for all of it."

She crinkled her eyebrows, and he realized it was the first time he'd ever seen her actually surprised.

"How could you? You weren't even born yet. Your parents weren't even born yet. How can you feel guilty about something that's not even your fault?"

He smiled. "I can feel guilty about anything. That's what it should say on my tombstone. It's quite a talent when you think about it. Empathy's for pussies. There's no use sympathizing with someone and not doing anything about it. What's the point?"

She stayed quiet.

"And so the thing I wanted to be was the person who, when the next time there was something like that going on, would do something about it. I would stop it. Me. On my own."

"That's a lot for a person to put on himself."

He shrugged.

"So how has that gone?"

He swallowed hard, afraid if he didn't that his next words would combust into tears.

"What you see is what you get."

There was a lull in the conversation as they reset. The iPod was onto the next manifestation of his OCD. Bob Dylan's voice singing about hard times was everywhere and nowhere all at once.

She sat up a little and the sheet slid down her chest exposing her breasts. He would live in this moment if he could. Honesty cancelling out hopelessness. Four walls all his own. The will to use joy for what it was.

"Ask me again," she said timidly. "What you asked me when

you first saw me today. Ask me again why I'm here."

His heartbeat sped up as he willed himself to look away from her.

"Daisy, why are you here?" His voice was barely a thing.

"I never left the Children of Light, Henry. Maybe you've already figured that out. I'm still part of them, and I've been sent to ask you a very special thing. Can I ask you that thing?"

The words sank into him like gunshots, but he nodded nonetheless, not really thinking about what she might be about to tell him, but rather thinking about the words to come as his life leading up to this very moment. Everything a prelude to this.

"I want you to come to Pottersville with me. Something very special is going to be happening there tomorrow and we want you to see it. It's important that you see it. Will you come?"

"Who's we?" he asked her, still not looking at her.

"All of us. The rest of us. We want you to come and see this thing, and then when it's over we want you to write our story. Will you do that?"

"What about Potter?" he asked. "Is he there?"

She smiled.

"Oh yes. He's there. And he knows all about you. He's eager to talk to you, Henry. There's so much he wants to say."

It wasn't even a choice really. He stood up and before he realized what he was doing he started getting dressed quickly and in silence, eager to get there now, overwhelmed with the feeling there was no time to waste.

Daisy got off the bed and began dressing, too.

"We had a hard time finding you," she said, pulling on her shorts and her tank top. She was dressed in just a few seconds.

"After your house blew up, we didn't know where you had gone. It took a while."

"I guess you shouldn't have blown up my house then."

She looked surprised.

"We didn't blow up your house. The Children of Light? That's not how we do things. In fact, after your place burned down, it made it a lot harder to find you. Luckily Oscar got in touch with me."

Now that she was speaking for the group, using the word "we", he noticed that her voice had become something different, more rigid, hotter, an automatic indignation that went along with constantly being put on the defensive.

Blood rushed to his brain as he leaned over to tie his shoes and just as he was about to give himself over to the idea that his place had been bombed at random, just as he was about to commit to the level of apathy it took to buy lock, stock, and barrel into the notion of the universe as being nothing better than a series of random chaotic events; events like apartments that spontaneously combusted and world-famous cult leaders wanting the pleasure of his acquaintance, the truth that it had been Truman struck him painfully, and he stopped tying his shoes and stormed into the living room. Looking around in the fragile light of late afternoon, it took him a moment to spot Alberto and Truman who were sitting next to one another on their new purple couch, their slack forms utterly transfixed by whatever movie they'd decided to give themselves over to this time, and for a brief instant, as he ran over to where they were, his fist already cocked back like a hot piston, he thought to himself they looked like they were floating in a sensory deprivation tank. Truman saw Henry first and instead of blocking as Henry's fist connected with his chin, teeth, and upper lip simultaneously, he chose instead to pause the TV, a decision he strangely didn't regret even as he bent over and spit out, along with a puddle of blood, one of his front teeth.

"You blew my house up, didn't you, Truman?"

They felt like ridiculous words to say, a sentence that was never supposed to be, but there they were, as straightforward as he knew how to put them. Alberto stifled a chuckle and then put his eyes back on the TV as though that would somehow save him.

Truman put his hand over his mouth, then took them away to spit again. More blood. *There couldn't be enough blood*, Henry thought, the lust for it something new in him, something genuine. Maybe even meaningful.

"Jesus, Henry," Truman speech was a garbled thing, a computer program full of bugs. "I did it for you. I did it to get you out of your funk."

"My funk?" Henry was yelling now, each decibel felt like another in a quickly growing lists of good reasons to hit Truman again. Kick him. Break him in fucking half.

"I thought it was what you wanted. Secretly. Admit it, you were relieved when you had nowhere to go but here."

Again, the urge to hit Truman swelled in him, but now it was different. It wasn't so much about simply hurting him as it was passing along a curse that would kill him if he didn't get it out of his system.

"You don't know what you're talking about," he shot back as he tried not to crack or cry. "Nothing about you is sincere. I want you to admit that. I want you to admit that all this is about you and what you want. And in twenty-four hours, or however long it's going to take for Oscar and the police to wipe this place out, when all these people are being taken away in ambulances and body bags, maybe then you'll realize that all you are is a selfish asshole who'd trade everybody and everything to prove a point. You're an idealogue, and the ironic thing is you're too stupid to even realize it." He took a deep breath, but his body was a shaky vessel adrift on a vast blue sea of adrenaline.

Truman stopped nursing his wounds and stared at Henry. His eyes, Henry noticed, were incredibly clear, maybe more so than he'd ever remembered seeing them before. Everything was silent for a moment and then a helicopter swooped in low, palpitating the windows with its fleshy percussion.

"Where are you going to go then?"

Henry turned and grabbed his bag from the room. He walked back out and pointed an aching finger at Daisy. Throwing a good punch hurt a lot more than he remembered it hurting.

"I'm going with her. Back to the desert. I'm going to finish my story, turn it in to Ken, and then start a brand-new life. The life I've been waiting for. The life that everything up to now has been a test to see if I deserve…" He waved a hand at Truman as he reached for the front door. Words didn't often fail him, but this time he was at a loss, and the best he could muster was something like a doctor's murky pity for a patient for whom there were no more sensible options for treatment. Behind Truman he heard Alberto devouring bellows full of blue energy as though he were in the Nathan's Hot Dog Eating Contest, something beyond hyperventilation, a coping mechanism gone all HAL 9000.

Henry turned and left the apartment, not looking back to see if Daisy was following or not. He assumed that she needed him now more than he needed her. She had lied to him about CHoSEN, and maybe that meant she owed him something. In his heart, he knew it didn't really work like that. People deceived one another all the time, and motive rarely figured into it. Like Truman, she probably chalked it up to resourcefulness, legitimized it as a means to an end. If that were the case, then why couldn't he do the same? What was stopping him from populating his own little world with useful tools? They went down the elevator in silence and left the building through the front door, where they were greeted by a phalanx of reporters who shouted a thousand questions at them all at once, word soup out of which he caught certain phrases that made him smile in response. *Powder Keg. Catastrophe.* It felt to him like some weird drinking game religious zealots might play when they got bored awaiting the Rapture.

The questions went on but as soon as Henry and Daisy had gotten in and closed the doors of Henry's car, the reporters instantly peeled off, buzzing back toward the building in search of another piece of shit to hover around.

Before leaving he took one last look at the building and noticed that a number of flags had been draped from a number of windows on various floors. Among them he saw the Confederate flag, The POW-MIA flag, a Grateful Dead "Steal Your Face" flag, and perhaps strangest of all, the Saudi Arabian national flag. The banners waved leisurely as a slight breeze lifted them, their colors reminiscent of passengers waving from a departing cruise ship. Up and up they went right to the top of the building, which meant their ideas weren't just spreading haphazardly as he had first thought, but were actually ascending, rising higher and higher like the Tower of Babel, words and ideas they were stacking like a high and careful staircase they believed would one day get them to the truth.

It was twilight as they drove south on La Brea toward the freeway, the part of the day Henry had always thought of as having no integrity. Nothing honest happened at twilight. Even the city itself was a lie. Not even a city, the silhouette of a city. It felt good to have a real reason to be leaving for once, not fleeing a mistake, but headed toward something important. And it wasn't until they hit the 10 East—no music on the radio, no conversation, just the respiration of traffic, the deep bellows of chronic movement—that he realized what he had said back at the apartment.

"Did you catch that?" he said to her, breaking their reverie.

"Hmm?" she asked lazily. She was deep in dreams, awake but gone, her mission was 98 percent of the way done.

"What I said to Truman. Did you catch it? I said that I was going 'back to the desert.' Weird slip, huh?"

She smiled and rested her hot hand on his thigh, stroked it lightly, igniting a forest fire of shivers across the forest of his skin.

"Not so weird," she said drowsily, neither here nor there. "I mean, we all belong somewhere, sweetie."

Chapter 14

THE NEXT FEW days of school were an exercise in guerrilla warfare as Henry did everything in his power to avoid running into Cal. He still hadn't gotten over what had happened at the airport, but more than that, he was perplexed that Cal hadn't seen what a fucked-up thing it was to do in the first place. The great lesson of powerlessness, or at least the lesson he had gleaned from listening to all that punk rock, wasn't that you were supposed to fuck people over just because you could. Rather, there was a responsibility to stop assholes in their tracks, to grab the baton from the next runner and jet off in the opposite direction, not club the next guy in the relay race over the head with the fucking thing.

Instead of trying to explain it, he chose instead to hide wherever he could, discovering an old janitorial closet that, judging by the paraphernalia he found on the ground, had long since been forfeit as official school property and given over to a kind of two-foot-square red light district. Used condoms, the bitter ends of joints, even a switchblade, which Henry pocketed as he waited out a nutrition period. He thought twice before taking it, though, as a worry bubbled up from his Neanderthal brain that protested that they must be holy objects, left there as offerings to some greater deity. Shiva the Crammer who rewarded kids with good grades on exams they barely studied for, or St. Trevor who could mystically prevent or terminate teenage pregnancies.

There were other hiding places he tried, too, but none were as exquisitely bleak as the closet. He gave the old athletic equipment shed at the end of the football field a try, tiptoeing through cobwebs that had been strung between ancient pieces of athletic equipment, which, in the sour light of the place, looked more like ancient implements of torture than the foundations of a physical education. Tackle dummies that had long since had the foam ripped out of them showed the sharp and rusty edges of their metal infrastructure. Blue and white poles for pole vaulting, the school's oceanic colors, were caked in places near their points with what could only be the bloody imprimatur of past student bodies' good tries and near misses. One lunch period was spent in an old electrical shed on the catwalk above the stage in the school auditorium. He watched from on high, with the switches from the fuse box digging into his arm, as kids, more cheerful than he ever knew kids could be, practiced their lines for whatever theater production they were bound to be taking way too seriously this semester. The surge of scorn he felt made him feel a little too much like the creature in the *Phantom of the Opera*, some terrible monster with jagged skin caught up in the soft palate of the place, so he left that space as soon as the end-of-lunch bell rang and skulked along to his next class, grunting past the actors who wondered, magnanimously, if he wasn't there to try out for a role.

The next day at lunch was spent in a supply closet deep within the recesses of the school cafeteria, a culinary industrial complex where the cooking smells ranged from disinfectant to burnt, there was no in between. He leaned against a box of frozen hamburger patties as his mind wandered to what it would be like to be in solitary confinement twenty-three hours a day. Not so bad, he reasoned longingly, raising his feet so that they were resting on a carton marked "burrito meat."

The janitorial closet was definitely the best option and he was deep in resigned reverie one lunch period, resting comfortably in his toxic hammock, when a knock at the door upended his thoughts and almost made him fall on his face. He stayed stock still for a few seconds hoping whoever it was would go away, but the knock came again, this time louder, and he stood up and put an ear against the heavy wooden door.

"What?" He tried to sound authoritative and threatening, but instead of the desired effect, and because of his current residency in the wonderful world of puberty, it came out sounding like the squeeze horn on a child's bicycle.

"Henry," a girl's voice answered, "it's Grace. Are you okay? Let me in."

"Leave me alone," he said, embarrassed that she had found him here. "I'm fine. I'm happy. Go away."

"Come on, Henry, open the door. I want to see you."

"No," he yelled. "Leave me alone. I'm hiding and you're going to give me away."

"Give you away to who?"

Her voice was all patience, empathy, and he knew she wouldn't go anywhere until he'd opened the door and showed her that he was all right.

"I'll open the door so you can see me, but then you have to go away. Okay? I'll tell you about it later, but right now I just want to spend the rest of lunch period here. Promise?"

"Fine," she said.

"Say you promise," he repeated again, confident that they weren't so far out into the international waters of their lives that the old childhood pinkie swears and oaths of their youth weren't still in effect.

He unlocked the door and opened it a crack so she could see his face.

"See. I'm fine. Now, go back to..."

Before he could finish the sentence, though, she pushed her shoulder against the door and fought her way through the narrow slit as he tried to slam it on her. Once inside, she turned and locked the door and looked at him.

"You promised you wouldn't do that," he said to her, out of breath and angry, but more embarrassed that she had been able to outmuscle him. *Would he ever be stronger than her?* he wondered.

"What's going on, Henry? Erica was doing detention in the cafeteria and saw you sneak in here and close the door. She waited a bit to see if you'd come out and then she got worried and came and found me."

"Don't worry about it," he said. It was nearly dark in the closet except for some light that filtered through a transom at the top of the wall. It was enough to see that she was wearing her worried/angry look, the one he referred to as her "mom face." He held back calling her that, though. He'd made that mistake before and had found himself in strange arm holds that made him wonder if she wasn't receiving secret agent training somewhere on the side.

"This is weird, Henry. Who does this? Who hides behind mop pails and roach traps?" She bit a fingernail as she watched him. "Is this part of your Cal thing? Are you hiding from him? That's it, isn't it?" She was forever problem solving. "Did he do something to you?"

"No," Henry said, already resigning himself to defeat and the fact that she was going to take over and insist on solving this for him. "He didn't do anything to me. I just don't want to see him. I know he wants to have a conversation with me about what happened and I don't feel like having it. I thought if I could disappear for a few days, like completely disappear, he'd forget about it and move on. I know, stupid."

She sat down on a box and he heard her sigh. "Oh, Henry. What are we going to do with you?"

"Nothing!" he erupted, frustration finally getting the better of him. "You don't have to do anything. I'm taking care of this by myself, Grace. I don't need you to solve all my problems, okay? Besides, you're leaving next year. What happens then? What happens when you're three thousand miles away? It's not us vs. them anymore, is it? So just pretend like you're already gone, okay? That's how you can help me the most. Pretend like you're not here anymore. Can you do that?"

Outside, the bell that signaled that lunch would be ending in five minutes rang abruptly and then stopped, its echoes pinging off the walls for an extra few seconds, a constant reminder that the sounds you thought were only in your own head actually belonged to everyone at once.

"Do you not want me to go away? Is that it? Just say it and I won't go. I told you I'd always be there for you. I wasn't lying, Henry. If you want me to stay, I will. I can tell Brown that I won't be coming and enroll at Santa Monica College and then transfer in a couple of years to UCLA. I don't really care, Henry. If that's what you want, I'll do it. I can be like Erica and get busted for going to class with a piece of a joint caught in my braces, and then go to junior college and date a guy who drives a motorcycle who gets me pregnant and then leaves me to start dating a chick in junior high. Maybe after I have the baby, I can get a job at TGI Friday's and bring home uneaten potato skins and jalapeno poppers to you and the baby. We can have a nice life together, the four of us. Oh wait, I forgot about Mom. She'd be there, too. She's another one who doesn't want me to leave her. She can have the master of our one-bedroom. Gotta respect your elders, right? Hopefully the bed will support her enormous girth as she balloons up from eating all the TGIF leftovers. She won't want to move, right, since she'll have everything she needs right there. Our happy little family."

Her voice was a tired glassy thing, its sharp edges of anger and frustration replaced by good ol' American resignation. He never realized just how tired she was until that very moment.

"You've really thought this through, haven't you?"

"No. Not really. I'm just as lost as you are. I know you don't believe me, but it's true."

He hugged her as he thought of reassuring things to say.

"I didn't know that Mom and Dad were making things so hard for you. I thought they were too busy being disappointed and worried about me to pay much attention to you."

She chuckled. "You're the one worth saving. To them I'm already gone. All grown up. Self-sufficient."

He watched her as she dried her eyes on her shirt sleeves. Her nose wrinkled as she said, "Jesus, it smells awful in here. What is that?"

"I'm not sure. Bleach, maybe?"

"How have you been spending all of your free periods in here? Doesn't it make you sick?"

"It's not my only spot. I know about closets and sheds all over the place. I'm an expert."

"Little panic room *pieds-à-terre* everywhere, huh? It's like an Underground Railroad for social delinquents."

He laughed. "I guess we should go. Fifth period."

"Yeah," she said, standing up, "but let me go first. You come a minute later. Last thing either of us need are incest rumors.

That's kind of the apex of teen bullying ammunition.""Agreed," he nodded.

Her hand on the doorknob, she turned to him one last time before leaving.

"What did we figure out here? Anything?"

He thought seriously, but the only thing he could think of was a line from the Saturday morning cartoons he still loved to watch.

"That I love you and you love me and we're a happy family."

"Okay," she smiled back at him. "Okay."

*   *   *

Disappearing became fun, a new way to play war. Cal had been right when he said it was easy to be overlooked. It was. It became a game to him to find new places to stash himself between classes; corners to snuggle, trees to grope. He hung on the outskirts of the most anonymous of cliques, feigning enough of an interest in the most subterranean of the subterranean to keep himself hidden for fifteen or twenty minutes before moving on to the next. During those moments he received cursory introductions to anime, veganism, and puppetry, and he wondered at the number of teenage obsessions that could exist in such a small area, and if like a buildup of toxic gases, it was potentially a dangerous situation. Even more subversive was his discovery of a chess club and a debate team, activities he believed only existed in movies and novels about high school, his parent's school. To know they existed in real life was astounding but also reaffirming, like finding physical proof that the world wasn't all black and white before he was born, but that color existed, life was as it always had been and always would be.

But he was outside it all. Truly. When he first started

toiling away at his disappearing act, he wondered how long he would be able to keep it up for. Now, though, a week or so into it, he felt sure that he could keep it up forever if he wanted. That could be his "thing." He'd be the guy they'd remember in high school as being around during class but completely gone otherwise. They'd start to think of him as a narc, an illusionist, or a superhero; some might remember him fondly as a hallucination or a ghost. If he had to choose between urban legend and living legend, there was no doubt in his mind which one he'd opt for.

One afternoon, after a rather lengthy lie down in the dusty ivy up at the top of the student parking lot, where he found himself feeling drowsy from the surprisingly dulcet sounds of school adjourning, laughing kids, plans being made, both for the long and short term, half-hearted threats, the scurrying of rats in the plants around him, he arose and saw that he was not alone. Sonny Armour was leaning against his car—an old, battered, grey Honda Accord pinstriped in rust, one headlight missing as though it had gotten an eye knocked out during a barroom brawl—smoking a joint. If Henry rising from a patch of ivy in front of him like Jack's Beanstalk with light acne was surprising, he didn't show it. Taking another hit of the joint, he smiled as Henry blinked away the light of day. "Whoa," he tapped the ashes on the ground and nodded knowingly as if what he was seeing somehow legitimized every hope he'd ever held dear about smoking pot. "That is fucking rad. What are you doing? Jungle warfare or something?" He took another stoned drag from the joint, inhaling as though it were a matter of life and death, and then held it out for Henry.

"I was hiding from someone," Henry said, as he brushed himself off and took the joint.

"Bully?" Sonny asked and laughed at his own joke.

"No, not really. More like a version of reality I'd rather just avoid for the rest of my life."

"Perfect timing then," Sonny said as Henry took a long hit off the roach.

Handing it back, Henry started laughing as something occurred to him, which quickly and unsurprisingly turned into hard coughing, as if there couldn't be one without the other.

"Hey, I thought you were supposed to be straight edge," Henry said as Sonny took another hit. He certainly looked the part with his ripped jeans, black Converse and stained white tee, which, Henry thought, would make one hell of a Rorschach test after another hit or two. Already his insides felt like a monkey scurrying up and down the trunk of a coconut tree.

"Fuck that," Sonny said dismissively, waving his hand around as though he were casting a spell that made anything he said sound reasonable. "It's just music, man. Straight Edge. Punk rock. Deadheads. Who cares? It's all the same. No one acts like that when they get home. You think your buddy Cal yells, 'Anarchy!' at his mom when she tells him dinner's ready every night?" Henry laughed and beckoned for the joint. "Besides," Sonny went on, his mouth and brain were on a stoned, if not entirely synchronized, roll, "most of that punk stuff is for fascists. Do this...do that. Anthems. Sounds like the fucking army to me, dude."

Henry handed the joint back and nodded in agreement. Well on his way to oblivion, he might as well have been nodding at the news that a bowl of Cheerios had just been elected President.

Situated at the top of a long canyon road, surrounded on all sides by mountains and state park, the school acted as an echoing mechanism for loud sounds, dispensing shouts of joy, anger, and over-solicitous greetings to all corners equally. Even when things were quiet, he felt the air around him sometimes vibrate, eager to burst into life, quivering the way spring did as it emerged from winter, or the beginnings of public restlessness as a new epidemic claimed the first of its many victims. Ominous or eternal, the school radiated a constant sense of expectancy, and so it was no surprise when their silence was suddenly interrupted by loud shouts from the athletic field at the other end of campus. It was impossible to tell what sport they were playing, the shouts were completely anonymous, but it soon became apparent that they had some anger behind them as certain voices rose above others, because enthusiasm eventually and quickly faded, until finally, as though it had been an exercise in sonic evolution all along, one voice rose above all the others with the clear message that a fight was about to begin: "Fuck you, faggot!"

Henry tensed and looked quickly at Sonny. Every fiber in his body wanted to run and watch whatever was about to happen. Real violence was such a unique occurrence it was hard to resist. But Sonny made no sign that he was interested in going to check it out. He just kept on leaning against his car like his life depended on it, his head thrown back, eyes closed, soaking in the sun with a broad smile on his face, perfectly content to be where he was. Contentedness was an unfamiliar posture for someone his own age, and Henry stopped to marvel at it, aware as ever that he was high as shit and that fact probably added to the mystery of it all, but still taken aback by the confidence he saw, jealous of it in a way, a kind of untoward envy that made him perfectly aware that he was ungrateful for every good thing he had in his life.

"Let's go," Sonny said, and Henry looked around, surprised, as Sonny opened the car door and got in instead of heading toward the fight.

Dazed for a moment, the sound of the chaos still swelling

around them, Henry stood motionless, unsure which way he was supposed to go.

Sensing his hesitation, Sonny smiled, leaned over, and opened the passenger side door for him. "It's okay, man. Let's go." That smile reached over and nudged him playfully in the ribs. "Get in the car."

They drove out of the parking lot at a leisurely speed and again, mercifully, there was no need to talk as the tape player filled the gaps with something tuneful and bright. Henry leaned back and closed his eyes, not caring where they were going, focused instead on the music, sounds that were the same temperature as his blood, the stale smell of cigarette smoke, the words Sonny had used to draw him away from wanting to run down to the field and see the mayhem. *Get in the car.* They were the most wonderful words he'd ever heard and from that moment on it was the phrase he would always dream of uttering to a girl, more to the point than "I love you," which was really nothing more than a verbal fait accompli. *Get in the car* was so much more; it was an open invitation to conspiracy, a way to put the fix in on destiny.

Friction didn't exist. It was a thing of the past. He wanted to be this high all the time. This weightless. A slide guitar came in out of nowhere, swooping in like a superhero to save the day. "What is this music?" he asked, truly amazed, a recent convert seeing the light for the first time. His eyes were shut tight against the pleasure of the moment. If he opened them, he told himself, and found they weren't floating on air it would be the biggest disappointment of his life.

"Are you kidding?" Sonny asked him from what felt like a million miles away and in his head at the same time.

"No," Henry felt himself smiling wider and wider. Joy was a homesteader settling across the terrain of his face.

"It's Neil Young. *Heart of Gold*? You've really never heard this?"

"Nope. I told you. It's been all punk for a while."

"Your parents probably fucked to this song." He smiled mischievously. "Jesus, you've really missed out, man."

"I know." He'd have to remind himself later to blame somebody for that.

The music became louder and Henry felt himself pressed back further into his seat. Further. Further. And further still until he became the physical embodiment of the reclined position. He heard the turn signal begin to click, felt the wide arc of a left turn, but still wouldn't allow himself to open his eyes. It was one thing to know where they were going and another altogether to understand that they were the very articulation of softness and that the violence they held in such high esteem had no parallel in their everyday lives. It was just another fantasy or an inside joke that no one laughed at anymore.

*   *   *

When the car stopped, he had to force himself to open his eyes. It took him only a second to realize they were parked at the entrance to the state park a few miles away from school. At the entrance to the park, near the ranger's station, was a public pool where the swim team practiced, an archery range, and a piece of fallow land that was used seasonally as a pumpkin patch, a Christmas tree lot, and a place where the Boy Scouts held their periodic car wash fundraisers. He'd learned to swim at the pool and gotten his Archery merit badge at the range. Every year he came with Grace and his mom to pick the perfect pumpkin, their mother indulging them while the kids inspected each and every one before making their selections. One each. The two most perfect pumpkins in the place. Grace liked the oblong ones while he preferred the short stout ones. What it said about their personalities he had no idea. What he did know, though, was coming to the patch was one of his favorite things in the world to do; to hike up the path from the parking lot, the smell of farmed earth growing in their noses the closer they got, the feeling of leaving that other, inferior, world behind, because what could be better than this? What could be better than the smell of rich soil, trees shedding leaves making them a ticker tape parade, and finally coming around the corner to that commotion of yellows and oranges, magnified and polished to a brilliant sheen by the sun. This was his youth, here, in this place, and it had been a happy one. The ground under his feet was the topography that proved it, the well-worn path he'd forgotten about but had been here all the time. Whose fault was that?

"Did you used to get your pumpkins here?" Sonny asked him as if reading his mind.

"Uh-huh," he answered a little surprised. He had forgotten he was with anyone.

"Me too," Sonny said. He pointed at the pool. "And swimming lessons and, wait, let me guess," he closed his eyes and put his fingers on his temples pretending to be deep in thought. "Archery!"

"Guilty as charged." Henry forced a smile to his lips, despite feeling like Sonny had just read his mind and torn apart his memories as though they were the paltry first draft of a much more complex work in progress.

"Everyone," Sonny chuckled, more to himself than to Henry, "the same."

They continued up the path in silence. It was hot and still.

Every once in a while an escaping lizard would cause a little landslide of dirt to drizzle down the side of the mountain to their right. An endless forest of dry and brittle bushes populated the hillside leading down on their left. At the bottom was a dry riverbed his mother had once told them used to have water in it, but it sounded like a fairytale. He wasn't much for the outdoors. Maybe hiking in the Himalayas or in South America would be different, but this felt more like they were scientists assessing the aftermath of a cataclysmic event.

Lost in his thoughts he didn't think to ask where they were headed until he looked up and realized where they were. Skull Rock was a landmark in town, as much a physical point of reference as it was a not so subtle code for getting high. For most kids it was as much a part of the collective memory about the park as the pool and the pumpkin patch, a physical and metaphorical move up the mountain to maturity, but Henry had always thought of it as a place for popular kids, or in his less paranoid moments, a spot where he wasn't welcome. Besides, he'd never understood why they called it Skull Rock in the first place. The resemblance had always been lost on him. Until now, that it. Now, as they approached the cave, which was about a hundred yards up the side of the mountain, with two smaller, uninhabitable holes above it, he saw it as plainly as he'd ever seen anything. In fact, he couldn't believe that he'd never seen it before, it was so obvious maybe in much the same way a newly minted convert can't imagine a time when god was never there. It seemed almost impossible to him now as he stood below it, flat-footed, his mouth hanging ever so slightly agape the way it always did when he was this high and deep in thought.

Without a word Sonny scurried up the side of the hill taking for granted the hand and footholds he knew so well, that he should avoid the poison oak shrub halfway up on the left, that the trick was to keep moving or else you'd slip backwards. In a few seconds he was up and had disappeared into the skull's mouth, the only proof that he'd ever been there the dissipating clouds of dust and a set of shoe prints that stamped the ground with the Chuck Taylor waffle sole every few feet or so.

Shielding his eyes from the dust, Henry gazed up at the mouth of the cave for some sign that it was his turn to go up. A rope ladder. Thunder and lightning. Any kind of invitation, really. But when Sonny's voice finally emerged from the cave's mouth, swollen and puffy with echo and the tailwind of distance, and asked him, "Are you going to come up or what?" he chastised himself for stalling. He needed no invitation to ascend. The hill and the cave were his rite of passage to claim just as they were Sonny's or Grace's or anyone else he'd ever heard talking about hiking up there. If it existed as a symbol, then it was a symbol in his mind alone.

He took a hard run at the hill and tried to put his feet where Sonny's footprints were, and other than a few minor landslides and the displacement of a family of lizards who, like gravity-defying refugees, he sent scurrying in his wake. Making it to the top was easier than he thought it would be, and in that moment, as he hoisted himself over the lip of the cave, he felt a strange twinge of regret and sadness that what he'd always assumed was so unattainable was actually much easier than he ever could have imagined.

Inside the cave it took a moment for his eyes to adjust to the sudden darkness, for his nose to acclimate to the turgid moldy smell, for his skin to accept the quick reversal in temperature. The air was damp, and the close quarters gave form to every little sound, turning the scrape of his foot along the dusty floor, and even his ragged breath, into skittish animals that brushed against his legs and arms in a crazed attempt to find freedom.

"Is this your first time here?" Sonny asked, and Henry swore he could feel the words rustle past his ears. "You should sit down. The ceiling's not very tall."

Whatever paradise of debauchery he was expecting, the reality was a very small space with room for around four people, he guessed, six if you were tripping and two of the six were phasing in between this and another dimension. Sloppy graffiti that reminded him of something a toddler left alone with a set of crayons might come up with decorated the walls and ceiling, a healthy mix of sexual propaganda and an almost pagan devotion to drug references. A bouquet of pot leaves and a picture of a teardrop with the letters *LSD* artfully arranged inside it took up the entire back wall, and underneath it someone had erected a makeshift shrine to Jah that was adorned with a broken bong and a crushed can of Cactus Cooler that had been reappropriated as an incense holder. You had to admire the resourcefulness of stoners, he thought as he took it all in. It wasn't impressive, but it was replete with sincerity, which, to those at impressionable ages, was often a much more important marker of significance.

He wasn't sure what he expected to find here, but after all the buildup he had to admit to himself that this was a disappointment. Maybe in the back of his mind he had pictured lava lamps and huge hookahs that fumed day and night, an inexhaustible combustion engine that could save the world's energy problem but was kept secret for their own nefarious purposes. Vast conspiracy theories of which he was the linchpin suddenly occurred to him, and he was relieved when Sonny passed him a joint he hadn't even seen him light. He took a deep hit and watched as the expelled smoke clung tightly to the atmosphere instead of dispersing like it did when he smoked outside, confirming his recent belief that the cave was immune to the law of physics and when the government finally found out the truth about this place they would all be labeled enemies of freedom and put into concentration camps that had secretly been built throughout these canyons.

"I can't believe you've never been here before," Sonny said to him. "How is that possible?"

Henry wasn't sure if he was being asked a question or if Sonny was merely considering a surprising piece of data he'd just collected for an ongoing science experiment.

"Never gotten around to it I guess," Henry said, choking slightly on the sentiment as much as the weed.

"Your sister sure has."

At the mention of his sister, his body suddenly went rigid.

"What's that supposed to mean?"

Sonny laughed.

"Nothing. Just that I've seen her here before. Relax, man."

A quick and ominous thought passed through Henry's mind. It was irrational, but what if Cal was right about everything, and Sonny had lured him up here so that he and his friends could jump him and beat him up? He tried to think back on the last couple of months, wracking his brains trying to think of anything that might merit an ambush. He'd stolen no one's girlfriend nor had he besmirched anyone's honor. What else was there?

The damp chill of the cave sent a shiver up his back, and he turned quickly expecting to see a gang of his classmates tip-toeing behind him. Sonny let out a laugh that came out more as a giggle, a consequence of being stoned, and Henry had a quick notion of what he might have been like as a little boy, weed doing the thing that weed did when it was working at its best.

"Don't worry," Sonny said, "there's no one back there. I've already checked like three times."

He laughed again and Henry, feeling himself relax into the camaraderie of shared paranoia, laughed with him.

After that they were silent for a while, sitting side by side, cross legged, at the mouth of the cave. The weather was perfect. A slight breeze played at the edges of their vision, rustling, now and again, the brush covered mountains that were half of their view. Mountain ridges formed a healthy patient's EKG line, and above that, the sky bristled with alternating currents of pure blue electricity. Henry had the overwhelming urge to deliver a soliloquy, or maybe it was an elegy. He wasn't sure which. But before he could make the mistake of pontificating aloud, a large bird of some sort drifted into their line of vision and hung in the sky for a moment like an eyelash in the sky's perfect blue eye, riding invisible currents, of air or electricity, he couldn't be sure. Simultaneously, he and Sonny both reached up to wipe away the hair from the eyes, saw each other doing it, and then broke down into convulsive laughter. The bird, meanwhile, had found its motivation somewhere beyond their field of vision, pumped its wings a couple of times, and flew decisively out of view.

"A few mornings ago," Sonny began, apropos of nothing, "I started my car and there was this kind of weird noise from under the hood. I didn't think much of it. My car is generally a piece of shit. When things start to go wrong, I just crank up the stereo a little higher until I can't hear the problem. I call it my audio mechanic."

Henry laughed, and Sonny looked over at him quickly, a serious look that changed into a smile when he realized Henry wasn't making fun of him but only laughing along at the joke.

"Anyway, I drove to school and there was this weird smell.

I don't know how to describe it really, but it was coming through the air vents, like something was burning. Not plastic, though. Skin. Skin and hair. You know the smell." It wasn't a question. All boys knew that smell and the smell of every other substance on earth after it had been burnt. "Finally, I got to school, and I couldn't really ignore it anymore, because it was so bad, I started to feel nauseous from it. So once the parking lot emptied out I popped the hood and pushed it open and do you know what was there?"

"No," Henry said. He wasn't laughing anymore.

"At first I couldn't tell what it was, because it didn't look like the thing it was supposed to be. It was just all this hair and skin and stuff. But then when I looked closer, and I remembered that there was a big pregnant cat on the street, I put two and two together and," Sonny's shoulders heaved as a sob went through him, a single catastrophic breach like a hole in a levee, "I realized the cat had climbed up under my hood and had her babies on the engine block. She must have left to get them food or something. And while she was gone, I fried them all. They couldn't move yet so they couldn't escape. They must have been so small. Small bodies. Small noises. Hopefully they were still so young they couldn't open their eyes yet. I'm not sure how many there were, because they had melted, you know? They were different..."

Tears flowed freely down his cheeks, and he lowered his head, let the sobs roll through him, inhuman moans, beyond mourning, breathing the death.

Unsure of what to do, Henry carefully slipped an arm around Sonny's shoulder and pulled him close, ready to yank his arm away in case Sonny wasn't cool with it. He'd never had to comfort anyone before, so he wasn't sure if there was a certain amount of time that had to go by before they were ready to be reassured. Body language was a tricky thing if it wasn't telling you to run.

Laying his head on Henry's shoulder, Sonny let himself be patted and cooed at, "It's okay, it's okay," Henry repeated each sentence twice like Grace had always done with him whenever he got upset. Repetition was its own special kind of incantation. "You didn't know. You didn't know." As if saying it two times made it true. As if saying anything might help.

After a few minutes, Henry noticed the sobs starting to subside, breath returning to its mortal rhythms. The sounds coming out of Sonny were starting to sound less primal and more what sad was supposed to sound like. He picked his head off Henry's shoulder and looked up into his face. The gaze that met Henry was unfamiliar and with good reason; he'd never felt that glow of excitement ignite in the pit of his stomach before, never felt the mass of eyes full of so much longing, desire's magnetic pull. Their lips met and stayed locked for a few seconds and in that time Henry's mind raced with excuses for why this was happening. He was only trying to comfort Sonny. He was stoned. It was his first opportunity to kiss someone. They were all good justifications, but none of them were as good as want.

The kiss ended as quickly and mysteriously as it had begun, and before Henry knew it they were headed back down the hill and then down the path toward Sonny's car. They walked single file, Sonny in front while Henry trailed behind him trying to match him footstep for footstep. Silently they emerged from the trail and climbed into Sonny's car, the car that had killed the baby cats. Sonny drove without music and Henry heard all of the knocks and pings, the cacophony of malfunction he hadn't noticed earlier. They said nothing to one another except as Sonny pulled up in front of Henry's house when Henry, halfway out the door, turned back, and out of sheer curiosity asked, "What do people say about me?"

Sonny looked confused.

"What do you mean?"

"I just mean, what do people think of me? What do they say about me?"

Sonny thought about it for a moment and then shook his head.

"Nothing," he said with no emotion in his voice. "People don't really talk about you."

Henry stood in the driveway and watched Sonny as he drove off, unsure now what to think, wondering sincerely if the last few hours were real or if he had made them up in his head, a fantasy to fill the fallow time between days, the moments he knew he should think of as his life.

*   *   *

The next couple of weeks at school were marked by a loneliness the likes of which he'd never experienced before. It wasn't the usual kind of loneliness where nothing seemed worth doing, where nothing was fun enough, nothing interesting enough. Nor was it the kind of loneliness that brushed by you in the halls, people so near yet so far, raising the hairs on your arms in anticipation of a touch, or you'd even settle for a hint of recognition, a reflection of existence. Matter on matter. Mass on mass. That kind of loneliness, at least, had an antidote, which was you could wait it out and eventually it would pass, and you could force yourself to believe that it had been in your head the whole time. Because loneliness wasn't in the atmosphere, lingering and foreboding, the proof of omens like earthquake weather, nor was it a germ or a virus or any other karmic inheritance. It took patience to exist, that was all. Patience solved everything.

What made this loneliness worse than any other was that

he was so painfully aware of its origin. Since that afternoon at Skull Rock, Sonny did everything in his power to avoid Henry. He shot Henry withering glares if he saw him coming toward him at one of the breaks, and in class, if Henry took a seat near him he'd get up and move as far away as possible. Once, Henry tried to ambush him after school in the parking lot, and Sonny, smoking a cigarette, picked up his pace, pretending not to hear. When Henry had almost caught up with him Sonny had spun around and flicked his lit cigarette at Henry so that a spray of sparks exploded off his jacket. "Get away from me, you faggot. If you don't stay away from me, I'm going to fucking beat your head in with a baseball bat until it fucking explodes. Are we fucking clear, faggot?" His voice sounded strangled, choked with hate, like the words were something in him that would kill him if he didn't get them out.

It was as clear as crystal, but it didn't help the fact that all Henry wanted to do was talk to him. Just two minutes. That was all the time he needed. He didn't want to say much. He wasn't interested in Sonny, not in that way. He was sure of that. What had happened between them was an anomaly, two people needing two different things who happened to be in the exact same place at the exact same time. He wanted to explain that to Sonny, that the chances of what happened were astronomical—astronomical in a cataclysmic way. Meteor hitting the earth astronomical. No more dinosaurs astronomical. What he wanted was to tell Sonny that it was okay with him if they never talked again, but he wanted him to know that he didn't hate him and hoped Sonny didn't hate him, either. That was it. If he could just say those few sentences he'd be happy for the rest of his life. If he could just say that, he'd feel like he was a human being again.

One night after his parents and Grace fell asleep he raided

the liquor cabinet and started drinking everything he could get his hands on. Gin, vodka, Tia Maria, it didn't matter. After the first ten or so gulps none of it tasted like anything anyway. He took a bottle of cheap vodka up to his room and put a Bob Dylan tape he'd swiped from his sister's room in the tape deck. He didn't know the name of the song, but the words made him cry, and when he was done crying, he started laughing, and when the laughter petered out it was time to puke. He rushed into the bathroom, knelt at the toilet, and made his ablutions, loudly enough to wake his sister, apparently, because suddenly there she was, rubbing the sleep out of her eyes, her hair strewn this way and that.

"Henry?" she asked. "Are you okay?"

And then her eyes settled on the bottle and she heard "Visions of Johanna," a soft rebuke from his room, and she let out a big sigh and sat down on the floor next to him.

"Oh, Henry," she said, rubbing his back lightly.

Her first instinct was to commiserate. It was what made her great, he thought, a true humanitarian. When he was done puking, he would tell her that.

"What am I going to do with you, Henry?"

"Could you…hold…my hair back for me?" he said carefully between eruptions.

She looked at his buzz cut and laughed as he emptied the contents of his stomach into the toilet. So many colors, he thought, rather rationally, as his body made the noises of a fomenting revolution.

When it was over, and she had forced him to drink more water than a sinking ship and had helped him brush his teeth and change his pajamas, and tucked him into bed, she tiptoed out, and as sleep was closing over him, he remembered he hadn't yet thanked her, and called out to her one last time in a loud whisper, "Thank you, Grace. It doesn't seem like it's enough sometimes. I know how hard I am."

"I love you," she whispered back, and he could tell she was smiling.

"You know, sometimes I wish that I was blind so that I'd have to touch your face to know what you were thinking," he said, and suddenly the loneliness began to lift. He could see it behind his closed eyes, drifting away, wisps of smoke, a drunkard's soliloquy. "I hope that doesn't sound weird. Is that weird?"

He fell asleep before she could answer, though, or maybe she never did. He never would find out, though, because the next day was the day that everything would change forever.

Chapter 15

DÉJÀ VU WAS invented by the desert.
Mile after mile stretched before them in a remarkably unchanging pattern of rocks, road, and the occasional
cactus that sprang up here and there like an afterthought,
part of the land's own collection of knick-knacks. The sun
stayed high and the road ran flat until it disappeared into
a puff of vapor somewhere far into the distance, a point on
the horizon that didn't really exist, because even the horizon
itself was a trick of the light. A real horizon at least offered
some promise of completion in the shape of a vanishing
point. But not the desert, vague to say the least, offering,
for free, the worst views money could buy, complete with all
mod cons, including the terrible, sinking feeling that you'd
been here before and would be here again, forever perhaps,
not just experiencing déjà vu, but starting to anticipate it, a
loop of unimaginably dismal proportions. Imagine thinking
about death as lurking not only around every corner, but
around every corner you've just passed as well. Death in front
of and behind you! To cement the suspicion, every once in
a while a car would emerge out of thin air on the opposite
side of the highway and barrel toward them at what seemed
like impossible speeds, speeds that to Henry made him feel
like they were driving from something devastating that he
was stupidly headed straight toward. The desert in a nutshell.

Mile after unchanging mile and he started to get antsy. Although it felt like they were practically standing still, Henry knew the distance was peeling away and in no time at all they'd be there, at Pottersville. Knowing what awaited him did very little to alleviate his anxiety, but he would have to rein that in if this was going to work and he was going to get what he needed. It was hard to believe, but he was being brought in to do a job, an important job, like a medical specialist who's flown to some foreign hospital to perform surgery on a rich sheikh or someone who might reward him with jewels, or women, or a private Lionel Richie concert, or whatever people that rich did to show their appreciation to people who saved their lives. In this case, though, he'd already received his reward and he looked over at his traveling companion and experienced a sudden twinge of longing and loss as it dawned on him that he would never get to be with her again. She'd done what she had to do to get him to come along, to soften the blow of the truth of the matter, and in a way he felt a bit like a sucker for taking the bait so easily. He couldn't help but think of Grace in moments like these, how she'd probably softly scold him for acting like a typical male. When he was younger just the thought of that disapproving look would have flushed him with shame. But now, things were different. Now he was at that age where rhetorically asking "Why not?" felt like an acceptable response to almost any moral dilemma. It wasn't about being less thoughtful. It was about being economical with his good judgment, as if there was a finite amount of it, a diminishing national resource he had to conserve for when it really counted, for when the shit really hit the fan.

Next to him Daisy sat without making a sound, without moving a muscle, languishing in apathetic conspiracy with the sun as it illuminated the fine little blonde hairs along her

legs and arms and the wind that threaded its way through
the small crack at the top of the window whipping the long
blonde strands of her hair into a frenzy. She stared off into
the distance as a faint smile traced its way across her lips.
Every once in a while he'd look over at her and try to guess
what she was thinking, but it was useless, she gave nothing of
herself away. Her eyes were her own, and with her feet pinned
up lazily against the cracked fake leather of the dashboard,
her posture said even less. She was a firecracker soaked in
kerosene, the danger being she'd blow up before she got to
do her pretty thing.

At the beginning of their drive he'd put on some music but
had quickly turned it off. Nothing seemed to fit. Nothing
seemed to be big enough. He'd tried to engage her a couple
of times, once by pointing out the jail where Evel Knievel
had gone just like his father had done to him when he was
eight. Maybe his dad had just been trying to make conversation, too, and the notion that trying to find common ground
could lead to the worst kind of desperation gave him a sudden
lump in his throat that stayed there for what felt like hours.

An hour or so outside of Pottersville he pulled over at one of
those exits that advertised lodging, fuel, and food, everything
but an answer to the question that had always nagged him,
which was where the fuck the people lived who worked at all
these places. He scanned the horizon for domiciles, and seeing
nothing, not even a small cluster of trailers or yurts or pre-fab
mud and shit condos, came to the conclusion that he always
came to, which was there was an underground community of
fast-food workers who burrowed into the cool sand at night,
where they hunted bugs and culled moisture by sucking on
the used Big Mac and Burrito Supreme wrappers that littered
the landscape. What he hadn't figured out yet was how they
got there in the first place. He was stuck between the possi-

bility that they were genetically engineered ears of corn by Monsanto that had become sentient and resentful of their destiny as biofuel for Chinese automakers or that they were a colony of swingers created in the seventies and had spawned too many love children to exist any longer in polite society. Either way, it wasn't an altogether bad destiny, he thought, laughing to himself. Daisy looked over at him and smiled and squeezed his hand. It was the first time she'd acknowledged his being there in the last two hours, and he wondered what she would say if she knew what had made him laugh.

At the top of the freeway exit he pointed left and then right. "What'll it be? Tacos, burgers, or Denny's, which, in my opinion, kind of defies classification. It's more like a state of mind than actual sustenance, you know? Like nihilism or polygamy?"

"Hmm?" she asked. She hadn't heard a word he'd just said and he was fine with that. Instead of repeating himself he pulled into a McDonald's drive-through and ordered a Big Mac, fries and a Coke. It had been a long time since he'd eaten at a McDonald's and the idea of having it now seemed to him appropriate somehow, an indulgence at the precipice of something great.

"Want anything?"

"No thanks," she answered. He assumed she'd say no, but thought it polite to ask. Women like Daisy didn't eat McDonald's, not even once in a while. He saw now that hers was a life of discipline and order, which was probably one of the reasons the COL had seemed so appealing to her in the first place. Order out of disorder. He understood the appeal, but he knew that kind of thing wasn't practical for him at this point in his life. For now he needed his exceptions; they went along nicely with uncertainty and doubt. Perhaps when he got back home, after he'd interviewed Potter, he'd look into something like TM or fatherhood or one of those other cult-light things people were always boasting about on social media. He would treat himself to a fresh start. The final exception.

At the drive-through window a pretty, young girl with her brown hair in pigtails handed him his bag of food. "$7.49," she said and it instantly made Henry think she had just told him some important password. Maybe it was the code word to get into the underground bunker?

"You're in a good mood," Daisy said, examining him closely.

"Is that against the law?" he said, teasing back. God, she was pretty. Her eyes were wide open and effervescent. Her smile sweet enough to break the heart of any day.

"Not against the law," she laughed. "No."

Eating as he drove he felt a surge of self-confidence, the likes of which he hadn't felt in a very long time. They didn't speak again until they reached Pottersville three hours later.

*   *   *

The desert's last dose of déjà vu came as they drove down a small dirt road into the foothills, which from the freeway had seemed a million miles away. They followed the narrow road past a few cacti and little else into shade cast down from the mountains, which suddenly loomed above them like a quickly moving storm. All the while he could sense Daisy growing more and more agitated as they went and unkindly he thought of a dog wagging its tail for a master it hadn't seen in some time.

"This is it," she said, as they drove down the final stretch of the road toward a simple iron gate, above which was painted the word *Pottersville* on a wood sign that swung delicately in the non-wind that was always found in the desert, the gentle impulse to sway at the risk of not being able to stay put against the heat, the phantoms in the distance, and all the other things that conspired to scare one away. Pottersville. A threat as much as a location. A promise to some and the end of the world to that many more. He had been here before. In his imagination, wondering what had become of the little girl who ran away that night out into the desert and straight into his dreams. When he and his family had enjoyed Armageddon with a light snack as they let their attention flick between the Olympics and the police raid on the compound more than thirty years before. He tried to remember if Grace had been there that night and then recalled that she had stormed off at a certain point up to her room too disgusted to stick around.

"This is it," she said again, and he resisted the urge to tell her, "I know," because that would be rude. But he did know. He knew it as well as he knew anything in his life.

"Honk your horn," she told him as he pulled up to the gate. "Just once." He could sense her excitement, that for her this was a homecoming long in coming. He was about to ask her how long it had been since she had last been here, but before he could speak he saw the first few tentative faces of people begin to cautiously appear from inside the dilapidated sheds and dorms he guessed constituted the guts of the "town." Slowly, soul by soul, they stuck their worried faces out of doorways and up against window panes and when Daisy stuck her head out of the window and began to wave, and they saw that it was her, smiles suddenly ran roughshod and they ran from their hiding places and began to cheer, and, he couldn't be sure, but it sounded like they were singing, too. Someone pulled the gate open and he inched the car slowly into Pottersville as a crowd of happy cultists swarmed them, pulled Daisy out, and absorbed her into a group embrace that metastasized as more and more people, men and women, joined it. In a few moments the whole of them were a single organism overcome by a singular emotion. Happiness. He had never felt anything so beautiful in his entire life.

After a few minutes the group began to disperse, and as people went off a group of a dozen or so young women, all about Daisy's age, stayed behind for an extra moment of fellowship, their heads pressed together, a most solemn congregation, and when they split up they each took a moment to recognize Daisy and thank her for her great work. Or maybe it was a sacrifice, although considering he'd be the thing she was sacrificed for, he chose to think not. "You are the light amongst us, Daisy." "No, Rose, the light reaches you before any of us." "May you grow so high you touch the sky, Daisy." "No one will grow as high as you, Heather. Your petals will kiss the sun. I know this." "There is no sweeter smell than the Daisy in its bloom." "No greater smell has ever touched the world than the scent of the Lily." On and on it went until they had all had their turn with her. Their voices were biblical, rich with the sincerity of true believers. Many kissed Daisy's hand as they left. Some her forehead. If there was a hierarchy at play, or cynicism, it was lost on Henry. The sun took care of that. High and hot in the sky it was a filter for honesty, the logic being no one had the wits to waste or the energy to lie in such brutal conditions. It was enough just to survive.

The girls left to do whatever tasks it was that occupied the days of a cult member. Henry thought about what those might be the way he wondered what it was a lawyer did all day. Or a politician. How did anyone really fill the hours of their day? He imagined them going to rinse out the tubs for the poison Kool-Aid or cleaning the sacrificial knives for the ritualistic bloodletting ceremony. Order, after all, was order.

Daisy, her fingers entwined around those of a woman around Henry's age, led her to where he was standing. The woman followed Daisy sheepishly like a shy shadow. Even though she was older and taller than Daisy, she seemed much smaller, weaker, the kind of person who might have to be convinced that it was okay to have defense mechanisms. The woman kept her eyes pinned to the ground in front of her, and as they approached, her tentativeness made Henry imagine he was meeting the woman whose hand his parents had once been promised to him in marriage.

"Henry, this is Flora. Flora, I'd like you to meet Henry."

Flora slowly picked her gaze off the floor as if it was something heavy and precious, and when he could finally see her entire face he felt his breath leave him in a soundless gasp. Blonde hair cut short, skinny nose, light dark circles under her eyes. Bony shoulders peeked up from beneath a tank top. He pointed a finger at her, "I know you from somewhere. Where have we met?" She was on the tip of his tongue and it killed him he couldn't place her. Did she work at the paper? No, further back than that. High school? Oh god, not that. Anything but that.

The women looked at each other and giggled softly.

"I don't think so," Flora said. Her voice was tiny, but not without its own kind of assured strength. It was the voice of someone conserving their energy, someone pacing themselves for the long haul. "I get that a lot, though." She saw the pained look on his face and was immediately empathetic. "Don't let it bother you, Henry. If you were meant to remember, you'll remember."

"If he wills it," Daisy chimed in. He had almost forgotten she was there.

"Yes," Flora agreed. "If he wills it."

A loudspeaker he hadn't noticed before suddenly cleared its throat of phlegmy static, followed by four chimes in ascending order that reminded him of the PA at school announcing the dreaded tardy blitz. People everywhere stopped what they were doing and looked up at the loudspeaker nearest to them as a man's voice suddenly emerged, chipper and bright, but also dreamy.

"Good morning, Flowers. Isn't it a beautiful day?"

"Good morning, Father," they bellowed back in unison. "It's a beautiful day."

"Today, as you do your work, as you honor yourselves and God with the tasks you have before you, I want to share a thought with you. Well, not a thought exactly. It's something I read once a long time ago, one of those things you listen to and then store in the back of your head and forget about until one day, POP, it bursts in you like a seed pod and suddenly it's everywhere you look, infused in your every breath, burrowed and germinating in every one of your thoughts. I guess what I'm saying in my old man way is I just can't get it out of my head." The voice chuckled at itself and around Henry a sea of similar chuckles spread throughout Pottersville. It was his first "sighting" of Potter. A gigantic lump of anticipation formed in Henry's chest, and he instinctively froze, afraid if he moved he'd somehow scare the voice away as though it were a skittish fawn foraging in the woods. But the voice wasn't going anywhere. Slow and comfortable, it went on. "So, Children, when I woke up this morning, and this thought was bursting in me, alive in me in the way only the most beautiful things can be said to be alive, I just knew I had to share it with you right away. Well, after my first cup of coffee that is."

He chuckled again, and the Children of Light laughed along with him, an all too willing audience for what sounded to Henry like a well-practiced vaudeville act. Real "take my wife" kind of shit. But when he looked over at Daisy and Flora, and saw their faces starched with the kind of contentment he imagined might only exist between mother and newborn, he thought maybe he'd been mistaken in thinking that this was schtick. They were submerged in the man's folksy soliloquy, happily drowning, and waited for every word to sink them further beneath his ocean of love.

"When I was a younger man, still searching for truth in my life, still holding out hope that the true word could be found in a book or upon the lips of some holy man, instead of right before me, in the ground, infused in the soil—long before I realized that god's love was something that had to be nurtured and loved and helped to grow—as you know, Children, I was a simple gardener. Maybe they'd call me a landscaper today. I don't know." More laughing. "I had a friend who was in school, and this friend sometimes worked with me to earn extra money to pay his tuition and to buy books. I admired him for his enterprise and his work ethic. It impressed me not only to know someone going to college, but someone who was there because of his own hard work and not simply as the child of privilege."

The Children of Light had stopped working and those that had gone inside came back outside, all of them listening voraciously to every word Potter said, eating his story up with their hungry eyes and acres of smiles. Henry had no way of knowing if they had heard this story before, or if it was better in some way than the ones they usually heard, but as he listened he tried to open himself up to the influence of not just the man's words, but the quality of his voice as well, a resonant act of contrition and modesty that teetered carefully on the brink, but never quite fell, into the valley of apology. It struck him that it was the voice of his making or his unmaking and so he closed his eyes and listened as he began to mentally prepare the questions he would ask.

"One day, my friend did not come to work as he was supposed

to. It was a hard day because I had to double the work, and when it was finally over long past daylight, I went to sleep feeling exhausted but utterly fulfilled. Exhausted because I had done the work of two men but fulfilled also because I had done the work of two men.

"The next day, he again did not show up and I called him. Yes, Children, we had telephones back then." More laughter from the living laugh track. "He didn't answer and I became worried. For several more days he was not to be seen until finally, one day, he showed up at work right on time at eight a.m. I was shocked when I saw him, although it had only been a few days, and I asked him where he had been. Well, Children, he looked at me, and I could see right away that something had changed in him. His color was not the same. He was paler than usual even though we had spent so much time out in the sun tending to the soil and he was beset by a calmness that seemed to me like an illness rather than a real peace.

"He first apologized to me for his absence and then went on to tell me that his mother had passed away the week before and he had been seeing to the funeral arrangements and visiting with family members who had come from out of town to pay their respects. His father was already dead and he was the only child, so all of the responsibility had fallen on him. It was a great burden, he told me, and after the funeral the rabbi had asked him how he was and he responded honestly that he was tired and he was heartbroken. The rabbi, he said, had thought for a moment and then said to him that it was important to consider one thing upon the loss of the second parent, which was that in Judaism one wasn't said to be an adult, a real adult, until both parents had died. The words struck me, Children, and I didn't know how to respond. I waited a moment and looked at my friend, wondered if it was this knowledge that made him seem so different to me, and then asked him what he said. 'What did I say?' he asked me as if he were searching me for the answer and not speaking rhetorically, 'I said nothing. What is there to say when you feel a piece of yourself die?'

So, Children, the thought I wish to leave you with today as you go about your busy beautiful work is more a question really than it is an observation. And that is, why can't we be children forever? What's to stop us from living each day as if it were our first? What's the matter with each day being perfect because it is the one and only? Children, I ask you this," the voice was a rising, booming thing and emanating from it Henry could feel tension growing in the air, a fleshy excitement breeding on the wind, gathering enough energy to be its own natural disaster. He felt it in himself. His insides were a conductor for chain lightning. If he coughed, he would breath fire and burn the whole place down. The desert, too. The voice had a power all its own. This place. These people. A desert wind blew in and it coated him like a second skin. Yes, even the wind was in on it. "Will you always be my children?" his voice had gone soft again and the effect was pure emotion. Henry heard a woman sob and a man answer with a resounding 'Hallelujah!' that bled across the camp and out into the desert where the desert gave back the only thing it was capable of giving. An echo.

*   *   *

Dinner that night was a simple and tasteless affair of chicken, rice, and stewed vegetables. These people were obviously not concerned with the quality of their cuisine and seemed more than happy with the bland offerings. In fact, they were full of joy, busy with it, dizzy even. The outdoor dining area where they ate was nothing more than a dozen or so picnic tables beneath a wood awning that was strung with white Christmas lights so the feeling was festive. Brainwashed cultists or not, atmosphere was atmosphere and it was clear to Henry that, in the way their hands moved like fluttering insects when they talked and their eyes wide as saucers, they were anticipating something huge and great.

Henry had a table pretty much all to himself and he pulled out his small reporter's pad and pen and began jotting down a few notes, questions he would ask Potter when he was finally able to talk to him. He'd asked Daisy at least ten times since they had arrived and she had kept putting him off, telling him "Soon. Soon." She had walked him to dinner and then immediately taken off once he was situated. He could see her across the room, chatting excitedly with Flora and the other girls whose names were flowers, whose necks bore the same tattoos. She was dressed like them now, too, and he had to admit she looked spectacular in the gauzy white dress, like a wisp of something real.

He got up and walked across the room to where she was sitting with the others. He wasn't as self-conscious as he thought he'd be as the only outsider in Pottersville, in fact he felt quite the opposite, he felt almost invisible, as inconsequential as anything happening outside of these gates.

He tapped Daisy on the shoulder and when she turned around to face him, she was all smiles. The other women immediately stopped speaking and turned their attention to him as well, a baker's dozen or so of the most cheerful people he'd ever laid eyes on.

"Daisy," he whispered, but she interrupted him.

"You don't have to whisper. These are my sisters. They know everything I know. They hear everything I hear."

His ears reddened at the thought of their love-making. How

many of the details did they know? He guessed probably all of them and thought that after this was all over he'd write an advice book about dating cult women and make sure to stress they were terrible at secret keeping.

He cleared his throat.

"I just want to know when I'm going to get my interview. You know I have to get this thing to my editor in a couple of days and I want to make sure I have time to write it up the right way."

He added that last part in there to try and get on her good side when in reality he wasn't really sure how he was going to maintain his objectivity. It wasn't going to be easy to erase the things he knew about what had taken place here. He flashed on his childhood, watching the standoff with his parents, Grace storming out of the room, offended by the notion that what they were watching was entertainment. She'd been right about that, of course, but in reality when had Grace ever been wrong?

"It's going to have to be tomorrow, Henry. He's so tired tonight and not feeling very well. He's already asleep, but he asked me to ask you to get all your questions ready," she glanced at his notebook and he understood that she knew exactly what he was doing and thinking, "and that tomorrow he'd be all yours."

Around the table, women continued to smile up at him without saying a word and, after a few seconds of silence, Flora got up from the table and took him gently by the arm. "Let me show you where you're going to sleep tonight," she said, gently guiding him out of the dining area and back into the main part of the town.

It got very quiet very quickly once they moved away from the tables and the silence, he felt, seemed to devour them with its heartless jaws. Dim lamplight lit their way, forcing shadowy impressions of the wooden buildings they strolled past spread-eagled on the ground like criminal suspects. The moon was large and bright and was the only reminder he had that life existed outside these gates.

"You seem agitated," Flora said, her eyes looking forward instead of at him.

"I'm distracted."

"Isn't that the same thing?"

"No. Not always. Distraction doesn't necessarily lead to agitation. It can be a good thing sometimes."

He turned to her and was struck again by how thin she was, how angular. In less light she would be mistaken for a monster from a nightmare, something that could wedge its way into whatever small space you were hiding from it.

"Are you enjoying yourself here?"

He shrugged. If this was the part of the evening where she tried to psychologically corral him into joining up with them, he had bad news for her. He was more than able to shoulder the burden of his demons without the help of a group of people whose version of paradise was a living ghost town in the middle of the desert. Besides, group thought wasn't his thing. He could imagine Truman and Alberto here, though, living like kings in a delusional utopia. Perfect for them.

"We're happy here, Henry," she said, and her voice had gone from light and bashful to something now with a harder edge. Something that lived in reality. "We have something that we love, a person that we look up to. We have companionship and purpose. We have a system of beliefs that fit who we are. That's a rare thing. Not many people can say that. What would you trade for all the happiness in the world? Because as far as I'm concerned, being out here is not a lot to ask."

For the second time that night he pictured Grace, smelled the chemical smell of microwave popcorn, felt a tension he couldn't name. It was as if he was home. Home again. No place like home.

He said, "There's no such thing as all the happiness in the world. We all have an agenda and we're uneasy until we've completed that agenda. 'All the happiness in the world...' Give me a fucking break. The most we can hope for is a little objectivity, don't you think? Moments of clarity. Yeah. Little moments of clarity to light the path along the way."

He could almost see them, those little lights, as they walked along in the near dark, and when a man and woman passed them on the dusty trail, soundless save the scrape of their feet along the dusty ground, he became giddy with the thought that every soul he came across had the potential to be a nemesis, the yin to his yang, and it gave him a sudden sense of hope he hadn't felt since arriving here.

"Objectivity?" Flora laughed. "Are you trying to tell me you're able to be objective here? That you're not going to let what you think you know about us sway how you see us? What you write about us? Daisy has a very good feeling about you, and she convinced us that you could be the one to do justice to perspective. I was against you coming here. But she insisted and I finally relented because that's what you do for people you love, Henry. Sometimes you relent. And when you do, it's that act of surrender that builds the love between you."

Without realizing it, they had stopped walking. He tried to see her expression, but it was too dark for that, too dark to get a sense of things.

"You're about my age, right? Around forty?"

"Thirty-nine," he said after doing some quick subtraction. The older he got the more figuring out his age became a parlor trick rather than a simple biological fact.

"And let me guess," she continued, "you were watching Mary Lou Retton when the news broke in about the siege here. Am I right?"

She didn't wait for him to nod.

"And a few weeks later you watched the little girl on *20/20* talk about escaping and running through the desert. You pictured it in your head, didn't you? The little girl in her gauzy white dress, her bare feet torn up by the hard ground, being chased by the bad guys. Did you think she was cute? Helpless? Did you want to save her, Henry? Did you save her in your dreams?"

He felt his body stiffen as he suddenly realized where he'd seen her before. She was mocking him, but she had that right, he supposed. She'd earned it, hadn't she?

Trying to sound as normal as possible he asked her, "Why did you come back?"

"See," she said as she shook her head in disappointment, "there's no objectivity." She waited for him to see it, to see that she was right, but it wasn't clicking. Finally, she sighed as though she'd been speaking to a child whose bedtime had long since passed. "Who said I ever left, Henry?"

Chapter 16

THE KNIFE CAME from nowhere, Grace told him later when they were home, but that's the way it was with knives, that they were always just coming out of nowhere. In movies and books the guy would have nothing in his hand and then suddenly—Abracadabra!!—a knife, like stabbing someone was an amazing magic trick, three-card Monte sleight of hand. So that was how he imagined it when Grace told Henry the story, and she was shaking and babbling, trying to make sense of it all in her rational mind because, hey, everyone knew that magic wasn't real, right?

"Slow down," he begged her, putting his hands on her forearms to keep her from floating away, "tell me again what happened."

"Cal," she said, taking a deep breath, "your friend Cal just stabbed Peter. They were arguing, and then all of a sudden Cal had a knife in his hand and..." she took a breath and finally her wild eyes settled on his face, "he stabbed Peter with it."

Henry felt his blood freeze. "Is he okay?"

"I don't know. I mean, they don't know. They had to take him away in an ambulance. Oh my god, Henry," she started crying, slowly at first, and then in huge choking sobs that drowned her words, "what if he dies? What will happen?"

He let his hands drop and rubbed his temples. *No no no*

no no. It had to be some sort of mistake. His mind did a quick inventory of things that could be easily mistaken for a stabbing, but there wasn't much that sprang to mind. It was the first thing she'd said to him since earlier in the day when Peter and Cal had gotten into it. In fact, the only thing that came to him as he watched her, as he tried to put the pieces together that had made up the last two days, was the urge to tell her that he hadn't meant to ask how Peter was, that he'd been asking about Cal. He couldn't care less about Peter. But he knew he couldn't say that. Saying that would ruin things forever, however long that was.

He loved her so much, but he was paralyzed by the idea that he should be doing something different than just standing there. Shouldn't he be patting her shoulder, saying "there, there," or at the very least offer her a Kleenex? But he did none of those things, just watched the top of her head bobbing gently, uselessly against his leg. At the end, standing still was the best he could do for her. After everything she'd done for him, all the times she'd comforted him and taken his side unquestioningly, that was the most he could offer. And with that hatchet of information now buried in his head, he had the unexplainable, yet terrifying thought that he was still watching a movie he started ten years ago and that was his life now. Whether that was more or less real than the real thing was anybody's guess.

*   *   *

It was only two short weeks ago that Sonny had driven him home after their day in the hills, an awkward silence jammed between them in the front seat like a huge stuffed animal won at a state fair. Night was coming and dusk was busy doing a vandal's work, painting over another perfectly good day. There were a million things Henry wanted to say, but he resisted. What he really wanted to know was if they were going to be friends, if tomorrow he could sit with Sonny at lunch and when he did would Sonny clap him on the shoulder and introduce him around as his new friend or, hope against hope, maybe say something like "welcome to the club." And then Henry would shake hands with all these kids he'd known since kindergarten, kids he'd never actually talked to in ten plus years of close proximity, and that would be that. All those years of feeling separate from them, a nameless difference, would suddenly dissolve and colors would shift before his very eyes, deepen, grow in luster, and he would see things for what they really were and life would be the real life he'd been waiting for; a life of parties and dates, of staying out too late, of harmlessly fucking up and being forgiven for it by his teachers and parents again and again, sins brushed off and chalked up to the vagaries of youth as if it was a lifestyle choice that demanded to be respected like any other. The thrill of a whole new set of rules, new music to listen to, new clothes to wear. Jesus Christ, how he longed for someone to wind him up and let him go. But that was a lot to ask for and even more to expect. Silence was better than the truth, Henry conceded, soaking it in. The sun was almost completely erased now, and when Henry looked over at Sonny all he could make out was the dark outline of his profile, and he must have still been a little high because to him it looked a little like Skull Rock, and it took him everything he could not to laugh, not to make a joke about two tiny boys perched on the top of his lips, kissing softly, innocently, so fully lost in a moment as to be submerged in it, drowning in the displaced time.

"Are you moving?" Sonny asked, his voice came out of nowhere.

"Huh?" Henry dumbly replied as he slowly emerged from

his thoughts.

Sonny pointed over his steering wheel and Henry looked at him blankly. He jabbed his finger repeatedly and impatiently at a spot outside the car.

"Your house," Sonny said losing his patience. "Jesus. There's a U-Haul in your driveway. Are you moving?"

Henry looked and saw that he was right that there was a U-Haul in front of his house with moving boxes scattered around it. There were a full three stoned seconds when he stared at the van and couldn't for the life of him figure out what it was doing there. They weren't being evicted, he knew that much, and there didn't appear to be any damage anywhere. He certainly didn't remember an earthquake or a flood, although anything was possible. Then, suddenly and calmly, he remembered.

"My parents are getting a divorce. I think my dad is moving out."

Sonny kind of nodded and said, "Weird."

Henry shook his head in agreement.

Sonny pulled a U-turn and when his headlights splashed over the driveway they saw Henry's dad come out of the house, a big moving box in his arms, stop, put the box down, and shield his eyes. He looked so small out there among all his stuff, the sum parts of a life lived poorly, and Henry thought that this was how a sculptor should shape him if given the commission to make his dad into a monument, standing stupidly in a driveway, blinded by light, and towered over by decades of possessions that were too much of a burden for him to carry. Too numerous to mean anything.

The car stopped, and Henry panicked inwardly for something to say, anything to put a dent in the awkwardness. In the driveway, his father stayed in the exact same position, his hand cupped over his eyes, and Henry wondered what it was he thought was about to happen. He was a man so used to being saved by the good graces of others, and more specifically, the uniquely feminine sense of duty that bordered on pity. Henry had no doubt that he expected this idling car was here to save him, too, maybe to whisk him away to the not so distant past for an asshole mulligan or to deliver him a sexy divorcee around his age but with fewer wrinkles and skinnier than his mom and she would just saunter up to him and link her arm in his and they'd go off together like the last twenty-five years had never happened, and he wouldn't think twice about it. He wouldn't doubt it for a second because that's the way things were supposed to go.

"Later," Sonny said suddenly and flatly like a preemptive missile strike.

"See you tomorrow?" Henry said weakly and in spite of himself, and he as soon as the words left his lips, and Sonny stayed quiet, Henry knew deep down that there was no way in hell he'd be seeing him tomorrow or any other day for that matter. He knew better than to want a thing too much, that saying it was the surest way not to get it.

He got out of the car and walked to his dad who still hadn't moved.

"New friend?"

Henry shrugged as the car sped off down the street.

"Come on," his father said, squeezing his neck chummily. "Help me load the rest of these boxes in the truck and I'll take you to McDonald's."

Henry nodded, picked up a box, and was immediately overcome by guilt that he was somehow betraying his mother. He glanced up at the house to make sure neither she nor Grace were watching and he saw nothing. His worst fear was that they were watching in the dark and to them this would be his picking a side and he was suddenly off their team, which is where he really wanted to be. Hopefully they'd give him a chance to explain himself, to tell them about "fathers-and-sons" and "quality time." Maybe that bullshit would work on them, because it was better than the truth, which was that he didn't know how to say no to his father even though he knew in his heart of hearts that every decision the man made was the wrong decision, every piece of advice he dispensed tainted by a worldview that was based on the narrowest of perspectives.

Once they'd loaded the truck up they headed west on the 10 freeway, their windows down, cold air devouring them so his dad could smoke a cigarette. Silence except for the sound of the wind until his dad looked at his watch, threw the cigarette out the window, and turned the radio on to catch the call from Santa Anita.

"Annnnd away they go…" the familiar British voice of the announcer crooned, intoning the action in a quick monotone that just reinforced for Henry that the races were a purely transactional thing for his father, as were his baseball cards, his deep obsession with football…all of it consumed with a studied absence of joy and enthusiasm. It was nothing more than a careful impersonation of responsibility. His dad really had nothing to take seriously. Never had. He knew that now.

They pulled off the freeway and stopped at a McDonald's drive-thru in the marina. Big Mac, fries, and a Coke for each of them. Eating in the parking lot, they stared out the windshield at a couple of homeless guys reclining on a grassy knoll. The oblivious drunks passed a bottle back and forth, laughing, clearly having a better time than Henry and his dad.

"Throw this crap away," his father said, stuffing all their garbage in the empty paper bags. He lit a cigarette and blew the smoke angrily out the window.

Henry walked to the garbage can that was next to where the homeless guys were sitting, and they both watched him carefully as he dumped the stuff in the can.

"Anything left in there?" One of them asked.

"No," Henry said. "Sorry."

There were actually a few french fries he hadn't finished and he immediately felt guilty for lying to the guy.

"I've got a problem," the guy went on, his voice wavering between sincerity and an oil slick. "I had some money for a bus ticket but I got robbed by this guy I used to know. Then I had to come down here to meet another friend and he robbed me, too." Henry watched him studiously because he felt like it was the courteous thing to do, but in just these first few sentences his story already made no sense. Henry was transfixed by the deep grooves of living and worry that ran every which way across the man's face, lines that people in his life didn't have and certainly his father didn't have. They were proof of life, physical evidence of intention and meaning.

Henry dug in his pocket and fished out a dollar bill, which he gave to the guy. He poked it into his shirt pocket and nodded. "Thanks, buddy. You're okay in my book."

Walking back to the car, he suppressed a smile because he knew his dad was watching him. He wouldn't be happy that he'd given his money away like that and when he got in and closed the door he wasn't surprised when his dad turned to him, his eyes narrowed to judgmental slits, and asked him in that tone of voice of his that was worse than a shout and more of an exaggerated incredulity that was like a magnifying glass focusing the sun right on Henry's ego, "Did you give money to that bum?" His father shook his head dramatically, like he was shaking away the cobwebs of a concussion.

"Don't, Dad…"

He couldn't stop himself, though. Delivering a life lesson via shaming was his specialty and squarely in the wheelhouse of all the most magnificent assholes down through the ages.

"Don't 'don't Dad' me. It just shows you don't know the meaning of a dollar. Still, after all this time. You're sixteen now, Henry. It's time to grow up and stop being such a pushover. Do you want people to take advantage of you for your whole life? Because they will. If you let them, they will."

They were driving down Lincoln Blvd. now. It was around 7:30 and the rush hour traffic was just beginning to die down. Henry rolled down the window and inhaled. He could smell the ocean, and it surprised him as if he had forgotten where he was. Or maybe he'd just forgotten who he was. Either was possible under the circumstances. He had this habit of dissociating when he was angry, making his mind disappear from his body like a cheap illusion, sleight of hand as defense mechanism. Maybe it was the day he'd had with Sonny, or the fact that it had finally sunk in that his parents' divorce was a real thing, but instead of saying nothing and staring forlornly out of his window as he might have done any other time he and his father were arguing, he said.

"I don't want any more life lessons from you."

It was silent for a minute before his father said, "What did you say?"

Henry repeated himself.

"I said, I don't want any more life lessons from you. I don't need them anymore."

"Oh, you think you're too old now to listen to me, is that it? You know better?"

"No, I'm not too old. I just don't want them from you. I've

realized that I don't care what you have to say about anything. You think you're trying to help me, but you're not. I'm not dumb. I know you've always thought that I'm gullible and weak. Too sensitive, I think were the words you used to use. Now, I know you just don't like me. You have no respect for me. Admit it. It's okay, Dad," Henry turned to face him, but his father kept his eyes fixed firmly on the road in front of him, "you don't have to like me or respect me. I really don't care anymore. Just don't tell me how to live, because I know not everything I'm doing is wrong. It can't be."

They turned off Lincoln onto one of the side streets that had a Polynesian name, Bali or Tahiti, it was hard to remember which. Tall, morose apartment buildings lined the street, identical in the overblown austerity of their architecture and the menace of their promise. Henry imagined them all full of men like his dad, men incapable of doing their laundry and resigned instead to roaming the halls in mumus and soiled undergarments like unsanitary apparitions; men eating unidentifiable meals out of cardboard containers and from wrappers, the disintegration of their livers and immune systems completely in sync, like a fraternity house's catastrophic binge-drinking circulatory network.

They pulled up in front of one of these buildings, *Neptune's Castle*, the sign over the front door said in a barely conscious attempt at nautical whimsy. Underneath it were the words: *Welcome home*, and it made Henry shiver just thinking about it as he and his father silently unpacked the boxes onto a waiting trolley.

Still not speaking ,they pulled the trolley through the lobby, his father in front guiding it, Henry in back steering it, and out through the back into the pool area. Although it was dimly lit, Henry could see a couple of ducks (bachelors too?) floating in the leafy water, ducking their heads into the water every once in a while in what to Henry looked like deep shame.

"See," his father said breaking the silence, "we've got a pool here. You don't have one of those at home," the insinuation being he had taken Henry and Grace into account when he signed the lease. "You and Grace can come over whenever you want and lay around. Sunbathe. Swim. Whatever. Nice, huh? And over here's a little gym where you guys can work out…" Henry didn't say anything but laughed to himself. He didn't think it was possible the extent to which his father didn't know them, but there he was, proving it by giving him a tour of amenities he'd be disappointed to find in jail. As they walked, Henry reached out his arm to pluck a kumquat off a tree, and as he did so a huge cloud of black dust shook loose making him cough as he inhaled the neglect. Oblivious, his dad kept on talking.

The elevator opened at the eighth floor and immediately Henry was greeted by the overwhelming stench of cheap cologne. The hallway was eerily silent as they pushed the cart down to his dad's apartment, number 809, the second to last door to the right.

His dad fumbled with the key in the lock for a minute until finally managing to open the door. "Ah-ha!" he said, with a proud smile of sincere accomplishment decorating his face. "Here it is."

The best that could be said of the apartment was that it was clean. Otherwise, the only thing really remarkable about it was its extreme drabness, its many shades of white competing for the eye's attention like an insane asylum's color palette. His father kept pointing out the banal features as Henry worked as fast as he could to pull the boxes off the trolley. All he wanted now was to get out of there and never come back. It wasn't only that it was depressing, but he could see how staying in a place like this might completely overwhelm him, make him forget there was an outside, a reality all unto itself.

After thirty minutes or so the boxes were all off the trolley. Henry put his hands in his pocket and looked at his dad.

"I guess that's it. I'm going home now."

His dad stared at him. "Don't you want to stay for a little bit? Hang out? I have a bottle of good Scotch somewhere. Have you ever tried Scotch? I mean really good Scotch?"

"That's okay, Dad. I have to get home. I have some homework I still have to get done. You know, finals and all that." He clenched his fists in his pockets.

"Okay, some other time," his dad said. "Let me find my keys so I can drive you home."

"That's okay," Henry replied. "I have a friend coming to pick me up. We're going to study together."

"Oh," his father said, nodding, "is it that guy who dropped you off at the house earlier?"

"Mm-hmm," Henry lied.

"Okay. I want to give you a couple of bucks and something to take home to your sister. Do me a favor and tell her how nice this place is, okay? I want to make sure I see as much of you guys as I did before. I don't want anything to change between us. This isn't about you guys. It's between me and your mom and that's it. Understand?"

He was already using that phrase *your mom* that divorced parents used when talking to their kids about their former spouses.

"Okay, Dad."

His dad turned to go into the other room but then stopped himself and turned back to Henry.

"About what you said earlier. I don't hate you, Henry. I don't think you're stupid or weak or any of those things." His dad's eyes roamed the walls, refusing to find Henry's face. "I know things, though, that you don't. I have a lot more experience than you, and I know that when you're older you're going to understand that I was right about a lot of stuff. You probably think I don't know anything. I was probably that way with my dad, too. When you're older, though…" he trailed off as he finally let his eyes meet Henry's. "Then you'll see."

"Fine," Henry said robotically. Time was slowing down, and he felt tiny beads of sweat coldly running down his back and his sides, like the point of a sharp knife cleanly slicing him open. No pain yet, but it was only a matter of time. In just a few seconds it would be overwhelming. But until then he was all anodyne awareness.

"Fine?" his father said. "That's it? 'Fine?'"

"Yeah. Fine."

"Henry…"

"What do you want me to say, and I'll say it? I want to go home now. If it makes you feel better for me to agree with you, then I'll do it. If you want me to smile, I'll do that, too. A pat on the back? A bear hug? Fine. All of those things? Fine. Fine. Fine. Just tell me, Dad. Tell me." His voice was coming apart, and tears were beginning to form. In a few seconds he wouldn't be able to hold it in anymore, any of it, and he would either have to take his hands out of his pockets and hit his dad or he would start sobbing so hard and so loudly it would shake this building down to its pathetic foundations.

His father walked back into the bedroom to get his wallet and when he did Henry noticed that the box at his feet held some of his dad's baseball cards, including the prize of his collection, the '52 Mantle. Without thinking, he unclenched his fists, picked up the card in its hard lucite case, and slipped it into his back pocket, and despite his well-honed sense of guilt, it didn't feel like stealing at all. It felt like payment for something, a long-standing debt that was his due for as long as he could remember.

His dad walked back in with two twenty-dollar bills, folded them, and handed the money to Henry.

"Put this in your pocket. One for you and one for Grace."

Henry took the money and shoved it into his pocket.

"I hope I'll see you sometime, Son. I really do love you. You know that, don't you? Even if you say you don't, you really do."

Henry bit his lip and nodded. Once again, his father was telling him how he should feel, and Henry realized that he couldn't help himself, that he would always have to impose his will on others to get what he wanted, that he lacked finesse, that he'd never learned to be selfless.

When he was back outside a few minutes later, he wandered aimlessly for a little while up and down the quiet Polynesian named streets and then headed back up to Lincoln to grab the bus. It was around nine o'clock. Rush hour had ended and now the streets were eerily vacant, laid open like a gutted animal, hollow of its traffic, a shell of something once great, but rendered silent, assigned a new purpose for the time being. Everything was alive until you decided it wasn't, he thought to himself, boarding the bus, already pushing the night with his dad to the back of his mind where it belonged with every other hazy memory he'd accumulated throughout his life, shapes and blurs with no hard edges.

When he got home, his mom and Grace were waiting for him in the family room, the TV tuned diligently to *Jeopardy*. There was a stillness in the house he hadn't anticipated, like sound was a trapped bird colliding with a window again and again as it tried to make its escape, dully pounding the ears but possessing no real resonance, no shape to testify to its substance. He wondered if they felt it, too, but there was no chance to ask them because when he came in they were instantly up and around him, asking him what it was like over there, how his father had been, what had he said.

"Wait, wait," Henry said getting anxious. "I'll tell you." He heard himself speak but couldn't feel the words. It was like they had no meaning. "There's not a lot to say other than it was really sad. He thinks it's going to be one way, but I don't think that's the way it's going to be. Also, I don't know if he's ever done laundry before."

Instantly his mother was in tears. Grace and Henry stared at her, bewildered, and she glared back at them angrily.

"What? I did live with him for twenty-five years," she said, her voice quivering like something flimsy, "and I loved him for most of it. It breaks my heart to hear about him not doing well. What if he never has clean clothes again?"

Grace pulled her mother to her and put her head on her shoulder and rubbed her back.

"There, there," she said gently as she stared at Henry to show him she had absolutely no idea what she was doing.

*   *   *

The whole next week at school Sonny kept his distance from Henry, turning around when the two made eye contact in the halls between classes, averting his eyes as Henry walked to where he was sitting with some other people at lunch, purposely being the last person to come into class so he could find a desk as far away from Henry as possible. After a week of that Henry kept his distance. At least, he thought to himself, Sonny had the decency not to hide in a closet the way Henry had done when he was trying to avoid Cal what seemed like months ago now.

Henry ate his peanut butter and jelly sandwich by himself; it was April and the sun was everywhere, spilled across the campus like red wine on a white carpet, staining everything with the fresh smell of spring and those wavy-colored lines that crawled in front of his line of sight every time he turned his head, lines he once thought were worms in his brain when he was little, but now knew to be bits of blood, a thought that made him sick to his stomach when he thought about it for too long. Chess club was closed and so was the band room. Lucky for him he found a shady patch of lawn and picked at blades of grass with one hand while he fed himself the sandwich with the other. When he was done, he toyed with the idea of ditching fifth period (geometry, which he was getting a D in anyway) to go up to the gas station and buy some candy and maybe a magazine, when someone stepped in front of him, a huge form backed by the sun so Henry couldn't see who it was. He felt a shock of adrenaline pulse through him as he put his hand up to shield his eyes, but when the figure knelt down he saw that it wasn't Sonny, but Cal, come to pick over the carcass of the recently friendless.

"Where's your friend?" Cal asked.

Sometime in the last day or two Cal had given himself a Mohawk, a short one, like De Niro at the end of *Taxi Driver*. He also was wearing his green Army jacket buttoned up all the way to the top so that he looked a bit like a militant Eskimo.

"Where's your hair?" Henry answered back as matter-of-factly as possible.

"Ha ha," Cal replied as he started to go through Henry's lunch bag for scraps of food. Before he could snag it, Henry popped the last corner of his peanut butter sandwich into his mouth and smiled as he worked the dry hunk of food around in his mouth.

"Where's your friend?" Cal asked again. He took a pack of Marlboro Reds from his jacket pocket and offered Henry one as what felt like to him a small bribe.

"He's not my friend," Henry answered, taking a cigarette although he didn't really smoke.

"No kidding," Cal answered, and they walked together, silently, behind the administration building and lit up. They smoked in silence and just as Henry was crushing his butt out beneath his heel, Cal looked at him and said, "I'm thinking of starting a band. Do you want to be in it?"

Henry laughed, shouldering his backpack. Almost time for another hour of living up to his own sub-par expectations of himself.

"I don't know how to play anything and neither do you. Won't be much of a band."

"That's okay. None of these guys do when they start. The Clash. The Germs. The Circle Jerks. They just start and then they learn as they go. We can do that, can't we?"

"So it's going to be a punk band?"

"What else would it be?"

"I don't know," Henry said. "Ever listen to Neil Young?"

Cal laughed.

"That fucking hippie? Yeah, right. Nice one."

Henry didn't try to go any further with it.

"Fine," Henry answered, "I'll be in your band. Don't we need a third, though? Drums, guitar and bass? Who's going to play what?"

"Nothing says you have to start with three. We can do it,

just you and me, and then if we find someone we like, then great. Otherwise, we'll just be a power duo. Like Simon & Garfunkel, only we'll sing about murder, mayhem and anarchy instead of our feelings."

Henry laughed. He was starting to feel good for the first time in a week.

"Are you saying those things aren't feelings? I feel mayhem-y all the time."

"You're right," Cal laughed. "I can barely contain my anarchy sometimes."

They went back and forth discussing possible band names, beginning first with funny-sounding diseases, dictators, and then moving on to serial killers. It had to be menacing, that much they both knew, but it also had to take the piss out of menace at the same time. A good name needed to have both those elements so people didn't know if you were joking or not, which was where the real menace came from in the first place.

"How about 'Half Mast'?" Cal suggested brightly.

Henry shook his head as he twirled a plucked piece of grass.

"Too much room for dick jokes."

"True," Cal said, a little deflated.

The lunch bell rang and in a few short moments they were enveloped in a sea of legs marching off to their fifth period classes. A fog of noisy chatter clouded the air above them as they sat there looking skyward, the high afternoon sun bleaching out the faces to whom the legs belonged.

"I like it like this," Cal said, one hand shielding his eyes and the other propping himself up. "When I can't see their faces. I like them more when they're just legs. I think I connect to them more this way. This must be how guys become leg men later in life. Maybe fetish is all perspective."

Henry laughed and then stopped. Something in what Cal had just said, perspective and anonymity and all that.

"I've got it! I've got the name," he was squeamish with delight. "Neighbor Kids."

Cal was silent for a few seconds as he processed it, he plucked some grass, threw it down.

"It's perfect," he said, his face serious and pensive. "It's perfect because you don't know who these kids are, right? They could be us, they could be them, they could be anyone, and because they're so invisible you don't know where they are or what they're going to do."

Henry nodded. "You don't know what they're capable of."

Cal smiled. "Exactly. You don't know what they're capable of."

Cal repeated Henry's words with relish and then quietly pondered its greatness. There were so few times when you happened upon a perfect thing, and when you did, you just had to kind of sit there and admire it.

They grabbed desks next to one another at the back of the geometry room and spent that period and the next working on song lyrics, album names, logos…all the ephemera that made a thing real. After school they went to the public library and found a table deep in the stacks where they continued to trade ideas, draw, and laugh. It was only after a couple of hours that Henry realized they were near the reference section where his favorite books were shelved, Nostradamus and the Jane's volumes, and he saw the proximity as a good omen.

It was almost dark when Grace and a couple of her friends suddenly came around the corner.

"Henry!" Grace squealed, genuinely glad to see him.

"Gr-race? What happened?" he asked, stunned.

She laughed, stuck her arms out to her sides, and twirled around.

"What do you think?"

He'd left for school after her that morning but apparently a couple of hours was all it took, because where yesterday she was the sister he always knew, today she was dressed like a punk rock chick; half of her shoulder length hair had been shaved off and she wore a black tank top and tight-fitting black jeans. A studded belt circled her waist and dark mascara clouded her eyes in a sensual haze.

"It looks punk," he said softly, not sure what to say.

"Thanks," she said, a little puzzled by his tepid response.

"Sorry," he backpedaled, "I'm just surprised. When did you do that?"

"It's not like I killed someone, Henry." Her friends laughed at this. "I'm just trying something new. I'm out of here in a few months. Nothing says I have to go back east next fall looking like I grew up at the beach."

Her confidence, as always, astounded him. What she decided in a couple of hours would have taken him months of fretting, weighing, and agonizing so intensely that in the end making a change wouldn't be worth all the aggravation.

She smiled but then recognized that it was Cal he was sitting next to him and her smile quickly dissolved.

"What are you guys doing here?"

Unexpectedly, the question rankled him. There, deep in the library, was the one place on earth he felt a little provenance, a semblance of belonging that was absent everywhere else in his life, including his own skin. He felt embarrassed to tell her that they were starting a band. It felt too predictable, too pathetic in a way. He was about to tell her that he'd talk to her when they got home, but Cal had no hesitation.

"We're starting a band," he said in that voice of his that was a line being drawn in the sand of a beach that no one ever visited. That no one even knew existed.

As Cal said the words, Henry felt a shiver of embarrassment icily trace its way through his veins, creating within him a sketch of something illuminated and starkly ashamed. He wished he could have told her this in his own way, to minimize the questions that would come next, the conversation that was going to feel like an accusation. He knew how to handle her, he knew the finesse it took to win her over. Not to convince her of a thing, because she was too smart for that, but to move her far enough that she'd take his side. It was a short distance, the measure of their love. *Let it go*, he willed her in his head. If they were at all connected, she'd be able to read his most desperate thoughts, right? Like the way Leia and Luke knew when the other one was in trouble even all the way across the universe.

She scratched the side of her neck and then pulled absentmindedly at the three or four earrings that dangled from her ear. Those were new, too. All of her was new, he thought. Now he'd have to spend the short time they had left with one another going back and excavating what remained of the old part of his sister, the part he could depend on more completely than he could any feeling that resided in his own flimsy body.

"But you don't play an instrument," she said looking now at Henry and Henry alone, boxing Cal out of her line of sight and out of her awareness generally. That was one of her skills, making Henry feel as though he was the only person in the world.

He shrugged. "I'll learn."

They stared at one another until it became uncomfortable, and one of Grace's friends made a stupid joke to break the tension. It was the end of the year and the girls were there as part of their yearbook committee duties to find some funny pictures to use in the margins of the Annual. Sometimes Henry forgot that Grace was part of the whole high school industrial complex thing. She didn't take it seriously, she could be whoever she wanted to be despite all that other shit that made her seem to other people like a cog in that machine. As an explanation, though, that wouldn't work on Cal. Henry knew exactly how Cal saw this. To him she was wearing a costume, dabbling in something he took deadly serious. From her side, she was just being the over-protective big sister, and he appreciated that instinct of hers, loved her for it, but it also made him feel voiceless, invisible, a motive and not really a person at all.

The silence grew louder, became the shape of something vicious, panting, producing a slobbering noise that was the buzzing of the fluorescent bulbs, its heartbeat the adrenalized echoes of footsteps that came back to surround them from other sections of the library. Henry felt his own heart start to beat faster than it should, instinctually fearing a confrontation that now felt inevitable, the proportions of which had no relation to any part of reality as he saw it.

"Can you just leave? Please. I can't..." He was about to say that he couldn't take it anymore, but he resisted the urge. He didn't want to sound too dramatic even though that's exactly what his nerve endings were egging him on to say.

Grace looked at him like she'd just been slapped. He was still the only one that could reduce her to rubble like that, melt her down for spare parts with just a few words or a hurt stare. He'd never taken advantage of it before, but he had always wondered *why me?* He had an inkling that it had to do with the empathy she had flowing through her, deep reserves of pity and pathos she could dredge up just for him when the mood was right, when words failed them both.

"Don't forget we have dinner with Dad tonight," she said, finally looking away from both of them. "He's taking us to the Cheesecake Factory in the Marina. It'll be a hoot." Her words trailed off and were captured in a pit of hurt feelings. She plunged her hands into her pockets, blew a loose strand of hair out of her wide blue eyes, and followed her friends as they marched like a doomed expedition deeper into the stacks.

When she was gone, Cal began to furiously shove all the papers they'd been working on into his backpack.

"What the fuck..." he sputtered. "Why was your sister dressed like that? Who the fuck does she think she is?"

Henry was stunned. There had always been a tension between them that he guessed was mistrust on her part and some kind of never-gonna-happen crush on his, but he had never guessed there was so much anger mixed up in it, too. Clearly he had missed something. "I suppose you gave her the mixes I made for you, too," Cal spat.

"So what?" Henry looked at him and noticed for the first time all of the tiny nicks all over his scalp from where he'd cut himself shaving off his hair. There must have been a lot of blood, he thought.

"So what!?" Cal was yelling now. He was losing control.

"That music is for anyone. Not just us. I know you think it's our thing, but to some people it's just songs. Not everyone gets into it the way..." he stopped himself from saying 'you,' "we're into it. Fuck, Cal, don't make this into something it's not. My sister's not a poseur. She's not like all the others." He started to feel hot. Too hot. It was probably just him. "She knows what it's like to feel different. In three months she's out of here. In three months she'll start college and that'll be it. I know she's counting the days and it kills me," his voice began to crack, just a little, just enough so that he couldn't count on himself to not become completely undone. "It kills me because whether you want to see it or not she's just like us and she has been since the beginning. And both of you are idiots for not seeing it." There was nothing really else to say, and he trembled for having come to the end of it.

"No!" Cal growled at him getting right in his face and Henry smelled gum on his breath and cigarette smoke beneath that. "She's not like us. Don't ever say fucking say that! You're either us or you're not. There's no 'like us.' That's not a thing. It's all or nothing. You're such a fucking weakling, Henry. Pick a fucking side, why don't you. Stand up for something in your shitty little life."

The librarian rounded the corner and said in her best firm voice, "I'm going to have to ask you boys to leave the library right now."

Cal got right up in her face, and for a second Henry was worried he was going to hit her.

"Fuck you," he said viciously and walked calmly out the front door.

Henry followed, fumbling through a litany of apologies like a novice priest as he grabbed his things and took off after Cal. He didn't have to search hard for him, though. Cal was sitting on the curb right in front of the building, his face buried in his hands.

It was getting on toward dark now, six o'clock, a time of day Henry had always associated with despair. Everywhere people were getting into the rhythms that would lead them into nighttime. Men were leaving their offices, their top buttons undone, neckties loosened, pinched faces dreading the commute, dreading their families, and most of all, dreading knowing that tomorrow they'd have to do it all again. Likewise, moms with their whining kids were leaving the library or karate class or the orthodontist's office or whatever thing it was they felt would make their children more well adjusted. As if that was a thing that could be learned. As if that thing could be practiced. And the kids themselves? The kids were beyond exhausted, nothing more than well-tempered leather that had been worked by force into a usable shape. Kid wallet. Kid belt. What about one of those leather masks that had the zipper over the mouth? They made those, too. Whatever you wanted. They could make it all.

Days stuffed to the gills. Nights slashed open to spill out the guts of the thing.

Henry didn't want to choose, but he knew that Cal was right in a way. Even if you didn't want to pick a side, one day you'd be forced to and there would be no getting around it. Sitting next to Cal, he pulled from his shoulders the grey Dolt backpack he'd owned since the fifth grade. Reaching into it, he felt around the lint, scraps of paper, and uncapped pens that collected at the bottom until his hand closed around the thing he was looking for.

Pulling out the baseball card he'd stolen from his father's collection he held it out to Cal and tapped him gently on the shoulder.

"Know what this is?"

Cal slowly uncovered his face and looked at the card tucked away in its hard plastic case.

"No."

Henry smiled. He normally wasn't the one flush with knowledge, and it felt empowering, for once, to be in control, to be the one who had the information to give instead of always being at the simpleton's end of a conversation. Fucking small victories. "This is the 1952 Topps Mickey Mantle baseball card. Notice the corners. No bends at all. No wrinkles anywhere on the card and the back," he flipped it over gently, slowly, like he was revealing the greatest secret of all time, the fucking Rosetta Stone for all their teenage woes. "No gum stains, no nicks, no rubber band marks anywhere from where some dumb kid might have bunched it together with a bunch of other cards. When a card like this is in this kind of condition, do you know what they call it?"

Cal shook his head.

"Gem mint. Isn't that funny?"

"How do you know all this?"

Henry shrugged. "I had to." That wasn't quite right, but they were the words that popped into his head.

"What's it worth?"

"About five thousand dollars," Henry answered nonchalantly. "It's enough to buy us all our instruments, amps..." he wasn't sure what else they might need so he stopped rather than make a fool of himself.

"Did you steal it from your dad?"

Henry shrugged. "Technically. But I also felt..." Dangerous waters those grey areas, because once out there they'd have to be defended until the end.

Cal nodded as he gently took the card into his own hands, weighed it, trying to make sense of its relative value. "You felt like he owed it to you, right? Is that what you were going to say?"

Henry shrugged.

"If you feel that way, then you're probably right. He probably did owe it to you. And more."

Cal handed the card back to Henry and smiled. It was all going to be okay. Larceny, as well as pale reasoning, would see to that. But justifiable, Henry thought to himself, as the two friends stood, said goodbye, and parted ways for the evening, a decision worth its weight in gold.

*   *   *

The next few days were the most perfect of Henry's life.

Back at it with the song lyrics, the record cover illustrations, and—new to the calculus—they'd added magazines like *Guitar World* and *Bass Player*, because pretty soon they'd have the money in hand to own the things they suddenly couldn't live without. They pored over the pictures of Gibson SGs, Fender Telecasters, Gibson Flying Vs and their heads spun with the possibilities. They'd decided somewhere along the way that Henry would play guitar because he had smaller fingers. He was dead set on the SG. Black. It had to be black. No special reason other than no other color made sense. Cal was going to get a Fender P-Bass. Classic and practical.

It took Henry a few hours of obsessing over the details of the instruments before he realized that what he liked about it was how much it reminded him of the *Jane's* books he used to compulsively memorize when he was a kid. The pictures in the magazines, the shiny instruments with their high-gloss finishes, streamlined and beautiful, posed around the necks of the rock stars in the ads reminded him of the weapons he once longed for, and he was struck, after all these years, that it wasn't the weapons themselves he was interested in, but their details. It was details he was hungry for. Facts and measurements, the proof of a thing, the weight and feel of it in his arms or strapped around his neck. String gauge or ammunition caliber, it didn't matter. As long as he could put his hands on it. That's what mattered.

The plan was that on Friday they'd ditch school after lunch, hop the RTD to Hollywood, and go to a baseball card shop he knew about off Hollywood Boulevard. After that they'd go directly to Nadine's, the music store on Santa Monica Boulevard, and get the gear which they'd store in Cal's garage until they figured out where they would practice.

"Won't your parents want to know where you got it from?"

"They never go in the garage," Cal assured him, circling pictures in *Bass Player* magazine. "It was supposed to be for me and my hobbies. They wanted me to have space to be creative or some shit like that."

What an amazing concept, Henry thought.

"Did you ever use it for anything?"

Cal's eyebrows bent into a suspicious arc. "Are you kidding me?"

The next few days their excitement continued to grow as a religious fanatic might work himself into a fervor feeling the end of days were right around the corner. Friday. Friday. It was a holy relic that possessed all the answers, every shallow promise would be borne out, would be the first few wailing infant breaths of their new life. When they weren't together with their heads bent close over top-secret documents, knee-deep in ecstatic conspiracies, Henry worked on his own developing themes for their albums with an enthusiasm that could only result in self-immolation. This was adolescent bioluminescence at its finest, sincere and toxic. In their planning they were already on their third album and in Henry's opinion it was time for them to loosen up a little bit, the first two having been focused on alienation and politics respectively. Number three would be more about girls and relationships since by then they'd both probably have had a couple of serious girlfriends and enough sexual experience to speak authoritatively on the issue. Henry wouldn't go too crazy, though. He'd be the more constrained of the pair, sow his wild oats early on, and settle down with a nerdy-looking girl with a page-boy haircut that had a blue streak running through it and a pair of thick black glasses and a penchant for writing anonymous erotica.

Even the weather was perfect those few days: slate grey skies nailed to the earth's ceiling like two-by-fours bracing the windows of a general store before a tornado came and did its own chaotic inventory. Some higher power was agreeing with them, supporting them like a medieval arts patron, and though he'd never considered himself a superstitious person in the past, he took these things collectively as a sign and he put his faith in that.

*　　*　　*

Thursday night was when everything blew up. He was up in his room and the phone started ringing, and even though it was easier to think it after the fact, he remembered feeling that the phone sounded different somehow, a little more urgent than usual, maybe the space between rings was a little shorter than it usually was, the ring itself tinnier and higher pitched, the machine channeling panic through its morbid wires. Those were easy things to think in retrospect so he never mentioned them to anyone, but he did lift his head from the desk where he was busy scribbling lyrics for a song about the similarities between class warfare and prom, heard the groan of Grace's bed as she leapt off it, footsteps and complaining floorboards as she ran across her room to grab the receiver. Silence from the room after that, a deep silence that was the collection of all the tension in the house, the neighborhood, quite possibly the world, and then the scream.

When they finally got her to calm down, she told Henry

and their mom what had happened. There had been a car accident earlier that night. Four kids from school were speeding home after swim practice and the car had blown a tire, gone up onto the tree-lined median, and smashed against one of the massive coral trees planted there. To say there were no survivors was an understatement. Grace, of course, knew all four of the victims. They were kids from the senior class, all friends of hers, all with plans for the fall. "Berkeley, UCLA, Arizona, and Colorado." She recited the names of the colleges they were planning on attending in the fall over and over like a prayer, already trying to remember them, keep them from fading the way the dead do. "I don't understand," she moaned as their mom stroked her hair. "I don't understand."

He knew who they were but didn't really know them. He knew them by sight, by the Oingo Boingo T-shirt one of them used to always wear, by the way another squealed whenever she saw her friends and threw her arms around them and hugged them tightly as though it had been ages since she'd last seen them instead of a day. The other two he wasn't sure about. One of them might have been the one who rode the red scooter to school and used a whole space to park it, a thing which drove Henry crazy even though he didn't own a car. The last one might have been the guy who said, "Nice shirt," to him in the hallway once when he was wearing his Clash T-shirt, an approval that had carried him through the day.

Their mom held her in her arms and rocked her until the flood of Grace's sobbing slowed to just a trickle, a consequence of fatigue and in no way a symptom of acceptance. Henry sat at the foot of the bed and watched them, unsure of what he should do, and had the hilarious realization that he was now the man of the house and as such should be doing something. He put his hand on Grace's ankle and squeezed it gently and she picked her head off their mother's lap, looked down at

Henry, and gave him the shadow of a smile.

He was reminded of the previous year when his friend Tyler had died. He knew the emptiness she was feeling, the breath-snatching cold wateriness of it all, the regrets and the guilt that made no sense but were suddenly the only accessible emotions, the only feelings that made sense to a body going through the first throes of grief. He sympathized with all of it and remembered how grateful he would have been if someone had been there to articulate it for him, but something shy in him made him hold his tongue, a quick round of second guessing himself about whether or not what he'd felt would have any bearing on this situation, that this was somehow worse and completely out of his range of comprehension. But grief was grief, he argued with himself, and before he could fully assess just how stupid of a thing that was to think, the doorbell rang, and he was glad to have a real reason to get up and move away from them and not just because he was starting to feel uncomfortable.

He opened the door to a handful of teenage girls, all of whom were in a different stage of despair. They moved past him like a runaway passion play and ran up to Grace's room in a scrum of sobs and sniffles.

Henry went to the kitchen, grabbed a six-pack of Diet Cokes out of the fridge (he wasn't exactly sure how many women were now upstairs but he figured it couldn't be more than six), took a box of Kleenex off the counter and headed upstairs.

Grace's room was awash in tears and the low constant rumble of moaning. He put the drinks and the tissues on the floor in the middle of a sort of half-circle they'd seated themselves in and said, "I thought you guys might need this."

Grace and his mom, who had also caught the crying bug, beamed at him as though the gesture was the most perfect thing he'd ever done in his entire life, and the girls began to grab the drinks and tissues en masse, cracking them open almost simultaneously so that the sound of the cans made him picture an enormous monster gleefully cracking its knuckles before inflicting whatever kind of horror struck its fancy at the moment.

One of the girls, he couldn't remember her name, stood and put her arms around him.

"Thank you," she said, and he felt her warm tears fall on his shirt, her body pressed firmly against his as though she was trying to fold herself into him. "You're so sweet," she whispered. He pulled away, asked if they needed anything else, and went next door into his own room where he could still hear the whimpering through the walls, the gut-wrenching agony. But they were only muffled sounds to him once he was in his room, kind of like a wave machine if the waves were a tsunami wrecking a small helpless fishing village somewhere on the other side of the world. He lay on his bed, felt the sound wash over him, through him, and without thinking too much about it, let his hand wander into his pants and jerked off right then and there, coming in no time. He hadn't even used lotion or spit and maybe that made it better, that he had done it dry, kind of like a punishment for the bad timing of it all. When he was done, he turned over and fell asleep immediately and didn't wake again until his alarm went off at seven the next morning. He hadn't slept so well in years.

*　　*　　*

The next morning he woke up to find the rain gone and the sky scraped to a perfect blue, the crystalline color of which had its own distinct resonance which was the tail end of something piercing, a vibration made long ago.

There was no sound coming from Grace's room. Either

they'd all left or they were still asleep in there, afraid to get up and face the monster grief hangover no amount of Advil or cranberry juice could cure. He smelled the jeans crumpled in a ball on his floor, pulled them on, and did the same with a shirt. Stains were one thing if they were dry, but bad smells were where he drew the line. Decency was a compromise you made with yourself.

Downstairs and still no sign of anyone. No congregation in the kitchen standing over the sink spooning cereal into their mouths, no yogurt with Grape Nuts, no Mom urging jackets or chewable vitamins that tasted like the rind of an old grapefruit.

He ate a quick breakfast and when he saw that his mom's car was gone, which probably meant she had left early to take Grace to school, he sighed and started out by foot to the bus stop. He couldn't blame them for forgetting about him considering everything that had happened, but he still wished they had just woken him up because, honestly, he was worried about Grace and wanted to see her before they got to school and went their separate ways. Whenever she cried, which wasn't often, he felt as though something was being torn out of him, something vital with a pulse, and he immediately became hopeless that there was anything he could do to fix things. If he saw her, though, and she wasn't crying this morning, he'd feel a little better about her being out of his sight for the rest of the day.

A slow dribble of cars trickled by. No one drove crazy in the morning because no one was in a rush to get to where they were going. In a cruel irony, all of the big car accidents he could remember seemed to happen at night when people were on their way to a party or home from a fun night out. Never in the morning when it might get you out of a day at school, laying around on the couch, legs propped up like a crippled aristocrat watching *Twilight Zone* reruns and sucking on lemon drops until the roof of your mouth hurt as bad as your sore back or whatever. There was a certain reverence, however, reserved for the morning, which was, in and of itself, a fickle god to be feared and appeased. You could never be sure which way the day would take you so it was best to stay under the radar if possible. Drive slowly, stay quiet, masturbate unenthusiastically…whatever it took not to be noticed.

Lost in thought, he didn't notice a car had pulled up next to him until the window was lowered and he heard Sonny call to him, "Yo, Henry, do you want a ride?"

The sun was already high and hot and the first few drops of sweat were already tickling his scalp. By the time he got to school he'd be a sweaty mess. He hesitated, though, because part of him couldn't help but be suspicious.

As if he'd read his mind, Sonny said, "Come on, man. I'm sorry I've been a dick the last couple of weeks." He looked at his watch. "Did you hear what happened last night?" And then more impatiently. "Just get in."

Henry opened the door, threw his backpack on the floor, and got in the car. They drove for a few minutes without speaking. The radio did the small-talking for them. Neil Young again, singing about love as if it were a protest song. Just to be a dick, Henry almost said *They're playing our song*, but decided against it. He didn't have it in him to be cruel to anyone but the people he loved best.

As if he were thinking the same thing, Sonny reached over and turned off the music. He cleared his throat and asked the same question again, "Did you hear about what happened last night?"

"Course I did," Henry said, looking out his window. "I had half the fucking girls from school at my house. Fun times."

"Fucking crazy, huh?"

Henry wasn't sure what Sonny wanted from him, so he stayed silent. He really had nothing to say, didn't feel particularly sad. In fact, the only real thing he felt was agitation because he knew that when they got to school everyone was going to be all sad and destroyed whether they knew the kids who died or not and the thought of it was balling itself up inside his chest more and more the closer they got. All those fake fuckers going into dramatic hysterics, turning themselves inside out with grief and agony, and it turned out Sonny was one of them. What a disappointment. What a fucking sham.

"I didn't know them," Henry said, tracing, nonchalantly, the outline of the sun on the window with the tip of his finger.

"Yeah," Sonny said, looking at him in surprise, "but still."

"Do you remember this kid named Tyler in our class who died a couple of years ago? He was short, had a bad limp. I think he had MD or MS or one of things with an M that makes you sicker and sicker and smaller and smaller until there's nothing left of you at all. Not even the disease is there anymore. There's just nothing." He closed his eyes and swallowed. *Why?* He asked himself. *Why do this now?* "Do you remember that guy?"

"No," Sonny said. He sounded confused.

No. You don't, because no one remembers him except for me. No one cared except for me and no one even pretended to care. So why should I care now? Why should I feel anything when my heart is telling me not to feel anything. Isn't that the only thing I should be listening to? Words better left unsaid. Or maybe only said to Cal. Yes, Cal would understand. He smiled and opened his eyes. The sun was still there, he hadn't traced it out of existence.

"I wasn't trying to get you to say anything when I kept trying to talk to you after…" *after what?* "…after last time. I didn't want anything from you. I didn't want you to do anything. I only wanted to be your friend."

Sonny reached into his shirt pocket, fished out a cigarette, and lit it without taking his eyes from the road. He leaned forwards and switched the tape back on. Neil Young was keening in his soft and beautiful way about a place called *Sugar Mountain*, just the tail end of a dream, a reason for longing.

"You say that like it's nothing," Sonny said, pulling the car into the school parking lot. He took a deep drag and flicked the cigarette into the ivy next to the sidewalk.

It didn't take Henry long to find Cal. He was hanging around the perimeter of a huge cluster of sobbing students. He looked puzzled and was trying to get as close as possible without being noticed.

Henry came up behind him and clapped a hard hand on Cal's shoulder. He jumped a little, turned, and then laughed when he saw it was Henry. A few of the kids in the grief amoeba threw caustic glances their way so Henry grabbed Cal by the strap of his backpack and pulled him into a hallway off the main quad.

"What the fuck is going on?" Cal asked.

Henry told him what had happened as they walked slowly through the halls. A light drizzle began to fall, soundlessly decorating the asphalt with careful circles as Henry told him everything he knew. And when they turned the corner at the end of the E Building, and he caught sight of the flag already lowered to half-mast, he told Cal the rest of it, too. About Tyler, about the fakeness… he was on a roll. If he kept going, he could have linked every fucking terrible thing that had ever happened in the history of the world to this accident. JFK, the Challenger explosion, everything that ever happened to Jodi Foster ever. He felt like he had the power to connect it all if he wanted, show how the pieces fit together, that tragedies were joined by how we reacted to them as a society, if by nothing else. The equal and opposite reaction being the threshold for what people were willing to accept the next time got higher and higher, as well as the associated expectations. The worse shit got, the more justified people felt to exercise their indignation, their self-righteousness, in whatever way they wanted.

"Shit," he said, winding up what had become a sermon of sorts. "They'd be fucking disappointed if this shit didn't happen."

Cal suddenly stopped and looked up.

"Wait, why hasn't the bell for first period rung yet?"

Henry looked around. Cal was right. There was no one in this part of campus, and all of the classroom doors were still locked.

Henry shrugged, and they circled behind the classrooms and walked past the utility field where they were stopped in their tracks by the sudden appearance of a wrecked car in the middle of the field. Its make and color were indistinguishable, as was its original shape. All of the glass that had once been the windows, windshield, back window, even the rearview mirrors was completely gone. Not a shard or a speck remained anywhere. The two tires that were left were both bent at impossible angles and the interior space had been compacted to the size of a hamster cage. The idea that four people had been sitting in it less than twelve hours ago seemed impossible, like the laws of physics had been somehow subverted for the sake of a joy ride. Fire had scorched the car body and there was a smell that he couldn't place. It was the smell of gasoline, and of burnt rubber, but also something tinny. Earthy. But when Cal pointed at the dashboard and Henry bent down to look inside and saw the wine stain of blood there, and down on the gear shift, and even on the parts of the seat upholstery that hadn't burnt up he realized that what he smelled was blood. What he smelled and couldn't place was everything coming together at one time.

"Hey!" a sharp voice yelled at them. "Why aren't you two at the assembly?"

It was Mr. Neville, the security guard. He had his walkie-talkie out and was pulling back his jacket so they could see the badge he wore on his belt as if they didn't know who he was.

"What assembly?" Cal asked, and Neville pulled a face like they were the two stupidest motherfuckers to ever walk the face of the earth. Before he could give voice to his revulsion, though, the doors to the main auditorium opened and kids began filing out, slowly, in what looked like two single file lines. They were preceded by the principal who was walking backwards at the head of the line, using a bullhorn to lead them toward the wrecked automobile.

"When you get to the car, I want you to really look at it. Study it. Think about what it must have been like for the four students who were killed in it because someone chose to drink and drive."

Henry saw his sister toward the front of the line. She had a Kleenex pressed to her nose and he could see, even from several feet away, that her eyes were full of tears. She was doing everything she could to hold it all together, physically and emotionally.

Grace and her pack of friends walked toward the car and, arm in arm, began to circle it. They moved slowly, carefully, penitents performing a cleansing ritual or maybe praying for a miracle. Either way, it was too late. That was the hardest fact to swallow. They would eternally be too late. The only noise was the principal's occasional bullhorn admonishments and little sobs that bobbed up here and there like the chirps of insects hatching on a perfectly warm summer's night.

Grace looked up and when she saw Henry, she pulled the Kleenex away to flash him a little smile, a brief show of teeth to let him know that she was still there, that she hadn't disappeared completely behind the snotty tissue and the low moans of regret.

Henry smiled back but suppressed the urge to wave, and as he turned around, saw Peter step out of the line and walk right up and stood in Cal's face.

"Were you smiling?"

Cal looked at him quizzically.

"Don't look at me like that, you fucking freak. I asked you if you were smiling."

"I wasn't smiling," Cal said, pointing at Grace who stopped, along with everyone else, to see what was going on. "She smiled at us so I was just saying hi…"

"No. You weren't saying 'hi'," he said 'hi' in a fake lisp. "You give a little wave when you're saying hi to someone. Or you tilt your head. That's how you say hi when people are dead. You don't smile."

Peter's voice was becoming a low growl, and looking down Henry saw him clenching and unclenching his fists. The adrenaline was almost palpable, as real as the smell of gas and the sound of smashing glass.

Henry wasn't the only one who felt it. Kids began to fall out of line and form a tight circle around the two would-be pugilists, the gravitational pull of the potential violence was undeniable. In just a few seconds nearly everyone had abandoned the car wreck and were crowded around Peter and Cal, and just like that they were mourners no longer; they were kids again, just kids, in the prime of their lives as far as being susceptible to immediate gratification went. They didn't lack empathy, but they were wide open, too far gone to ignore what was right in front of them.

Henry looked around for Grace and saw her still standing by the car. Abandoned by nearly everyone, it couldn't really even be called a car wreck anymore. It had been that for as long as they filed past it in their somber lines, trying to guess what "self-reflection" looked like, and what the correct walking speed for showing respect was. But as soon as they walked away, it became nothing more than a pale stand-in for tragedy, a monument. But Grace stayed, not ready to abandon her vigil. She was a true penitent, a keeper of the faith, and what was happening between Peter and Cal was sacrilege. It was the violation of a holy place and also maybe the realization that holy places were not in as plentiful supply as they once were. Every day there were fewer and fewer of them and stupid people, violent people, were the architects of their destruction.

Henry pushed his way through to intervene, through a sea of bodies that didn't want to part, that clung fast together in a contracted muscle of anticipation. Ducking his head down and using it like a steam shovel, he pushed whoever was in his path, incurring a slurry of "Watch out's!" and "Fuck you's!" along the way that he imagined, for some reason, were appearing in comic book word bubbles above his head. The sharp point of an elbow hit him square on the top of the head, making his skull ring and radiate pain down his neck. He stopped to catch his breath and then went back to it. He felt something wet, which he imagined was blood, begin to wet his hair and then delicately trickle down his forehead in a way that was almost relaxing.

When he finally made it to the center of the circle, he was out of breath.

"Peter…Peter…I saw the whole thing and he wasn't laughing. He was just smiling because Grace smiled at me and he was right next to me. Don't worry…"

Peter interrupted. "What the fuck happened to your head?"

He touched his face and his fingers came away sticky with blood.

Peter went on, not waiting for an answer, "Stay out of it, Henry. It's bad enough you hang out with this guy." He never took his eyes from Cal, and the sound of Peter's voice was like nothing Henry had ever heard. Low and deep and far away, it was a thing of tension, an animal trap hung together with the tautest of wires, trembling for the chance to collapse and smash bones.

Peter took a step closer to Cal so that their noses were almost touching and when Cal reflexively put his hand up to make some space between them, Peter immediately brought his arms up to his chest and shoved Cal as hard as he could, sending him flying to the ground. Cal's backpack must have been open, because suddenly their band stuff was everywhere. Drawings of their logo, song lyrics, lists of their possible stage names, fake tour itineraries, all of it was cartwheeling and gliding everywhere. Students began to step out of line to pick it up and as it dawned on them what they were reading, they began to smile and then laugh, handing the papers back and forth among themselves.

Henry and Mr. Neville both stepped forward at the same instant. Neville, with a surprising amount of spryness, went for Cal and Peter at one time, grabbing both of them gruffly by the arms, and led them away, reminding Henry that, in the great scheme of things, they were actually still kids.

Henry, for his part, started ripping pieces of paper out of people's hands and scooping them off the ground. Shame fueled him, a deep embarrassment that he'd done something terribly wrong by having this dream. He felt himself moving faster than he ever moved in his life, panting as he shoved the papers into his bag. A couple of seniors held sheets of paper over his head and pulled them away at the last second, so he snatched at air when he leapt to get them. He was jumping like that when Grace and her friends made their way in to him and when she started to mouth *What are you doing?* he didn't even wait for her to finish the sentence when he answered her back in silence, *It wasn't his fault! It wasn't his fault! He didn't start it!*

But it wasn't what she wanted to hear, and she walked away.

*   *   *

"Cal stabbed Peter, Henry! He fucking stabbed him!"

What preceded the stabbing was that, given the "emotional stress" of the day, both Cal and Peter were each let off with a stern warning. Future repercussions were mentioned, permanent records hung in the balance.

The next day, sitting in geometry, Henry tried to calm Cal down, tell him that it didn't matter, but nothing Henry said seemed to help and Cal continued to fume. "It's not fair," he kept muttering to himself. Henry watched him as he ground his pencil into his paper until the lead broke and he balled up the paper. "No, it's not," Henry answered, trying to be a good friend, but really he was only thinking about himself and the fact that Grace probably hated him now, not to mention that everyone knew about their band and how stupid they were for thinking about starting one. "It never is."

"They never notice us unless it's something bad. We're the human equivalent of fly-over states." Henry thought the comparison ridiculous but he kept his mouth shut. He still wasn't convinced that being invisible was a terrible thing. Some of those fly-over states seemed pretty nice to him, miles of nothing but green and brown boxes with a lonely house and baseball diamond thrown in for good luck. Sometimes you'd see the name of the town printed in all black caps on the side of a water tower. Always a stately name, something heavy with history and pride and not at all complicated.

Cal tried to get him to ditch after geometry, but Henry needed to get to sixth period. He'd been late with a couple of English assignments and he didn't want to give Mrs. Arnold any more ammunition to use against him. Real life loomed large, after all, and Mrs. Arnold's propensity for using literary references to describe their class performance had led to his being called 'Piggy' from *Lord of the Flies* longer than he'd care to remember.

"Did you get all of our band stuff back?"

"Most of it. I think," Henry said sheepishly.

In truth, he didn't want to even do the band anymore. It felt spoiled now, and for once, Cal was definitely not being paranoid. They were the laughing-stock of the school, and while he was sympathetic to the need for comic relief given the recent tragedy, he just wished they didn't have to be its source.

By the time he got home from school, Grace was already in tears and screaming about the knife, and he had a moment where he suddenly wondered if he'd gone back in time a day and there was still a chance he could undo everything that had happened between Peter and Cal after the assembly.

The story, when he finally got her to calm down enough

to tell him, was that on his way home from school Peter and a few of the other senior boys had jumped Cal. He'd been punched in the face a couple of times before he had the good sense to fall and cover himself up, but instead of stopping, Peter had kept on going, kicking him in the ribs and the head until someone had pulled him back and declared ambiguously that Cal had "had enough."

They turned to leave and hadn't taken more than a couple of steps, when Cal ran up behind Peter and slid an 8-inch hunting knife into the small of his back. He was trying to pull it out, apparently to finish whatever job it was he felt compelled to complete, when the other kids tackled him and held him down while one of them ran off to call 9-1-1.

"I'm going to the hospital now. He might die, Henry."

She grabbed her purse and stopped in front of the mirror in the entranceway to pinch her cheeks and dry and her eyes.

"I hope..." he started to say, but she cut him off.

"What's wrong with you, Henry? Why would you hang out with someone like that? And why did you act like that at school? Do you think this is funny? Do you think people dying is something to laugh at? My world is fucking falling apart, and you don't even seem to care. I thought you were always going to be there for me. I don't understand..."

Outside a car sounded its flimsy little horn.

"I have to go," she said, shaking her head, and made a large circle to get around him to the front door. She pulled it shut hard behind her as she went out and the door rattled noisily.

The house was dead silent, he couldn't even hear a creak and he felt more alone than he'd ever felt in his life.

As if on cue the phone rang, and before he picked it up he knew it was going to be Cal.

"Hello?"

"Can you come over?" It was Cal but it sounded like his voice had been dipped in glass and rubbed over a cheese grater.

"And when you come, bring the baseball card. Okay? Will you?"

"Sure," Henry replied. A cold spike stabbed down Henry's spine.

*　　*　　*

Amazingly, he'd never been over to Cal's house. He knew vaguely where it was, that it was a street called Charm Acres, and that it was north of school somewhere, one of those small twisting streets that when you reached it was like a world unto itself with trees and shrubs running wild and overgrown, a car or two rusting gently in front of one of the houses, feral cats scampering into shadows with such sudden mania that it made him wonder if an earthquake wasn't about to strike.

The only thing he did know about Charm Acres was that a bad thing had happened there once long ago, but that wasn't unique. Each of these streets was a legend more than a place, navigable in the sense that history was navigable, that stories were navigable, and that those legends, and not their physical location, was their true geography. All teenage related, of course, because it wasn't tragic unless the terrible thing happened to someone young and beautiful. Their little suburb was a map of tales like that, places with feelings, an atlas that needed a shrink and an exorcism, if only insurance would cover both. There was Bestor Street, where Doug Wilson took five hits of acid and went running down the street in the dead of night without any clothes on screaming about werewolves and Reagan, somehow conflating the two in a steadfast fit of socio-political paranoia. On Herradura,

Lindsay Renault ran into a sliding glass door, the shards exploded into her skin, punctured her lungs and drown her in a sea of her own budding blood. Charm Acres was famous because it was the street where a girl named Angela Fenner had gone crazy and lit her mother's little yapping Maltese on fire in their backyard.

Henry wasn't exactly sure where he was going when he walked onto Cal's street. He wished he had remembered to ask, but he had other pressing things to consider.

"Are you looking for the weirdo's house?"

Henry stopped and turned around looking for where the high-pitched voice had come from.

"Over here. No. Next one. Look up. In the window."

Swinging his head around, he caught sight of a kid staring at him through a screened window. He had one of those haircuts the surfer kids had with his hair dripping over his eyes like a wave collapsing over the appearance of intelligence.

"What'd you say?"

"*What'd you say?*"

The kid mocked him in a voice that was a natural disaster. Puberty, vitriol...whatever concoction of hormones that opened the ground under your feet at that age, dropped the ceiling on your head, turned you into a slathering refugee who'd just as soon kill someone for a copy of *Penthouse Forum* than to look at them. Whatever that natural disaster was, that's what the kid sounded like.

"Who's the weirdo?"

"*Who's the weirdo?*" There it was again. An aftershock. The kid looked like the type of moron who could keep this up for another thirty years.

Henry decided to ignore him.

"Which house is his?"

The kid swiped the hair from his eyes and pointed to his left.

"It's right here. Right next door."

Henry looked at the house. It seemed normal enough. A low white fence surrounded a well-kept lawn. Did Cal mow the lawn? he wondered. Was that one of his chores? Did Cal have chores? Jesus, he knew nothing about him.

"I didn't know the weirdo had any friends."

He felt the kid's eyes on him as he walked up to the front door. This must be that kid's haunted house, the place where he and his friends dared each other to ring the doorbell and run away. A place that was filled with creatures and murderers, that had hidden doors that led to torture chambers, maybe a retarded incest baby chained up in the kitchen they fed scraps of meat to when they were feeling generous. And there he was, walking up to it calmly, like it wasn't anything. *What do you think is in here, you scared little fuck?* He only mumbled the words, though, in case Cal's parents were right on the other side of the door listening. What a first impression that'd make.

He knocked and heard the sound of his fist echo through the house that gave back a sound that made him think it must be hollow and cold inside.

He looked back over his shoulder and saw the kid still staring at him. Maybe he was a quadriplegic or, better yet, brain-damaged and was only able to communicate through insults. Henry liked the idea that it was a cry for help. Everything became instantly relatable when you saw it through the lens of pity.

Elegant little footsteps could be heard approaching the door from the other side. He'd never tried to imagine what Cal's parents might look like, but suddenly notions of obese chain-smoking trolls with prominent scars and gargantuan appetites for abuse and neglect swirled in his head and he involuntarily flinched as the door opened.

But the woman who answered the door couldn't be further from his hysterical premonition. Cal's mom was short and, while not old exactly, gave off the vibe of someone who was happily embracing the prospect of aging. She wore a long navy skirt made from some long-outlawed petroleum-based fabric that hung to her ankles and an immaculately ironed beige blouse. Conservative high heels in flesh-colored stockings, and makeup and hair fit for being a witness at an execution completed the look. But it was her smile, more than anything else, that was the heartbreaker. Sincere and loving, it was clearly the mask of someone broken, someone longing to be kind and caring, but with no one to bestow her natural impulses upon. He could instantly tell she was a good person but also incredibly sad.

"You must be Henry," she said in a prim English accent.

"Hi," he said lamely, caught completely off guard.

"Come in, come in," she backed away from the doorway to make room for him to come in. "Cal is going to be so happy to see you. He's been so sad lately."

He stepped inside and waited for her to tell him it was okay to walk in.

"Go, go," she said, shooing him into the living room.

The house was immaculate and quaint, a perfect vessel for channeling anxiety. It was like stepping into a living room in 1950s England. Wood paneling, an uncomfortable-looking beige sofa that looked firm enough to torture someone on, a row of plates with bird illustrations mounted on the wall. All of it seemed designed to make one feel uncomfortable. Not deeply so, but enough that he was instantly seized with the fear of breaking something priceless or irreplaceable.

"Would you like a cup of tea, dear?" Her accent was a perfect blend of colonial and matronly, and it made him feel like she was just as likely to give him a hug as she was to cane him.

No one had ever offered him a cup of tea before and he thought of saying yes, if for nothing else but the novelty of it, but was worried he wouldn't know the right way to drink it, or worse, that he wouldn't like it. She'd stand over him with that accent and ask him what was wrong with it and he'd have to say nothing and sit there and drink it all while she watched, knowing that he hated it, but not willing to let him off the hook because 'that wasn't the way they did things in this house' or 'god save the Queen' or whatever reason for suffering he couldn't quite imagine.

She led him down a hallway and pointed to family photos on the wall along the way.

"Look at Cal," she said, pointing at a picture of a little boy about five years old, a smile a million miles long stretched across his face ending in adorable dimples, Superman's *S* displayed proudly on his T-shirt. "He was such a cute little boy, wasn't he?"

Almost the exact same picture of Henry hung in his house. Same Superman shirt, same luscious brown hair, same indefatigable smile. How they had gone from there to here in just over ten years was a mystery to him, just as how the heart stretched and bent yet still survived was also a mystery.

In another picture, an even younger Cal was at the beach with his parents. They were all smiling against the glare of the sun, as if their happiness was something that had to be proved, and little Cal, his sweet white head protected by a little bonnet, clenched a plastic pail and shovel in his chubby little fist. Behind them was a sign that said, 'Shuffle Your Feet for Stingray." Henry smiled. What a fucking great name for an album, he thought, but he quickly corrected himself. Who was he fooling? There would be no band now. There weren't going to be any albums or tours, nor would either of them would learn an instrument. Those plans were over, a piece of a different life.

"Very cute," he offered politely. "The cutest."

She smiled at him and said, "Thank you."

The hallway dead-ended at a narrow staircase and as he followed her up it, he looked above him and saw a beam overhead and decided that this was where Cal had imagined hanging himself. There didn't seem to be any other place to do it. Besides, the drama of it would be hard to deny. His mother would come home after work one day, make a plate of cucumber sandwiches for him, and then, at the end of the hallway of family pictures, there he'd be, swaying slightly in an invisible breeze, a purple-faced metronome with a 'Fuck You' note stuffed in his pocket.

At the top of the stairs she knocked softly at the door. There was no answer, so she knocked again. The voice that came back was the one he'd heard on the phone earlier, the one that didn't belong to Cal.

"What?"

"Darling, your friend Henry is here."

"Come in," he said, then added angrily. "Henry only!"

She smiled at him and then they did that awkward trying to change places in a tight space dance.

"Try to get him to eat something, Henry. Maybe he'll listen to you."

Henry smiled and went into the room.

"Close the door, man," Cal spat at him as he walked in.

Henry's heart beat nervously as he quickly shut the door

and turned around.

The room was nothing like he imagined it would be. Instead of the punk rock posters, floor strewn with dirty clothes, empty cans of beer and overflowing ashtrays he expected to find, what he saw instead was what felt like the New York apartment of a Yuppie. There was an oval floor rug covering the wood floor, a Monet print on the wall, a stereo with LPs, CDs, and tapes stacked and organized neatly in alphabetical order, and then there were the books. Row upon row and shelf upon shelf of books. Henry scanned a few of the titles and found, to his surprise, they were self-help books, books on religion, books about cults like the Hari Krishnas and the Children of Light. Not a Douglas Adams or Stephen King novel among them.

"Look at me, Henry."

But Henry didn't want to turn around. He didn't want to see what they'd done to his face, because then it would be impossible to say no to whatever else Cal might ask him to do.

Cal started crying. "Please, Henry." There was so much desperation in the voice Henry was afraid Cal would drown in it.

When he turned he flinched involuntarily at what he saw. A black and blue baseball-sized contusion rose from Cal's face calling to attention the specific shape of his orbital socket. His nose was clearly bent to one side and finger-shaped bruises crisscrossed his neck where someone had obviously tried to choke him. Henry stifled a gasp.

"They tried to kill me," he said softly. "You see that, right?"

Henry nodded and let his eyes drift to the window where outside trees moved lusciously, languidly, proving beyond the shadow of a doubt that god had not a care in the world.

"Did you bring the card?"

Henry put his backpack down and took out the card, handling it carefully as though it were a bomb that might go off.

Cal sat on his bed and stared intently at it, studying first the front and then the back.

"Five thousand?"

"I don't know if that's what you'll get for it, though. If you take it to that store near Nadine's, you can probably get a thousand."

"Where is that?"

"Right off Hollywood Boulevard."

"Right, right." Cal's gaze drifted away. "All I ever wanted was…"

His words trailed off, but Henry knew what he wanted to say, because it was what he was thinking, too.

"What?" Henry asked. "Say it." He needed to hear it. He needed to hear someone else say what he was feeling, what he'd been feeling all along.

"How do you know if the way you feel love is the way everyone else does?" He sounded so innocent when he asked it, so helpless, that Henry felt legitimately guilty that he didn't have an answer. He understood, though, the need to know, to feel as though there was some parallel to you out there, a moment in amber, a meridian running under the ground connecting your feet to someone else's. "I can't stand not knowing, because if you don't know that, then what chance do you ever have of being happy?"

"Grace isn't talking to me. She thinks you're crazy and that I'm crazy for being friends with you. I know what's going to happen. She's going to stay away from me all summer, and then in the fall she'll go off to Brown and that'll be it. I'll never see her again."

"I'm sorry if I…"

"You didn't do anything."

"You know what I'd like more than anything?" Cal said, staring vacantly ahead as though he were looking at a map, studying it, trying in vain to achieve some modicum of location. "I'd like to go to another place and just start over. New friends, new clothes, new everything. I think I could get it right next time, knowing what I know now. Do you think I could do it?"

"You mean really disappear and start over someplace else?"

"No, I know that I can't really do that. I'm just asking, if it were possible, do you think I could force myself to be someone else? And do you think that would make me happy?"

Henry picked at his nails as he thought of what to say. From downstairs he heard the thumping of a dryer and thought of Cal's mom down there, dutifully trying to get the blood out of Cal's clothes, the incident only a temporary setback, because in the back of her mind he was sure it was only a matter of time before everyone else saw what a sweet boy she had.

"I don't think it works like that," Henry said softly as he thought of Grace, who would be leaving to go off to a college in just a few months. "It'd be nice, but I think in the end you'd always just wind up being yourself. That place you're talking about doesn't exist."

Nodding, Cal shifted his gaze so that his eyes met Henry's. He'd finished trying to find the Fountain of Youth, Atlantis, El Dorado or any of those other places that existed almost exclusively in the minds mistaken for atlases of those who tried to find them. His ship had crashed, and he was stranded there with them, awash on an island as much hostile as it was indifferent, and the problem was, it wasn't clear which bothered him more.

"That's what I think, too," Cal said. "Stuck, stuck, stuck. Like a rat in a trap."

"It doesn't have to be like that," Henry said, trying to cheer him up. "Disappearing isn't the only solution."

Cal thought about it for a minute.

"You're right. I guess I could also kill them all."

The hair on Henry's arms stood up as he searched Cal's broken face for traces of humor, sincerity, anything. He'd take anything at this point if only to know where exactly he stood. But Cal's face wasn't easily read anymore. Peter and his friends had seen to that.

"Don't look so worried, Henry. Jesus, I'm kidding."

The dryer stopped and they heard his mom begin to hum something that sounded familiar to Henry, but couldn't quite place. It was an earnest tune, wistful, but before he could figure out what it was, Cal put on a Misfits record. "20 Eyes" tore apart the silence like a thing with claws.

"What are you going to do with the money?" Henry asked him, wishing that Cal would turn the music down just a little.

Cal shrugged.

"I don't know, but I need to get out of here."

"Where are you gonna go?"

Cal shrugged again. That subtle show of apathy and nonchalance was becoming his signature move.

"Maybe England. I have a British passport, because," he gestured at the floor, "my mom."

"Right," Henry said as he tried to imagine Cal in London, sporting a spiked mohawk and giving the two-fingered 'up yours' salute to every twat that walked by with a briefcase. But then he remembered that no one really dressed like that anymore, and besides, he couldn't really see Cal going overseas. There was something about him that seemed quintessentially American.

After a few minutes more of silence, Henry got up, said goodbye to Cal, and headed down the stairs. Cal's mother was waiting by the front door. Her eyes were red from crying but the smile was there. He imagined it always was.

"Going already?"

"Yes, ma'am. Homework," he shrugged.

"Good lad," she said. "I do hope you come again." Her voice was sweet and spindly, as fragile as a sugar sculpture. "Cal really does speak highly of you. A boy needs a best friend, don't you think?"

He smiled in response and closed the door behind him, hoping with everything in him that the boy next door wouldn't see him. That he'd just be left alone.

*   *   *

At home, Henry ignored his mother's entreaties for him to "have something to eat" and went straight to his room. Out of nowhere, a burst of adrenaline surged through him, pinning him against the wall like a school bully demanding lunch money or some other token tariff of humiliation. He surrendered to it and stalked around his room. Circle after circle, ticker tape breathing, he wanted to destroy everything, but that would bring his mother and Grace up to his room. Then they'd want to talk, and he would be helpless against that, against their wanting to love him.

The next few days flew blurrily by, shapes of days, of things to do, not the real thing at all. Not in the slightest. School was suspended for the next couple of days as administrators tried to figure out how to handle the incident. Parents were frantic, deluging the school with calls, demanding to know whether or not their children were safe, and in the next breath, wanting to know how something like this could happen. It was the serve and volley of outrage: attack, fall back, defend, repeat until exhausted or until the bigger, better outrage came along. Victimhood was the new sainthood, and it seemed everyone was looking for a piece of the immortal pie.

*　　*　　*

A few days later school was scheduled to start back up on a day that was sunny and warm, the sky blue enough to touch, with just enough of a breeze to stir the air slightly. He dressed, brushed his teeth, and combed his hair, all like he would any other morning. But it wasn't like any other morning. He knew that. School was going to be different from here on out. Peter had seen to that. And so had Cal. It would be a long time before things were normal again. This year was certainly off the table. Maybe by the time his senior prom came along, he'd be able to show his face on the quad. He was there, but not there. What did hippies call it? Disassociation? He stopped brushing his teeth and let a frothy mouthful of spit trickle over his lower lip and splash, flatly, into the sink. Staring into the mirror, he willed himself to leave his body. How much easier this would all be if he could rise out of himself and watch over this first day back from above, digest it as a spectator might, objectively and with a perspective that was wise beyond his years.

Downstairs, he poured himself a bowl of cereal and ate standing at the sink. He heard his sister and mother come in behind him, but he didn't turn around. He'd been avoiding them pretty successfully for the past few days, and he wanted more than anything not to have to talk about any of this with them. They'd try to understand, and maybe even say that they did, but they didn't. They couldn't. How could they understand what Peter and his friends had done to Cal when all they knew were the reports coming out of the hospital about Peter's recovery and his bravery. It wasn't like he felt that Peter deserved what happened to him, but neither did Cal.

"Henry, are you okay?" his mother asked, concerned and cautious. "I've barely seen you the last couple of days. It's like you're a ghost."

Hesitating a second, he turned and drew in a deep breath, ready to tell them everything. That he'd stolen his father's prize baseball card, that Cal was going to use it to run away, that Peter and his friends were bullies and that he and Cal were the real victims. A large, frothing part of him wanted to say all that, to vomit it out like poison he'd drunk but wished he hadn't. But he didn't. He didn't say any of it. What was the point?

He stared doe-eyed at his mother, who had his chin in her hands, turning his head this way and that, as if inspecting it for structural flaws or relative freshness.

"You look okay," she said, letting go of his face and smiling. "Stay away from the junk food today. I know you won't, but at least try. Okay, Henry?"

He nodded, unable to speak.

"They call that the mother's CAT scan," Grace said, walking up to him and taking his face in her hand and turning his head this way and that like his mom had done. "Very technologically advanced diagnostic tool. They'll be using it in ERs all over the nation soon."

She smiled and, letting his face go, stared at him carefully.

"Are you okay? Seriously?"

"I'm okay," he whispered. If words could kill, then people

asking other people if they were okay would have the power to wipe out every man, woman and child on the planet.

"I'm sorry we've been fighting. I really am," she whispered back, inviting him into another secret, another way she showed him how she loved him. "I don't want us not to be friends."

He forced his lips into a smile.

"Look," she stepped back, "I'm wearing the keffiyeh you gave me. I love this thing. So cozy." She closed her eyes and smushed the thing up to her face as she shook her shoulders back and forth. "Mmmm."

From the street a car honked. Her ride.

"Let's do something after school today. Just you and me. Okay? Something fun for a change."

"Like what?"

She shrugged. "I don't care. As long as it makes you smile."

After she left, he rinsed out his bowl and yelled out, "I'm leaving, Mom. See you later." Usually he left without waiting for her to answer, but today he stayed by the back door for an extra few seconds, his fingers hooked underneath his backpack straps.

Her voice came booming with affection from upstairs. "Bye, Henry. Have a great day, love."

CIRCA

Chapter 17

JUST THEN THE loudspeaker crackled back to life and Potter's voice once again bled into the air.

"It's been another long day, Children, and there is still lots to do. But, as we all know, little flowers need their rest as much as they need sunshine, as much as they need water. Tomorrow is another day. In fact," he chuckled deeply as if the purpose of life was an inside joke known only to him, "tomorrow is the only day that matters. In the history of the world tomorrow is the most important day of them all. Do you believe me, Children?"

"Yes," he heard Flora murmur along with a chorus of assents that reached them across the night like a sandstorm rolling through the desert.

"Good. Now go to sleep and remember, Father loves you."

The speaker switched off and the last haze of the voice evaporated into the evening. As far as bedtime rituals went it was fairly benign.

"Father says it's time to go to bed, so," she shrugged and without any trace of self-satisfaction, "it must be time to go to bed."

As she pulled her hand out of the pocket (to what? Shake hands? Hug? Perform some sort of nighty-night bloodletting ceremony?) of her breezy linen pants, something small fell to the ground. He bent to pick it up and as he stood he realized the thing he handed back to her was a bullet.

"Thank you," she said, putting it back in her pocket, her tone without embarrassment or explanation.

"This is where you'll be sleeping." She nodded toward the rickety cabin they had stopped in front of, a structure that in his mind was the essence of what he might describe as a journalist as emergency housing. "Choose any bunk you'd like. You'll be the only one in here tonight."

"Is that it?" he asked her, slightly incredulous, when it appeared as though she was about to leave.

"What do you mean?"

"I mean…" He wasn't sure how to tell her their security seemed a little lacking or if it was any of his business to do so but certainly something wasn't adding up.

"Are you thinking that I should be more wary of you, that I should maybe put a guard in front of your cabin, or tell you to mind your fucking business. Am I not sinister enough for you, Henry? Is that it? Do you want to be threatened? Will that make it feel more authentic to you?"

If she was kidding with him, or threatening, or merely piteous, her expression gave nothing away, her countenance was stripped down to its barest essentials as he imagined other parts of her life to be, portable, a go-bag of a face.

When he didn't respond, she grinned.

"Go to bed, Henry. Tomorrow's going to be a big day." And then, as if as an afterthought, she added, "You might want to save your paranoia for your dreams. That's how I take mine."

As she took her leave from him, he watched her wrap her arms around herself, carefully cradling her own chest, and he realized for the first time that he was cold as well. He went in the cabin and looked through the small bag of stuff he'd grabbed on his way out of the apartment and found an old flannel shirt he'd owned since high school. It still fit him, and the used cottony feel of it reminded him instantly of Grace, of watching movies with her in their den, trying to figure out how to be as monumental as the classics they loved, how movies like *Lawrence of Arabia* and *Casablanca*, made them feel.

Later, when he was alone in the bottom bunk of a bed that was too short for him, he tried to take his mind off what tomorrow might be. He did some deep breathing and then performed a full body scan on himself, a relaxation technique some New Age girl he'd once slept with showed him how to do after a brief and disappointing experiment with Tantric sex that he found more exhausting than erotic. Neither worked. He switched on the flashlight on his phone and aimed the beam at the bunk above him. Whatever he'd expected to find there he was sorely disappointed. There were no pleas for salvation carved in the wooden bed frame, no initials, no desperate graffiti of any kind in fact. Whoever had slept in this bed before him had been willing. They were all willing, and that was perhaps the most difficult thing to accept. He tried to conjure in his mind the person who slept here before him, to conjure their neuroses, their state of mind, their troubled past, abuse or neglect, too much or too little. But apparently that wasn't the case. He himself had tried on a million disguises in his life. Maybe he was just jealous that they had found one that stuck. The California Dream wasn't a dormant thing, lazy and curdled, just waiting to be snatched away like buried treasure. It was its own engine, and if you didn't come after it in due time, it would one day take the initiative and come for you, just dream you right up. Everyone had their job to do. There would never be any getting around that.

Somehow he fell asleep, and when he awoke in the middle of the night, it wasn't because of any dream he was having. After what Flora had said to him he'd expected nightmares of some kind, intrusions, or at the very least a token boogeyman or two. But none of those things came to him. Instead, it was the desert itself that woke him, the desert that had changed its form in the middle of the night, grown fatter, crowded and dense with emptiness, looming close and drawing nearer by the second, growing out of spite for having its wide openness taken advantage of during the day. It was the absence of the thing that roused him, the great void that was as much a substance as any other.

He looked at his phone. 3:15a.m. Instead of trying to fall back asleep he swung his feet over the side of the bed and was starting to put on his shoes when he remembered something about checking for scorpions first. He peered into them and found nothing but a little sand. Why couldn't that system work for everything in life, he wondered. Just take a peek inside; no scorpions, no problems.

He took a leak at the side of the cottage and set out in no particular hurry back toward the dining area where they'd eaten dinner. The stars shined wildly above him, constellations that barely made a dent in the city sky out here looked like the irradiated blood oaths of vengeful gods that nature intended them to be. It was easy to see how early man found god first in the sky, where there was nowhere to hide. He followed the cheerful chirping of people giggling through the maze of low buildings and thought to himself that under different circumstances this could be a summer camp, that in the morning these people woke up and went sailing, tied knots, made tie-dyed shirts, and at night, after the grown-ups thought they were safe and sound in their bunks, the boys snuck carefully into the girls' side where curiosity met its inevitable and awkward match. So many possibilities in life. So many roads to choose from and they all wound up in the coils of the same tight concentric circles. Communities shrank; they never grew. They were open and permeable, but they were defined by specific and tight-knit groups, assigned meanings that would never make sense to anyone except those who were there at that exact time and place. In his own life, how many disguises had Henry tried on himself? How many times had he imagined himself a punk, or a little brother, a journalist or a soldier? He'd tried on all those hats, but none had ever stuck. Under the right circumstances that might be him giggling in the warm and starry night, carefree and delirious with the promise of a thousand new lives ahead of him, a thousand times to fuck it all up and be forgiven, rinse and repeat. Yes, Father. No, Father. Hallelujah, I'm a plant!

This is how it happened, he told himself, this was how objectivity left you. While empathy might be what was missing out there in the real world, it was without a doubt the natural enemy of the journalist. There was no room for empathy in the interpretation of facts, no room for feelings, for optimism. He'd never deny that under even slightly different circumstances he could be one of the Children of Light, but that thought, while useful as catharsis, wouldn't get him very far with the task at hand.

A light breeze blew in from a direction he couldn't quite pinpoint and ran through him like a ghost, a buzzing that was simultaneously warm and cool, the feeling of drugs just starting to come on, and it was just about to be revealed whether it was going to be a good or bad trip.

Emerging from the tight cluster of small structures, he wandered into a clearing and saw a trailhead he hadn't seen when they first came in that led away through the low hills

that seemed to be everywhere and nowhere at once, camouflaged until he came right up on them, when suddenly
they loomed big and threatening like a surprise party for a
100-year-old. He looked left and right, listened for noises,
which, out here, had as much substance as little rodents the
way they skittered across the desert floor and in and out of
the canyons that led back through the center of the earth,
back to the beginning of things, when the closest parallel to
the meaning of life was to be on the right side of the buffet
line at the Soup Plantation.

It was an easy hike and after five minutes or so, before
the trail spat him out at another clearing, he could hear the
busy sounds of voices, footsteps and the ever-present growl
of generators. He crept into the clearing and hid behind a
huge boulder just as two people walked by, their arms laden
with all types of different flowers, their chatty voices full of
excitement and anticipation. He followed them silently as
they made their way further back into the hills, and for the
first time since he arrived, he had the distinct feeling he was
in a place that was not for him, a secret part of the desert he
hadn't yet earned the right to visit. Flush with adrenaline,
his breath came now in quick clouds, his heartbeat a global
distraction, he stalked them into another part of the hills,
where he suddenly pulled up short as they continued their
work. In front of him, looming like a UFO, was an enormous
greenhouse lit up from within by scalding white lights. Everywhere around the greenhouse people seemed busy preparing
the building for some kind of event, bringing armfuls of
different types of flowers inside, leaving to get more, and then
coming back. Convivial chatter adorned the air with a festive
noise like party decorations, and if the sinking feeling in his
stomach hadn't told him otherwise, he could have sworn they
were getting ready for a high school dance.

Careful not to be seen, Henry crept to the far side of the structure where the light was lowest, and looking around to make sure no one could see him, peered into the greenhouse, not sure what he would see but confident it wouldn't be good. How could it? A secret place within a secret place. He felt like a child imagining such a place could even exist, that people had things they needed to keep so hidden. But they did.

His breath steamed the glass as he pressed his face close and he cupped his eyes, a real pervert's pose, he thought, but shame only had a moment to cut a rug before terror elbowed its way onto the dance floor that was his imagination. He counted quickly. Twelve. He counted twelve girls inside, all around Daisy's age, all wearing the same gauzy white dress she wore, all marked with the same neck tattoo, crowded around a table. They were giggling hysterically, and even though the glass was too thick to hear anything through, he imagined he could hear the laughter, the excited chatter, what he knew in his heart to be the sound of children. He moved a few feet to the left to get a better look and saw what it was they were doing at the table. One of the women he hadn't yet met, whose name he was sure was a type of flower, was sitting at the table in a folding chair. Standing behind her, Flora held a pair of barbershop clippers which she was using to shave all of the hair from the woman's head. Her beautiful blond locks slid to the floor as section after section of her head was shaved without any noticeable strategy, the haphazard runoff of beauty and vanity, and instead of looking upset she smiled hugely, bouncing up and down on her chair and clapping her hands like a little girl about to blow out the candles on her 6-year-old birthday cake. When her head was bare Flora turned the clippers on the woman's face, removing her eyebrows in quick efficient swipes, and when that was done, the woman stood up, let her dress fall to the ground around her feet, and the rest of her body was trimmed so that after a few moments she stood there, completely naked, without a hair anywhere on her. When it was over, the others helped her back on with her dress and hugged her tightly. It was then that Henry saw that a few of the others had already gone through this process, and when they had settled down, Daisy took her place on the chair and the whole thing was repeated on her.

He moved from the window. He didn't want to see this, whatever "this" was. Even though the women looked ecstatic there was something about the act that chilled him because what they were doing felt very final, the culmination of something long and hard fought.

The rest of the greenhouse was still bustling with excited activity. Every detail had to be perfect because they earnestly believed that if they didn't miss a single thing, if no detail went unnoticed, then they would undoubtedly have the best night of their lives. And maybe they would, but what Henry would tell them if they would just ask him, was that their youth, in the end, wouldn't be enough to save them, neither the associated good intentions nor the dreams that still felt like kinetic energy, destinies waiting to be fulfilled. He knew because he tried once, long ago. He put that theory to the test but found out the hard way that youth can't stop a bullet, can't keep you from getting trampled, can't stop you from slowly bleeding to death and the life leaving you in gigantic sighs until the light of the sun became the light of the room and they there nothing but light, which in the end was the thing that stopped you from talking, from living. All that light. He'd seen it. He'd witnessed all of that and more, because he was there for the disappointment that came afterwards: the silence, the smoke, the rebirth that wasn't the rebirth of life, but the rebirth of a pain that had been there all along, hidden in plain sight, hidden in a backpack, on a T-shirt.

People continued to move in and out of the entrance with armfuls of flowers they would lay down lovingly in piles of the same type that were growing and growing. Twelve piles in all. Twelve women named after twelve kinds of flowers. He didn't have to look to see if there was a pile of daisies, but he did. Large and overflowing, sitting between a pile of roses and tulips, the pristine bouquet was fit for a royal wedding. And in front of each pile there was a simple wooden bar stool, remarkable only because of its plainness. He was beginning to understand that nothing was to overshadow or even distract from the beauty of the flowers. They were what mattered. The beautiful flowers laying in piles and the beautiful flowers shaving their hair—as what, he wondered? An offering to god? A stab at modesty? He looked again at the pile of roses. They were perfect specimens. Each one had been carefully pruned, de-thorned, made ready for offering. So that was it. That's what they were doing. The women were being pruned as well, being made ready for the thing they felt was inevitable. But that was silly, because of course he didn't need to guess what it was they were getting ready to do. That part was suddenly the clearest of all because it was why they existed in the first place. Like when he had looked for the daisies, he didn't need to look up at the ceiling, but when he did, and he saw the twelve nooses dangling above the twelve stools, he wasn't surprised. You couldn't make an agrarian, Utopian omelette without first cracking a few human sacrifices.

As though they were channeling the ambient energy, the speakers once again crackled to life with no warning. The Children of Light stopped what they were doing and those that were inside now came out to better hear Potter's voice when he once again began to speak.

"Oh, Children," he crooned, his voice was no longer giving a barbiturate soliloquy, no longer the sound of meat marinating. Now it was tinder; tinder in the excited hands of a teenage firebug. "It is time…"

All around him they cheered on the end of the world. He tuned out Potter's voice as he watched their faces light up, their bodies go slack with relief. Near him a woman his mom's age clasped her veiny hands together underneath her chin. A grandmotherly smile ran roughshod over her face as she swelled with pride. Who knew how long they'd been waiting for this, how long they'd known what the end would look like but not when it would finally get here. They were settlers who had waited for decades for the railroad to decide to put tracks through their small town, with the promise of connecting them to the rest of the world, and now the train was finally coming and it would take them all exactly where they longed to go.

Henry used his phone to take pictures of them, of the greenhouse, which, now that he looked at it more closely, resembled in many ways, a prism, as it absorbed the lights they used to illuminate the valley, and threw it back off in colors so bright and pure each one became a parable, a holy version of some ugly truth. Out of habit he selected a few of the kitschy filters he had on his phone, framing the Children of Light in sepia, black and white, an oversaturated seventies snapshot that reminded him of the pictures in his family's own photo albums, their own shared reality that now seemed about as authentic as …No, authenticity wasn't the right word. Authenticity was a quality like lightness, or newness. Anything could be authentic if enough people believed it was. What he was thinking of was something different. What he was having trouble with had more to do with reality, the complete dissociation he felt from certain events and where he was now, the line from there to here. He'd seen the end of the world once before and as the crow flies it wasn't that far from where he stood now. He watched Flora walk over to Daisy and squeeze her shoulder. Daisy, her eyes wet with joyful tears, put her head on Flora's shoulder and the women stood there together, swaying lightly, ecstasy in lockstep, as if Potter's words were a breeze. Grace would be about Flora's age now, he reflected, noticing the age spots on her hands that were gently patting Daisy's shoulder, threads of grey running through her hair, the virus of age consuming her slowly but surely, eating away at her until one day there would be nothing left. Aging gracefully was capitulation.

He tried to post the pictures to Facebook and Instagram, but there was no connection out here, and besides, he couldn't believe that was his first impulse. He had to find Potter, and he had to find him now. That could have been Grace out there. It could have been anyone he knew and loved. He thought of Truman and Alberto, of the men in the building who had gotten in over their heads because they were bored and needed something to believe in. Nothing mattered anymore but sitting down with the man and trying to talk some sense into him. Henry didn't want to try and convince him he was wrong, or that the things he believed were foolish, because that time had come and gone if it had ever existed at all in the first place. The sense he would try to talk to Potter was the sense of mercy, and if he couldn't put that across, he'd find another way. That's what the *Jane's* book had always been for, he reflected. When you needed another way.

Potter's speech ended just as the sun started to crease the sky with dawn's subtle colors, Impressionist's colors, the illusion of substance where none existed. In the distance over the hills they had climbed through to get to this part of the desert, he heard the silly scurrying sounds of animals hurrying to take refuge from predators and the heat, the surest proof that night had its own set of rules that were different than what passed for order during the day.

When Daisy walked outside for a moment to watch the sunrise he felt a careful, inaccessible part of himself snap, rushed up behind her, and clapped a rough hand over her mouth. It took that touch to remind him how smooth her skin was, how soft people could be. She struggled against him and was able to turn slightly and see that it was him and then she began to struggle harder.

"Stop," he hissed at her. "I don't want to hurt you. I just want to talk to you for a minute." She kicked backwards and caught his shin with her heel. The pain made him wince, but it wasn't enough to make him let go. "Just stop," he whispered into her ear. "I won't hurt you. I won't hurt anyone. I need you to take me to Potter. Now. You promised you'd do that. And if you don't, I'll fucking leave. I swear to god. I don't care what you crazy fuckers are doing. I'll take off right now. And I know you don't want that. That'd defeat the whole purpose of bringing me here in the first place." Suddenly clarity was its own thing and he latched onto it. "Isn't that why you got to know me? Why you fucked me? You wanted me to fall for you a bit. Not totally. Not head over heels, but enough so that I'd follow you out here and…what? Not say anything to stop you all from killing yourselves? Or no…that's not it. You wanted me to watch," his voice lit up and then continued getting higher as he spoke, his thin lips stretching wide to make room for the spite flowering widely the way a plant opens up to fulfill its obligations to ecology. "You want me to see it and then write about it. Oh my god, that's even worse." What she didn't realize, and what he understood now, was that his obligations lay with the past where the dead lived, debts that weren't quantifiable, unfortunately, which made it difficult to know when they were paid off. Also, those debts demanded flesh and blood, he realized now, human sacrifices made willingly and without malice.

Her muffled invective grew less intense and then her struggling began to subside a bit. She needed him to stay. *They* needed him to stay. Leverage was something new to him, but he knew he had it, so he let her go and she spun around to face him. She touched her lip and saw that he had drawn a little blood there when he had clapped his hand over her mouth, cutting it on her front teeth. She let a string of red saliva hang off her lip and dangle to the ground, but it wouldn't break and she had to grab it with her hand and pull it off to get it to fall. Her eyes found him, and with her hair all gone, she looked like a feral animal, fierce and desperate, and he stared back remembering someone's advice about mad dogs and that the only way to break them was to stare back, plant your feet, and hope for the best, while demonstrating with your posture that you weren't afraid to have your face bitten off your head.

"Fine," she spat at him. Her anger was substantive, and it scared him deeply, but he held his ground, made himself remember that just a few short hours ago, before they had shaved off all her hair, she was just a girl excited to see her friends, a girl making plans by giggling as if optimism was all it took to create the perfect day.

Without another word she turned, not waiting to see if he was following, and walked back through the canyon and over the short foothills, which he now saw, ringed the place like a set of sharp teeth. Back at Pottersville she led him through the makeshift streets, past her comrades' confused faces as they wondered what was happening, what wrench this outsider had thrown into the day. Even though it felt as though he'd just seen the first signs of the sun breaking back at the greenhouse, when they got back to Pottersville it had become a boiling frenzy sending heat waves dancing everywhere he looked making it seem as though the earth was being wetted down with the overflow from the sun's roiling cauldron. As they walked, he searched for a tune to hum, something appropriate for the situation, but nothing came to mind so he just whistled instead, a nameless tune, something quick and bright and eager to please. He knew it was the right melody when he heard a bird start to sing it back to him.

Finally they arrived at the largest cabin he had yet seen. It was the same off-white as the rest of them, paint peeling here and there in nostalgic patches, but it had a few homier touches the others didn't have; a wraparound porch with a couple of rocking chairs for settin' a while and sippin' lemonade while the kids were doing their mass suicide thing and a big stone chimney poking up from the roof that was just ready for Santa to come and drop off gifts to all the good little girls and boys.

"Are you ready?" she asked him, and he couldn't help but laugh a little at the sight of her. With all her hair gone she looked like a gigantic penis and while he didn't know much about what they were doing here, the one thing he was fairly certain of was that he wouldn't want to go to his maker looking like morning wood.

She opened the door and, taking a deep breath, he followed her in, patting his back pocket to make sure he still had his notebook and his pen. The only thing missing was the fedora with a press card poking out of it. His heart raced madly in his chest, and he wondered if it was normal to feel this nervous before an interview, if it made him somehow less professional. He didn't have long to ponder the question, though, as Daisy flipped on the lights and swept her hand toward rows and rows of bookshelves all lined from floor to ceiling with boxes full of reel-to-reel tapes.

"Meet Father," she said lightly as if her voice was a thing that had been erased and was only faintly there.

He turned quickly expecting Potter to suddenly be there, looming, healthy and large, a façade of a man. A man with windows and a revolving door. A bucket for umbrellas at his feet. He expected a man big enough to contain all of these lives and more, galaxies, but when he turned around he saw no one. He turned again, round and round like a tourist on a New York street corner, until finally he stopped and faced her. Daisy had her hand to her mouth where she was stifling a little girl laugh, the kind of laugh that gave no credence to correlation between age and wisdom, a laugh that was meant to mock and only mock.

"No, silly," she said, the smile still there like light from a star that had collapsed eons ago. "Here. You're looking at him. At Father." She walked to the empty desk in the corner of the room and switched on a large reel-to-reel tape player that looked more relic than instrument. Potter's voice instantly came to life mid-sentence. He was preaching about the importance of soil.

"The soil must be rich, Children. Dark and nutritious. As the winter once again approaches what I recommend is this…"

She turned the volume down so he could let it process. But he didn't need the silence. He already understood.

"How long?" he asked, looking more carefully now at the spines of the tapes, reading the labels on the boxes which he saw were divided by week. The last box in the bottom right corner of the last shelf was missing. "How long ago did he die?"

"We don't think about it like that. To us he's not dead, he's just…"

"Stop," he interrupted her. He was out of patience for all of it. The lingo, the justifications, the coyness. All of it. Why was it so fucking hard to get a straight answer from anyone? "Just answer the question. Please."

Her smile dropped and her pale red lips made a slight, unreadable crease in her otherwise wrinkleless face. "We don't know. We don't think about it like that. That's what you're not understanding. We have him because we have these tapes. He's here with us all the way to the end," and then a smile lurched back onto her face. "And now we're there, and it's wonderful that you're here with us, Henry. You're the only one who's going to see it, and it will be beautiful, and it will be terrifying," her dainty fingers began to tremble with excitement, "and then you'll tell the world about it. You'll tell them why we did it and you'll tell them that we'll be back, and when we come, we will bring more beauty and more peace and more love than they could ever imagine." Her face shone up at him, round and pale and without hair, she looked like the moon to him, pure ecstasy, love's greatest favor to mankind. She was in her teenage place. What the airport had meant to him that long-ago day with Cal was what Pottersville meant to her.

For a minute he stood silently, watching her, his stomach doing backflips and his skin pricked entirely by the burden of knowing. And for a minute he thought about it, for a minute he actually considered what she was saying, and for a minute it actually made sense. It would be so easy to let them die and then write their story. In fact, if he didn't write it, it would still write itself. All he had to do was channel it.

She had all the hope in the world, genuine hope. He was the one who wanted the world to burn. It had always been that way with him. The other thing he knew was that there was no point in killing something unless it was young and pretty. That he had learned the hard way.

"No," he said softly, letting the word echo into the past. He looked at the ground as he said it, afraid to meet her eyes. "No, I'm not going to do it. I'm not going to sit back and just watch you take your life. Watch twelve girls take their lives. I can't write that story. I won't write that story."

When he looked up, her smile was gone. The steel brace of her jaw bulged from sunken cheeks.

"You want to know when, is that it?" Her voice was equal parts desperation and exasperation, panic's perfect pitch, a last-ditch elixir he'd come to know all too well over the years. Flat-out anger would be next, and it would be served straight up and as wrathful as they come. "If I tell you when he died, will you stay and write the story?" she screamed at him. "1988, okay? Write 1988. Or 1994, 2006. Write whatever the fuck you want, Henry! Write circa 1990 or 1920! It doesn't matter. The important thing is nothing like this is ever going to happen again. Don't you understand that?"

He turned and began walking toward his car. He was done fighting, because he knew how wrong she was. Of course it had happened before. He had seen it with his own eyes. Circa 1990. And it would happen again if he didn't do something. He thought of Truman and Alberto, of Oscar and all the men back at the building who were about to discover that their reason to live was no reason at all, but a countdown to a time indeterminate. *Circa*, he thought to himself. *What a funny little word.*

He checked his cell phone. No service. He would call Truman as soon as he could. It was still early in the morning. He should have time.

Behind him he heard Daisy hurrying to catch up, her bare feet scratching the loose sand and gravel, another skittish animal when all was said and done.

"Henry!" she called loudly, "Wait. Don't go. Please! Henry!"

He ignored her as he continued on to his car, and once there, he opened the passenger door and motioned toward her with his head. "Get in the car." The words reminded him of that stoned day with Sonny so long ago and the pledge he had made to himself that one day he would say that sentence to a girl and it would be irresistible to her. It would mean more than "I love you" or anything else his unromantic brain could invent.

"No," she said. She had gotten her dress dirty, her face and arms. She didn't look pure anymore. Now she just looked worn and tired.

A crowd of Children of Light had gathered and were watching them from a distance of a dozen or so yards. He saw Flora begin to slowly walk toward them.

"This is your last chance," he said so calmly he shocked himself. "Get in the car."

"No," she repeated, folding her arms, willing to indulge his pointless standoff.

But he didn't have time for a standoff. He looked at the fifty or so COL members gathered around, and at Flora who was moving toward them at a fast pace, her body tense, and made a quick calculation in his head. In a single movement he clicked open the car trunk and ran at a dead sprint at Daisy, who barely had time to register the fact that she was about to be kidnapped. He grabbed her by the shoulders and threw her into the trunk, closing it quickly and firmly, and then ran around to the driver side, got in, and started the ignition. Time had slowed down to one of those mid-falling moments and he let himself steal a glance out the window as he threw the ignition into drive and saw the entire encampment of COL running at him at full speed. Leading the charge was Flora, whose face he saw was a smudge of panic and fear, the same panic and fear he had seen in his childhood dreams of her first dash though the desert all those years ago.

The car shot gravel and sand out behind them as he pushed the accelerator, and when he looked back again in the rearview mirror, he saw only a brown cloud that had eaten them up, one and all, in its powdery mouth. He didn't hesitate for a second as the car rammed the fence they had driven through yesterday, but what seemed now like a lifetime ago. Hitting the open road, he pointed the car toward LA and pushed the accelerator down as far as it would go. The car shook with the effort, but that was okay, if a cop pulled them over he would just tell them that there were fifty people about to kill themselves just down the road a piece. *Down the road a piece!* He'd always wanted to say that.

He checked his phone. Still no signal. As soon as he could he would call Truman and tell him about the wonderful day he was having, tell him they had to get out of the building before anyone got hurt. It was hard to get Truman to do something that he didn't want to do. That he'd learned from experience. *But*, he thought, *when he hears my voice, he'll know. He'll know that I have it all figured out and I know how to save them all.*

He put the phone next to him and started to compose Potter's obituary in his head, and as he did it he started with him and Grace, with Cal and anemic afternoons where he didn't have a name to call whatever it was he felt deep inside himself, a hollow illness he prayed someone would give him medicine for and make him feel better. That was the story he began in his head, the story of Potter's life and death, because it was his life, too.

Chapter 18

WHEN HE GOT to school, he stopped at the front gates, near the smiling porpoise mascot he never could quite get his head around, waiting for someone to point him out. But no one did any such thing. It was business as usual as students walked around smiling and yelling to one another, laughter and the steady pulse of lively conversation wove through clusters of kids sitting cross legged in circles on the grassy center quad as rowdier kids chased one another through the maze of cafeteria tables, grabbing each other affectionately and then reversing the chase so the one who was caught was now the chaser. Retribution, it seemed, was an endless but joyous game. Campus was slowly returning to its normal state after the accident, not to mention what had happened with Peter and Cal. The car wreck had been moved after a few of the parents complained that it was enough and their kids didn't need to see "that" every day. The black armbands some of the students wore were also all but gone, black again the sole property of the Goths who didn't know what to make of the last several weeks. Real tragedy had thrown a monkey wrench into their collective raison d'etre and moping finally felt like an appropriate existence again. The only reminder was the flag, which still flew at half-mast, hanging limply against the flagpole in the absence of any wind.

The first period bell rang and for Henry it was history class. Mr. Jackson, their tired-looking, overweight teacher who, by the looks of him, was the veteran of at least seventeen armed conflicts, lectured to them for fifty minutes straight about the Civil Rights movement, covering everything from Jim Crow to MLK in the time it took to defrost a chicken.

"Tomorrow we'll do Vietnam," he yelled out to them gleefully as the bell dismissing class rang.

He took a seat in class near the back of the room of his second-period class, civics, and as the teacher began to discuss the subject of voter's rights with them, he raised his hand and called out, "Can I go to the bathroom, Mr. Willows?"

Mr. Willows stopped the lesson and took off his horn-rimmed glasses to peer at Henry.

"I don't know, Henry. *Can* you go to the bathroom?"

The class chuckled sleepily at the old joke, and Henry gripped the sides of his desk to keep himself from tipping over onto the floor.

"May I go to the bathroom, Mr. Willows?"

The teacher put his glasses back on and turned back to the board.

"Go. Take a pass."

He left his seat and his sweaty palm slipped off the door knob as he went to open it. The knob made a loud sound, which made a few of the students near the door jump in their seats a little.

"Everything okay, Henry?"

He forced a smile as all eyes turned and landed on him like a swarm of locust. He rubbed his palms along the leg of his jeans and twisted the knob again, this time with success.

The door closed behind him with a heavy thud, and he worried for a second that Mr. Willows might storm out after him to accuse him of some sort of delinquency he hadn't intended. But no one followed him. He was in the clear, so he decided he'd take his time getting to the bathroom and back. There was a certain sweet spot when it came to using the bathroom during class. Too quick and you really hadn't maximized the time out of class. If you took to long you were seen as fucking around and the next time you needed to go you might get an answer like, "I thought you went enough last time to cover you for the rest of the year." Ten minutes felt pretty reasonable, he thought, as he began to hum some nameless tune, basking in the way the sound echoed around the halls as though it were a bumble bee zipping from flower to flower, looking for just the right one to pollinate. Next, he stopped at a water fountain and drank deeply from the rusty spigot. The rumor was there was lead in the water you got out of the fountains, but that didn't stop anyone from using them. What didn't kill you made you stronger.

Thinking about a version of himself that was made of lead and whatever corrosive chemicals made iron nails disappear overnight in a can of Coke he suddenly found himself smiling for what felt like the first time in forever. Maybe things would be okay, after all. Maybe Cal would leave, and everyone would forget that the two of them were friends. Maybe by the time summer was over the whole thing would be an urban legend, something so stretched out and manipulated that it didn't look anything like what had actually happened. And maybe in that version of the story he wouldn't be friends with Cal. Maybe in that version he would still just be a ghost to them. Yeah, that'd be okay.

As he rounded the corner, though, all those thoughts disappeared from his head as that narrative was disrupted by the sight of Cal at the other end of the hall, dressed all in black, carrying a rifle in one hand and a pistol in the other. They looked at one another for a few seconds, and it took that long for Henry to process what he was seeing, to understand what was about to happen. Cal had a duffle bag strapped across his shoulders and Henry wondered, staring at its bulging sides, just how many guns you could buy with a '52 Mantle. How much ammo? Cal began slowly walking toward Henry, who found himself frozen, not with fear exactly, but with confusion. Even though he knew what was going on, what was about to happen, he just couldn't comprehend it. Somehow Cal with those guns didn't compute. The chrome of them. The weight. When had he learned how to fire a gun let alone load one?

Before Henry could decide whether to turn and run away or rush toward Cal and beg him to leave before anything happened, Mr. Neville, the school security guard who had been their detention minder the day they took acid and went to the airport, rounded the corner behind Cal.

Without thinking, Henry gestured for Cal to turn around. Henry saw Cal's forehead crinkle like an overripe piece of fruit, and he remembered thinking that it was such a strange expression for someone armed to the hilt to be making. As Cal turned to face Mr. Neville, Henry stopped walking and watched them argue, hearing their voices steadily rise as their exchange got more heated. And then, in what seemed like a scene from a movie, Cal stepped back, held the gun up and Henry heard a loud crack ricochet around the concrete halls. He put his hands over his ears, but he wasn't sure yet that Cal had really fired the gun. The sound was more like a firecracker than a gun shot, but isn't that what people always said? That it sounded like a toy?

It took a second, but Neville slowly sunk to his knees looking more like he was about to propose marriage than take his few final breaths. Henry watched, transfixed, as Neville grabbed Cal's shirt and Henry couldn't tell if he was doing it to keep himself upright or if he was begging for his life. If it was the latter, he needn't have bothered. Cal raised the gun again, pressed the barrel to Neville's forehead, and then, without even a hint of hesitation, pulled the trigger.

As soon as he heard the noise, Henry looked away, but he was sure if he had been looking he'd have seen the man's brains and bits of his skull sprayed onto the ground as though someone had turned a hose on in his head. He looked back around, and Neville was laying there at Cal's feet, his legs bent under backwards beneath him. Cal was staring at the body, too, and to Henry's surprise no one had come out to investigate the noise. How was it possible that the two gunshots hadn't lured anyone out of their classrooms? No teachers. No students. Just the two of them.

Cal was the first to look away from the body. He turned to Henry and motioned him over with the gun.

Henry shook his head.

Cal took a couple of steps toward him and waved him over again, this time much more angrily, and hissing his name. "Henry! Get over here! Henry!"

Henry took a couple of steps backwards. If this was a movie, he thought, he'd be saying a prayer in his head, maybe begging with a crinkled voice, multilingual in all the ways it took to stay alive. If it was a movie, this would be his redemption moment, his one and only chance to die for his cause, for Grace, for whatever random thoughts popped into someone's head as they were looking down the barrel of a gun still smoking from recent use. It was his opportunity to be a hero, the kind he'd read about in so many books about soldiers who made the ultimate sacrifice, music swelling in the background, beatific looks on their faces as they majestically dissolved from this world to the next. Instead, he took a couple more steps backwards.

Cal approached him, slowly, and raised the gun. "Henry! Don't make me do this!"

Without thinking, Henry began to walk backwards, slowly, step by step, feeling as though the next would surely set off a landmine. Cal continued to follow him, matching his pace, in no rush to hurry this up, the gun still pointed at Henry, who could already feel the bullet entering his skull, his chest, his arm, crushing everything within him into a fine powder indistinguishable from any grain of sand or bit of dirt you'd find on the ground.

Cal said his name again and this time it sounded like an apology, like the last chance Henry would get before he'd be dead. Without thinking, Henry turned and started to run, not sure where he was going, not sure it mattered. He ran and ran until his pulse pounded behind his eyes making him blind, and then he reached the cafeteria and the janitorial closet he'd locked himself in the month before when he was hiding from Cal. A simple game of hide-and-seek compared to this.

He threw himself into the closet, pulled the heavy door shut behind him, and threw the deadbolt. Despite not having heard the gun go off again he couldn't be completely sure if he'd been shot or not. Every ounce of energy he possessed and had ever possessed was currently swirling with no apparent design throughout every ounce of his body, short circuiting him, making him twitch and yelp uncontrollably all at once.

It took a couple of minutes for him to calm down enough to pat himself down and realize he hadn't been shot. And just as he was starting to wonder what Cal was doing now, he heard the first shots that would not stop for the next ten minutes.

He tried to count but stopped at eight or nine when he heard the first of the screaming. He never knew there were so many kinds of screams. Screams of terror became moans of pain, and those were screams too, only they didn't have the force behind them anymore to sound like the terror screams. He heard pleading and praying, all of it their own kinds of screams, all of it, strangely in tune. A perfectly pitched suicide machine.

A few times someone tried the door handle to the closet, shook it a few times, and then ran off. He could have opened the door, because he could hear the shots still popping off in what sounded like the other side of campus. He should have opened the door.

And then, just like that, it stopped.

An eerie silence descended like a fog, thick and wet, and that was the most terrifying part of the whole thing, because it was impossible to tell if the shooting would start up again or if it was over for good. Every once in a while there'd be another scream, lower and more plaintive, fat with the weight of retrospection.

After that, sirens. And after that, a bullhorn, telling everyone it was safe to come out. Henry unlocked the door, and the sunlight shocked him. That it was still bright and clear seemed almost impossible. Surely the fog he imagined he'd heard was hanging off everything like the branches of some sad Southern tree.

He wandered a bit and froze when a cop pointed a gun at him and commanded him to "Lie down!"

Gladly, he thought, as he pressed his face into the cool grass and stretched his arms out in front of him.

Around him the kids who'd been cleared by the cops wandered around in a daze, still too shocked to seek solace in one another or to articulate even the most primitive of thoughts. They didn't know they were glad to be alive yet, or that they'd come closer to death than they might ever come until they were old, surrounded by their families who would be leaning in close, farming last looks, noticing the lights flicker as the last breaths left their bodies. That would be a long, long time from now, and far away from here.

After he'd been cleared, he was ordered to run with his hands behind his head to the front of school and as he crossed the quad, he couldn't help but think about the day the kid had punched him in the face as part of his gang initiation, introducing Henry to the practice of random violence, of victimhood and all those affiliated vocations. He glanced at the bodies on the ground as he ran, kids his own age and younger, clutching wounds they'd live with forever, intrusive narratives into what were up until then perfect little stories. He heard them whimpering and groaning, their small voices addressing the thin air in front of them as they made their pitiful peace with whatever apparition they could conjure on such short notice.

Some of the dead were already covered with sheets, cheap shrouds flapping noiselessly in a breeze that seemed to kick up from nowhere, splashing the campus with the faint scent of salt water, the beach so tantalizing yet inappropriately close. In a quick flash of skin he saw a body that looked like it could be his sister and making sure none of the cops were watching he ran over to it and knelt, his knees instantly damp from the dew that reminded him it was still morning, that there was still a whole day ahead of him. And after that more days, days drawn out to their edges, corpse still, days and days he would spend on his knees, contrition no match for the remorse that was already fully formed in him, a pulpy new organ he couldn't live without. From what felt like another planet birds spoke vividly to one another, scandalized by what had happened, and then the bell rang dismissing them from third period. Long and sharp it trilled and then just the miserable echo of it, high-pitched and sustaining until that too faded into the overarching silence. Again the wind reared up and peeled back the sheet in front of him and suddenly there she was, just her head, her hair still shaved in that new style she was so fearless about trying on, lipstick still straight, the skin on her face perfectly unblemished, and he thought, *They have it wrong. She's fine. Look at her. There's nothing wrong with her.* And for a moment there was relief that she was still alive, that she'd played dead, or had somehow fallen into a deep sleep like a fairytale princess, but when he threw back the rest of the sheet, greedy for her life, to fulfill the mortal debts he would always owe her, he understood in an instant that there was no mistake. Bejeweled in death, a deep red amulet of blood rested against her chest, regal somehow, and below that three more holes in her stomach completing her coronation. It was what *Jane's* referred to as a tight grouping, when a series of shots struck their target like that, academic until now, he thought, taking in the whole of her, the elegant red welts, the awkward turn of her hips, her legs at sheepishly odd angles, all of it bringing to mind a coquette trying on pretty poses, and not a corpse at all, which is exactly what she now was. A body and nothing more.

"You're not supposed to be doing that," a woman's voice said, and he looked up and saw a policewoman walking toward him, a walkie-talkie in one hand, her other hand hovering over the gun in her holster. Her eyes were buried deep in the shadow of an LAPD baseball cap, and although he couldn't exactly see her face, Henry felt that she was afraid of him, and for a moment he considered how easy it would be to scare her into drawing her weapon and shooting him dead, blessing him with a matching set of vestments that would confirm his birthright as a member of this royal family.

"This is my sister," Henry told her plainly, and she came over and lifted him gently by the arms, put an arm around his shoulders, and guided him to the front of school where yellow tape was already stretched out in all directions, because the school wasn't a school anymore, it was something else, a crime scene, but more than that, too. A battlefield, he thought.

A sea of parents' faces rippled behind the flimsy barrier, every one of them wrecked by pain, deep lines inscribed grief on them, their eyes wide and made of fear, and none would ever be the same. It was one of the ways we get older, he thought, by dying a little and in bits and pieces.

One by one kids were sent across to their moms and dads, everyone in tears, groups collapsing in avalanches of hugs, the children buried so far beneath they'd have to lower in food and water to sustain them until authorities could figure out how to one day dig them out.

When they saw him, Henry's dad ran forward through the tape, grabbed him, and crushed him into his chest. He'd never remembered being hugged so hard, not even by Grace. Tears from both his parents wet his hair as they clutched him, held him at arm's length, their eyes searching his body for wounds, and then pulled him in again, over and over like that, this mirage of a son of theirs they could barely believe existed.

"When will we know something?" Henry's dad screamed at a cop.

The cop walked over and put a hand on Henry's dad's shoulder. "Shouldn't be long now."

The size of the group began to thin out as more and more kids were delivered safely to their parents. Only those with kids still unaccounted for remained as the paramedics began to do their work, rushing in and out with their stretchers and instruments that seemed to Henry now completely beside the point. And then later the gurneys with the dead, the white sheets eliciting a gasp every time one went by as if they were floating ghosts or anything but what they were, which was children they'd never see again. Parents were directed to go to St. Joseph's hospital where the injured were being taken, that there would be more information for them there. St. Joseph's, where Henry and Grace had both been born.

He could have told them that Grace was dead, spared them the agony of waiting for the news, but he didn't want it to come from him. He kept his mouth shut as they drove to the hospital, a long, panicked motorcade speeding behind the blaring ambulances as they swerved in and out of traffic. Looking out over the ocean Henry saw a small plane dragging behind it a banner advertising Coppertone, complete with the famous illustration of a dog pulling down the bathing suit of a little girl in pigtails as she helplessly watched.

At the hospital they waited with all the other families on vinyl furniture in the waiting room that was choked with tension and the nauseating smell of antiseptic. No one spoke, the only noise was an episode of *Sally Jesse Raphael* on a TV hung in the corner that no one bothered to turn off, Henry suspected, because no one but him even realized it was on. After a while the doctors began to come in, little by little, calling out names, and delivering news about emergency surgeries, prognosis, and in some cases, when the mother would scream and a noise came out of the father that sounded like life itself catching on a barbed wire fence, that there was nothing that could be done. He watched their faces but heard only Sally Jesse's voice.

When it was their turn, he watched in slow motion as his mother collapsed into his father, both of them stunned by the words they'd never properly register. The crying came later. The shock. The recriminations and the questions of Henry, who they never quite forgave because of his relationship with Cal.

Henry's parents sent him to another school for his own good, but he dropped out a few months later and took his GED. His parents didn't care. They were happy he was taking care of himself because neither one of them really had it in them to watch him.

Grace, though, always stayed with him. She was there when he worked: she was there when he drank. And when he tried to send her away, like when he was trying to pick up some drunk chick two gin and tonics too old for him, that's when it was the hardest to get rid of her. But even then he didn't really want her to go away, not if he really got right down to it, because if she left him she might never come back, and that he couldn't live with. He'd tried. God knows he tried.

At community college he took some journalism classes and liked that. It let him write, but it didn't force him to use his imagination. He wanted to be based in a world of facts. The less chance he had to let his mind wander the better.

And when he got his first newspaper job, compiling information for the obituaries of notable people who hadn't even died yet, she was right there with him, too, and he heard her laughing that he was going to be a natural at it.

He promised her, when she showed up in his head late at night, that if he ever had the chance to save her he would and she'd laugh at that, too, and tell him it was too late.

Why don't you ever write my obituary? she asked him all the time, and he told her that to him she wasn't dead. *But I am, Henry. I'm as dead as they come.* She had an amazing sense of humor for a dead person.

Okay, he told her finally after years of her asking, *I'll write yours. It won't be easy, but I'll do it.*

Thank you, Henry. I love you, she told him in her softest voice, the one that felt like feathers.

I love you, too.

Acknowledgments

I'd like to thank Ellen, Harper, and Sasha for all their inspiration, love and support. Abby Weintraub for the cover design, constant encouragement, and enthusiasm for my many neurosis. Monica Corcoran Harel for reading early and often. Mark Givens for his patience and intelligence. Thanks to my mom for giving me my love of reading. And last of all, thanks to Ron Greenfield, Cory Berg, and David Jones who we lost along the way.

www.ingramcontent.com/pod-product-compliance
Lightning Source LLC
Chambersburg PA
CBHW030842030726
47495CB00005B/1336